# House of Seven Days

By Juniper Ellis

House of Seven Days

Limitless Publishing, LLC
Kailua, HI 96734
www.limitlesspublishing.com

Formatting: Limitless Publishing

ISBN-13: 978-1-68058-116-4
ISBN-10: 1-68058-116-3

# Dedication

For Tim, and for my mom,
with love, thanks, and laughter.

# Monday

## *Francine Millicent Pond*

"Who are *you*?" Pond asked, as she rounded the bend of the staircase and took in an unexpected occupant of the window seat that adorned the landing.

Francine Millicent Pond was the owner of not only a magnificently awkward name, but also a recently inherited house to match. Her great-aunt Gertrude had departed after a long and eccentric life, and had surprised everyone by bequeathing her rambling, intricate Queen Anne to her great-niece, the member of her family least likely to become a homeowner.

Before moving to Baltimore to take possession of the house, Pond had known her great-aunt from a distance, and mostly remembered her laugh. Gertrude poured forth cascades and fountains of nickers and brays, cackles and caws. Meanwhile, she looked both astonished and delighted that such sounds could proceed from her own tiny, delicate body. Anyone who witnessed Gertrude's laughter could not help joining in, even though it wasn't always clear what set her off. Her entire life had been a mystery, like her house, both beautiful and strange—as was her obscure reasoning for willing her odd mansion to her grandniece, who was known for moving every few weeks or months.

Pond had lost count of her moves, but believed relocating to Gertrude's Baltimore pile of sticks might be the fifteenth move she had made since the previous time she had lost count. Pond was just beginning to make her acquaintance with her new abode, and was continually being startled by some strange contraption or other. Doubtless many of them even had a purpose, but most were decorative, or at least Pond kept supposing that was their intended effect.

The new occupant of the window seat appeared to be quite purposeful, although she was seated, eyes fixed steadily on a book perched on her lap. "Who are you?" Pond repeated.

"Nareen," the girl said, not looking up from her book. "Hello, Francine."

"The name is *Pond*." Everyone who knew her in Baltimore seemed to have a very regrettable habit of calling Pond by the annoying first name her parents had given her, the name she had long ago rejected. "Surely I didn't inherit *you* along with the house. Where did you come from?"

"My mother." The girl smiled.

Of course Pond was imagining it, but she could almost hear Gertrude's laughter. Pond stifled a grin. "True for all of us," she admitted. She studied the girl, who was ensconced amidst a fantastic spread of pillows of all colors and patterns. The stripes, squares, and paisleys should have clashed, but somehow formed a perfect backdrop for the girl and her dark orange shirt. "Who's your mother?"

"You know her as Colleen."

Pond could see the resemblance now. Colleen, the woman who cleaned Gertrude's house, was dark haired, tall, and formidable, and Nareen would be too someday, although at the moment she appeared to be peaceable and all of fourteen. Colleen's daughter had glossy brown hair, clear golden skin, and dark eyes that remained focused on her reading.

In all directions Pond looked, upstairs and down, surfaces gleamed. Even the air stood up and took notice when Colleen moved through the house. Pond could appreciate that, and had allowed the arrangement to continue. It was certainly the only way the house would be cleaned as long as Pond had anything to do with it. The money that went with the house seemed endless, so there was no reason to do otherwise.

"But she left?" Pond asked. "She's done with her work. You'll have to call your mom and tell her to come get you. She couldn't have forgotten you."

"Oh, she never forgets me," Nareen replied. "That wouldn't be possible. I'm her daughter."

"Good. Then call her and get her back here. Don't want you missing your mom."

"I never miss her, either."

"So call her." Pond reached into her yoga Capri pants, to which she had sewed on a pocket or two, patch style, and pulled out a cell phone, so far the only purchase she'd made with her great-aunt's money. She proffered the phone to the girl.

"My mom doesn't answer her phone," Nareen said, looking up at Pond.

"Then how are you supposed to reach your mom and tell her she's left you here?" Pond demanded.

"That's a good question." Nareen again became absorbed in the page in front of her.

"You can't *stay* here," Pond retorted wryly, stating the obvious. Gertrude's money paid Colleen to make the house gleam, insofar as its abstruse arches and whimsical towers and spindles could admit enough light to permit its confusing corners to gleam. But throwing a bookworm daughter into the exchange was not part of the deal.

"Why not?" Nareen turned a page.

"Because it's not possible."

"You have six extra bedrooms," the girl pointed out in a neutral voice. "In addition to all your other dens, pantries, offices, and dressing rooms."

*They're not mine*, Pond almost said. But she caught herself in time. If they weren't hers, why was she so set upon not sharing them with an unexpected houseguest? "That doesn't mean I want you staying in one of them," she said aloud, stating what was so evident it ought to remain unspoken. "You're *not* invited."

"I never am," the girl replied in a steady voice. "But somehow I still get to see a lot of the world."

"Oh my God. You don't mean your mom does this all the time, picks a house and leaves you there?" She didn't know whether to laugh or cry at the idea. The footloose part of her approved, while the part of her that had once been a young girl shivered.

"*I* pick the house," Nareen corrected her. "Yours is very beautiful, you know. I've stayed at some of the finest houses in Baltimore, but there's something different about this place. I've decided I like this house better than all the rest."

"You're serious." Pond squinted at the girl. "Well, you can't hang out with me, and that's that."

"But I've decided to stay here this week." Nareen smiled with determination, her teeth white and even. At the moment, she looked very much like her mother, who intimidated Pond. Pond found the experience unsettling, as she was otherwise accustomed to either intimidating everyone else, or not quite managing to mind what others thought.

Pond nodded, as if she were unfazed. "What if I called Child Protective Services?" she offered brightly. "A perky, caring professional can come out and collect you. That would surely be much more stable. You don't want to grow up in strangers' houses. Very disruptive, moving all the time." She suppressed a smile. Moving all the time *was* disruptive, but there was also something habit-forming about it. Still, fourteen-year-olds were too young to develop their own habits. Adults got to determine such matters for them.

"Besides," she added, bluffing a bit, "I'm not at all nice. CPS has *got* to be nicer than I am." Undermining her own point, she refrained from saying aloud, *Plus, they want to help you, and I don't.*

"CPS doesn't know what to do with me," Nareen

said. "I take care of myself. And I won't stay anywhere they put me."

She had to give the kid credit for aplomb. "When did you say your mom is coming back?" Pond asked, maintaining an even voice. The light streamed through the bay picture window and added its own stripes across the multi-patterned pillows. Pond ran her fingers through her hair, one of the few features she let herself like when she glanced in a mirror. At the moment, reflected in the window, she could see glints shining off sleek waves of dark brown, red, and gold.

"Next week, of course," Nareen said agreeably.

Of course. Colleen cleaned Gertrude's house every week. "Look," Pond told the girl, "it's the cops or CPS. Which do you want me to call first?"

But before anything could be resolved about who would be called, Gertrude's phone rang. Nareen closed her book and placed it with care into an embroidered bag she wore slung across her body as if it were part of her wardrobe. She looked at her host and leaned back into the pillows, apparently prepared to absorb all the sunshine she could, as independent and used to taking care of herself as an outdoor cat. Right now, Nareen was indoors, and luxuriating in the life that streamed in through the windows.

Pond was not accustomed to being in a position where anyone could summon her. She hadn't given out her new cell phone number, and didn't plan on answering it if anyone called. Nonetheless, the house phone continued jangling, jarring Pond's already sensitive nerves. What was she supposed to do, answer the call, as if she were a normal person, a commonplace type who could be reached by *telephone*? She scrambled downstairs, glared at the clangorous machine, and then picked up the receiver.

"Pond residence," she said, her voice as stiff as her spine.

On the other end of the line was Gertrude's lawyer, Bertram Something-Something, Esquire. Before she had quite registered what was happening, he was reading a codicil to the will. From beyond the grave, Gertrude was enjoying a bit of a joke. This part of the will wasn't to be read until Francine had stayed in the house three nights.

The lawyer cleared his throat twice. "She told me from the time the codicil is read you have seven days to take possession of the house. Otherwise it takes possession of you." The attorney read part of the codicil aloud. "The first part of the answer resides in one of the books you will find while staying in the house."

"*Ha, ha,*" Pond said. "That's a good one." Everywhere she looked, she could see books. Books were stacked on shelves and piled on the floor. She knew from pulling out several drawers that looked suitable for containing linens that they, too, held books. Books were everywhere. And the answer would be found in one of these tomes. Gertrude was enjoying a good laugh, but Pond wasn't. "What was the question?" Pond asked.

"I'm only reading you what the codicil says," Bertram told her, as kindly as someone who billed by the minute could manage. "There's more," he went on. "'You have only seven days to figure out the secret of the house. After that, the ship sets sail, with you or without you.'"

"You've got to be kidding."

"She told me something else," he said, his voice taking on a thoughtful tone. "It wasn't part of the codicil, but after we had written this addition to the will, she said, 'I want her searching as if her hair is on fire and the only way to put out the fire is to search.'"

Pond felt her scalp prickle, and she patted the top of her head to be sure no flames had arisen. Her hair didn't seem to have combusted. All felt cool and quiet. Except a sense of burning heat was now rising within her—part curiosity, part anger, and part something else. Fear? Excitement? "Thanks for telling me."

"If I were you," the lawyer offered in a helpful manner, "I'd find the secret of that place and get out of there as soon as possible. Sooner than seven days, if you can manage. She was...unusual. Very interested in end-of-days things."

"The end times."

"Right," the lawyer affirmed. "The old ways pass away, the new ones arise. I could be wrong, but I wouldn't want to stay in that house if I were you."

"I'll leave then," Pond vowed, with a sigh of relief. "There's no reason for me to be in this place."

"Except you only have seven days to figure out the secret, the one you can't get away from in any case."

"*Gaa*. So, I have to stay here in this ticking time

bomb of a house."

"It's not so bad," the lawyer said, attempting to comfort her and only making it worse. "We're all living in a ticking time bomb, in a manner of speaking. Yours is just more definite."

"I'm not going to *die*."

"Probably not. Because you're going to figure out the secret of the house. Besides, she didn't say anything about dying. She said something about rising."

"What?" Pond demanded.

"I can't remember." The lawyer coughed, as if he had realized he'd revealed more than he was supposed to.

"Seriously?" Pond said, in complete bemusement. She drew a deep breath. "Fine. I'll look for the secret. Starting in books, it sounds like. But what do I do about this house? I can't stay in it after seven days. I never stay that long in one place. Not unless you really want me dead."

"Sell it," the lawyer advised, his voice becoming smooth and taking on a more routine tone. "Figure out the answer and sell it."

"Can't I sell it now?"

"Alas, no. You have to live in it seven more days first."

"I'll give it away," Pond declared.

"There can be no transfer of title until you live in it for seven days first." The lawyer drew a deep breath. "And today is day one."

\*\*\*

Pond ought to have felt independent and at ease, but after her conversation she felt trapped instead. She placed the receiver back on the phone, which had to be vintage World War II era, complete with ancient rotary dial. The ring was more than loud enough. Maybe she ought to have ignored its summons. Now she had to find the answer, which would put out the fire all these questions were creating within her.

The light in the house had shifted. The sun was overhead, its rays no longer streaming through the same windows. Before she decided what to do in response to the phone call, she fled to the front porch. Right now, being on the porch was as close as she could come to fulfilling her first choice— outright leaving the house behind.

After she had ruled out all other options, Pond began canvassing all the books. Books were in the parlor area, and the living room. They were even in the entry foyer. Dining room, check; pantry, check; kitchen, check. In the pantry, she ran into Nareen, who was closing a cabinet and looking self-satisfied, though Pond was too annoyed with books to spend much energy being irritated with Nareen. Bathroom, check.

*Who leaves books in their bathroom?* Pond wondered. Conservatory, check. Books were in every room on the ground floor.

"What are you doing?" Nareen asked, who had begun following her from room to room.

"Looking at books. One of them contains an answer I'm supposed to find. The answer will reveal some sort of secret to the house."

Pond ran up the service stairs, which led from the kitchen to the second floor. Books adorned the master bedroom, and the library of course, as well as the dressing room, the office and guest bedrooms, and the upstairs bathrooms, too.

She growled and ran up the stairs to the third floor. The third floor contained books in four bedrooms, a den, a dressing room, and more bathrooms. By the time she ran up the winding stairs to the extra half floor, which was round and consisted mostly of glass, she almost knew to expect what she would find—a window seat built into the round wall, and books lining every square inch of space beneath it.

"No problem," Pond said sarcastically. "I'll just breeze through these buddies this afternoon, find the answer, and be done with it."

"I can help," Nareen offered, beginning to page through the nearest volumes.

"There are probably books in the basement too." Pond wondered where it might be best to begin looking—at the house's top, bottom, or somewhere in the middle.

"You know what I wonder…" Nareen spoke in an aimless tone of voice, as if she were talking about nothing that mattered. "How well do you know this house? You might be interested in some of the things I've discovered while helping my mom clean it." She looked at Pond, and smiled, before adding a cutting glint to her grin. "You might not want to stay here alone, you know."

"Sure I do." Pond had always lived alone; it was one of the things she loved about staying in motion.

Besides, she had stayed three nights in the place, and slept like a happy log each night. "Time for you to move on, Nareen." She'd always been the one to go, so how in the world was she supposed to get someone *else* to leave?

"Where would I go?" the girl asked, as if it were the most reasonable question in the world. She copied Pond's movements, ruffling through books, seeming to work with much more facility than Pond did. She discovered an old library card, and an old calling card, but that was it. She set them aside in a neat pile.

"*I* don't know," Pond said. "School. Where does your mom go? Go with her."

"It's summer, of course," Nareen said, rolling her eyes. "School's out. And my mom has to work all the time. She's all over the place. Really, this is much more settled for me."

"CPS could give you a settled arrangement. A permanent one. You could live in the same house *all the time*. Like other people do." She held back a shudder as she threatened Nareen with such a horrid possibility. Houses held phones where lawyers could reach you, and massive piles of books to look through, and other torments that had yet to reveal themselves.

"Sure," Nareen agreed. "Do you know how boring that sounds?"

*Actually, kid, I do.* Aloud, Pond said, "I didn't know this was about your entertainment." Somehow, having to provide for a young girl's amusement felt even more absurd than letting her turn Gertrude's house into an involuntary bed and breakfast.

"Of course it's not," Nareen replied. "I have my book for that. I can read anywhere, you know. In any conditions. I have read in the midst of cat fights, dog fights, and sibling fights, and while spouses threw vases at each other over my head. I am very focused."

*This girl picks quite the houses*, Pond mused. At the moment, the house they stood in was peaceful, full of echoes of Gertrude's laughter, along with the precious bric-a-brac of a lifetime, piled into three and a half stories. Too many of Gertrude's treasures were bound between covers Pond now had to open.

"There aren't a lot of fights in this house," she said, wanting to brush away the distractions provided by all those books, and by this girl.

"I can tell." Nareen gave an equivocal shrug.

"Not unless you're planning on starting them."

"I read," the girl said. "Other people fight."

"Here we go." Pond discovered a twenty-dollar bill which had fallen out of the volume she was holding, a book about gardens in the eighteenth century. By reflex, she was thrilled as she thought about the meals it would buy, before she remembered Gertrude's money would buy all the meals she would ever need. But Gertrude's money would also make her go through all these books. Whatever the question, twenty dollars probably wasn't the answer.

"Really," Pond said. "Why in the world would I let you stay here this week?"

"Why *wouldn't* you? You have a very big house all to yourself."

"I don't even know you," Pond spluttered, holding a volume on topiary upside down and shaking it. The spine creaked, but nothing else happened.

"Not yet."

"But I'm not your mom," Pond protested. "I don't know what parents do. I don't know how they do it."

"Some of them don't."

"You're right about that." Pond glanced up in bemusement from a book on obscure handmade coins. This girl had an answer for everything. "You are way too smart for your age."

She shrugged. "I've had to be. Look, you won't even notice I'm here. The only thing you'll notice is how helpful I am. Give me two hours, and you'll thank me. You'll *ask* me to stay the rest of the week."

It didn't sound like much. Colleen was a formidable house cleaner few would dare to challenge, and Pond wasn't sure she could either. If stubborn grout stains couldn't resist her, what hope did Pond have against Colleen's daughter?

"Two hours," she agreed, hoping she wouldn't regret it. She began to notice and to appreciate that Nareen was moving through the book stacks with great efficiency. Maybe the girl would find the answer, whatever that meant.

And then Nareen got up and left, her footsteps vanishing into the vast house, and Pond felt a flash of annoyance. *You don't actually want her here,* she reprimanded herself. *You don't want to know what she's doing.* Pond got up, too, and lost herself in the house, although she returned to the upper half-story sooner than Nareen.

"See," the girl said, reappearing some time later, proving she had been to the pantry and kitchen, at least.

Pond was seated on the window seat cushions, staring at the ground level book stashes, and wondering why her aunt had such arcane taste in literature.

Nareen held out a tray, one Pond thought she remembered having seen before, tucked away in one of the ground floor pantries or sculleries. It was an expanse of bronze painted with fine cloisonné work or something similar, featuring little sprigs of blue, yellow, and white flowers along a border. The tray held an array of food Pond never would have thought to combine.

"I'm a much better cook than your aunt," Nareen explained.

"You would have to be," said Pond dryly.

The one meal she had eaten, or attempted to eat, at Gertrude's had been a debacle. Gertrude had meant to serve roast duck for a winter holiday meal. She was too nontraditional to celebrate Christmas, which she figured other people had more than covered with their usual tedious parties, but was glad enough to summon up festivities for Yuletide or the winter solstice.

The only trouble was, she had gotten so involved in festooning her house with greens she had neglected to turn on the oven until fifteen minutes before dinner. The result was predictable; everyone admired the dining room, which made it look like multiple trees had sacrificed their lives, or at least their limbs, to drape every available surface with evergreen branches and swags, wreaths and bows. Many surfaces which were not available had been pressed into service anyway, for the greening of halls and walls, windows and doors, ceilings and floors.

And everyone had taken a few bites before realizing their optimistic mistake, then poked dubiously at raw duck, which Gertrude served and ate with as much delight as if it had been golden brown and braised with delicious plum sauce. Pond still wondered if Gertrude had known about her culinary disaster or not. She also wondered which possibility pleased her more—that her aunt was oblivious to cooking or to politeness.

Either way, whether she didn't know about oven thermometers or didn't mind serving uncooked fowl, Gertrude reveled in freedom, rejoiced in the raw or the rude. By now, of course, the resulting stomachache was a long forgotten twinge stored somewhere in Pond's digestive system neurons.

"How did you know my great-aunt wasn't much of a cook?" she asked, straightening her shoulders and studying Nareen's concoction.

She'd taken organic corn chips and what had to be the only fresh grapefruit in the house, and placed a tiny sliver of the fruit atop a single chip, adding a single dried shaving of something or other to the delicate pyramid: it looked like artisanal cheese, or sun dried mango, or maybe both, and then atop the whole pyramid she had sprinkled little green tendrils of what smelled like lemon basil from the kitchen garden. Pond popped two in her mouth, and chewed, delighted. But she wasn't going to admit it.

"Not bad," she said.

"I'm a much better cook than you are, too." Nareen's face took on a mischievous expression, so that she looked for a moment like an imp.

"How can you say such a thing?" It was true, though. When it came to eating, Pond was an accomplished food connoisseur, but she remained a barely competent chef. One of her temporary abodes had been in a culinary school basement, so she could tell the difference between fennel and anise in a single bite of a perfect dish, but she wouldn't know what to do with a fennel bulb if it walked up and introduced itself to her. Just like she didn't know what to do with this disconcerting girl. But how could Nareen know Pond suffered from an appalling lack of knife skills?

*For good reason*, Pond assured herself. *I am far too reasonable for cooking.* Sometimes life made it necessary to eat cold beans out of a can, standing over a sink. Freedom was more important than consistency.

"I know your kitchen, from before it was yours," the girl explained, "and you haven't changed it. Only one baking sheet. No real cook has fewer than four."

*So, I'm not a real cook*, Pond thought defensively, *but it's not exactly your place to tell me so. Besides, I've only been here three days. Give me time, and I can add cookie sheets. Not that I would know what to do with them.* "How did *you* get to be a cook, anyway?" Pond asked aloud.

"I've had to be," Nareen said again, and for a moment her eyes looked ancient in her youthful face. She placed the tray on an antique side table and disappeared again, moving downstairs, and out of Pond's sight.

She'd vanished into the vastness of the house, no doubt to accomplish something delicious and productive, if nothing else. Pond made a sour face and decided to focus on accomplishing nothing at all.

But even the appeal of reveling in complete non-accomplishment couldn't draw her away from the search for long. When she went back to it, she also took stock of her own place in the mansion.

*I've really got to make my acquaintance with the full repertoire of Gertrude's pantries,* she resolved. It was a bit embarrassing to have Nareen already know her way around Gertrude's kitchen and supplies better than Pond did. *But then, Nareen investigated the place and counted its cookie trays before I came on the scene, before I even knew I had a visitor.* There would be time for Pond to know Gertrude's kitchen goodies. *Or maybe they're my kitchen goodies.*

One of these days, she would have to meet them all.

Pond sighed and stared at the bronze tray in dismay. *These things are tasty,* she thought, enjoying them against her will as she turned back to the books. She didn't want the hors d'oeuvres to be good, didn't want to like anything associated with her peculiar visitor.

Her aunt's books distracted her from Nareen,

absorbed her. Maybe she could understand her aunt by the titles she'd read. But something about these works made her frown. She pulled out the volumes and stared at several, reading the back covers and studying the fronts.

This area of the book stacks covered obscure and popular volumes on Julian of Norwich, St. John of the Cross, Valmiki, Milarepa, the Bhagavad-Gita, *The Serpent Power*, tomes on Kabbalah, yoga, tantra, and Kundalini. Some of them looked awe-inspiring, promising to transform a reader's life with a single prayer, or a non-prayer, a single act or a non-act. Many of the volumes featured covers that suggested reading them would enable you to ride a rainbow to a seven-turreted castle made of gold, or drink four leaf clover tea with leprechauns, or close your eyes and ascend on rays of white light that looked something like a carnival ride Pond had favored when she was about twelve.

But ascend *where*, Pond didn't know. And who did you meet after making your ascent? She doubted it could be an old white-bearded Big Daddy in the sky. And it had to be better than a carnival barker or a ticket taker, but so far that was all she had been able to conjure up in her mind. And Pond wasn't at all sure she had a ticket in her pocket. Maybe that was what Gertrude had meant her to find, but so far it was eluding her, whether she looked inside books or outside them.

Whatever the answer was, she wasn't sure it could be found in books. But she wanted to understand her great-aunt so she could understand how to get rid of this house and all its money, which were posing a major inconvenience.

*Cramping my style,* she thought, *holding me down. Not that anything's* ever *going to keep me fixed in one place.*

Yet, here she was, in Baltimore against her will, having to deal with a ridiculous mansion and *finances*, for God's sake. Not to mention what seemed like limitless towers of books and a secret she had to discover. Or was it a threat she had to disarm? She couldn't tell, from the lawyer's words.

Nareen materialized at Pond's elbow, this time holding a tray of beverages. She recognized this serving implement, as well—carved hardwood, probably antique. Another item she would have to meet. She could then proceed to dispose of it.

"What's this?" Pond took a glass.

Nareen smiled. "Pineapple fizz. Something I came up with. Just from things most pantries have piled up anyway. It's very adaptable."

*I know adaptable when I see it.* The drink was a tall glass of pineapple sharpness, softened by other elements that were creamy, and also a bit sparkly. *It doesn't taste bad,* Pond admitted to herself, but aloud she said nothing. *In fact, this drink is severely delicious*, she thought to herself after a second gulp.

"What are you reading?" the girl asked, seeming to notice Pond had shifted tactics. No longer was she just plummeting through the pages.

"Books." Pond was surrounded by tall stacks she'd already looked through, some of which she'd studied a bit. But she felt like she was mowing an enormous lawn which grew even as she mowed it. More volumes loomed on all sides than were piled around her.

The girl nodded, her eyes ironic.

Pond softened. "What about you. What are you reading?"

"Only one book. It's called the *Eighth Book of Secrets.*"

"Must have enjoyed the first seven volumes, then." An unfamiliar and quite dusty compartment of her mind approved of kids who read, not that she was going to let on.

Nareen shook her head. "It's the only volume I have. I don't know about the first seven."

"Look," Pond said, fired by a genuine impulse of generosity and self-preservation, "I would *give* you this house if I could, and all its books. But I can't." A look of misery crossed her face.

Nareen nodded. She seemed to know about giving things away, just as she knew about things that were impossible to let go of. "My mom always said she was the daughter of the wind," she remarked. "Her dad was freer than the wind."

"I get it." For Pond, having someone consider her a homeowner made as much sense as someone willing a house to the wind, or to a tree, or a river. She resumed looking through books, working through one after another, back again in the mode of hoping whatever it was she needed to find would fall out of the pages into her lap.

"He was a preacher," Nareen said, and Pond's smile diminished. She had walked away from the extravagant names her family had bequeathed to her, and away from their money and possessions, but not from their suspicion of men with clerical

21

collars.

"He couldn't own anything longer than two days." Nareen seated herself cross-legged on the floor, working with steady care through all the volumes around her. "Anything in his possession, he had to give it away. Money started burning a hole in his pocket, and so he would give it to the first person he saw who needed it. Even the clothes on his back."

Pond ached with understanding, and longed to throw her current volume against the wall, not that it was very offensive, a book on ladders and ladder designs. Her main problem with preachers was they'd figured something out for themselves, and felt no qualms about telling everyone else what to do. She wanted to figure everything out for herself, and didn't presume anyone else wanted to know about it once she had. And she also reserved the right to figure out nothing at all. But giving everything away—*God, yes.*

"Did he end up naked, once he gave away his clothes?" she asked eagerly, despite herself. She herself had a pack she could carry on her back, and nothing else. She would have preferred traveling lighter, but this country didn't understand being skyclad—adorned only with air. Pond contented herself with yoga clothes, to which she added pockets and random thermal layers as necessary.

"Not naked," Nareen said. "Everything he needed, he always found. He said, 'I own things, things don't own me.' And when my mom asked him what he meant, he told her, 'Things serve me, I don't serve them. You have to make a choice.' So, I guess my mom made her choice."

"*Aaaah.*" Pond made a strangled noise in the back of her throat. With her entire being, she felt the weight of all the items she didn't even know the house had, whole stashes of kitchen and dining accouterments, not to mention three and a half stories of fine furniture and entire rooms well-stocked with clothes, books, music, and wine. Not that she drank anymore, but that just made it *worse*, didn't it? And books beyond books. "There are a lot of things in this house." She moaned.

"I know there are. I've helped my mom dust them all."

"You can have them all, except you can't. Gertrude's will won't let me give them away."

"Sell them," the girl offered, looking up from a tome on evergreen trees.

Pond shook her head. "It's more dire than that. I can't sell them, either."

"So, don't accept them. They're not yours."

"Except they *are*." Pond sighed. "It's a terrible problem to have."

"I've seen worse." The girl grinned, her gaze remaining on the other glass on the serving tray.

"Help yourself," Pond said automatically. She wondered if despite herself she'd slipped across some invisible line, and now she and Nareen would have to coexist in peace, at least until two hours were up. *But I don't coexist in peace with anyone,* Pond thought. And she crossed her arms to prove it.

Nareen was either quite bad at reading body language, or quite good, and she looked past Pond's sullen posture. "I can tell you about one of the problems I've seen. It'll make yours look like nothing."

"Nothing looks like nothing," Pond complained. But despite herself, she listened, and she paged through the books, her pace taking on the rhythm of her own breath.

"I was staying at one place," Nareen began, settling herself into the rhythm of talking while ruffling through pages. The light streaming in through the windows settled on her face and shoulders. "It wasn't what it appeared. From the outside, it was a mansion, with more glass than this house, and a tennis court, both outdoors and indoors, a movie theater all its own, and a lap pool. But it actually was more of a prison."

"I *know*," Pond said, frowning at a plain piece of paper that had been relinquished by a volume on monkeys. "That's what this house is. That's what I've been telling you."

"No, it's not. You can be locked out of somewhere as much as you can be locked in. The boy who lived in the house was supposed to turn sixteen, but his parents used all the deadbolts on all the doors, keeping everyone inside safe. The boy, they locked outside. He spent his birthday pounding on all the doors, shrieking that he was having the worst birthday ever."

"Why did they lock him out?"

"To keep everyone inside safe."

"What was he going to do to them?" Pond asked, curious despite herself. She'd had bad birthdays, but they involved people almost forgetting the occasion, rather than tormenting her. At least, so far as she knew, any birthday afflictions had been more accidental or providential—extra garnish on the sometimes nonexistent cake.

"He was going to have his birthday," Nareen explained. "If *he* got to be one year older, then everyone else in the house did, too, and that couldn't happen. That was the house time didn't enter. The mom didn't grow older, the dad didn't get gray, the children didn't grow up."

"Yikes." Pond was holding a book on graveyard monuments, which did not make her feel particularly comfortable.

"No one in that house had birthdays. The children weren't quite allowed to exist. The whole house pretended everything had always been the same exact way it was at that precise moment. No one had ever been any younger, and of course no one would ever get any older. The boy's sister went along with it. She told me, 'It's easier to pretend than to go off on my own. If I go off on my own, what do I get, reality? Who wants reality?'

"But the boy wouldn't give in. Every year, he insisted on having his birthday. I couldn't quite figure out how he knew when his birthday was, if his parents pretended things had always been the way they were. A birthday admits that your life began sometime, you know? And if your life began sometime, then it would also end sometime. I could actually see the parents' logic. They had a point. A weird one, but a point.

"So, I asked him. He said he'd chosen his birthday because he liked the date. July seventh. Seventh day in the seventh month of the year. And then he said he chose another. Since no one else in the house had birthdays, there was a major shortage of birthdays, so he might as well have two. And he liked the date November eleventh. Eleventh day in the eleventh month. And then having a birthday was so interesting he chose another—March third. Third day of the third month.

"'I see a pattern,' I told him.

"'Well, it's better than *their* pattern,' he said.

"'So, you have three birthdays,' I said. It sounded fun at first, if your birthday was something to be celebrated. But if your birthday became a battlefield, then maybe not.

"'Better than none,' he told me.

"'But you're asking for a fight,' I said. 'You practically know they're going to do something like lock you out.' We were talking the next day, after he had been let back in the house. His fists were bruised from pounding, and his throat was sore from shouting, but he was more cheerful than I had yet seen him.

"'Wouldn't you rather fight than give in?' He smiled at me, but his eyes were very serious.

"'I don't like fighting,' I told him. I'm honest. 'Reading is more my style.'" Nareen looked at the now spiraling piles of books looming over her, and her eyes took on an amused gleam.

"And what did he say?" Pond asked, intrigued despite herself.

"He said, 'Sounds like an escape to me.'

"'Well, it's not my battle,' I said. 'I'm just visiting.'

"'That's my point,' he said. 'You're here for a

26

while. Which means you aren't locked out of or locked into time. Time is yours. If my parents have any say in the matter, time isn't mine.'

"He went on celebrating his birthdays—all of them, all by himself. That takes a lot of strength, going out on your own like that."

"But he hadn't left home," Pond reasoned. "He wasn't on his own."

"He *was* on his own," Nareen said. "And happy about it." She paused to munch a few of the culinary compositions she had made—edible art formed with corn chips as a foundation. She looked placid amidst her piles of books, as if she belonged, as if she were right at home.

*She looks more natural here than I do.* Pond felt like their proper roles were reversed, like she were the gangly one who didn't belong. Gertrude's house and money were as ill-fitting on her as clothes on a teenager; she hadn't grown into them, any more than a teenager had become accustomed to her own body.

Pond wouldn't have minded inheriting just the carriage house out back; that felt more familiar to her, and was probable home to spiders and other comfortable creatures. Old lampshades and ugly discarded furniture she could deal with. Streaky windows and drafty doors were no problem at all, and she could always hope the carriage house held no books. But this magnificent place would give her nightmares if she let it.

She thought about the living room, with its mullioned glass, its transom and transom lights over all the doors, the fine hardwood floor, honey-colored oak bordered by a double strip of darker maple. She considered the paintings, some of which looked objectionably valuable—a few original Chagalls, Rothkos, and several by other celebrated artists. It was all whimsy and color fields, cows dancing over the moon, lovers embracing violins and one another amidst the stars, reds and blues that saturated her if she let them.

The only one she liked was a frowning dark faced woman in the corner, whose hair featured a single red flower, and whose brow met in the midst of her stormy forehead, and Pond was almost certain *that* painting was just as famous as the rest. So, she would have to disapprove of it after all.

"It didn't work," she told Nareen with grim satisfaction and a baleful glance at a book on red birds. "I still think this house is a total problem. That kid had it easy. Time went on ticking by, even if his parents didn't admit it. He was going to get older, and when he got older, he could leave. And then he could go out into the world and find reasonable people who admitted things like birthdays exist. That's what I've always done, gone out and moved on when things got unreasonable. And now I can't." She groaned. "Gertrude had it in for me. If his parents really had it in for him, they would have given him their palatial house. It's by far the best way to afflict someone."

"You might be right," Nareen said, surprising Pond.

She felt gratified, but also disappointed, as if she had expected the girl to argue with her, to attempt to show her that Pond's lot was not one of sheer pain after all. And now Pond had gotten her way; she was left holding a bucket of complaints, and found she didn't want to. She didn't want the house, didn't want any of the buckets it forced upon her. But she didn't know how to walk away from it all. Still, they were making progress. The stacks of books surrounding them on the floor now outnumbered the stacks of books yet to be looked through on all sides.

Pond sighed, a sound of high melodrama, and slumped her head back against one of the book stacks, which threatened to teeter and topple over. The room was all curves and rounded corners, and looked as if it should feel hideous and uncomfortable to Pond, but wasn't bad. Even that didn't suit her at the moment. She didn't want to feel at ease in Gertrude's upper half story, didn't want anything about the house to entice her or make her feel that impossible condition—at home.

"On the other hand, I always find the house I need," Nareen told her. "Might not be the house I want, but it's always the house I need."

"Good for you," Pond replied, her face sour. "You found this one. Can't see why anyone would want it."

"Then there's no problem with me staying here."

"Except that I'm here. I would be anywhere else, but here I am." Pond reminded herself Gertrude had loved this place, and giving the house to her grand-niece may not have been intended as a peculiar form of torture, even though that was often what families specialized in. "I mean, *thanks*, Aunt Gertrude," she said aloud, with false enthusiasm.

Nareen laughed. "Gertrude loved you."

That idea startled Pond into silence. Her gaze roamed from floor to ceiling, taking in the half walls of glass, the hand-carved details of the surrounding window seat, and again the bookcases lining the floor. "Strange way to show it. She didn't *know* me," Pond said.

Nareen shrugged. "Maybe that made you easier to love. Maybe she loved everybody. She was proud of you, anyway."

"That's terrible." Pond gasped. "That's the absolute last thing I want." She didn't want anyone to agree with her, condone her decisions—or worst of all, be *proud* of her. She was determined to do something so beyond the pale that no one would again refer to her as Francine Millicent. Everyone would shake their head and agree she'd finally slipped beyond reason, beyond the world. "I guess you'll have to stay here after all," she said, with such a wild, desperate outburst that one of the book piles tilted and began to scatter. Pond grabbed at it, stopping its descent.

"Yay!" Nareen exclaimed, dropping a volume on orchids to clap her hands.

"I don't know about that." Pond wished she could take back her words.

She felt confused by hearing Gertrude had been proud of her, and for a moment wasn't certain of anything. Maybe her family would *approve* of her hosting this homeless waif—not that the girl was technically homeless, any more than she was technically a waif.

But how was she to know what anyone else

might think? And why did she *still* care what her family thought, when she had spent all these years trying *not* to care? She slumped back on the floor and looked at all the books, which covered every last subject. Maybe one of these volumes could answer her question, not that she would confess some shadowy part of her liked books. She damn well wasn't going to read them all.

Pond fled the room, but it didn't work. She couldn't leave behind the questions that were rising up. She closed her eyes in bewilderment and leaned against a wall. Nareen was back there in that room, yet Pond was more alone now, in this house, than in all the places she'd ever been.

She returned to the half-story. The house wasn't letting her run from herself, no matter how much she attempted to lose herself in it.

In Texas she had picked up sand burrs and twanging phrases, and a cowboy hat she lost at the next stop or two, along with cowboy boots some silent man had given her off the back of his pick-up. She had also picked up the ability to eat almost anything and almost nothing—snakes, cacti, fried everything, and fried nothing.

In Arizona, and all across the great west, she had seen sunsets over deserts, mountains, and lakes. She'd watched the day wake over cities, plains, and visions that seemed like mirages but turned out to be actual abandoned castles in sandstone walls and canyons.

In Alaska she had been burned and baked by the sun, dried by the wind, wetted, flashed, and sizzled by storms. In Wisconsin, and Colorado, she'd frozen, shivered, thawed, and gotten both lost and found in water and rock.

In New York, and Maine, she had slept in places she couldn't remember because they were so uncomfortable they didn't bear returning to. She'd also slept in places she couldn't remember because they were so beautiful they didn't bear recalling, places that would make anywhere afterward seem like it wasn't worth seeing, make her feel like her real life had ended somewhere back on the road.

"I had to keep traveling," she told the girl as she closed her eyes.

Shards of light, color, and sound kept flashing before her, all she'd seen while journeying, and all she had not seen, but somehow absorbed in her bones, so that she now carried more than before she left.

Most of all, her family wasn't where she was traveling. Nowhere she went did she find them. Everywhere she looked on the road, they were not there. She was Pond, and she was free. At least, that had been the big idea.

"I didn't intend to learn a damn thing." She laughed. "I seem to have achieved my goal. And now I don't know if that's good."

Her whole life had been full of lessons and the very best schooling anyone could have, yet Pond was convinced she had learned absolutely nothing that mattered. She opened her eyes and without changing the position of her head, moved her gaze in Nareen's direction.

"I mean, come on, what have you ever learned in school?"

Nareen smiled. "Nothing that seems to have harmed me too much."

"Wish I could say the same."

"Of course I learn much more in other ways. Reading. Moving around. Watch out for the quiet people. They often see a great deal more of what's going on than they let you know."

"I don't let myself see what's going on," Pond growled, closing her eyes and holding them shut tight to make sure of it. But even after she had closed her eyes, she still saw the girl's face silhouetted against the wall, her stare penetrating, inescapable.

"So, you admit Aunt Gertrude had it in for me," she said, without opening her eyes. Even in the darkness behind her closed lids, she could not avoid Nareen's gaze, so she again looked out of the corner of her eyes at the girl. Then, to avoid her piercing glance, she resumed going through books.

Nareen shook her head; she had continued her search with no pause. "I didn't say that. I said giving someone a house might be a good way to give them something to think about. Like you said, you can't always walk away from a house."

"That doesn't mean it's going to make me think," Pond vowed. "I stopped thinking after I graduated from high school. They claimed to be making me think in college, but it didn't work, so I left, and brushed all that off my hands forever."

"Thinking doesn't hurt." Nareen laughed.

"It's giving me a headache talking about it," Pond insisted. She recalled the grim-faced veterans of education, who might have managed to be a little less annoying than the giddy teachers, and coaches who told her, *I want to see blood, and I want none of it to be yours.* She remembered principals who derived way too much pleasure from their own words, and seemed to see themselves as dictionary-spouting army generals.

"I had the very best of educations." Pond shuddered. "I hate to consider what the substandard kind would have looked like." Or felt like. "Why do you even go to school?"

"I don't always," Nareen said. "If I want to, I go."

"I like *going*. Not to school, just going anywhere to be going somewhere."

"I like learning."

"What a terrible thing for a young person to say. I worry about the future of the world."

"People have always worried about the future of the world," Nareen pointed out, "and we're still here."

"Oh, no…please don't. You sound like you're taking the Long Perspective. Besides, we can always hope the world won't be here much longer." Pond's aunt must have agreed; the lawyer had said this house might have something to do with the end of the world. "This *moment*, that's where it's at. Where can I go this moment that won't require me to learn anything or do anything."

"You're not in a bad place right now."

Pond didn't disagree, not that she was going to admit it. She liked this room much more with all the books out of order, jumbled together, tilting like a precarious tower toward the ceiling.

"I am dangerously close to being thoughtful right now," she observed. "At least it doesn't require me to do much of anything." Nothing other than be that dreaded thing, a homeowner, a manager of finances, someone who answered to the legal name of Francine Millicent Pond. Someone who couldn't run when the impulse came, couldn't fly when the next wind blew down from the neighboring mountain peak, couldn't drift along freer than the tranquil rivers.

Nareen had eaten all the chips she had assembled. Now there wasn't even food to compensate for all the trouble Pond was taking. She sighed. "Being thoughtful doesn't hurt you," Nareen offered.

"You sound like a teacher," Pond said, and her tone made it clear it wasn't meant to be a compliment.

"Not that." She shook her head in determination. "I've decided to be a student forever."

Pond made a face.

"That doesn't mean going to *school* forever," Nareen clarified. "Not unless you're learning."

That was a novel idea. For Pond, not going to school unless you were learning would probably have meant not going to school *ever*. And after leaving school, Pond had continued *not* learning with all the determination she could muster, which was quite a lot.

"If you're not a teacher," Pond said, "then maybe you sound like my parents. Except they always made me go to school."

"After age twenty-five, you're not allowed to

blame your parents for anything. I read that somewhere."

Pond was going to have to revise her earlier assessment. Reading was downright incendiary. Books ought to be kept out of the hands of young people. In allowing Nareen to go through these books with her, Pond was doing nothing less than handing the girl dynamite. Pond was twenty-six, and blaming her parents was as familiar to her as her own face in the mirror—not that she looked in mirrors often. She knew how the familiar litany went, all the things they had done, all the things they had not done.

What else were parents for?

She looked at Nareen, who was going to have quite a problem; she could either blame her mom for everything, or for nothing.

"There are too many mirrors around here," Pond said. Many of them were antique, and some of them were silvered, but they would all be relentless in showing Pond her own face.

Just then a book slid off one of the stacks Pond had been studying earlier. A hard-covered volume, one that hadn't caught her eye. Neither Pond nor Nareen had moved.

"Told you," Nareen said. "You don't want to stay alone around here." She grinned, and again her expression featured an unsettling gleam.

Pond rolled her eyes. She had been going through those books while the girl was in the kitchen opening cans of pineapple juice; they'd both been moving books that probably hadn't moved in decades. Of course the book had been dislodged from her earlier scrutiny of the piles. She nonetheless felt a shiver of interest, and reached over to grab it.

"The *I Ching*." The name meaning nothing to Pond.

"Sure." Nareen's eyes widened in excitement. "I stayed with a woman who taught me how to do that. It's kind of like fortune telling, but not exactly. You read sticks in the long version. Coins are easier." Nareen began digging through her pockets and pulled out three buffalo nickels. "A boy gave me these, at the last place I stayed in. He had so many buffalo nickels he lost count of them. He gave me three, which is just how many you need for consulting the book of changes. So, you ask a question, and then the coins tell you an answer."

"Okay," Pond said. "Where is your mother?"

"I expected you to ask something about what we're looking for in these books." Nareen had been shaking the coins in her hand, but now she stopped. "Anyway, you know she's working." A slight edge entered her voice. She shrugged it off and resumed shaking. "Ask another question."

"Sure," Pond said, with a sharp glint in her eye. "Where's your father?"

Nareen stopped jangling the coins together, and this time her face showed hurt and disappointment. "We're not talking about me."

"I don't know why *not*. We've had so much fun talking about me. And about parents. Ought to be your turn."

Nareen shot Pond a glare. "Ask a question about something relating to you. If I have any questions

37

about me, I'll ask them."

"You'd better. Fine. How do I get rid of this house?"

Nareen shrugged. She grabbed a pen and paper from an exquisite Victorian-looking roll-top secretary. She bent over her coins, a look of concentration coming over her, and giving her face the quality of a wise statue. She cupped the coins in her hands, shaking them, and then allowing them to spill forth onto an ivory inlaid table in front of her.

For a moment, while the coins clanked together in Nareen's hands, Pond caught a trace of a fragrance in the air somewhere, some sort of penetrating essential oils—citrus and cedar, floral and woodsy. The look on Nareen's face reminded Pond of a fortune teller she'd visited once in New Mexico. The fortune teller's hair had been long and unrestrained, an image of time made visible.

"What do you do to read the coins?" Pond's natural impatience wouldn't let her wait and see for herself.

"Hold the question in your mind. Let the coins fall. Watch the patterns. Read the designs."

Pond watched the different arrangements of heads and tails that spilled from Nareen's cupped hands, wondering what significance they would reveal, or if they could mean anything at all. But Nareen seemed to see something in the coins' fall. Every arrangement inspired her to draw definite lines on the pad of paper. For a moment, it even crossed Pond's mind perhaps the coins could speak with more clarity than human beings did. Perhaps the lines Nareen was drawing would provide a clear pathway into the future. On the piece of paper, the lines were transforming from broken into solid, and solid lines were warping into broken. And perhaps the lines formed a road Pond could travel, a map she could read that would let her escape this house.

After she had made six coin tosses, noting down the designs they formed, Nareen looked up, frowning. She grabbed the *I Ching* and flipped through its pages, making further notations. At one point, she seemed to be swallowing a laugh. At another, a slightly puzzled expression moved across her forehead.

Nareen's expressions increased Pond's anticipation. She wanted to be in on the answer. Nareen worked in a pool of quiet, while Pond leaned back against a stack, propping volumes into a wedge that supported her lower back, shifting her weight from one foot to another, crossing and uncrossing her arms, sighing.

"Ah," Nareen said, moving her gaze between the lines she had drawn on the paper and what looked like charts in the book. She flipped from one set of pages to another, and then to another. Then she looked up at Pond.

"About time," Pond snorted.

"The first answer it gives is gentleness. Wind carries away fog, mist, or clouds, as if they had never been. And then in the new clear air, religion comes into play, or something like religion, a force that unites people. That same force can be behind family, you know, or behind a country. And so the answer also involves cooperation among many people, who unite, who get rid of fixed ways of living because they join together."

"That's impossible," Pond spluttered. "All of that is impossible."

This book had it in for her, too. Wind wasn't gentle, it involved hurricane force gusts. It involved whipping up waves, tearing off tree limbs. It involved something more like Pond's mood, which was increasingly stormy. And the rest of it was nonsense, too. Religion didn't unite people, it divided them, and so did families, and countries. If any of those configurations united people, it was into rigidity, not the opposite.

Cooperation was impossible. Look at the first letters of the word: they spelled *coop*. "That's for chickens," Pond said aloud, "not people." Certainly not for her. Family had gotten her into this fix. There was no way they could get her out of it.

"The answer isn't finished," Nareen said. "The book of changes goes on to say the heart needs to be open, clear of judgment, ready to receive truth. The force of inner truth is what you're being guided to see. But you are right in one way. The book also says it's good to choose your close ties according to what is right. Even criminals share a strong common bond. You want your associations to be based upon clarity and truth, and then the invisible will manifest itself."

"I'm not a criminal," Pond said, who prided herself on having never stolen, at least not from anyone who didn't deserve it. And she never lied, unless she could tell someone was doing the same to her. And she never ever associated with anyone for long, so close ties would not be a problem. She would not be led astray by anyone at all, much less any common scofflaws.

"I don't think it's saying you're a criminal. It's just saying don't cooperate on any old basis. You have to choose a good basis on which to cooperate."

"The last time I cooperated with anyone, we ended up driving into a ditch." She relayed the story to Nareen.

Pond had been somewhere in Virginia, and had hitched a ride with a woman who seemed reasonable. She had met the woman at an ashram, which should have tipped her off to the fact the stranger had no chance of being reasonable.

As the woman drove along with a look of annoying good cheer on her face, through the rolling hills, Pond had been thinking how damn bucolic everything was. All of a sudden they came to a bridge, and the woman, providing no warning whatsoever, had closed her eyes and put her head down between her shoulders. She kept driving, shouting, "I can't look! Going over bridges terrifies me!" Meanwhile, the woman had accelerated, her foot sealing the gas pedal to the floor.

Pond had reached over from the passenger's side, grabbed the steering wheel, and done her best to keep them on the road. It almost worked. They made it over the bridge, but on the far side, when the woman had yet to open her eyes, they had strayed into the other lane, and would have hit an oncoming farm tractor. The farm tractor was orange, not green, and it was not made by John Deere, but by some Japanese company.

All those details were bright and vivid in Pond's

mind, along with the sliding thud of bumping along the shoulder and then into a ditch. The driver had felt Pond turning the wheel clockwise and had deepened the turn. "We wouldn't have landed in the ditch if the driver hadn't decided to overcorrect," Pond said.

"It's fine," the woman had said when she opened her eyes. "The universe always helps me cross bridges." She wasn't upset at all about finding herself in a ditch.

"What would you have done if I hadn't been there to help?" Pond had asked.

"The same thing," the woman said, "although I probably wouldn't have had the ditch experience."

"You can *have* your ditch experience." Pond had opened her door and was preparing to walk the rest of the way. She wasn't going anywhere in particular, anyway.

"Roads need ditches," the woman said, laughing, pulling her vehicle back on the road. "It's fine. We got to see both. Usually you just drive right past ditches without noticing them."

That wasn't precisely true for Pond. She had slept in several, in dry culverts, and liked ditches fine. She could still smell the sagebrush that had framed the last one. But she also liked choosing to be in ditches, rather than paying a surprise call. Pond waved silently as the woman went on her way. Every bridge Pond came to after that, she looked for skid marks or signs of a crash, but saw nothing. Maybe the woman had taken another road.

"Just because you cooperate doesn't mean you'll end up in a ditch," Nareen said.

While she was speaking, Pond had paused in her search through other books, but Nareen kept going. She had now accumulated a tiny pile of bookmarks, none of which seemed particularly notable. Some of them had tiny jottings of page numbers or quotations on them, but nothing jumped out as being of any significance.

"*You* don't cooperate with anyone," Pond said defensively.

"Maybe I cooperate with everyone. You can ask another question if you like."

Pond shook her head. But despite herself, she asked, "How will cooperating help me get rid of this house? We could burn it down, I suppose. It would go much more quickly if we both worked to set the fires."

Nareen seemed to ignore the suggestion of arson, and turned herself to the question about cooperation. Watching the girl as she shook the coins in her hand, Pond found herself drawn into the girl's calm absorption. Nareen spilled the coins onto the ivory inlaid table, and the girl's stillness was so powerful, Pond felt herself transported back to a potter's studio in Oregon. The potter had worked clay with the same alert focus, creating a quiet so absorbing that Pond had almost felt the shapes emerge from the clay, even before those shapes became visible on the wheel.

Now Nareen worked with steady quickness, drawing patterns on her paper, materializing solid and broken lines, making patterns out of metal and air and light. She recorded the lines, checked the book, checked again. Her face broadcasted amusement.

"Interesting," Nareen said. "What has been is going to be discarded, and what is new comes into view, but not by violence. It's a gathering of energy, people who share the same view come together, and work harmoniously, not selfishly. You don't have to hurry anything. Everything happens at the right time. Rest now, and then later movement will come. It will happen gradually, just as reconciliation comes slowly and with tenderness."

"Do you understand what that means?" Pond demanded, beginning to meander through the books still lining the wall. "Wait…my aunt told her lawyer something like that, too. The old ways are passing away, and the new ones are arising. But I don't know about the rest of it. Do you?" Pond didn't like the idea of working with others. She was ready to get rid of everyone *else*'s old ways, as long as she could keep her own.

"You're the only one who can know what it means. It sounds like the book wouldn't advise burning down the house."

"Figures. That would burn the book, too," she added ominously, looking at the *I Ching,* and at the arches, bridges, and buildings they were creating out of books. She'd once burned a book in the high desert, when the air got so cold her breath froze inside her nostrils. Some reflex, probably from her childhood, had made her shy away from burning it, but at that moment, the book had served a greater purpose providing physical heat and light rather than metaphorical. Pond had let herself forget what book she had burned, had left its name along with its form crumbled into dry ash and dust on a high plain not too far from the Tetons.

"The answer isn't finished," Nareen continued. "It also says, hold onto your internal light, even if things seem dark outside. But don't create needless enemies. You can benefit by being considerate in your behavior. Don't fight everything, but also don't be ripped off."

"*Humma humma humma humma*," said Pond, making her voice into a whining drone. The book said everything and nothing. One thing was certain, she was not going to be ripped off. And she wouldn't create needless enemies. Every single enemy she made would be perfectly appropriate, exactly right and fitting. She shoved away a volume on natural rubber.

\*\*\*

Without Pond's having noticed it, she and Nareen had settled into a comfortable conversation. Even if Pond was still all angles and elbows in her behavior, she had begun to accept the girl's presence.

That became apparent the moment the doorbell rang, creating a tingling chime that echoed all the way up and down, forward and back into the house's expanse. Who dared interrupt Pond? She was occupied, intent upon her tirade. And why had Gertrude arranged her house in such a way that even on the top story the jangling call of the bell intruded?

Pond rose and stalked down several flights of

stairs, through the grand entry hall, to the front door. She looked through the stained glass that framed the door vertically, finding a rude interloper, a man standing there looking at the door. He caught a glimpse of her gaze and raised his right hand, waggling his fingers in hello. She had to open the door now.

But that didn't mean she had to be polite. She opened the door a crack and stared at him, ensuring her eyes told him to be gone.

"Chimney sweep," he introduced himself, tipping his hat to her. He was very sooty. He was smudged, and dark, and very thin and tall, and appeared to have emerged from hot forges right at the center of earth's heart. He brushed his hands together, and his nails were chipped, and his palms thick with work.

"I didn't know there were chimney sweeps anymore," Pond said. "Thought they went out with gas lamps."

"See," said the sweep, "that's a common mistake. But your chimney's not safe if it's not swept."

"I'm not burning a fire. It's August."

"Gets to be August, means winter's not far away."

"I don't want you to sweep my chimney." In defending herself against the unsought sweep, the chimney had suddenly become hers, rather than Gertrude's.

"I'll come back tomorrow," he offered hopefully. "I'll check back after you've slept on it. Things always look brighter in the morning."

Pond closed the door. The man walked across the vast porch, his motions light and steady. He went down the steps, and got into his white van. The van had no logo on it, and appeared to have lived almost as long as the man, who wasn't young by any means. Pond went upstairs, trudging more slowly up than she had run down.

"That's funny," Pond told Nareen, who was going through the last volumes on this half story. "That was a chimney sweep. But he's got Arkansas plates." She knew all the license plates of all the states, even from a distance, and all their variations—the ones in honor of rare birds and estuaries, farmland and sports teams, as well as obscure and famous activities.

"Probably have more chimneys in Maryland," Nareen suggested, straightening her shoulders.

Pond stared out the window toward the house's front. The man had gotten back behind the wheel of the van, but he was just sitting there, not doing anything, not talking on a cell phone, not studying a clipboard, not eating.

"Is he allowed to do that?" Pond wondered, after more time had passed.

"Why not? I'm sitting here."

Well, how *long* was he allowed to sit there, in front of her house? But he continued to do so, while Pond slumped down, with her back on the floor and books towering over her, all around her, and stared at the ceiling. She half expected the ceiling to be made of books, but no such doom awaited her. She became very keenly aware of all the walls; their beauty and solidity loomed over her.

All that paint, glass, architecture and design, carpentry, and artistry. The walls were thick with planning and vision, money and labor. She considered all the walls in this house, which were laden with art and history. The walls towered from floor to ceiling—terrible things, heavy expanses unbroken by any horizons. Such walls separated her from everything, but especially from freedom.

In Samoa, they built sensible houses with no walls. Those houses let you breathe. Maybe she could stay a long time in a house with no walls. Probably not, but who knew? She had a better chance of abiding a wall-free house than she did this one, with its ominous stone foundation, at least three feet at the thickest point. That foundation wasn't going anywhere, and as long as Pond was the unfortunate legal owner of the place, neither was she. She considered finding a sledgehammer in the carriage house and doing some damage to the stones, but it made her shoulders ache just thinking about it.

She had worked in a quarry near the Badlands, and had learned how little she enjoyed hanging out with rock destined to become headstones. *I'm* alive, she had grumbled to herself the entire time. *Why hang out with graveyard rock? Or foundation rock,* she now amended her earlier policy. Really, it was all the same.

The roll-top secretary, which Nareen had left open after grabbing pen and paper earlier, suddenly wheeled its top down, snapping itself closed with a satisfying click. The movement was so smooth and inevitable it was almost unsurprising. As the desk shut, its wooden half-circle furling after it had unfurled, the sound it made was like a well-crafted lid fitting into its companion box. The movement spoke of going home.

Nareen looked up from her book. She didn't say a word, but looked significantly at the secretary, then at Pond, before holding out her empty hands. I *had nothing to do with that*, her gesture said, more loudly than if she had spoken. At the moment, Nareen's bared teeth were making Pond uncomfortable. There was something too superior about the glint of her smile. "Like I said," Nareen repeated her earlier words. "You might not want to stay alone in this place."

"Those Victorians were clever," Pond told the girl. "Must have rigged it so the top would close itself after a time, if you left it open. And you did." The girl's earlier activity had triggered the motion; that was the way things were. Things at rest stayed at rest, and things in motion stayed in motion, unless there was some sort of catalyst that changed everything. Like a dreaded will. Like an inescapable house. Like billions of books.

Pond hadn't noticed any noises at all until the girl mentioned she might not want to stay alone, but now while she leaned back against the floor, she became aware the house was not as silent and still as she had thought. She listened in the distance— and the house had a *lot* of distance, almost possessing its own internal horizon, its own sense of vastness, plains and mountain steeps.

Suddenly the house materialized around her as the great indoors, of all ridiculous things. She could hear creaking and settling, the house breathing. Far away in the distance she heard a knocking sound, wind blowing and banging a loose shutter. Or maybe it was a woodpecker attacking one of the many trees. Gertrude's house was very much in the city, but it was nonetheless in a forest. Woodpeckers, not to mention other birds, would enjoy such a grove. Doubtless they were doing so now.

Pond was used to staying in new places, accustomed to all the life a house had, apart from her. Sometimes when she moved into a place, she could tell something about the person who had been there before; perhaps they smoked, or they didn't. They had a clean fetish, or they didn't. They liked hanging things on walls, or tearing strips of wallpaper off at random, or they enjoyed gardening, or weeding, or not. They took their things with them when they left, or they didn't.

The chimney sweep's boots flashed in Pond's mind. She had noticed them rather than meeting his eyes, and they had reminded her of her favorite boots, which she had worn for three weeks in Seattle when she had lived in the University District. She had picked them up at a thrift store, and they were the best boots she ever had. But when it came time to go, she left, and her boots stayed there.

You had to be prepared to leave behind everything, even the good things. You had to be able to go. She no longer remembered why she hadn't worn the boots when she left. Doubtless her reasons were compelling. They always were.

Pond went to the window. The chimney sweep was still there, head leaned back against his driver's seat. What was he doing, occupying her street? She supposed it wasn't really her street, more the city's. But it was the space in front of her house, and it grated on her, having him there. She didn't want him sitting there, doing nothing. Why couldn't he just depart conveniently? She had already told him she had no business for him here.

\*\*\*

While Pond disappeared somewhere in the house and yet managed to escape nothing at all, Nareen scrambled together some food. When she presented the meal to Pond, she mentioned how she considered it inferior, due to the sparse fresh ingredients she had to work with, and the excess amounts of items with a long shelf life.

Pond reappeared for dinner, drawn by food into company. She rated the dinner quite high on her scale of recent meals, although she didn't say so. Pond did resolve silently to give the girl more ingredients to work with. Gertrude's money could stand to support something delicious. If Nareen was going to be here, they could at least eat well, since the girl didn't seem to mind cooking.

After dinner, Pond surprised herself by doing the dishes. At the ashram, she had to do the dishes or she wouldn't have been able to eat, and usually such compulsory duties triggered an equal and opposite response. Usually she would have stayed away from any cleaning activity for several weeks, or at least as long as she'd had to engage in whatever discipline it was. There had been weeks when she hadn't showered or done her laundry, weeks when she couldn't be bothered to eat, weeks when even speaking was something she disdained.

While she washed the dishes, Pond noticed what the plates said about Gertrude. The plates were beautiful, but they didn't match. In fact, the plates were exquisite, many of them painted with gold leaf or gold edging, so delicate Pond didn't want to breathe too exuberantly in their direction, lest they shatter. She didn't even want to imagine how much they'd cost or where they came from or what museum they should be in. And here she and that funny girl had used these precious plates for such an undistinguished activity as eating.

Pond looked around the kitchen. Hardback books occupied several bookcases, which looked modest in size, but which Pond now knew would take hours to look through. She pushed away the possibility that searching through books wouldn't be enough. No one could read them all. She would have to find the book, or the book would have to find her. Tomorrow. She was done looking through books tonight. Tomorrow would be time enough to pillage more volumes for all the truth they held, for that one particular answer.

On the shelves that ran the length of the kitchen, higher than she could reach, strange colanders and ladles and elegantly contorted metal presses piled on shelves that ran off into the distance. Most of the implements Pond could not imagine using, and she could not imagine Gertrude using them, either, based upon the roast duck dinner. But maybe Gertrude had enjoyed cooking, when she remembered to apply heat. Maybe she had acquired and then tested every one of these antique contrivances.

Pond liked that none of them went together. Steel and bronze, tin and aluminum, brass, gold, and silver intermingled on Gertrude's shelves. The delicate consorted with the grotesque. In Gertrude's kitchen, the pretty and the preposterous had flirted, before going all out and consummating their union.

*Oh dear Lord.* A realization came home to Pond. *All of that is mine. It can't be, but it is.* She didn't know what it meant, *mine.* None of these things had anything to do with her. But she didn't know how to walk away from such a plethora of items the law and everyone else called hers. *What in the world could one possibly want or do with such an arsenal?*

Many of the devices looked more appropriate to a medieval battlefield than to a modern kitchen. But not all the knights in history could wield so many weapons. Maybe she could stage a tournament, and to the winner would go all the kitchen goodies, the kitchen, and the house that held it, as well as the land that harbored the house. And who would enter such a tournament, if she hosted it?

The chimney sweep was still there after dinner, once the now living, breathing silence of the house had gotten to Pond and she had asked Nareen to teach her how to read the *I Ching*.

"No problem," Nareen said immediately. "I'm sure you'll learn quickly." The girl seemed to bite her own lip to keep from smirking. They were in the living room, and Nareen was reading, elegant in a green velvet wingback chair that appeared to be swooping and diving at the same time. Pond was comfortable on an asymmetrical couch that she told herself not to enjoy sitting on.

"You might be surprised," Pond replied grimly, studying the first fall of coins, and becoming familiar with the lines they formed. But she took to the coins, or the coins took to her, so she spent several long moments lost in contemplation, in wonder.

Some mysterious pattern was becoming visible to her as she drew the solid and the dotted lines, then read the codex they indicated. Lost years she had spent flinging herself at random across the land, running and rambling, avoiding everything that could possibly be avoided, suddenly threatened to become meaningful.

The coins and the patterns they revealed hinted at a geometry, a hidden language. All the times she had kept her elbows out, forcing everyone away, all the times she felt as isolated as a solitary rock looming up from a desert plateau, all the times she hadn't wanted to be who she was—all those times had brought her *here*.

The coins had caught light as they fell through air, and the angular figures she had formed of her own life became a secret grammar, one that spoke according to an inner logic, one that augured something startling. She'd caught a glimpse of wholeness. It was totally unintended, and yet the landscapes she had traveled had managed to also form a landscape of her life. These patterns now said all geographies had their own beauty and participated in their own order. Even the pitted landscapes of the craters of the moon, even the unearthly wilderness of her own heart.

She closed her eyes, and all the roads and unmarked ways she had traveled came back to her, visible now as solid and dotted lines, leading her to this place, where she sat in a circle of lamplight with a quiet girl. She opened her eyes, and the light felt soft and welcoming, showing her that solid and dotted lines were everywhere—in the marble hearth of the fireplace, in the grain of the wood floor, in the carved arches of the doorway.

For several long moments, everything was one long sentence that was almost possible to read. Her position on the couch, the girl's position in the chair, the whole house around her, the whole house holding her, and beyond the house a whole universe.

And then a door slammed somewhere—of course it couldn't be inside the house, for the only two inhabitants were right here—and she shook away the harmony. Next thing she knew, she'd be *singing*, which was something she hadn't done since third grade.

Not even the aching sweetness of mountain music had made her sing, nor the rough lyrics and bass laughter of bayous blues. Nor did the lilting melodies of hymns she had heard all across the land, or the sky-filling catcalls and yodels. Sophisticated syncopated city backbeats and throat-scratching scat, wild-driving rocking rhythms, plain song—none of it had ever made her sing.

She went upstairs without a word, and pointedly did not say goodnight, proving beyond a shadow of a doubt she was still the same old Pond.

# Tuesday

The next day was sunnier than ever, in strict counterpoint to Pond's mood. She was determined to demonstrate she was at odds with the world—with Gertrude, the house, books, the lawyer's instructions, advice, and perhaps most of all with Nareen, whose primary offense was being available to receive Pond's scowls.

Nareen continued cooking, seemingly calm as ever, when Pond stormed into the kitchen. "You'll feel better after you eat," said Nareen, who appeared to be intent upon making herself indispensable in one way or another for the span of the week.

Pond didn't bother replying, but she ate the omelet Nareen had prepared with chives from the kitchen garden and the last eggs in the house. She silently put money on the counter, hoping Nareen would find it and use it to buy more ingredients.

Nareen had gotten up early, she told Pond. "I already searched through the basement volumes on cooking." She'd waited until Pond finished eating to point out the pile of recipes she had gathered. None of them seemed particularly relevant.

The most interesting ones gave instructions on how to concoct supposedly edible dishes during years of war and deprivation. They looked like they were from both World War I and World War II, and probably the Great Depression as well. Those recipes were all about substitution—what to add if you didn't have the ingredients you really needed. "Mock apple pie, and mock butter. Please tell me you don't want to eat those. I hereby vow never to make any meals that mock good food."

"That's not the answer," Pond said scornfully, rejecting the recipes.

Nareen breathed a sigh of relief. "I'm glad I won't have to bake any war-time novelty pies. That rules out the basement books."

Pond trudged heavily into the living room. She was torn between two options. She could fling herself on the ridiculously comfortable asymmetrical couch, whose back was a high arch on one end swooping to a low arch on the other. Or, she could take a giant stack of books from the nearest shelf and spill them across the floor.

A third option came to her. She could take armfuls of the books and climb the nearest staircase, dumping the books down the steps, so as they tumbled, slid, and fell, they would open their covers, reveal their hearts, let loose any secrets they held. And as Pond read aloud the resulting sentence, the answer would appear midair in golden glowing fiery letters, which Pond could then throw more books at.

"I'll just be a minute," Nareen told Pond, grocery bag over her shoulder. A book was slung across her chest, as it had been when she was cooking. "Is there any food you especially like?"

Pond froze, holding a stack of volumes to her chest. No one as far back as she could remember had ever asked her such a preposterous thing. In the days when she'd lived at home and had plenty of money to buy groceries, her mother had appointed their food habits, which mostly involved barely digestible health packets, such as brown rice and broccoli cooked the same length of time, which resulted in uncooked grains countered by unseasoned pasty green mush. Even the cats had to choke down grated carrots and other distinctly non-feline items. To Pond's mother, food was fuel, and she indeed managed to make everything taste similar to gasoline. Both at home and on the road, Pond ate what was on hand.

Now she swallowed, envisioning as much dark chocolate as she could ever hope to eat, and ginger in sweets and savory dishes, curries, stir fries, stews, breads, cakes, and cookies. Black tea, steaming hot so it burned her tongue and the back of her throat.

"Whatever," she said, more stiffly than the tomes she held in her arms felt. The edge of one book was cutting into her inside forearm. She looked at that volume in irritation. She knew she didn't like quilting, and this book wasn't doing anything to convince her otherwise.

They were a short walk away from a gourmet market, so Nareen was gone and back quickly, plunging into the living room books alongside Pond. Gertrude hadn't read all of these volumes, Pond knew. It wasn't possible for one person to read so many. But one of the books would reveal something important, so she continued seeking, biting back annoyance so she wouldn't go all the way and choke on it.

Pond, who never followed directions, was finding it absurd to see how well she was doing at following her aunt's instructions. *Why?* If she was agreeing to look, the least she could do was comply with as ill a will as possible. She made a point of slamming every book down so it released a poof of dust from each binding. Dust was something Pond was comfortable with, recognized, didn't mind rubbing all over her skin. Dust was an old friend. If Pond couldn't muster up enough courage to stay on the run, she could at least coat everything with an extra layer of grime.

By the time the phone rang, she was almost eager to answer. At least it wasn't another book, which could only be relied upon to produce a very limited amount of dust. She ran to the rotary dial monstrosity, while Nareen staunchly went on searching.

"Bertram Something—Something," Pond grumped.

"My favorite client's favorite niece," Bertram replied. "I see why she left you her house."

"Really?" Pond was silent, imagining that, like Nareen, he could see some congruence that remained invisible to her. "I'm not anybody's favorite anything."

"You're like your aunt."

60

"I'm not like anybody," Pond insisted.

"There you go. That's what I mean."

Pond snorted. Even if she was right, that didn't mean she wanted anyone to agree with her. Now he was making it so she would have to disagree with herself, on principle.

As she waited for the attorney to explain himself, multiple possibilities flashed through her mind. He had the answer, and was going to share it with her now. Gertrude's codicil had been a joke, and here was the punch line. There was no answer, and she could stop looking.

She began thinking of fire again. No one could live in a blazing or a burned house. But she didn't want to go to jail for arson. Jail might well be even more confining. Maybe she could convince Nareen to light the flames.

"So, you have the key to explain what you said yesterday," Pond prompted. He was lost in legal silence, which was no doubt very dignified, and also highly lucrative for him, but didn't help her at all.

"I have another codicil to read you," said the lawyer, his words seeming to come with reluctance. "It might be some kind of joke. I don't know if she's laughing at you or at me."

"Oh, good," Pond replied sarcastically. Something had to make sense. Maybe today would be the day she would find the key. When the lawyer had handed her the key that unlocked Gertrude's house, she had felt she was opening something new. Instead, she was now wandering into a deepening maze.

"Ahem," said the lawyer, then paused. It

sounded as if out of nowhere a laugh had erupted in his throat, except his own tongue obstructed the emergence of mirth. The resulting noise he made was nowhere near a normal laugh, producing something closer to a strangled cough. But it was a start. Pond listened, and received the impression some kind of an engine was being restarted after years of disuse.

He seemed to almost strangle on choked back laughter. "So, this codicil says," the lawyer paused and drew a deep breath, "You *can't* find what you're looking for by looking, but you will only find it if you *do* look."

There was a sound like a melon falling to the floor. "Did you just whack your head against a wall?" Bertram asked, to no reply. Pond had done exactly what he'd said, but wasn't going to dignify his question with a response.

He repeated the codicil, but it seemed to make even less sense than it had the first time.

"Now you're just adding to the billable minutes," Pond accused.

"I am providing a scrupulous reading of what the codicil says."

"I was hoping you'd have the answer." In one statement, Pond had conveyed her lifelong disappointment in all things official and predictable. They were bound to let you down, she knew from experience, yet given that legal rigmaroles had created her current predicament, she had been hoping they could also help solve it. "Of course, that would be asking nonsense to explain itself," she added.

"The words make sense," Bertram said defensively. "They're written in English. The sentences have all the required elements. It's one of the things included in my price."

"That doesn't mean it *means* anything," Pond retorted. "Putting the two bits together, we know the answer is found in a book, but *can't* be found in a book, but will only be found if I look."

Bertram harrumphed loudly, apparently attempting to cover over a gale of laughter, and sounding like a choking goat in the process. "There's more," he said. "The book will open, and the key will reveal the most valuable thing in the house."

"Of course it will." Pond's reply was bitter. That's what Gertrude had said she wanted, for Pond to search as if she were on fire. She made a face and mentally wished upon her aunt flames of ongoing torment, piled upon crackling blazes of more acute agony. She patted the top of her own head to cool down.

"Good luck," Bertram said, hanging up.

"Luck doesn't have anything to do with it," Pond told the telephone after she had hung up. "Gertrude was a mad woman." She frowned. It was anyone's guess what else this house contained—quite possibly a guillotine, doubtless historic.

*After you lost your head, would you mind less if your hair were on fire?* And then all the books came into view again, and she groaned.

\*\*\*

She stalked back into the living room and updated Nareen, who shrugged and continued searching. She had gone through several piles while Pond was talking on the phone, and had begun building stacks into temporary monuments along the enormous marble hearth.

"Convenient for burning," Pond told her, picking up a fire wand, a butane lighter that could be flicked on or off. *Click, and there was your fire.* Pond studied the flame. It offered a definite appeal.

Nareen shook her head as she moved onward through all the volumes on French aristocracy, medieval chivalry, and astrology.

Pond stared at the books moving through Nareen's hands. She didn't quite believe in any of the subjects they covered, not the aristocracy, nor chivalry, nor perhaps even stars, at least not that their arrangements portended anything much, but it didn't bother her that people wrote books about such imaginary elements.

She believed in taking fate into your own hands, as much as possible. Of course, there were some things you couldn't control, but then you could always leave. Except now she couldn't.

"We could listen to music or something," Pond said desperately, after spending some indefinite amount of time with a pile of paper that was devoted to explaining metals and metallurgy.

"Gertrude doesn't have a radio. It was one of her things—no radio, no television. She would say, 'No wireless, no waves.'"

"Damn." Pond thought back over her tour through all the rooms. "No computer, either."

Maybe Gertrude had been completely disconnected from the modern world, just like Pond was. Her gaze fell on the *I Ching*. Pond had kept the book close to her, carrying it down to breakfast and into the living room afterward. Now she paused and went to the volume. *Might as well ask,* she thought. *Can't be any less helpful than the lawyer.* She sat down and formulated her question.

*How do I find what I'm looking for?* She shook her head violently at the first answer. Courtship and marriage had nothing to do with anything, especially not with her.

*The book can be as wrong as anything else,* she decided. But she continued reading. It went on to say affinities attracted, and being receptive to good advice would help. *Maybe it doesn't mean a literal courtship.* An actual courtship was out of the question. But maybe she would find some friendship or good advice somewhere.

She looked at the books, with metals topping the nearest rise. The answer Gertrude was telling her to find had to involve more than metals. Although keys were often made of metal.

The book of changes wasn't finished speaking to her. It went on to say gathering together, like a family, would do the trick. And that only collective ethical commitment can unite a group of people. "Oh, *family,*" she said aloud. "Since when has family ever solved anything?"

"It happened once," Nareen said. "I saw it."

Pond had never seen it, and she said as much with a roll of her eyes. Nareen shrugged and kept going through the books.

"So, tell me what happened," Pond said unwillingly, just as the doorbell rang. She looked back over her shoulder as she rose and stalked through the living room, and through the entry foyer to the door, which she flung open.

\*\*\*

## Gruenbaum

He stood on the front porch, waiting for her to let him into the house. It would work this time. He would make it work. The pay was too good for it *not* to work.

"I *told* you I don't want the chimney swept," she announced.

"That's what you think," said the sweep.

"Why are you here?"

He brushed at the front of his shirt, knowing his movements were awkward, and hoping they covered for his unconvincing words. "I'm looking for my mother," he said, mumbling a bit in embarrassment, and telling part of the truth. "When she left my daddy, she said she was going to Baltimore. It was always one of her dreams."

"Good Lord." She snorted. "Most dreams tell people to get out of here."

The chimney sweep was new enough to town that he didn't know what she was talking about. "I thought cities help you find what you want to find."

"This particular city inspires most people to leave, and go on searching elsewhere," said the woman. He studied her face. His employer had told him her name was Pond.

He shrugged. "For my mom, Baltimore was it."

She offered a snarky reply. "My great-aunt said all the Southern eccentrics were going to New York and they ran out of gas in Baltimore. She was quoting something. Although, she knew about eccentric better than anyone."

The Arkansas traveler endured Pond's gaze, guessing she was a naturally curious person, or she wouldn't be carrying on a random conversation with a stranger at her front door.

"You don't look like you belong in New York," she told him, and her tone announced she wasn't giving him a compliment.

"New York was no part of my mother's dream," he said. "I'm here."

He told her how much it cost to have the chimney swept. She said he could help her go through books for the same price.

"Books?" the man asked. "Last book I read, I was thirteen."

"Good for you," Pond congratulated him heartily. The man studied her, surprised. He was used to disapproval. Everyone said education was so *good* for you. But she seemed sincere. He decided he liked Baltimore. Last night, sleeping in his van and wondering how to get inside the house, he hadn't been so sure. This morning, Baltimore was striking him as an interesting place to be. Besides, entry had been much easier than he'd expected.

"You'll want me to wash my hands," he said, looking at his palms, which were blackened with work.

It turned out he moved more quickly than the young girl, whose presence in the house he didn't understand. He could maintain a diligent pace, since he didn't much like books, and he kept his attention fixed partly on other matters.

While he went, he considered what books could be used for. Maybe insulation, if you were building with thick walls. You could stack them up inside. Or you could shred them and blow them in, like fiberglass. Or make clothing out of them, if you didn't mind something that could dissolve. You could always shellac the fibers, of course, mica-thin layers of varnish.

Soon he began focusing his attention more carefully. He had to find literary criticism, whatever that was. He cast his gaze around all the shelves. *You could use books to store things in*, he realized suddenly, *if you hollowed them out.* Maybe that was the point.

Right now the only thing between the covers were pages, and they were just taking up space. There, for instance. He peered at one thick volume on democracy which was taking up a gigantic amount of shelf. A person could open the front cover, slice into the middle with a carpenter's knife, almost all the way to the back, carving out an empty treasure chest right in its guts. And then you could store all kinds of things there—jewels, money, anything you wanted to hide. No one would think of looking there. What thief would search books, for God's sake?

Not five minutes later, he found what he was

looking for, although he still wanted to know what the big deal was about literary criticism. Someone before him had the same idea about using a book as a vault, and had glued all the pages together and then cut into them in a rectangular pattern that mirrored the book's shape, leaving an edge of pages, a border around the empty center. And the middle was all hollowed out, and held a small box.

"Hey!" He had thought this idea was *his*, and now someone had gotten there before him. He held up the box and shook it. Something rattled.

\*\*\*

## Pond

Pond's heart pounded with possibility. Maybe this was what the *I Ching* meant by courtship; she was about to find an answer.

"Go on," she urged him.

He handed her the box. She opened it and only afterward realized she had been holding her breath. She drew forth a tiny golden key and let loose all her air with a giant sigh of pent-up frustration and relief. The golden miniature was labeled in a delicate handwritten script.

*Everything*, the key said. Pond laughed, and then frowned. She stared at the chimney sweep. It wasn't right *he* had found the key, and she hadn't. If someone else found what you were looking for, didn't that take away some of the joy of discovery?

She gripped the key and its edges bit into her. It was in her hand, after all. Surely that was what mattered. "We still have to find the lock this key opens," she grumbled at the man from Arkansas. "Do you have a name?"

He squinted. "My daddy just called me All Y'all. He called all us kids by the same name."

"That's not an actual name," Pond said. "You must have a real name, but I'll just call you Gruenbaum. That's the author of the book I just looked through." She held the book up, then placed it on top of a stack.

The man shrugged. "Been called worse."

Pond presented him with money for his time. "Goodbye," she said, meaning it. On an inexplicable whim, she held out her hand to shake his.

He hesitated about taking her hand. He looked at his hand, and Pond noticed it was still black with work, despite all the washings he had administered.

Pond expected him to leave, now he had his money, and had helped her locate the key.

"I can help you find the lock," he said. He shoved the money Pond had given him deep into his pocket, where it would be hard to dig back out again. When he saw Pond hesitate, he added gruffly, "At a reduced rate. Got to see what that key goes to open."

Pond studied him. His face seemed sincere, and looked less shadowed than it had earlier. "Suit yourself." She decided to pay him in full, get rid of some of her aunt's money, but didn't bother mentioning that detail.

\*\*\*

They began in the living room, going through all the cabinets, curio closets, bureaus, and portmanteaux. All of these containers had their own locks, but all opened freely without a key.

They found a remarkable variety of tiny boxes in the cabinets. While Pond had been seeking books, books were all she had noticed, and books were everywhere. Now that she was looking for a lock to open, she found locks everywhere—locks on little jeweled containers, tiny wooden cases, metal compartments, and receptacles. Ornate chests served as bookends for several shelves they hadn't gone through. Plain, sturdy chests stood staunchly in corners. Many of the end tables had delicate drawers complete with a lock or two.

"Oh, good," Pond said. "I was wondering what to do with my day."

"I've spent worse days," Gruenbaum noted.

"We all have." Not that this wasn't bad enough, which made her remember the *I Ching* and its impossible pronouncements. "*Family*," she complained to Nareen. "I told you family created predicaments."

"Sometimes," Nareen said. "Sometimes not." Her voice took on a different tone, as if she were reading out of a book, as if every word were inevitable. Now when she spoke, she sounded less like a teenager and more like an oracle—no pauses, every word fitted into its own place.

"One house I stayed in told me family can solve problems sometimes."

"Houses don't talk," Gruenbaum said. There was something about the look on his face that Pond didn't like. It was *her* right to make such pronouncements, not his.

"I didn't say they did," Nareen said. "But that's what I learned in that house. It's difficult growing up without a mother," she told Pond, who thought, *Try growing up* with *one.*

Meanwhile, Gruenbaum nodded at Nareen's comment. While she talked, he seemed to be studying Nareen out of the corner of his eye, but his face still held a question. He didn't seem to understand the young girl.

"Growing up without a mother," Nareen said, "gives you a lot of freedom. I found that out at one house where the kids slept when they wanted and ate when they wanted, and went to school when they wanted. It all sounded great, until you tried it."

"*You* only go to school when you want," Pond told Nareen sharply.

"I'm learning all the time."

Gruenbaum shook his head, and Pond felt a flash of sympathy. This smart girl had an answer for everything. It was disconcerting.

"But these kids," Nareen said, "they weren't learning anything. They never left the house. They lived in the dark, with curtains drawn. That made it easier to sleep and eat whenever." Nareen paused, seeming to gather her momentum. "It was similar to living inside a video game. That's what the kids did all day, in the dark, and all night, which didn't look any different from the daytime.

"But for them, the game never ended and never began. They only ever played the game, stopping to eat and sleep when absolutely necessary. Because there was nothing else to do. The dad was there, but he wasn't really there. He would leave for work, and stay away. He would be home for a night and then gone. Maybe on the road. The kids didn't know, and by the time I understood he had left, he never came back for me to ask. They had their house, which was safe and quiet, and clean because of my mom and me, and they had their games, and plenty of food. But otherwise..." She shrugged and looked at her empty palms.

"Why'd you stay there?" Pond asked, before she could stop herself.

"I go where I'm needed."

Pond scowled. She certainly didn't need Nareen. Nareen was the one who needed her—or more specifically, required a place to stay.

Nareen seemed to catch Pond's skeptical look. "I'm not saying *you* need me. The house does. Makes it a fair exchange. I visit here, and give what I can in return." She nodded significantly toward the boxes she had been opening. None of the closures had been locked, and all the boxes had been empty. Now she began inspecting the bases of the boxes, tapping on them, apparently looking for signs of a false bottom. One box rang like a bell when she tested it. Solid metal. Pond frowned. Not that brass was bad, but it didn't reveal any secrets.

Gruenbaum cleared his throat and managed to remind Pond she ought to object to his very presence. She looked with skepticism at the two of them, standing in her house, the tall, young, dark haired, bright eyed girl, and the skinny old gray Arkansas grizzly. A perfect unmatchable pair to decorate her new home.

"The kids were just going through the motions of living," Nareen continued. "Then their world ended." She grinned sharply. "I opened the curtains."

"You've got to be kidding," Pond said, whose world had ended every time she moved. The end of the world was a bracing experience. If she stayed in one place, she was bound to forget. But remembering always involved much more than curtains. She had to *go* somewhere.

"Daylight came pouring in," Nareen said. "Made it much harder to sleep all day long. Made the kids stop and think, then notice all the people walking by. Who were those people, and where did they come from, and where were they going? And then the kids started wondering who *they* were. Ask a question like that, and everything changes."

"There's no house that doesn't let *some* daylight in," Gruenbaum protested. "Those kids can't have lived without any sunshine."

"You would be surprised what people get used to. Living in the dark is not the worst thing I've seen."

"Who were the kids?" Pond asked.

"Family. That's the shortest answer."

"You have siblings?" Pond wanted to know. She had a brother with whom she didn't speak, even when they talked.

Nareen shook her head. "Just family. That's what happens if you don't talk about brothers and sisters and cousins and relations."

Pond scowled. "You're saying everyone is your

family." She felt a bitter laugh well up within, but managed not to show it. Pond had too much family as it was, without taking on anyone else.

Gruenbaum shook his head. He looked like he didn't intend to say anything, but blurted out, "Are you all crazy? Not that I mean that in a bad way. You just don't look like you belong here."

"Of course not," Pond retorted. "As if you do, either."

Nareen shrugged. "The kids went to the park. They met other kids. They slept at night, walked in the sunshine, and played catch. They figured out they were themselves. Nothing fancy, only themselves."

"What happened to them after that?" Gruenbaum asked. "Watch out, when kids grow into themselves. Changes everything."

Nareen smiled. "They got to decide. But I didn't stay to find out, exactly. After that, I was in another house." Nareen studied Pond's face.

Pond turned away from the girl's gaze. Despite herself, the stories had a strange beauty to them, the way Nareen's cooking did. Pond didn't want to like the stories, any more than she wanted to like anything about her visitor. And yet she found herself developing a strange hunger for the conversation, as for the food.

Something about the way Nareen combined unexpected elements suggested it was possible for there to be order, meaning, and beauty present in the midst of chaos. In the midst of moving around, it was possible for there to be peace.

Now she examined a box that appeared to be

s, it was so fine. A minuscule lock
nto it, but its lid lifted effortlessly.
ier was empty like so many of the
must have hidden her jewels and
elsewhere, if she had any to hide.

ill empty," Pond sighed, following
Nareen's glance, "then how are we supposed to find
anything?"

"I see a lot of houses in my line of work,"
Gruenbaum told Nareen, asserting his presence. By
his tone of voice, it was easy to tell that he didn't
usually speak up. "Never seen a house quite like
this one. Most houses I'm in a very short time. Then
I move on. Most houses I don't want to stay in."

"Tell me about it." Pond snorted. Then she
turned to Nareen. "I still don't see how family
solves anything." All the curtains in this house were
open, just like all the locks. Maybe she could close
the curtains, and that would help. Maybe she could
lock all the locks. For a moment, she wondered
where all the keys were that fit these locks.

"You know how you know family," Gruenbaum
said. "It's who you fight with."

Pond blinked hard to keep sympathy from filling
her eyes. His tone made it clear he knew what he
was talking about.

"At least, that's what people mostly did in the
houses where I've worked," he rushed to add, as if
he had to explain himself. "Maybe the happy ones
stop themselves until after I've left."

"I don't fight with my family." Pond put his
comment behind her. "I don't say anything at all."
When they had come to the lawyer's office for the

reading of the will, they had spoken to her, but she'd pretended she was still at the ashram, keeping silence, or that she was in the desert or on a mountaintop, doing the same. She was still traveling, still alone. Silence said what you needed it to say.

She could tell her mother had been disappointed Pond had inherited the mansion. Her father had been amused in a distant way, and her brother was blank with surprise. She hadn't bothered noticing any of the other relatives. They were as featureless to her as wallpaper. Gertrude had changed Pond's plans that was for sure, but only for the time being. She would get back on the road.

"I don't fight with my family, either," Nareen said. Pond saw the girl eyeing Gruenbaum, seeming to calculate how and whether he would complicate her plans.

Gruenbaum looked at Pond, whose head was bent over a little cloisonné enclosure. It was more like a locket than a box. "Maybe we can check jewelry," he suggested.

Pond blinked. He was right. The little golden key was that tiny. "Lockets, that kind of thing," she nodded. "Let's do that later. Finish the larger containers first."

They finished the living room containers, which were all beautifully empty, in contrast to the accumulating chaos outside the boxes, items in haphazard piles. Books and boxes had seemed to multiply as they were opened, inspected, and then heaped together.

Pond dismissed the mess, although she grumbled

to herself about not being able to move away from it once and for all, abandon it as she had all the other messes she had made and tired of. For now they all went searching, moving in separate directions, scanning the house from top to bottom for things that locked, and reconvened some exhausted hours later amidst the living room disorder.

***

Pond was sitting in the living room when the chimney sweep clomped down the steps.

"I checked out the attic," Gruenbaum reported. "You can see the chimney from the attic window, so it's a lot like my usual work. Less soot. More mothballs and dust. Didn't find much. What you would expect in an attic. Other people's stuff. Old lampshades and chairs with one broken leg. All the chests were normal, unlocked and full of what no one in their right mind would wear. Although, you're all set for Halloween."

"You didn't find your mother," Pond observed, letting her eyes challenge his presence.

"Wasn't looking for her in the attic."

"I went to the basement," Nareen said. "All sorts of old storage containers for food. But all of them empty. Miles of shelf space. You ever want to feed an entire household for a year, you're good. You've got the room to lay in the supplies."

Pond had ambled out to the carriage house, which also wasn't locked. The carriage house was misnamed. It was really a gigantic barn—wide open rafters, an enormous tall roof reaching up two and a half stories high, and hay.

She had no idea what Gertrude had wanted with hay. Maybe she used to have a horse. Maybe her gardener used it when planting. Maybe Gertrude liked to lie on her back on a bale of hay, which is what Pond found herself doing. She justified it by saying the barn was free of containers of all kinds, and the air was clean and sweet, like a meadow in sunshine.

When she returned to the living room, she was exhausted—not from searching, but because she'd wanted to nap on the hay bales.

***

Pond agreed when Nareen suggested they look for jewelry, too sleepy to defend herself.

The master bedroom held several jewelry boxes, including several filled entirely with lockets. Pond had been sleeping in the master bedroom, although she left no signs of her presence, making the bed army neat, as if Gertrude were bound to return for a surprise inspection to see how much she'd been muddling everything. Pond's pack was so small it tucked under the enormous bedstead, out of sight.

Still, the room was a retreat, an interior space. For a moment, Pond felt awkward inviting Nareen and Gruenbaum into the room. What were they all thinking, running their fingers through jewelry boxes?

Gruenbaum must have picked up on her hesitation. "You don't mind me helping?" he asked.

Pond made a face. He had a point. Maybe she

was crazy, here in such strange circumstances, in Baltimore of all places, looking through this treasure chest. For that's what it was: nothing locked away in a safe, or a bank vault, everything just sitting on top of a bureau, strands of pearls and gold and diamonds and lapis lazuli and greenstone and emeralds.

Pond didn't know all the rocks to name them, but the stones themselves spoke of dark light glinting in precious veins of earth, and mines where the earth's heart glittered and shone, lifted into daylight so it could adorn the throats and fingers of all the beautiful ones who walked the halls of power and delight.

And here she was, one who disdained appearance and riches and power, working with these two, a string bean of a man from Arkansas, grimed with a lifetime's work, and a homeless waif of a girl, who also obviously didn't wear many gems, pawing through this collection.

Pond felt a momentary reflex that reminded her she didn't want to be fingered a thief, not that she was taking anything. But none of it felt like it was hers. It was as if she was an intruder.

"Suit yourself," Pond told Gruenbaum. She could see the loveliness of the chains and rings, all the bright gleam of metal and rock, precious for its scarcity, although here you wouldn't know such a thing as scarcity existed. Gertrude's dresser tops were now piled high with the things, as they emptied the contents of jewelry boxes into plain sight. None of the jewelry boxes were locked, either. This loot made the room look like a lair.

Maybe her great-aunt had been part dragon. More stuff for Pond to get rid of.

Then her breath caught in her throat. A ring with a plain green stone, uncut, unpolished, called to her. Never had she worn a ring. She didn't want to proclaim anything: no signs, no markers, and no allegiance to anyone or anything, not even beauty. *Who got to decide what beauty was, anyway?*

And now her finger ached to try that ring. She turned slightly away from Nareen and slipped it over the fourth finger on her right hand. A part of her insisted she couldn't wear Gertrude's ring, but it fit exactly. And it was her style, matching her patch-pocket yoga pants and her favorite tunic t-shirt.

Gruenbaum looked up from the piles of precious metal he was inspecting. "Looks good," he croaked.

Pond clenched her fist, as if to hide the ring, and only brought it into greater relief. "Thank you," she said. Then she wanted to throw the compliment back, as if she had been fishing, and caught a striped perch she didn't want. But tossing the fish away would entangle her even more, so she hastily told Nareen, "Gertrude didn't seem the jewelry type."

"Neither do you," Nareen offered. "But that's good on you."

Pond did not take the ring off. "I can't *give* anything to either of you, but pick something and wear it in the house. Pick the whole thing if you want. Drape yourselves in necklaces and bracelets and rings." She made her voice roar. "Wear so much you get tired carrying it around."

She grinned like a hungry wolf, warning away anyone hapless enough to be near that fierce smile. The jewelry was bad enough. Worse, Pond was letting herself be forced into semi-close contact with other people while she went through the loot. "I can't believe Gertrude had all this."

"She didn't really have it," Nareen commented. "She owned it, but she didn't mind it much. I was working in here one day dusting, and she asked me to go through all these boxes, and clean the contents. I told her I wasn't a jewelry cleaner, and that was fine. I told her most people didn't want a regular old house cleaner to handle their gems, and she didn't bat an eye. I asked if she wore these pieces, and she said she did when she thought about it, which wasn't often. Although there was one pendant she seemed to enjoy wearing, an old European diamond, A huge one. And then she asked me to pick a piece, any piece I liked, and it was mine. I looked through everything as I worked, and what I saw was this chain."

Pond noticed now that Nareen wore a delicate, deep gold chain, so fine she had to almost squint before she identified it.

"Gertrude said, 'Yes, pretty wee thing, isn't it,' and put it around my neck.

"'Thank you,' I said. She liked surprising me, and often came up with a good way to do it. 'Where'd you get the chain?' I asked.

"'Oh, my dear little mother gave it to me,' she told me.

"I told her I couldn't take her mother's chain. If my mother ever gave me anything like that, I would never let go of it. But Gertrude said, 'Of course you can't, but it's not my mother's chain now. It's yours.'"

Pond shook her head. It wasn't fair. Gertrude had given things away so freely, and now Gertrude's will wouldn't let Pond give away anything. She took a handful of jewelry and threw it on the bed. It wasn't a very satisfying toss. The jewels jingled, polite as they landed on the down quilt. And now Pond would have to untangle chains to look through lockets.

"I don't wear jewelry," Gruenbaum said, opening another heart-shaped pendant.

"Neither do I." Pond sighed, staring at the ring on her hand. She liked it. "But wear something while you're in this house, if you want." She knew it wasn't likely. The jewelry was very feminine. Gertrude had never married. And Gruenbaum was so sinewy and whittled by time that he wasn't the type for delicate jewels.

"Who's this, in the picture?" Gruenbaum held out a heart-shaped locket that held a portrait. "Everything else has been empty, but not this one."

Pond stared at the tiny picture. "Gertrude, my aunt. The lady of the house."

She who had caused all this ruckus looked not unlike a tiny bird Pond had seen once in a nest in a cottonwood tree in Arizona. The nest was small, but the bird was so much smaller that its home seemed like an entire world. Pond had been climbing a tree out over a little lake, when she saw the bird and its nest. She stared at the miniscule feathers, the diminutive beak, the penetrating dots of eyes, and had almost lost her balance, something that never occurred to her, and something she could not allow. She had to be rock steady to clamber everywhere she needed to go.

But the bird had been so light, so dainty, almost disappearing into its nest, that Pond lost all sense of perspective, forgot she was inching along a tree limb, forgot she was mimicking the deftness of squirrels and birds who perched up high with ease because they had no fear of flying or of falling. Looking at the bird, she became almost airborne, so light she nearly let go.

Gruenbaum looked again at the portrait. "Quite a lady," he said.

Pond nodded. Seeing the photo made it seem like Gertrude could pop up suddenly amidst all her deep and shimmering treasures.

Gruenbaum set the locket down. "Can't clean chimneys if you're all draped with stuff like this," he told Pond, his voice rough, but his gaze kept returning to an orange ring, set in a thick masculine band. He reached out for it, closing his eyes as he touched the stone. He placed the stone on his left middle finger.

"What do you think?" he asked, his manner shy and stiff.

"Great." Pond's lack of enthusiasm had to do only with her, and not with the man or his borrowed ring, which matched him the same way the green ring went with her. How had she slept four nights in this room and not noticed she was spending time in a hideous jewelry vault?

The contents of the safe-deposit boxes her

mother kept wouldn't have a tenth of what was stored here. And Pond's mother's jewels, which had been secured in a bank for thirty years, had been enough to send Pond running for cover to all the culverts of the land. She had to evade the perfect pearl conformity of the jewels, the wealth they represented, and the fact they came with her family.

Pond had run for seven years, and now she was back again, and more jewels than she had run from were showering down upon her. And she could no longer run. She sighed, her face dismal. *Surely nothing here is the most valuable thing in the house. It can't be. The key has to reveal what was most valuable, and nothing here fits the key.*

In the meantime, she hadn't noticed the disappointed expression on the man beside her.

"Don't listen to her," Nareen told Gruenbaum. "She likes moping." She studied the ring on his hand. "Wear that. It makes you look like a prince."

It was true. The stone and band were simple, but very proud and strong. On his hand, it turned his darkness into wise experience, his roughness into grace.

"I was a prince," Gruenbaum grinned. "When I was a boy. In the apple orchard behind our house, the trees were all green and gold. My brothers and I held tournaments."

"Skill and bravery," Pond teased, and then bit off her joking train of thought. "I was never a princess," she continued, making her voice fierce.

And she still wouldn't be. But she felt her fierceness become tempered as she continued working through the lockets, opening them as automatically as she had shucked clams at a shop in Oregon one week. The clams had been almost as big as her hand, which she thought was very objectionable of them, but it meant people filled up on fewer of them, and so there were fewer to pry out of their shells. Unlike these lockets, even the clam shells had not been endless.

\*\*\*

While the others continued working, Pond went and explored all the extra bedrooms. Each held a regrettable number of canisters, bins, and tins that locked. Pond let all the locks escape her scrutiny, and flung herself angrily in turn on each guest bed, first the two on the second floor, then the four on the third floor. They were all deplorably comfortable, even the one with posts that went as high as the ceiling, and four steps she had to climb up to reach, so she had to sort of catapult herself onto the mattress.

Even the one with mosquito netting was cozy, or maybe it was meant to be chiffon drapes. So was the one with velvet curtains, which appeared to be older than the house. Gertrude must have liked guests, or at least wanted to be prepared for the possibility of their imminent arrival. Unlike Pond, who would do everything possible to ensure she kept her guests at a limit of one.

Pond tested the beds, resenting every one of them, finding their luxuriousness intolerable, and telling herself again no one would ever use these beds, except Nareen if she must, for a brief time.

Nareen was working for her room and board, and Gruenbaum was receiving a handsome hourly wage. It was fine for them to work while she reclined in comfort. That was how it went, wasn't it?

She rolled over and reached into her pocket and counted out the bills that would cover Gruenbaum's time. She rolled back over onto the flat of her back and glared at the pay with the superior, scornful gaze of an employer. She hooted a catcall at the ceiling and decided to send Gruenbaum packing. She couldn't stand being anyone's supervisor.

"I'm not your boss," she announced, after thundering downstairs and running back into the master bedroom.

Gruenbaum looked up at her with a sardonic expression. "Of course you're not," he agreed, his face quizzical.

Nareen didn't bother replying, thereby proving she also was quite clear about bosses.

Pond gave him a handful of rolled up bills, his full day's rate. So what if his pay suggested he had already cleaned the equivalent of an entire day's worth of chimneys and it wasn't even lunchtime yet. What did she care? It was all Gertrude's pile. No matter how she went through it, there would be more there to burn.

Pond did wonder why she had found Gruenbaum hovering over the phone stand. "That's a 1992 Baltimore phone book," she told him. "Not likely to be much use."

He ignored her implicit question. "I can stay on and help out the rest of the day."

Pond frowned at him. "*Bah*," she said, her

expression grudging and severe. But she didn't tell him to leave. Was she imagining it, or did she catch a glint of humor, perhaps triumph, in Gruenbaum's eyes?

*\*\*\**

Pond sighed again, and then again, until Nareen announced lunch would be served in half an hour, and drinks in the interim. The girl didn't ask, she announced, and waited until Pond and then Gruenbaum left their labors. All the precious metals were strewn in piles, partly sorted, all the lockets partly examined, all the gems winking at their backs, as if they were mocking Pond, in on whatever joke Gertrude was enjoying.

"I can go eat in my van," Gruenbaum said. "I've got peanut butter and a knife. All set."

"You can't turn down my cooking," Nareen told him.

Pond didn't say anything, one way or another. At the moment, she didn't object to his presence any more than she objected to everything else. And so all three of them pulled chairs up to the table. Pond noticed Gruenbaum, like her, ate with as much relish as if he had been living out of a grocery bag before arriving here.

They sat at a table in one corner of the enormous kitchen and drank the Italian sodas Nareen served with a flourish. Pond had heard people call such a spot a breakfast nook, or a tea table, or a butcher's counter, depending upon what they used it for.

When the food was ready, they ate in silence, but

it wasn't uncomfortable, at least not until someone knocked on the back door. The kitchen door led out to the gardens and the back yard. Pond expected Gertrude's gardener might report someday, so she went to the door with that idea in mind.

The yards were beautiful, and Pond couldn't imagine a tiny old lady keeping them that way herself, so she half-thought a strapping nut brown lad might show up, not unlike the ones she had met working an organic farm in California, only maybe with fewer odd ideas about seeds. The ones in California believed you had to plant barefoot, when the moon was at a certain stage, first placing the seeds with reverence into your mouth before you planted them in the earth.

Instead of a nut brown lad, a beautiful platinum haired lady rushed in without waiting to be asked. The lady was older than Pond, an indefinite age, with a youthful face, bright eyes, and a blur of energy.

"Oh, you're eating," she called with delight. "Might have fancied you'd be eating. We're not lunching at my estate today. Workers won't let me. They interrupt everything. You know how it is." Then she paused, studying the three gathered around the table. "Are *you* workers? But what you are eating looks so *delicious*," she said.

"What makes you think workers don't like good food?" Pond asked, pitching her voice between innocent and snarky.

"What are you having for lunch?" the new arrival asked, borrowing the words, voice, and gestures of a little girl, before putting her hand over her own mouth, as if she had not been able to stop herself from speaking. "It's just it smells so delicious."

Pond said nothing. Nareen got up and put together a plate for the woman. She mock curtsied as she held it out to her.

The woman almost turned away from the plate, looked as if she knew the girl was teasing her as well as feeding her. Pond smiled. But the food clearly smelled so enticing the woman took the plate and began placing food into her mouth, at first delicately, with the little finger on her right hand crooked, and then eagerly, with all her fingers curled around a fork, and as if she hadn't eaten in a long time.

The woman ate standing, leaning against an island in the kitchen. Pond noted the physical distance the woman maintained—along with the social. But like all of them, the newest arrival also couldn't help losing herself in bites of frisée curled amidst walnut vinaigrette, tiny flat crab cakes that were apparently all jumbo lump and no filler, and not one but two handmade aioli sauces.

Not until she had cleaned her plate did the woman look with suspicion at the trio around the table. "Gertrude didn't usually eat such lavish lunches. I know. I used to visit her at lunch all the time. And what are you doing with jewelry?"

"Good question," Pond said, her voice dripping with irony.

"I know a thing or two about jewels," the woman said, presenting her aquiline nose in the direction of Pond and the other two.

"Bully for you," said Pond.

"So sad, about True," the woman followed up, dabbing at the corner of one eye to broadcast the idea of grief.

Pond and everyone else around the table looked blank.

"Gertrude," the woman said. "Always wanted to be called True."

Pond had not known, but she liked the name much better. "Crazy old bat," she said, her voice harsh, and it wasn't an insult but a compliment.

The woman sniffed, conveying disapproval this time. "They say she left this place to a renegade niece."

"How terrible," said Pond, with such utter agreement that the platinum haired lady seemed to be reconsidering her assessment for a moment. *Maybe this young scamp wasn't so bad after all*, her expression said. *At least she liked good food.*

"Francine Millicent," the woman said. "She probably goes by Frankie or Millie."

"The name is *Pond*," the new owner of the house said fiercely.

Something about Pond's intensity must have reminded the older woman of True. "Oh, dear," she said, "forgive me. You're the niece."

Pond nodded her head. "Much to my regret."

"You don't seem overcome with grief," the woman said, her voice disapproving, her eyes fixed on the green stone on Pond's right hand.

"You're right," Pond said. "I'm overcome with a house. And this ring is Gertrude's." She nodded to Gruenbaum. "That ring is Gertrude's, too."

The woman's eyes widened, eager and hungry. "You're not removing Gertrude's property, are you?"

"Good of you to care so much about Gertrude's property," said Pond.

"Oh, you know," said the woman, "one has to look out for the entire neighborhood, really. If one place goes on the decline, they all might. And I live right next door, so I've got a special interest."

Pond thought the woman was doing her best not to look greedy. She had seen that expression on other faces. She didn't bother pointing out the property was hers now, as she didn't want to remind herself. "You're welcome to wear anything you find here while you're in this house."

The woman looked down at her dress. She obviously had a personal shopper, and was arrayed in clothes that were brand new. Pond wondered if the woman ever wore the same clothes twice. She looked like the type who might not. Oh, well, more for the second-hand store.

"Not clothes," Pond clarified, although it was also true she didn't mind what anyone in particular wore. "You can borrow jewelry."

The woman threw back her head and laughed. "Oh, how funny," she said, when she stopped laughing. But her eyes grew very intent. "You're all playing dress up."

Pond glanced at Gruenbaum and Nareen, looked down at herself. "We are not playing at anything at all." Pond decided in that moment the three of them worked well enough together because they didn't play the games everyone outside this house asked them to play.

She neglected to mention Gertrude's game, True's game, which had them proceeding on a mad search through every open lock in the house. "To whom am I speaking?" she asked wearily, leaving out the untrue bit about it being a pleasure. It wasn't, and so she wouldn't bother saying it was.

"Duckie," the woman said, lifting her very beautiful chin to show it to its best advantage. "That's not my real name, of course, but it's what everyone calls me." She looked pointedly at the other occupants of the table, until Pond introduced them.

"My, you're a very young cook," Duckie told Nareen. She gazed at Gruenbaum for a long time. Pond followed her gaze, and picked up on what Duckie was seeing. He looked like a scapegrace, from one angle, and then from another he looked almost regal, as if he were royalty living in exile. Duckie turned away her eyes before he could catch her staring.

"I can't go too young," she said out loud, as if she were reminding or reprimanding herself.

"What are you talking about?" Pond said.

"There's that friend of mine, though," Duckie mused. "She's married, and she took up with that Greek man twenty-two years her junior. When *her* husband stopped bothering, she went off with Mr. Greek to Mexico. They're probably snorkeling at this very moment. And what are you all doing?" she asked Pond, her eyes bright with interest.

"We're having lunch," Pond said shortly. "It's nice of you to interrupt us."

"I only ever interrupt aristocratically," Duckie said, "in the politest manner possible, and with impeccable social grace." She looked down at what she was wearing, smoothed her skirt.

"It looks nice," Nareen told her.

"You're so good to notice. My husband never does. Not that he could notice right now, being in San Francisco. It happens to husbands in a shockingly short amount of time."

"San Francisco?" Pond asked, showing interest for the first time.

"First they stop noticing. Then they go. Even if they stay in the same room, they go." She cleared her throat. "Just like True. Not so long ago, I was talking with True. One day she was bright and cheerful and sunny as ever, eating happily, sharing her meal with me. 'Help yourself to anything you want,' she said. '*Anything*?' I said. But only later could I decide what I really wanted. And the very next day True was gone. No sign of illness, no sign of anything wrong. Just gone. Everything changes so quickly."

"Sometimes," Pond said. "Other times, you get stuck. Like now, in this house."

"It's not a bad house," Duckie said. "You just don't know it."

"We're getting to know the house."

Duckie narrowed her eyes. "Planning on selling?"

"Can't. True's will won't let me right now or maybe ever. For now, the damn thing is mine whether I want it or not."

Duckie stared at Pond. "You look surprisingly

good in your raggedy bits of clothing, and that green stone suits you." Then she put her hand over her mouth, as if she hadn't meant to say those words out loud.

Pond tilted her head in acknowledgment. "No worries. Honesty's not bad."

"Did you mean I could wear True's jewelry?" Duckie asked. "I don't adorn myself with pre-worn items, not even my own. But maybe I could make an exception. Or two. Depending on what I find." Duckie laughed, a genuine laugh, so that a look of surprise crossed her face. "Well, you do have your work cut out for you."

She was still chuckling as she left the kitchen. As she left, she looked at Nareen. "I might be back," Duckie said. "Cooking like that is worth coming back for."

Nareen closed the door behind her, clicking the lock into place.

"Good riddance," Gruenbaum said to the door, after it had closed behind Duckie. "She looked at me like she was buying a horse, and I was the horse."

"She's not so bad," Nareen said. "I've seen her before here, though I don't think she ever noticed me. She's scared."

Pond nodded in recognition. Duckie had all the signs of fear: the fake laugh, the perfect appearance, the desire to control the entire interaction, from arriving unannounced to leaving when she wanted.

"My mom told me something about her husband," Nareen added. "He showed up in a hospital in California after an accident, and the girl who had been driving the car was not licensed to drive, she was so young. Duckie was by herself in an enormous house. Her house is always under construction, full of workers. She doesn't like workers. She feels lost," she said. "You would, too, if you had to pretend things were one way, and it was obvious things were another way instead."

Pond nodded. It sounded like Nareen knew what she was talking about.

"I wouldn't do that," Gruenbaum insisted, and then he blushed.

Nareen saw the blush and grinned.

"What about you?" he asked. "You seem all proper, diagnosing everyone else's problems. But you're awfully young to be on your own."

"I am," Nareen said, her tone even. She got up to clear the lunch dishes.

Pond wondered what went on behind the girl's calm front.

Gruenbaum sat at the table and from his front shirt pocket drew out and stared at two items he had picked up from the jewelry: the small bird-like woman's portrait, and a cameo that depicted a young man.

Pond looked over his arm. The young man was gorgeous. He had to be a prince, or more than that, an angel, someone whose beauty was so striking it looked unreal, otherworldly. He was ideal, story-book, an illustration out of a myth, an honest-to-goodness hero.

"Tell me about her," he said. He held out the locket that held the woman's portrait.

"That's True," Pond told him. "Gertrude." She

took a deep, strangled breath. Gertrude looked so delicate, it was hard to believe she had landed this entire house on Pond's head.

Gruenbaum held out the cameo of the man, and Pond shook her head. From the sink, Nareen called, "That's Gene. He was the one Gertrude loved. He disappeared when she was young. Missing in action during World War II."

"I didn't know that happened to the beautiful ones," Gruenbaum said.

"Happens to everyone."

"I thought death like that was for people who have no other options." He stared at the man's face.

"I didn't know about Gene," Pond told Nareen. Gertrude had been so happy. How had Gertrude been so happy?

***

"Maybe we don't need to know exactly what we're looking for." Nareen was done with the dishes and now leaned against a wooden island.

Pond shook her head. Just because something sounded reasonable didn't make it so. "I'm going to ask," she said. She grabbed the *I Ching* and shook the coins right there at the table. "What am I looking for?" she said once aloud and to the coins six times in her head, shaking them and letting them fall. The patterns this time gave only a single answer, which ought to have made what the book said clearer.

But instead, her head fogged as she read it out loud. "Hold fast to the good. Bring oneself into

97

harmony with the universe. What happens on earth is temporary and binding, but if you recognize that limitation, the eternal can give certainty without harshness, and then you will find your place in the world and you will spread light."

"So that's what we're looking for," she told Gruenbaum and Nareen with sarcastic enthusiasm.

"Not me," Gruenbaum retorted.

"That's what you're looking for," Nareen told Pond. "You didn't ask what *we* are looking for."

"Same difference." Nonetheless, and particularly because she didn't know how she would recognize harmony, she sighed and said, "Fine. I'll ask." She frowned at the coins. "What are *we* looking for— Nareen and Gruenbaum and me?"

This time the book gave an answer she understood more. "Okay. It's a sign we will enjoy quick, smooth progress, much like a wise king and his faithful deputy working together for the good of all. Our original nature is bright, but because of everything this world has coated us with, it needs cleansing now so it can shine forth again."

Pond laughed as she read the next line: "Continue onward, and you will receive great happiness from your ancestress. Work together." She turned the pages to flip to the next answer. "Great surprise may be followed by celebration and laughter. Maintain steadiness internally regardless of what happens externally. Signs of God are not a danger to one who does so."

"I'm not looking for signs of God," Gruenbaum said, crossing his arms. "The only folks I know who talk about signs of God are those crazy people who handle poisonous snakes. They say that snake won't bite you, if you love God enough. So go ahead, might as well wrap it around your neck and the neck of your small child." He shivered and looked around the kitchen, as if a very long reptile might loom any moment out of the baskets and boxes and chests on hand. "Anyway, that's good your ancestress wants you to be happy," he added, nodding at the book.

Maybe True did want Pond to be happy. Sure had a peculiar way of going about it. "Could be it's talking about your ancestress," she told Gruenbaum. "Or yours." She turned to Nareen.

"*Yours* is the one who's giving us directions." Nareen laughed, and cleared away the last lunch items.

*Not very clear directions,* Pond thought, *but that was probably the point. If True had wanted to give better directions, she would have. True had had absolutely no problem determining what she wanted and then doing it.*

"Do we have to look through more lockets?" Gruenbaum didn't sound eager to resume the search, although Pond did catch his eyes resting again on the orange stone he was wearing on his finger.

"You don't have to do anything," Pond told him, half expecting he would hightail out to his white vehicle and be on his way. But she began trudging upstairs, step after reluctant step, and after a pause, Gruenbaum followed her, and then came Nareen, wiping her hands on the back of her dark green shirt.

Pond was still wearing the same clothes from the day before, but Nareen, who had arrived with no luggage that Pond had seen, must have had a little pack already tucked away somewhere. In any case, she had figured out how to change clothes: nothing fancy, another pair of shorts and another t-shirt. But she looked very clean and composed.

Gruenbaum was wearing his perfect boots again, the ones that reminded Pond of her lost Seattle pair, and the same rumpled outfit from yesterday. He appeared to believe in deodorant. At least Pond hadn't caught any sign of lack of hygiene from him, and she knew that wasn't an accident. You didn't sleep in a car and emerge smelling fresh without taking steps.

Pond had gone all out and showered this morning. Now, she stood staring down at the jewels, and they appeared to be winking at her. She glared back at them and refused to blink.

An indefinite time passed, which Pond measured by flipping at random through deep black obsidian boxes and bright pink-orange quartz containers. Then, because she was getting nowhere by considering all the beautiful pieces, she went pillaging the jewelry piles for the unbeautiful ones, and realized either Gertrude was again playing a joke on her, or a very severe joke had been played upon Gertrude—or upon all the women who had ever worn or been given such pieces. Pond gawked in amazement at a brooch featuring a ridiculous and elaborate Victorian woman's head in profile. It was unimaginable where in God's name a person would pin a thing like that on their body. Where could that person then go and not inspire laughter?

So, too, with an intricate spray of flowers, which appeared to be fashioned all of rubies and emeralds, sapphires and diamonds, and yet every color blared and clashed, so the flowers appeared to be fighting one another for supremacy rather than adding their brilliance to an overall bouquet. It was probably the most expensive thing Pond had yet touched in this collection, and yet its effect was to make her want earplugs for her eyes.

Pond ran her fingers over a monstrous chain, heavy loops of gold formed from an actual series of thick metal rings. The adornment looked more suitable for a prisoner or a knight into one form of bondage or another than for a nice society woman.

"Why would such valuable pieces be so hideous?" Pond asked out loud.

"Oh, they're not all valuable." Nareen snorted. She held up a bracelet that featured a purple paste jewel the size of her fist.

The fake purple jewel almost screamed "heiress" to Pond, because only one who had inherited such a thing could possibly wear it. The jewel was grotesque and baroque, an obvious glue stone set in a sunburst gold pattern, and the bracelet itself was fashioned of woven human hair in a basket weave pattern.

Pond groaned, hoping no woman had ever submitted to wearing such a thing.

"How 'bout this one?" Gruenbaum asked, pointing to a vintage tiara, a bright red one fashioned into a gigantic buckle shape, so its wearer's head would be transformed into a topsy-turvy version of someone's waist, as if a belt and its buckle had migrated upward, translated into rubies, and wrapped itself around someone's brow.

"I'm too ladylike to contemplate such a horror." Pond peered with exaggerated demureness into the nearest mirror. She almost didn't recognize herself, before she met her own gaze and identified it as herself. She flinched and turned away from the reflection, which carried too many questions for her to consider at the moment. *I'm not happy*, she assured herself. Pond insisted on being anything but a happy person.

Pond noticed Gruenbaum also avoided looking in the mirror, as if he knew well none of these adornments went with his rumpled work shirt, and especially not with his boots, and didn't know if he wanted to laugh at himself or not. But then he did look in the mirror, and he grinned with surprise.

"That doesn't look like me," he said, running his hand over his face. "I haven't seen that look since my brother and I played in the orchard. That was my brother's face, when he was just a little guy."

He whooped slightly and then put his hand over his mouth in mock politeness.

"Y'all are *crazy*," he called to Pond and Nareen, looking with apparent disbelief at his left hand, overflowing with gold and jewels. "Not that I like y'all, or anything," he added in a rush.

"As if you're *not* crazy," Pond said with disdain, ignoring the second part of what he had said, because it aligned so exactly with her sentiments. "You're a leading member of the club."

Just then she heard a pounding somewhere off in

the distance, and a voice calling, "Yoo-hoo."

"Oh, dear." Pond sighed, disburdening herself of an inconvenient mound of precious metal before traipsing downstairs to find the source of annoyance.

She knew it was going to be Duckie even before Duckie's coiffed platinum waves came into view. Pond heard Nareen and Gruenbaum on the steps behind her.

"Oh, my," said Duckie. "You all look surprisingly good." Confusion crossed her face, along with amusement and approval.

Pond looked at herself and the others on the stairs, seeing them through Duckie's eyes. She and the others were wearing their same old clothes, their same plain pieces of jewelry, which ought to have made Duckie sniff with condescension.

Instead Duckie now nodded and held out her own arm, displaying a bracelet. "Brand new," she said, like a child showing a new toy. "The diamonds are real."

"I wouldn't have dreamed otherwise," Pond said, and she meant it, even though the diamonds were so large they ought to have been fake. Duckie didn't look like a woman who would settle for fake jewels.

"Do you want to know how much it cost?"

Pond glared, and let her silence speak for her.

"More than my driver earns in a year," Duckie said, and yet a plaintive look crossed her face, and she seemed to forget all about her bracelet. "You know how it is when workers are around the house. Makes the place unlivable."

She turned her face in appeal toward Pond and

103

then toward True's house—the whole interior of it, in every direction. "There are *always* workers in my house. I can't bear it. The place is so beautiful. I can't bear it."

"You're not staying here," Pond told Duckie, staring at Gruenbaum so he got the message, too. Didn't matter how many extra bedrooms there were, Nareen was already one guest too many.

Gruenbaum told Pond in a stage whisper, "She can stay here. I can stay out in the car again."

Duckie turned to Gruenbaum. "You're a gentleman's gentleman. But surely there's room for both of us in this great big place."

"Neither of you are staying anywhere near this house." Pond glared at both of them.

"I'll just be in my van," Gruenbaum said, his voice confident.

Pond glared at him. She didn't think she could make him leave a city street.

"I'll stay in my house, then," Duckie said in a disappointed little girl voice. "Although I probably won't get a single wink of sleep." She paused a while and stared at the ropes of gold. "Are you going to eat a dinner as delicious as the lunch you had?"

Nareen shook her head, and Duckie looked far more chagrined than she should have. Then Nareen relented and announced, "It'll be even better."

Before long, Duckie had joined them, and Pond allowed her to help them look through all the jewels. She kept asking herself why and how she had acquired a third guest, who thought to invite herself to lunch and dinner at other people's houses.

But Duckie pawed through the precious goods with even more alacrity than any of the rest of them. Her eyes brightened like the jewels.

"I've never found a piece of jewelry I want to wear more than a day or two," Duckie complained. "But maybe there's one here."

Pond knew what she meant. Not that Pond sought it in jewels. But everyone wanted the gleam that lasted forever. For Pond, it meant always being on the road, always moving on to see something new. For a brief flash, Pond recognized her restlessness for travel was a cousin to Duckie's hunger for clothes and jewels, and it sounded like Duckie had a similar fondness for men, too.

"Men are the same way," Duckie said aloud, echoing Pond's thoughts. "They start off magical, and then become husbands. Husbands turn into inanimate objects." Her eyes followed Gruenbaum, who, now that Pond noticed it, never seemed to stop moving.

Duckie's eyes stayed on Gruenbaum, moving between him and all the lovely and precious and preposterous gems and metals, ornaments and adornments. She had the look of a child who didn't know whether to eat the mound of fudge or the mound of cookies. She did not place any of the jewels around her own neck or waist, wrist, hands, or ankles, even though Pond reminded her to wear whatever she liked.

Pond noticed Gruenbaum looked only at what was right before him. "I always work alone," he announced to the room at large.

"Fair enough." Pond wondered what he was

doing here, then. "Me, too," she added.

"I often work with people." Nareen looked pointedly at all of them, making Pond realize that without even talking about it, they had divided up the room and were systematically proceeding through all the containers, jeweled and otherwise.

"I don't work," Duckie said, her chin held high.

"You don't have to call it work," Nareen suggested.

"Yes, you do," Gruenbaum countered, "if you want to be honest."

"Really," Duckie began, "who do you think would wear such a thing? It would certainly choke a person."

"Suits you," Gruenbaum said. It was the first time he had spoken directly to Duckie.

She stared in apparent bewilderment at the jeweled noose in her hands, and did not place it around her neck. Then she fashioned her face into a picture of hope.

"Depends upon who's holding the other end of the rope," she said brightly, and Gruenbaum groaned, and despite himself glanced at her furtively, while Pond and Nareen laughed.

"I think these precious baubles are my second language," Duckie crowed with delight. "No, she corrected herself. "First is love, then English, then jewels."

And for the rest of the evening, Duckie let the noose lie, and stopped staring at Gruenbaum's dark grace, and he in turn did not ignore her, any more than he pretended to ignore anyone else, and all four sat together around the dinner table.

But Pond still did not wish anyone goodnight, as she stared at Gruenbaum's back and Duckie's as they left. She went up the stairs to get some sleep, insisting to herself nothing at all had been found that day, beyond a key that didn't fit any of the already-opened locks.

# Wednesday

The morning had begun fine and mostly quiet, and almost everyone had seemed to stay more or less on track with searching the room they were responsible for. Pond had begun the morning working through the jewelry in her room. To take a break, she tromped around the house, her irritability growing the more she thought about how many people were in the house.

When she had arrived that morning, Duckie had chirped on about something in the library. When Pond peeked in on her while making her grumbling rounds, Duckie seemed to be looking at everything but books, and couldn't quite hide a guilty expression behind the elegant dignified pose she took. Pond frowned when she *did* find Nareen in the parlor, even though the girl was looking diligent. Pond scowled when she looked in the dining room and *didn't* find Gruenbaum where he had said he was going to be.

Then in late morning a booming, a knocking, a banging, a thumping had begun, so loud it startled

Pond mid-motion, making her feel she was sifting through time and space as well as unwanted riches.

At first when she heard it, she thought she was in the midst of a waking dream, and couldn't tell if it was a torment or a wonder to have the entire house amplifying her own heartbeat. By the time she blinked and pinched herself and knew herself not to be imagining it, the sound had faded and the only thing remaining was her own heart, sounding in the stillness of her room.

And she told herself it had been nothing, nothing at all, and stared at a handful of platinum rings, almost believing what she was willing herself to believe. A wall of sound simply didn't come out of nowhere, and so clearly it *hadn't*.

She couldn't help herself, though: she sought out company. She poked her head into the library. "What was that noise?" she asked.

Duckie adopted a blank gaze, so Pond repeated herself.

Duckie shook her head. "All quiet here," she said, fighting to keep a straight face.

"You *had* to hear that noise. It made the floors shake."

Duckie smiled, her eyes not quite meeting Pond's, and Pond found herself wondering if perhaps her neighbor was not fully in touch with the real world. She went tromping off in search of understanding. If this house had to have so many people in it, at least that inconvenience increased the likelihood *one* of them might make sense. Didn't it?

\*\*\*

## *Duckie*

Duckie waited until Pond left the library before she resumed searching.

"Picky-picky," she told the absent Pond. "Wanting these old houses not to make noise. Just *try* getting something that old not to make noise. I'm almost as old as this house, and see if you can keep me quiet. Until he stopped paying me mind, my husband was always embarrassed by my charming enthusiasm. Try telling a fountain not to burble up," she said out loud to her husband, as if he could hear her all the way from San Francisco.

"Good luck to you," she told the direction in which Pond had departed, sniffing with exaggerated aristocracy. "*Although*," she mused, her voice slowing, "I *can* keep a secret when necessary. True told me about that lovely, perfect two-carat Old European diamond, and I haven't said a word about it yet to *you*, dearie. Catch me if I do."

Her eyes widened, her face brightened, and she dove back into her search.

\*\*\*

## *Nareen*

Nareen had been in the kitchen when the sound began, thinking about Pond and this house. *Wonder if it's my charm that made her let me stay here. Or my cooking. Or is she afraid?*

She smiled, remembering the way she had rigged the roll-top secretary, using a trick she had learned from her mom on one of their other cleaning expeditions to make the desk appear to close on its own. "You never know when it'll come in handy," her mom told her, eyes gleaming. Nareen thought Pond *had* looked alarmed when the secretary rolled itself up tight, putting itself away for the night. If it wasn't charm, it could be cooking, and if it wasn't delicacies it could be fear. All were convincing, in their own way.

When the noise began, Nareen whirled around, looking for its source. She was outdone, though she was not above suggesting other people's houses were haunted, and not beyond encouraging them to think so by adding a few strategic noises of her own making. Though the sound was so loud it had to be originating right where she stood, there was no sign of any noisemaker. And yet the sound was also ambient, seeming to emanate from the whole house.

Nareen was torn between fear and awe. She felt a twinge of envy. She had to figure out how to make such a noise. Her dear mom was right. Might come in handy one day.

And then she heard footsteps coming up the basement stairs and felt a flash of anger someone had preempted her plan, creating a ruckus before she could do so. But she would not let that throw her. She could turn anything to her advantage.

With real presence of mind despite the amazing noise and her anger at the individual she presumed had generated it, she drew a glass of water and began drinking it down, so when Gruenbaum entered the room she was standing with her back to him, looking out the bright window in the direction of the kitchen garden. There was of course nothing to see, and by now the noise had also halted.

"What are you doing here?" Gruenbaum asked, his voice as gruff as his appearance. He seemed to be hiding behind an exterior even more impassive and sooty than usual.

Nareen swallowed another elaborate gulp of water. "Thirsty. Would you like a tall glass of water? Maybe that's what you were looking for in the basement," she added archly.

"Checking the air conditioning," he said stiffly. He studied Nareen, a look of mistrust crossing his face.

"And how is the air conditioning?" Nareen said with false sweetness.

He grunted in reply. "Working. Dining room was hot. Might be my thermostat." He pulled at his shirt. He was wearing the same rumpled clothes he always wore.

Nareen, too, was wearing shorts and t-shirt, her usual attire. She hid a frown, and continued drinking her water until she had drained the glass. "Beautiful day," she said with exaggerated politeness.

"Sure," he said, his tone not hiding his challenge.

***

## Pond

Earlier that morning, they had all gathered

around the breakfast table.

"I put on my face much earlier than usual," Duckie chirped at the back door, using her hands to form a frame around her chin. She was unable to hide her anticipation, which Pond took to be directed toward Nareen's cooking. Duckie drew her chair up to the breakfast table with enthusiasm, just in time to be seated.

Gruenbaum had shuffled onto the front porch, looking a bit more diffident than Duckie. "I'm still here," he announced with a determination Pond didn't understand.

Sure, he could have a hot meal and another day's wages. Pond thought such determination seemed disproportionate.

Pond took some time getting used to the morning, and to seeing the others' faces over porridge bowls. The fragrant clouds of steam— which wafted cinnamon and cloves and something else, maybe a pinch of cardamom—made it easier, softening everyone's morning face, and at that point everything still seemed fine.

For a flash, Pond thought perhaps she could even call a truce—with these three, with herself, with the house.

The others seemed to be proceeding on the same basis, at least for the moment. Nareen and Gruenbaum stared at each other out of the corners of their eyes, but said nothing beyond a terse, "Good morning." Neither of them looked like they quite trusted the other. It was more like they were continuing to watch and study the situation, seeking a useful advantage.

Gruenbaum and Duckie also appeared to be at a draw. She wasn't staring at him, and he wasn't fleeing from her. Pond gazed into the depths of her bowl. This house was more bearable with three others there. Still, she wouldn't have chosen any of them if she had been asked. She would put up with them only long enough to solve the mystery. Their reward and hers would be freedom from this hideous, gorgeous mansion.

But only if she could contain her impatience. Every now and then she thought about owning the house and felt she would have to run screaming out the door and not look back. And then another odd part of her would recall the quest, and wonder what it was she was or wasn't going to find. The book had held the key, but so far the key hadn't opened anything at all. Every lock she had found had been already unlocked. And time was passing. Was disaster looming closer every day?

"Maybe there'll be more instructions today," she was saying, staring at her cup of tea, which seemed to be half full of cheer and half full of resentment, when there came a sudden knocking sound—a regular knocking sound, not a whole-house banging sound—somewhere off in the distance.

Couldn't be the back door, the one Duckie had used. They were seated near that one, and it was silent. Didn't sound like the front door, the one Gruenbaum had used, but Pond got up and checked anyway. *Most people would be inclined to start at the front door,* she thought.

Then she paused, wondering which of the side doors it could be. She traipsed through the conservatory, a room of solid glass interrupted only by a floor to ceiling sliding glass door that meant almost one whole wall could open to the garden terrace beyond.

The clear expanse revealed in full glory the new arrivals, a man so sleek and shiny he appeared to be made out of silk or carved from polished obsidian. He was all perfect planes and angles, all cut muscles and cheekbones, head shaved so clean it reflected light. And he was standing next to the largest, blackest, hairiest dog. Pond took in the man and dog and almost stopped breathing.

They were so beautiful, but so unusual. The dog was as furry as the man was sleek. The dog was large and robust and wobbling with happy signs of well-eating, while the man was trim and lithe. What they had in common was a steady, intent look. They were studying Pond as carefully as she was taking them in.

"Morning," she said, after opening the door.

"Who are *you*?" the man asked with amusement.

"What do you mean?" Pond shot back. "Who the hell are you?"

"I live here."

"No, you *don't*." Pond raised her eyebrows in imperious rebuttal.

"Hmmm. She doesn't usually have relatives visit, but that's fine. You have a resemblance, I'll give you that."

"It's not a resemblance anymore. She's dead."

"That's not possible," the man said, his eyes widening. "True would never do such a human thing as die."

"Tell that to the lawyer."

"I do live here. I'm back home. You're telling me the old lady's not here to welcome me?"

"There's nothing in the will about a permanent houseguest."

"I'm not a guest," he said. "I live here. We live here." He pointed to his dog. "We have the best suite in the house."

"There aren't any suites," Pond said, voice rising in triumph. *Should have known there would be fortune seekers calling.* She prepared to close the door and turn away.

"I'll show you," he challenged her. "Giselle," he called to his dog. "Where do we stay?" His dog took the lead, clearly familiar with the territory, and prancing with the easy grace of a show pony or a dancer, impossibly elegant for its enormous size and girth. He nodded at Pond, and floated while he walked behind the animal, his moves so smooth he appeared not to touch the ground.

When the supposedly familiar stranger entered the kitchen and saw the odd assemblage of folk gathered there, his face lit up with a grin brighter than the early morning sunshine. He looked around, and then did a double-take at all the faces around the table. "Don't see the old girl," he said. "A lot can change during a circus tour, apparently. I believe I've come home," he hooted. "This place doesn't *look* like a boarding house from the outside."

"It's not," Duckie said. "It's much better. Welcome." No one else was saying anything at all. Gruenbaum was petting the dog, which had gone to him immediately, and Nareen was dishing up another bowl of porridge, which she handed silently to the new arrival. There was still plenty of room around the table.

"What's he eat?" Nareen looked at the dog.

"She?" the man said. "Anything at all."

Pond thought of her mother's cats, growing up, which ate whatever they could find, and without a word handed Nareen money. The dog could eat what the dog wanted, whether that was porridge or something else. Meanwhile, Nareen searched through the cabinets and came up with a couple cans of potted beef.

"These aren't fit for human consumption anyway," Nareen told the dog, serving the beast in a filigree-adorned silver bowl, the least lavish serving dish she could find. The dog lay down and crossed its paws as it ate, an astonishingly delicate posture for such a gigantic beast.

"What's your name, dear?" Duckie asked. "I'm Duckie, you know."

"Charmed," said the man, bowing over her hand with impossible grace. "Ferdinand."

Duckie studied Ferdinand. "I've never seen anyone who looks like you," she said, her voice and face full of marvel. "I can't stop looking at you. Don't mind me," she waved her hand, and continued on, in a mad rush, as if she couldn't stop the words pouring out. "Your looks aren't classical anything, but I can't imagine you looking any other way. You look perfect. You're a model, aren't you?"

He grinned. "Dancer. Involves more movement."

Her eyes locked on his hips. "I bet it does," she said admiringly. "And what's your dog's name?"

"I'm her human, more than she's my dog," Ferdinand said. "She's Giselle."

"Must be hard traveling with her," Pond said, her voice full of grudging admiration. She had never let herself have a dog. This one was far too smart and nice for its own good. But imagine how much it *ate*.

Ferdinand nodded. "Only thing harder than traveling with her is traveling without her."

Pond let the murmur of conversation rise up without her. When she felt ready to dive back in, she spoke up. "Too bad there aren't any suites in the house," she said, almost wishing to be proved wrong, if for no other reason than the sake of the dog.

"Got distracted by breakfast," Ferdinand said, brushing his lips delicately with the back of his hand. "Let us show you. Giselle, we're home." And Giselle rose and raced up the service stairs, all the way up to the third floor, down a long hallway, and waited expectantly at a door. It took the humans a while to catch up with her. Their two legs did not work as quickly as her four.

"That's just the porch," Pond said impatiently. She had noticed and dismissed the screened-in area, probably once used as a sleeping porch. With the advent of air conditioning, such things had been rendered obsolete. Weather was too hot for her to imagine wanting to spend time there, and it got full sun in the afternoon, too.

"It's the porch, yes," he said, "but that's not all. Let me show you." He unlatched the door, walked out onto the wooden planks, around a little corner, and pointed out another door. "En suite, too," he said, opening the second door. Giselle leaped past him and almost skidded into place as she lay down on a rag rug that was braided all in varying shades of reds and golds, clearly returning to a well-known perch. "Welcome," Ferdinand bowed to Pond.

Pond was irritated at his graciousness and poise, frustrated by the presence of this suite she hadn't known about. Perhaps most annoying was this suite was what she would have claimed for herself, had she known it existed.

The area was cozy and comfortable, and had its own ambiance, apart from the elegance of the house. And it was clearly Ferdinand's. He had all the satisfaction of being the occupant, and none of the trouble of being the owner.

In fact, so distressed was Pond to discover the existence of the suite she forgot to ask all the questions that ought to have occurred to a rational person: Did he pay rent, did he have a key, and did he have his own kitchen?

Pond's face broadcast all her dismay.

"It's not that bad," he said. "We're unobtrusive. You don't even have to know we're here."

"I didn't know this place existed," Pond complained.

"Best part of the house."

"That's what's so terrible about it." She kept her voice from veering into whining only because she coughed mid-phrase.

Ferdinand studied her expression. "True said when she first inherited this place it almost made her go crazy."

"You don't have the foggiest idea," Pond said, crossing her arms. "I started out this way."

He shook his head, and she left. But then he followed her, and his dog followed him.

"What can we do to help?" he asked. "I believe in repaying my debts. I owe Gertrude many. If she's gone, I'll still do the right thing. How can I help?"

"Leave."

He paused, and then continued, his voice gentle, "Besides that."

\*\*\*

Lunch began with Pond pretending there had been no turf war about the third floor suite, nor any untoward noise throughout the house. She noticed Duckie didn't seem to want to meet her eyes, and that Gruenbaum and Nareen were wary of one another. They appeared to be bristling a silent challenge. Ferdinand and Giselle were studying everyone else, and were the only guests who met Pond's eyes in return.

Nareen offered seconds, and plates were held out with alacrity. Nareen looked at Pond.

"Thank you," Pond said, with exaggeration. She liked Nareen's cooking but didn't want to admit it, even if it was also clear everyone loved the food. Maybe the food was too good, and was keeping everyone here.

"Look," Gruenbaum said, "there's something we have to talk about." He clutched his coffee mug in his hand and swallowed several large gulps of coffee. "Ah. Too hot." But he forged onward. "That banging that came a little while ago. Can't be the only one who heard it." He bared his teeth at Nareen.

Nareen glared and crossed her arms. "I was in the kitchen."

"Doing what?" Gruenbaum challenged her.

"Cooking, of course," Nareen said, but her reply seemed too quick to Pond. And hadn't the noise come long before lunch?

Pond shook away her questions. "Boiler," she said out loud. She had stayed in several basement crash pads where she had not been able to sleep longer than fifteen minutes straight because the boilers had to heat an entire apartment building, which meant they were always turning off or on, clanging to a halt or clamoring on, and then pounding while they went.

"It's August," Gruenbaum pointed out. "We're not *that* far north. Who else heard the noise? It was very loud in the basement." He stared at Nareen, seeming to dare her to speak.

Nareen sent Gruenbaum a challenging look but kept silence.

Duckie patted her bright silver hair, and her face took on a blank expression.

"What about you?" Pond asked her.

"What?" She offered a dim, pleasant smile, and continued sipping at her tea. She added another sugar cube and stirred the hot liquid with great care.

"I worked in a haunted circus once," Ferdinand exclaimed. "One of my best gigs. Got to choreograph all my own routines and not one of them involved a fake unicorn."

"Do most of your dances involve unicorns?" Duckie's hearing seemed to zoom back into function.

"Not my idea. If I had to choose between working for a haunted circus and dancing with a unicorn, I'll take the friendly ghost any time. Save me from glued-on horns."

"I know exactly what you mean," Duckie said, her eyes wide.

"This is no circus," Pond explained, closing her eyes with tired exasperation. "And it's not haunted." There was always an explanation for everything. They just hadn't found it yet. "A shutter blowing in the wind."

Gruenbaum glared at Nareen, and she said nothing. And so he pushed back from the table, keeping his coffee mug in his hand.

\*\*\*

## *Gruenbaum*

Gruenbaum scoured the attic again, this time with the others following in his trail, and noticed it did have an air vent that flapped and banged, echoing wood against wood even in the slight breeze. He leaned out all the windows that opened on the extra half story, the third floor, the second floor, and the ground floor, demonstrating elaborately how silent everything here was. He had to halt that air vent, though, so he could get on with his own noisemaking.

From the basement he grabbed a hammer and a handful of nails, sticking the one through a belt loop and the others in his pocket, and went back up to the attic, but couldn't halt the air vent whapping along in the wind. If he approached the vent from the other side, outside, he would be in more familiar territory, and there he could nail the vent open, or nail it closed. Open was probably better, he decided, let more air in.

So he clambered up on his tallest ladder, the one that went almost as high as the pinnacle of the house. He did it as easily as breathing, so when he clambered back down after taking care of that vent once and for all, he was surprised Duckie seemed to be feeling faint.

She put her hand to her forehead. "It's just I'm a little dizzy from watching your feet float all the way down that big ladder."

He stared at her. Of course, she did her best to make *faint* appear *appealing*, not weak. He decided to ignore her.

"There," he declared, turning to Pond, placing his hands on his hips. "That won't bother anyone anymore. Took care of it flapping all around." If only he could say the same for Duckie's silver hair.

He scrambled down to the basement stairs and studied the heating and cooling system, which appeared to be geothermal. Steady humming, no noise. Next he went out to what he called the barn. No sign of anything there that could cause a disturbance.

He was walking around the outside of the house, studying the trees, when Pond caught up with him again. "Find anything?" she asked.

He shook his head. "All's quiet."

"This house just has a lot of unusual inventions," she said. "Even a roll-top secretary that appeared to close itself. There's a logical explanation for it. Some Victorian era automatic drum got wound too tightly years ago, and set itself off in the middle of the night."

Gruenbaum grinned. She was right, the whole house was full of odd contraptions. Trouble was, he didn't know how to prove a negative—that none of those contraptions had been behind the noise. Maybe he would just have to repeat the clangor.

***

## *Pond*

Pond had noticed most recently that Nareen refused to meet Gruenbaum's gaze, but watched his every move. What was going on with these two?

Some time later, he trudged into the kitchen, where Nareen was studying the mechanical gizmos piled on shelves along walls.

"Check this one out!" she exclaimed, turning a handle that rotated gears within a giant canister, closing a lid that then plummeted downward, downward, toward the bottom. It looked like a very elaborate and unfortunate antique trash compactor.

"Marvelous," Gruenbaum said, broadcasting a clear lack of enthusiasm.

"It's a duck press." Nareen continued wheeling the gears around. "After you cook your duck and carve it, you can extract all the juices from the carcass, using this indispensable device."

"Every house needs one," Pond said, mimicking a hearty television announcer's voice. "Not that I *want* any duck juice."

"That's what you think." Nareen shoved the press back high up on the shelf where it had come from.

Duckie came trundling and thumping into the kitchen. "You just missed a whole conversation about duck juice," Pond told her.

Duckie was pulling an antique wagon that contained a drummer boy, whose arm propelled a wooden stick against a skin drum head, the rhythm and speed tied to the wagon wheels' movement, so if you pulled faster, the cadence sped up, and became louder. "Look what I found!" Duckie said brightly, bringing herself and the banging to a quick halt in front of the kitchen island.

"That would explain everything," Pond said with elaborate sarcasm, "if only someone had been pulling a child's toy throughout the house under cover of invisibility. While hooked up to a megaphone, and running."

"No chance." Gruenbaum echoed Pond's tone.

"Well, *I* think it's a nice toy," Duckie said defensively, walking out of the kitchen and making a circle through the downstairs rooms to demonstrate. The thumping faded as she went into the distance, proving the toy drum could not have been the source of noise.

Ferdinand and Giselle floated into the kitchen. "Didn't find any noise," he announced.

*You and that dog are too elegant to keep company with cacophony*, Pond thought, *so what are you doing with me?*

"But I couldn't help seeing this," he said, holding up the golden key. "It was on a marble end table. Key to everything? I love me a good key to everything."

Pond shook her head. "Go for it. Search all the lockable containers in the house. Search to your heart's content." *Not that it will have any effect.*

\*\*\*

Nareen knocked on the door frame to get Pond's attention and let her know more ingredients were required, if everyone wanted to keep eating.

"Look," Pond complained, feeling Nareen was all but tugging at her elbow. "I'm no one's mother and no one's boss. And I'm no one's bank, either." Money wasn't the issue. Along with the house, Pond had inherited more than she was likely to go through in a lifetime of determined spending. But she resented the funds just as much as the house, and the thought she was now a conduit for money flow was enough to make her feel like clawing out of her own skin. She pulled a small treasury of bills out of her pocket and shoved it toward Nareen.

Nareen's eyes widened. "This handful of money you're throwing around will feed everyone for a whole week. I've never held so much money in my hands before." She glared at Gruenbaum, seeming to dare him to steal it from her. Duckie was paying no attention at all to such minor things as small fortunes. She glared at Ferdinand and then took a second look.

Pond's gaze had been following Nareen's, and so she, too, noticed Ferdinand's eyes were lit not with greed but with laughter.

"This is *some* kind of house," he crowed. "I still haven't seen any sign of the previous inhabitant. I'm looking, because I still don't believe it's possible for her to up and die. But I like it just as much as last year. Maybe more. One way or another, I'll figure out how to make good."

Gruenbaum shrugged silently. "That's nice," he told Ferdinand. He looked at Pond's yoga pants and patted his own pocket that contained his wallet. "I've got enough money right now. It will take care of bringing flowers to my mother."

"How sweet," Nareen told Gruenbaum, her tone belying her words. Then she addressed herself to the room. "Do you believe in ghosts?" She turned her head so her peripheral vision stayed with Gruenbaum.

"Of course not," Pond insisted, with absolute certainty. "Someone dies, they stay dead."

"So they wouldn't communicate after crossing over," Nareen said evenly. "For instance, through that noise." She glared at Gruenbaum.

"Impossible," Pond said. The phone rang, adding its ring to her decisiveness.

"Pond residence," she answered, in a strong voice.

It was the lawyer, with another message from Gertrude.

*Well,* Pond corrected herself silently, *maybe it*

was *possible for people to communicate after they had left, but they had to establish elaborate legal ruses to do so.*

Bertram Something-Something, Esquire, had been silent and composed on the other end of the line. But when Pond gave way to embarrassed snickers, he hooted, and then seemed to fake a sneeze to cover over his lack of composure.

"One can't go around *laughing*," Bertram said.

"Are you reproaching me?" Pond asked, so surprised she forgot to be annoyed.

"Laughter isn't dignified. It isn't professional."

"Excellent, then," Pond said, allowing her laughter to increase.

"If one can't contain laughter that suggests one isn't in actual control of one's body or mind or life. If chortles erupt in the midst of a phone conversation, what else can occur? Continents might shift, oceans flood, volcanoes blow, and all of it irresistible, like unexpected laughter. I do not approve."

"Of course not," Pond said, consumed by laughter. On the other end of the line, she heard the lawyer's seriousness giving way to waves of hilarity rising up and taking him over. It reminded Pond of Gertrude's laughter, astonished and astonishing noises of mirth.

Bertram's laughter reignited Pond's, so she began to shake, her stomach muscles starting to seize and protest, aching with the unwanted heaving hilarity. She attempted to hold it in, to halt it as completely as the toy drum had stopped its cadence when Duckie came to a stop, but instead, the laughter increased, intensified, until Gruenbaum, watching her, began rolling with silent chortles, his body shaking, but his voice making no sound. His face lost its fog of suspiciousness. Even Nareen chuckled, the wave of laughter washing away a look of uneasiness. Ferdinand surprised everyone by letting out what could only be described as a self-delighted cackle, entirely out of keeping with his dignity and grace; and Giselle pawed at the floor and bayed lowly, adding her voice to the din.

"Oh, my God," Pond said, when she could bring herself to speak again. "You can't be serious."

"Of *course* I'm not serious," he said. Pond wiped tears of laughter from her eyes, drawing a deep breath, preparatory to speaking. "If I were serious, I wouldn't be laughing. But I have a job to do. There's this message to deliver, a codicil to read. I have my professional distance to keep, for God's sake. I have spent *years* of my life enjoying an unbreakable composure."

"It doesn't seem to be holding up."

"It's shattered. I'm shivering in the wind over here. Let me gather up my fragments of certainty."

"Good luck with that. Good for you, not knowing what's serious for once."

"I don't know what's serious," he said, his voice still shaking, moving toward steadiness. "But Gertrude set up more directions to give you today."

Pond waited silently, and her silence allowed him to convey the message.

"It reads, 'There's nothing to find you haven't already found. You've just forgotten it's not lost.'"

Pond waited a long heartbeat of a moment, and

then she said, "That's it?"

"That's the opening bit. Then it says, 'Open the inner sanctuary and let one stand on all four corners of the world at once.'"

"My legs aren't that long." Even if she had mythic boots that traveled seven leagues in one step, she didn't see how such a thing was possible.

"That's to be expected." Bertram's voice conveyed a most professional sympathy. "I'm not crying. It's only that I laughed so hard water dashed out of my eyes."

"Of course you're not crying," said Pond, wiping the corners of her eyes. "Neither am I." She felt like the laughter had emptied her of all tension, and now she didn't know who she was any more. "What's True up to?"

"No one can claim to know," said Bertram, signing off.

*\*\**

"We have to open the inner sanctuary and one of us has to stand on all four corners of the earth at once. And, apparently, we've already found what we're looking for," Pond announced with exaggerated brightness, letting her voice bounce off the copper pots and ring loudly enough it made the stainless steel colanders vibrate in response.

"Not me." Gruenbaum vanished into the basement. He made a thundering noise on the stairs, but not a noise that would have carried to the bedrooms.

Ferdinand and Giselle also drifted away, as did

Nareen.

Pond stared at her own hands. What had she found she had thought was lost? Her stomach hurt from laughter and frustration. *True was completely mad,* she decided, *that was perfectly clear.*

But she still didn't know what she wasn't looking for because it had never been gone anyway. If you followed a mad woman's directions, did that make you mad? Or if you refused to follow them, if you fought against them, did you just become even madder?

A while later, Pond found Nareen in an office on the second floor. She was opening all the drawers in an old oak dental cabinet, her every movement meticulous. The dental cabinet featured more little compartments than Pond could count at first glance.

"What are you looking for?" Pond kept her voice neutral. She suspected Nareen knew much more than the girl was letting on, but Pond didn't want to begin with aggression. She could always build up to that, hold it in reserve, as if she were keeping a bundle of angry flowers behind her back to spring upon her first houseguest without warning.

"What you're looking for," Nareen said with a studied air of patience. "Whatever that key opens."

Pond didn't bother pointing out all the locks in the house were already open. Instead she asked Nareen what the noise that morning had sounded like, to her.

"I don't know anything about it." Nareen sounded very honest, which only served to make Pond think she was lying. "I get absorbed."

Pond frowned. Nareen's book pouch was slung

across her body, as it always was. *Book of Secrets*, whatever that was.

She was just going to ask Nareen about her book and her secrets, when Nareen said, in an offhand way, "Of course, not every house that has unexplained noises is haunted." She continued her meticulous opening and closing of drawers, peering in to note their contents: old stationary, pens, and ink; safety pins; tacks; candles; matches.

"*Ob*viously."

"But some are," Nareen continued.

Pond rolled her eyes, but despite herself she sat down at the desk and began checking out what it contained. Nothing very interesting. Old account books, receipts, correspondence. All those letters of a lifetime, sent and received. She pretended not to be listening to Nareen.

"One place I visited wasn't very clear." Nareen's voice was full of portent. "Could have been haunted, and then again it also could have been not."

"*Not.*"

"The house had a problem, one way or another. No one could live there longer than a few months at a time. The family who was there when I visited had only moved in weeks before, and still was living out of boxes. They had their dishes unpacked, and I put away the rest of their pots and pans. Both parents were scientists, the kind so focused on their work their eyes didn't really register what was going on out here, where houses and kitchens and kids existed. Their kids were growing up fine. It was eerie how self-sufficient they were. Of course, they had to be.

"The kids already knew how to cook dinner, even though they were about eight and six, cute little girl and boy. They had to eat, even if their parents got lost in the lab and didn't come home for dinner. The kids talked to each other and stayed on track. Their parents spoke to them in an absent-minded way, but didn't really notice what was going on. The kids told me, though, when they saw I was listening to them.

"They told me plates would disappear in the night. Not all of them, just one. You'd wash five plates, one for each of us, and leave them in the dish drainer, and in the morning there'd be only four. Same thing with cups. If everyone used a water glass and we washed them all, in the morning five might be there, but chances were it'd be only four.

"'Ghosts don't need dishes,' I told the kids, and they laughed. But they wondered what was going on, and so did I. I sat up one night, reading the whole time, and watching, and all the plates and glasses stayed exactly where they were. I got done counting them, went to the bathroom, and came back, and it took a little while to notice a plate was gone. I was tired," Nareen told Pond, in response to her skeptical look. "Had to have disappeared while I was out of the room."

*Or you miscounted*, Pond thought.

"So the kids and I took turns watching the kitchen, and the dishes kept disappearing, even though one of us was present. One of the kids must have been behind the dishes vanishing, or something else was going on. Then we watched in pairs. But the dishes still kept going, even though I saw none of the kids was taking them. Also, I never saw the dishes go. It was there one moment, and then it was gone.

"That was annoying enough, when it came to kitchenware leaving. Even if the parents didn't notice, *I* did, and it wasn't right having clean plates vanish. Dirty plates, maybe, but clean ones were supposed to stay where I put them. But what if other things started following? That possibility bothered the kids. I told them it wasn't likely to happen, but who knew? And then the girl's doll disappeared. She told herself she had lost it, let it fall in a park somewhere, or along a sidewalk when we were out walking. But she did understand that wasn't the case. And then the boy's favorite truck went, and he got tired of pretending.

"He said, 'It's what's been taking the plates. It got my truck.' I smiled and put my hand on his head and decided it was time. Nothing else could be allowed to fall out of existence. But then the dad's papers began going, and he finally noticed that disappearance. He came to talk with me, asking around, his eyes vague and not wanting to accuse me directly, not even with a look. He was a fairly polite fellow, and you could tell he was embarrassed. He was hinting I might be responsible. I told him flat out I had nothing to do with anything disappearing, not his papers, not his kids' toys, not their family's plates and cups and glasses.

"'I was wondering why we're eating on paper plates,' he said absently. 'And plastic disposable cups. I'm not much of a fan of those cups.' But his papers were months of research, maybe years.

"That happens, you know. Big loss. Sometimes an entire house is swept away in a flood or tornado. I've visited places where hurricanes have gone through, and taken away everything a family owned. But it usually goes all at once like that. Or in a fire."

Nareen shivered, and Pond decided not to joke any more about turning this house into an enormous blaze. If the place burned before they figured out what had made the knocking noise that morning, she would find it annoying. Besides, she hadn't discovered what True had set her looking for, and that might be even more annoying. For once, Pond found herself wanting the house to be there, and herself to be in it—at least long enough to resolve these mysteries.

Nareen continued. "Even when her husband tried to tell her his notes had disappeared, the mom didn't get what was going on. Then her manuscript vanished. She had brought it home from the lab to read through, before sending it out for publication, and in the morning it was gone. She had it on her lab computer, so she could get another copy, unlike her husband. His original hand-written notes had up and left. But she had lost the corrections she had penciled in, and it helped her understand why everyone in her house was upset. And then my backpack disappeared.

"'You can figure this out,' I told the two scientists. 'There's some natural process at work, that's taking things away. Things don't just vanish. Figure out where they're going.'

"The dad looked intrigued, and the mom frowned and attempted to focus her gaze on me, on something that existed in this world right in front of her. Her eyes almost registered what was happening here, and then they shifted away again, into absentness. I think maybe she was talking with electrons or something, and you know they can be in two places at once."

Pond shook her head in denial. "I do my best to know nothing about electrons."

"It's the truth. They can be in two places at once. But we all started watching now, and the way we did it was by being in the same room all the time. We ate in the kitchen together, and slept in the living room together, sort of forming a circle. We could put our backs to each other and look out, see what was coming. That worked really well, made things more comforting, until the couch disappeared. The little girl had been lying on it sleeping, and the couch was there, and then it was gone. Right out from under her. She was still sleeping, but now lying on the floor. The hardness of the wood beneath her woke her up. She sat up and rubbed her eyes and said, 'Not the couch, too.' She was laughing and crying at the same time.

"The mom got really excited at that point, and determined enough was enough. She put her arms around the little girl and said, 'We don't need a couch anyway, darling. I love you. You're safe. Everything is fine now.' And the dad came and put his arms around his wife and around his daughter, and pulled the son into their circle, and the son tugged on my hand and we all formed a big hug.

And when we weren't looking, when we had our eyes closed, leaning into the warmth and the comfort of holding on to everyone, the couch came back.

"No it didn't," Pond said.

"The couch came back." The mom whooped, and the dad hollered, and the kids began clapping. 'Test it,' I told them. 'Hug each other again.'"

"Oh, no," Pond protested. "Next you're going to say you sang 'Kumbaya.'"

"Never." Nareen laughed. "I like 'Jesus Loves Me' much better. We all walked into the kitchen, and we were holding hands, not wanting to let go once we grabbed on. We made a giant human chain, and in the kitchen we found all the plates had returned. In fact, it seemed like more plates had come back than had been there in the first place. I started packing away the plates, stacking them into the cupboards. And they wouldn't fit. One cupboard filled up, and then another, and there were still more plates.

"'We're going to have to give some of these away,' I said. 'There's more than we need.'"

"The mom nodded, hugging her kids. Once she had started hugging them, it seemed like she couldn't take her hands off her kids. 'I missed you,' she said. 'I missed you so much.'

"'We haven't been anywhere, Mom,' the little girl said.

"'I have,' the mom said, sniffling a little through her smile. The mom looked up at her husband. 'I'm not going *any*where,' she promised him."

"You mean she quit working?" Pond was

fascinated.

Nareen shook her head. "But she began talking to humans as well as electrons."

"People don't talk to electrons."

Nareen gave her a look that could have said anything.

Pond ran her fingers through a drawer filled with notebooks. True had apparently kept not a diary but quotations from things she had read. "Devotion to me blazes forth and consumes all obstacles," Pond read aloud. "One thing's for sure. True was not boring."

Who was that *me* she was devoted to, though? Pond hadn't seen many Bibles around. At least True's house wasn't haunted, any more than the house in Nareen's story had been.

"Might as well add talking with electrons to my list," Pond decided, her voice ranging between bitterness and amusement. "It's only one more impossible task."

Gruenbaum tromped into the office, blowing on his fingers with a satisfied look. "It's a geothermal heating system. It looks almost like a regular heat pump, but the heat of the earth itself is what powers it mostly. That old woman fitted out the house with a geothermal heating system. It's got to be what was clanking this morning. Even though the heat wasn't on, the same system cools the house. You noticed the house was kind of hot this morning. So there you go, something got switched on or off, or wires got crossed, and things heated up and began clanging along. But I fixed everything."

Pond blinked. Was it her imagination, or was he

keeping his fingers crossed behind his back?

"Things will be completely quiet now," he declared.

"Why, thank you." Pond made a show of elaborate gratitude, smiling with satisfaction at Nareen. She felt she'd proved something, though she didn't know quite what.

Nareen stared at Gruenbaum, her eyes uncertain. "I don't trust you," she muttered under her breath, loud enough for Pond to hear.

"Nareen was just telling me a story," Pond told Gruenbaum, ignoring Nareen's comment. "Maybe you know how to talk with electrons. That's what the mother in this story did."

Gruenbaum's happy expression deflated slightly, at the mention of mothers. "I'm pretty sure my mom didn't know electrons from electioneers," he said, his voice flat. "But she was gone too soon for me to be sure. I didn't have a sense of her as a person. As a mother she was all warm arms and smiles and food. And then she went to visit her friend in Baltimore. And she did not return."

"Lucky you." As soon as she spoke, she saw the pain on Gruenbaum's face, and the awkwardness on Nareen's, and she wished she could retract the words.

"Mind if I pick some flowers from the yard?" he asked. "I think my mother might like that better than some fake looking thing I picked up at the store."

Pond nodded. Gruenbaum began to propel himself out of the room, presumably to gather the flowers, but his every step sounded slower and more reluctant, and he remained in the room even after looking like he was about to depart.

*Figures*, Pond thought. *I wouldn't want to bring my mother flowers, either.*

Pond flipped through another of True's notebooks. "It is a foolish idea to suppose another can cause us happiness or misery," she read. "Do you think that's true?"

Gruenbaum grunted. "Not going to let anyone else make me miserable," he said, glaring at Nareen. "Does that also mean not giving anyone else the power to make me happy?" He shrugged, and stepped out.

Sometime later, Pond looked out the window and saw Gruenbaum seated in his van, gripping a bundle of blooms he had picked—it would have been Artemisia, hibiscus, a few straggling day lilies, and hydrangea, based on what was blooming then. Gruenbaum was staring at the flowers, staring out his windshield, looking like he wasn't going anywhere very fast.

Finally, he turned the key in the ignition and the engine ground and heaved to life. And then the van shook, ready to go, to be set into motion. It looked like only Gruenbaum was holding it back.

Pond had watched him depart, wondering what was keeping him in place in front of her house. *Good,* Pond thought, *he's gone*, although she understood why he might be reluctant to go visit his mother.

She became aware Ferdinand was watching her, and turned away from Gruenbaum to see her latest quasi-houseguests. Giselle was just as silent as

Ferdinand, and the two apparently couldn't look like they weren't on-stage. Right now they seemed prepared to take a bow at whatever performance they had completed.

***

## *Ferdinand*

"Ta-da!" announced Ferdinand, with an elaborate flourish of his arm. "I went looking with the golden key. Checked out what lock it would fit. I came at it from the perspective of a performer. What's most dramatic? What would build up to a culminating scene? I went to the top of the house and worked my way down."

In the third floor den, he'd admired the understated comfort, the leather sofas and the ever-present bookcases. In this room, the books focused on magic, not just old alchemical recipes and charms. Herbal preparations you could make under the light of a full moon; prayers you could offer to bring hope and healing, health and well-being; fairy tales and stories of elves and nymphs and water sprites. There were books on Old Norse legends about the spirit of the land and sea; advice about the god of mischief and the god of thunder; manuals on saints who helped you travel or come home, find love or recover from heartbreak. There was even a biography of Saint Walter, an abbot who had not wanted to be an abbot, and kept trying to quit his job so he could pray and meditate more. He went so far as to walk to see the pope, only to be told to trot back home again and go to work. Saint Walter had found out how to balance what he had to do with what he wanted to do, and would help the reader do the same. There were also volumes on knowing thyself, the deepest magic of all, taught by Greek philosophers and Indian sages and wise women around the world.

All that magic made Ferdinand think about the magicians he knew, who favored working with illusion in order to reveal reality. That was the best kind of magic of all. Give people the unexpected, and then show them how the ordinary was not separate from what they were watching. Performers had two choices: to make the extraordinary ordinary, or the reverse. Ferdinand enjoyed doing both.

It came almost as second nature to him to wave the key in the air and imagine where it might best fit. A small lamp called to him, tucked away on a bookcase. And in the base of the lamp, which was made all of brass and covered with scrollwork designs, there was a keyhole, of all things. And the lock fit the key, hand in glove, a puzzle piece clicking home. Ferdinand had almost smelled the bright lights of the stage, felt their heat, as he placed the key in the lock and turned it gently. Nothing rusty about that housing. Someone had kept the mechanism in fine working order, ready to turn, ready to reveal what was beyond the bookcase, what the lamp illumined.

He pulled at Pond's hand, silently urging her upstairs after him, and so Pond went up the stairs, walking between him and his beautiful beast of a dog. He sensed her watching him as he placed the key in the lock and turned it. The lamp tilted and the top bowed down and bent in half, revealing an opening in its base. That opening held a handle that called out to be gripped. "Go on," Ferdinand said.

She took a deep breath and placed her hand on the lever, which tilted gently and easily clockwise. A portion of the bookcase swung out from the wall, revealing a door. Pond swallowed hard and placed her hand on the doorknob, which was smooth, polished, worn. Ferdinand knew from testing it earlier the knob's grip felt like True had used this door often.

The knob turned silently, and the door opened into a chamber of stillness, a room mysteriously quiet and alive. It was not possible, as there was neither sight nor sound of anyone else, but the room gave off an impression someone or something had just left the room, had been lounging on the minimalist sofa, and then had escaped right before the door opened, vanishing into thin air before Pond stepped into the room, followed by Ferdinand and Giselle.

"What is this place?" she asked, her voice taking on a broadcast-loud whisper. To Ferdinand, it felt like being in someone else's heart, inside a hidden inner sanctum, hushed and wild, quiet and magnificent. "I hate it." Pond practically spit out the words.

Ferdinand raised his elegant eyebrows.

The sanctuary effect wasn't created so much by anything external about the room, although the room was beautiful and simple, perfect in fact.

"How could it have been that I didn't notice the existence of this room—or *your* suite—from the outside of the house? How are these invisible spaces possible in a finite amount of architecture?" Pond shook her head, and then shook it again, as if it felt full of cobwebs. "This house is too vast and rambling and asymmetrical. Which is what my head feels like right now. I feel woozy. This room shouldn't even exist," she wailed.

"You might let yourself appreciate the new discovery," Ferdinand suggested, suppressing a smile.

Three windows let in clear light, and the room was almost bare, so sparse were its furnishings. Rugs so spare they might have been woven bamboo mats, furniture so unadorned no one could rightly object to it, although it seemed that wasn't about to stop Pond.

A straight-backed couch, a couple of plain but comfortable chairs. A simple floor to ceiling wall-hanging showed three white cranes, one standing on a single foot, one taking off mid-air, another in full flight.

Ferdinand couldn't tell if the painting showed three cranes together in the same time frame, or one crane with a sequence of movement depicted simultaneously—a single crane that had been standing, and then took off, and then held up the air, making visible a line between heaven and earth.

But this room was a place where anything could happen. The invisible could become visible, the visible could vanish. Who or what had been here, and where had it gone? The place felt like a church and a forest, like a temple and a carnival, like a shrine and a lake, all at the same time.

True must have fitted the room with some elaborate ventilation system, because the air was fresher here than anywhere else in the house, despite the fact no windows were open. But there was a trace of scent, beautiful and unidentifiable, lingering in the air, a signature of whoever or whatever had been here.

"I don't like this space," Pond said. "It feels like being in someone else's skin, and about as comfortable, too. I don't belong here. This place makes me want to run more than any other place in the house. It's like antimatter to me. If I stay here, I'll stop existing. I'll get canceled out."

The room must have benefited from indirect banks of lights, for it felt like sunshine was warm upon Ferdinand's face, and True must have fitted the room with hidden speakers, for he heard a phrase or two of haunting, beautiful flute music, sweet and plaintive, aching with joy and longing and fulfillment. Ferdinand loved it. In other words, it seemed to create pure torment for Pond.

And then to make it all better or worse, depending on your perspective, next Pond noticed a tiny little calligraphy scroll, hanging on the wall to one side of the couch, with words that looked like Kanji characters from a distance, and only up close resolved themselves into readable English. She read the words out loud: "*The next part of the quest is hardest of all: sit still for five minutes. If you cannot sit still for five minutes, then be still for only one second, or even for one-half of one second—in total silence.*"

"That's impossible," burst out Pond, in a skeptical near screech. "I tried to stay still at the ashram. Damn near killed me. And that was for only a minute or two."

Ferdinand read the scroll for himself, over Pond's shoulder. "True was part wizard," he said. He didn't disapprove, but he could tell Pond did.

His statement was nonsense to Pond, and her expression showed her skepticism.

"The best wizards give *you* the magic," he said.

"Magic," she snapped, and he held up his hands in defense. "Try *hell*."

"Good luck with the quest."

"It's im*poss*ible. Of course I can't sit still for five minutes. No Pond can. As much as I have run from my family, I'm like them in that way."

"Not even one second?" Ferdinand shrugged and left the room. Giselle looked quietly at Pond, and then followed.

***

## *Pond*

Pond stared after him, listening to the quiet emphasized by his departing footsteps. Until now, she hadn't quite believed the lawyer when he suggested the quest True had set could be deadly.

Now she was convinced. The quiet was what told her so. For in the quiet of this room she became aware of all the sirens of her mind, all the horns and whistles and clanging bells within her. Every thought and desire and impression, every image and obstacle, every billboard she had walked by, which now loomed with advertisements of her utter inadequacy.

Pond hated things she couldn't control, and most uncontrollable of all was her own mind.

*One second*, one part of her mind said, *that's not so bad.*

*Forget it*, another part of her mind answered, *the old lady was a lunatic. She's dead and gone. How can you be bothered with what*ever *tricks she set up?*

*But it's only one second*, the first part of her mind said, *even* you *can be quiet for one freaking solitary second.*

*Oh, yeah?* sneered her own mind in response, and set up a frantic drumming and thrumming and beat boxing to prove its point.

*Shut* up! Pond told her mind, and it only made the mind take a sarcastic bow and then turn up the stage lights even brighter. She groaned and put her fingers to her temples.

"I'm *not* quiet," Pond said out loud. "This is not going to work." She fled the chamber of affliction.

*** 

Pond flung herself on the asymmetrical living room couch in a funk—a very unquiet funk—until she was interrupted by Duckie.

"Ta-ta," called Duckie, patting her hair as she entered the room. Then she looked around with great care, noticed it was only Pond in the room,

147

and stopped patting her hair. "My husband's back."

Pond blinked and sat up straighter. "Congratulations." She was unable to keep bitterness out of her voice.

"No, no, no. You're right. Commiserations are more like it. He asked me to come home." She crossed her arms.

"Of course he did. What else would a husband do?" That was one reason Pond was so set upon not acquiring one. "Of course, you'd want to help welcome him."

Duckie grinned a very slow and satisfied grin. "I ordered *all* the workers to stay on the job. *All* the time. That will give him a proper arrival home. Just imagine the banging and the sawing all through the night. Sweet lullabies. I'll have to order some jack hammering. The basement foundation could use some shoring up."

Pond managed a sour smile in automatic response to Duckie's grin, and then took in what she had said. Duckie wasn't going back to her husband. "What? That will keep you up at night, too."

"Not if I stay here," Duckie suggested brightly, and Pond frowned but didn't say no, so Duckie pressed her advantage. "Where else would I go? I have to help you look," she added hastily, and then began blurting. "Besides, I have something else to figure out about True's jewelry. Her collection adds up to some sort of a pattern. I just can't quite decipher it yet." She frowned and straightened her shoulders. "I'm on the case, but I don't know whether the case is a mystery or a joke. No *way* did our dear True acquire that collection for her own use. It was so far out of character for her. Where did it come from, and why? Did your great-aunt have any great romances?"

"Only one I know about is Gene," Pond said. "He's dead. Lost in World War II."

"Long time gone. It has to be something else then. Maybe there are papers that explain everything."

\*\*\*

## Gruenbaum

Gruenbaum came thumping in to find Pond, and didn't want to interrupt her while she was talking, especially not to that silver haired woman. Duckie. He sat down on a velvet nightmare of a chair and stared blankly at the bookshelves. Then he decided he had to interrupt.

"Hey," he said, "excuse me. I visited my mother. I took her flowers." He hoped she liked them. He saw himself talking to the man in the office and getting directions, following the steps carefully, and locating where she was. He saw himself placing the flowers near her head, even though in her condition she probably could not smell them or see them. He sat there, reaching out with all his might, sure she couldn't hear him, but saying anyway, "Mom, I'm here. I've come to visit you. I missed you."

And he listened, but no reply came, only vast stillness, and so after a time he arose and trudged back to the van. And he expected there to be great sadness, or a heavy weight lifting off him, or *some*thing. And instead, he felt just the same as ever, except maybe more himself. *That's done,* he told himself. Whenever his work at the house was finished, he would now be free to return home.

"How'd it go?" Pond asked indifferently. "I'm not really that interested in mothers. At least not mine."

"She was just the way I always imagined her."

"My mother always manages to surprise me." Pond didn't look as if she enjoyed the experience.

"My mom gave me one great big surprise, and that was it. I came home from school one day and she was gone. Went to visit her friend in Baltimore, as she had always wanted to do. Her best friend from school had come up here to work, and gotten married. My mom wanted to go but my dad wouldn't agree to it, so one day she took a bus. Her friend had sent her the money for the ticket. Her friend didn't have any kids, so she could save more than my mom could. My mom was going to come back," Gruenbaum insisted. "Her friend got her a *two*-way ticket. And then my mom caught a cold in Baltimore. You don't expect a cold to change your life, now, do you?"

"Oh." Pond's expression changed as she realized what Gruenbaum was saying. "You went to lay flowers on her grave." Pond, looking uncomfortable, placed a hand on his forearm, and then drew it right back as if she'd been stung.

"That's okay," Gruenbaum told her. He understood curmudgeons more than he understood kind people.

"What are we talking about?" Duckie asked,

smiling mistily.

"His mother's *dead*," Pond said.

He had spent the rest of his childhood without a mother. And now he had seen where she had gone, and a bubble rose within him, and popped, and he felt effervescent sadness and relief, and wanted to laugh and cry at once. *She is at rest, and has been this long time*, he told himself, *and I can be, too.* Not in the ground, not yet.

"You're done in Baltimore," Pond prompted. "You'll be on your way, right? On the road again. *I* would."

Gruenbaum felt her stare focused on him, but congratulated himself her eyes weren't suspicious, only expectant.

"You have the option to leave now," she said. "Don't know why you're not running madly away from this house."

He shook his head. "I've got the time set aside. I'm staying, if you don't mind. Help figure out this house."

"What's to figure out?" Pond asked sarcastically, and then seemed to let go of her sarcasm as a banging commenced. It was the same banging from that morning. "It's like that beautiful and maddening flute music. It sounds like the noise is in my head, not in my house."

"Maybe it's the same thing," Duckie said.

"But it also sounds like it's everywhere, not in a particular place. Like it's everywhere and nowhere all at once. How do you locate that?" She shook her head. "One thing, though. The noise is better than that blasted silence in that inner room."

Gruenbaum got up and raced out of the room. Convenient his second round of work in the basement hadn't taken effect until now. But he didn't understand *why*, and so he wasn't quite comfortable with it, even though he knew he had to be behind this noise.

\*\*\*

## *Duckie*

Duckie decided to let them pursue the clanging, while she pursued those two elusive carats. Besides, she wanted to decipher the message True had left in the form of jewelry no one would ever be able to wear. Too valuable, too awkward, metalwork and stones from all times and all lands.

"But we live in the twenty-first century," Duckie protested out loud. "It's not acceptable to wear such pieces to a luncheon, not even at the Engineer's Club, not even at the Hopkins Club." What were all those useless, precious baubles doing here? "This is *Baltimore*, after all." There was one precious piece she still wasn't finding.

She sniffed with satisfaction. Her husband could roll himself onto the couch all he wanted. She was otherwise occupied. He didn't need her there to watch him ossify. She crossed her fingers she would be able to stay here tonight.

\*\*\*

## *Pond*

Pond found Gruenbaum in the basement, tinkering with pipes. The noise had halted before she arrived, and so the air was silent for Pond, and yet she could still feel the sound that had been there, reverberating in her bones. Bertram hadn't been crazy after all. First the chamber of silent torments, and now maybe this house was rigged to blow. Perhaps Baltimore was the perfect place for the apocalypse.

Pond frowned. Now she thought about it, maybe the apocalypse had already been proceeding quietly in Baltimore for *decades*. Could be, True was just ahead of her time, and her house was at the leading vanguard for the new way of living, in which convention would be tossed out on its ear, no plates would ever match again, and pipes would set themselves ringing throughout all houses.

She didn't know whether to feel glum or proud this place seemed to be becoming some sort of epicenter of oddity. At least it distracted her from her own inner battles.

Gruenbaum grunted. "Quiet for now," he said. At the moment, Pond found his expression unreadable. Was it satisfaction he was feeling? He looked like he had laid something to rest.

Pond nodded, and her mind went skipping on to the next phase of the quest True had set. Pond was feeling increasingly antsy if she wasn't discovering *some*thing that helped her feel like she was moving forward. Now they had found the inner sanctuary, they had to find the world.

A flash of memory shot through her mind. She was letting Ferdinand in, and she was watching him and Giselle walk. She ran upstairs, through the kitchen, pantry, dining room, and into the solarium. Yes. The mosaic floor was abstract, but it definitely featured an unfurled world, a replica of an ancient map, from the days when people wrote in Latin, Here Be Monsters, along their drawing of the far side of the world. But the map, a globe flattened out as if an orange had been peeled in one whole swathe, and then unrolled, was huge. Way too large for one person to stand in all four corners.

*** 

Pond was kneeling on the middle of the mosaic, wishing she had never thought to inspect the world. What did the world have to do with her, anyway? She had spent most of her life not paying attention to it, which was proving to be by far the best policy. Look what looking at the world had gotten her. She was perched on a flat slab of slate—shiny flinty blue gray stone, and shaped like nothing more than an altar. And she was on the altar, and would become the sacrifice if this game didn't work out.

In the middle of the world appeared a game board, looking like an eccentric slightly off-kilter version of a checker board, its rectangular shape emerging into view with the game board's center right at the world's equator. All around the board Pond could still see the unfolded world, its edges banner-like, waving, and free. She was feeling imprisoned at the moment, suspended helplessly on one of the game board pieces.

The board consisted of twelve positions, all evenly apportioned in rows. Four rows of three positions each, one full row above her, two full rows below her, and a position to either side of her. Pond closed her eyes in disbelief, but even behind closed eyes, she could still see her current predicament: along the top row ran three colored squares, then in the second row came a colored square, Pond's altarpiece, and another colored square. Below her row ran two rows of three colored squares each. Pond opened her eyes and counted: three of the squares were gray-blue, three ivory, and three a red orange sandstone color. Pond's piece appeared to be immobile, but all the others were fitted on tracks. Two positions were blank, allowing room to move all the others from one place to another.

Ferdinand was standing on the life-sized game board, studying the movable squares. As soon as Pond had stepped onto the middle piece, the mosaic floor had revealed itself to be a giant stone game set. The slate pieces that formed the playing field had risen slightly above the rest of the floor, and above them had risen Pond's piece.

As Pond was lifted up, from beneath the large, square stone she stood upon, a smaller piece of slate emerged, containing chiseled instructions. She knelt down to read it: *Arrange the pieces into a fitting pattern, or into the void you will descend.* While the stone slab was still being raised into the air, Pond had shrieked, and Ferdinand had been the first to arrive. The rest were now watching from the edges of the room. The only one breathing at anywhere near a normal rate was Giselle, and she didn't look very happy Ferdinand wasn't dispensing ear rubs at the moment.

Ferdinand sighed and studied the board. The slightly irregular altar-shaped piece descended a little lower, its movement smooth. "My time," he said, his voice soft, "or maybe it's *your* time. It is not limitless."

Pond had first scoffed at the idea of the void, whatever that was, but was now treating the prospect with greater seriousness. "Come *on*," she said, her voice fierce. She had discovered if she tried to move off her stone piece, she plunged downward even more precipitately. From her memory of Gertrude's basement, the house's foundation footprint did not extend under the solarium. So whatever Pond was facing down there, it wasn't just a known cellar or musty air.

"I'm really good at Rubik's cubes," Ferdinand said, his voice helpful, and Pond groaned.

She had solved such a puzzle once, by accident, and had so objected to seeing all the colors lined up obediently—yellow with yellow, orange with orange, and so on in tedious rows of matching colors—that she had vowed never to repeat the experiment. But now she found herself hoping Ferdinand was right, and he could save her from the easy downward movement. She was in what she considered an actual, impossible, predicament. Her fate now placed her at the mercy of another person's actions and decisions, something she could not tolerate under any conditions.

And so she found herself perched between the impossible and the intolerable, suspended over a void. *At least the descent was going quickly*, she told herself, feeling glum. *The torment could not go on forever.*

Ferdinand, meanwhile, was trying all sorts of combinations. So far, he had lined the stones up in various arrays by color. He had worked in a clockwise direction, placing all the gray-blue together, then all the other colors in turn. That arrangement had made Pond's stone move even lower.

Then he had tried various patterns, but of course the number of colored squares did not exactly line up with the number of slots on the board, so he could arrange three of one color along one long row, and three of one color in another row. Then he had the third color to divide up among various rows, placing those pieces anywhere, and each position he tried seemed even less successful than the last. Pond was about eye-level with the board, and dropping quickly.

He had worked through various combinations, his movements quick and sure. He alternated gray-blue and ivory along one side, and then ivory and gray-blue along the opposite side, but there were three red orange pieces left over. Nothing fit. The existing squares didn't work with the existing spots allotted for them, and now the top of Pond's head was level with the board.

"You know what's terrible about this," she said. "Having to sit in one place while he does everything." She would have laughed if she could have mustered the energy. The house was more than out to get her. *The void will be not a big deal*, she told herself, *much easier than having to sit still and watch the dancer move the squares.*

And now she could see nothing at all, unless she raised herself up in a kneeling position. She did so, attempting not to topple over, and steadying herself a bit by reaching up to touch one of the game pieces. *I may be kneeling, but I'm still nowhere near praying*, she assured herself.

"It doesn't work," she exploded. "None of the pieces go anywhere, but how is that a surprise, anyway? Nothing in this house goes with anything else. Nothing matches. *I* don't match. *You* don't match. Why should the game pieces match?"

She had spoken out of anger and frustration, and the only one she had seemed to offend was Duckie.

"There's nothing wrong with matching," she said in protest.

"Let me try something new," Ferdinand said. "The patterns haven't been doing it. Let's randomize them. Put them wherever."

"*What* are you doing?" Pond demanded.

"Sliding the pieces along. Putting them in any order and in none. I think it's working." His voice rose with excitement. "The pieces are gathering their own momentum. When I'm not trying to force them to go somewhere, they're telling me where they want to go. They're helping me."

"Look at that," Duckie said. "They're moving in one direction, first quickly and then more slowly."

"Maybe it's magnets," Gruenbaum suggested. "Let your hands feel the stone."

"I see," Ferdinand said. "It is almost like the stones know where they're going, and they're telling me by how it feels to move them in that direction."

"Hurry up." Pond threw her hands up as she realized again there was nothing she could do to make anything go faster. Except she could attempt to slide off the altar piece, and the result would be obvious. She would bring herself to the void that much more quickly. She was beginning to contemplate such a move, confronting the void sooner rather than later, deciding to make the plunge herself on her own time. Then, the stone piece began slowing its downward motion, steadying and raising itself upward. "Thank *God*."

"That's right." Ferdinand grinned. "You don't have to thank me at all."

"Thank you," Pond said, speaking on automatic.

"No. I was just a pair of hands. The stones knew where they needed to go. You realize the pieces make no sense at all in this order. There is no pattern at all here that I can identify. The floor looks a lot like it did when we began. But I don't remember how things were, right at first."

"Thank you." This time, Pond meant it. Her legs and back were trembling. She didn't know what God looked like. Surely nothing like Ferdinand. But Ferdinand had stopped the descent, and now the game board returned to level. The floor was again a floor. Pond was no longer kneeling on an altar.

She collapsed backward in relief, arms and legs spread-eagled along the once again flat stones, and then she got up and ran through the house

159

whooping. The biggest relief of all was being able to *move*. The void could wait. She had had to confront something even more terrifying: stillness.

*Never again*, she vowed, half laughing and half crying. And to prove her point, she ran laps through the downstairs of the house, until she was so tired she could run no more and collapsed onto the asymmetrical living room couch.

Ferdinand and Giselle pranced into the room. "I talked with my cuz," he told Pond. "She wouldn't mind a place to stay, either. You've still got plenty of room." He marked off people and rooms on his fingers. "Three more bedrooms, and that's not even counting the dens and offices and libraries and all."

Pond blinked. "What are you talking about? You might be staying in your room, and Nareen in hers, but..."

Duckie grinned appealingly.

"Grrrr," Pond said, accepting Duckie. Gruenbaum nodded silently, making his own plea. "I'm not going to say no," she told Ferdinand, her voice testy. "But only because you helped me out."

Pond slouched back to the solarium and stared at the map built into the floor. Ferdinand and Giselle followed her. Surrounding the game board was the unfurled world. She felt like a moth drawn to a flame that had almost destroyed her, but she couldn't stay away. Damn quest was getting under her skin. She would get it before it got her. She shivered and decided not to focus on the game board but on its surroundings.

"I have to find some way to stand on all four corners of the world." She pointed in dismay at the

160

map built into the floor. "There's no way one can stand in all those places at the same time." She could appreciate the irony. It was the way she had lived her life until now, in a blur of motion. But motion required time. She didn't know how to jump into all places at once, or juxtapose instants of time to form a single whole that spanned the globe, even a map globe now arrayed before her feet, looking innocent and ordinary.

"Does it have to be a person who stands in all four corners?" Ferdinand asked.

Pond thought back to the instructions. "One must stand in all four corners."

"No problem," Ferdinand crowed. "Luvreen will be here, soon as she can get here. She's traveling at a more deliberate pace than usual. Walking from downtown."

Pond had walked from downtown plenty of times. It didn't take *that* long. "Does she know this house is knocking all about, banging and thumping?" It didn't seem to matter. "Any cousin of yours wouldn't care, I guess," she told Ferdinand, with an elaborate roll of her eyes.

"And there's another small guest. Like me, she travels with an animal companion."

Pond liked animals. She found them easier to deal with than most humans. Maybe the cousin was blind and had a companion seeing eye dog. "There's room," she said, echoing Ferdinand's earlier words without noticing it. Under no conditions would she let herself ask Nareen or Gruenbaum or Duckie to stand on the other corners. *Especially* not after being forced to cooperate with

Ferdinand to save her own life. But sure, a cousin and a dog, that could be considered.

Gruenbaum popped his head into the room. "Took care of those dials on the geothermal system, once and for all," he said. He crossed his fingers, and this time Pond caught the motion and figured he didn't really know what he was up to. At least they had identified what was causing the banging noise.

Back in the living room, Nareen was reading.

"Tell me about that book," Pond said.

"It's not a very normal book." Nareen's face lit up. "The same things I read happen in my life. Sometimes it's the reverse. Sometimes things happen in my life and then I read them in this book."

"What kind of things?" asked Pond, almost prepared to seize Nareen's volume and read it. She had to be able to find the answer somewhere.

"Sometimes the connection isn't very clear," Nareen admitted. "But I can still tell it's there.

\*\*\*

After a late dinner, Pond turned instead to the book she was beginning to think of as her own book, the one that told her things, sometimes before they happened and sometimes after.

*The I Ching is like a lens*, she thought. *It magnifies things so I can see them more clearly.*

Looking at the book, she mused, *The whole universe almost makes sense at random moments.* Life, to Pond, had been the dashes dividing a road, and then sometimes the solid lines in the road's middle, which only meant you couldn't overtake another vehicle in that stretch of road. No passing.

Pond tossed the coins. "What is it I have found because it's never really been lost?"

The book advised her to restore to its purity and pristine condition what had been allowed to fall into a state of disrepair and decay. Take vigorous action to remove stasis, it said. She scoffed to herself. *My life has been all motion. Not stasis. Besides, the ridiculous house quest had been advising stillness.* To Pond, those two felt a lot like the same thing. The book went on to recommend she provide peace and sustenance to others, and cautioned her that difficulties would bend her rather than break her, as long as she stayed within the truest part of herself.

"Help," Pond said aloud. "This book is telling me to restore everything to its original condition. Does it mean the house?" She gazed around at the house, which looked good to her, an observation to which she objected on principle.

Duckie was devoting herself to untangling jewelry. "Doing my best, dear," she said cheerfully.

"Maybe you need a good bath." Nareen laughed.

Pond snorted. She was already much cleaner than was her usual habit on the road. "What's the truest part of myself?" she asked out loud, not expecting much of a reply. That was one of those unanswerable questions.

"Easy," Ferdinand said. "The part that never leaves you."

Plenty of times, Pond had wished one part or another of herself would leave her. The impatient part, the angry part, the hungry part. The part that didn't know where it was going, so it always had to move on. Hoping the next view would be so magnificent, or so boring, that she could give up, conclude she had reached the end of the road. This was *it*, the destination so grand or so dull, that she could stop traveling. But her fiery emotional reactions hadn't gone. She hoped that agitated, demanding, incessant part wasn't the bit that never leaves you.

"It's not a bad part," Ferdinand told her, waving his hand in a dramatic flourish.

Pond made an attempt to still her expression. She hoped she hadn't been broadcasting more of her inner state than she wanted to. On the road, she had kept herself covered, her face closed.

"It's a steady part," he said. "That part won't let you give up. That part always keeps you going."

"I've got that one down," Pond said. She had always thought that was the problem, the bit of her that goaded her onward, the drive in her like a thorn in her side, never letting her rest in one place.

"Good for you, girl." Ferdinand cheered.

Pond made a face at him. "Everyone's always told me that's the bad bit of me, the black sheep in me."

"They're just jealous. Or they're trying to sell you something."

She grinned.

"If they're talking on about black sheep, that means they're trying to set themselves up as the white sheep." He hooted. "How do white sheep know they're white? They've gotta have a black sheep. So, they made you into the black one." He stroked his forearm. "Not that black's a bad thing to be, but don't let anyone tell you what you are. You get to say."

Pond opened her mouth. She had no idea what to say. She closed her eyes, wondering where she would possibly find the truest part of herself. The book had said, what doesn't break bends—and lasts.

\*\*\*

She remembered a storm in Arizona, where she had actually sought shelter in a cave, the only dry place for miles around, and huddled inside, away from the runnels of water, and looked out at the lightning tossed trees. And some of those trees had been brittle, and had broken. And some had been willowy and had bent almost double, so they were blown along the ground near to the horizontal plane, and then at the end, when the winds subsided, and the torrential water lifted, those trees had come right again. They had been still standing amidst the other storm-broken trees.

She had always thought bending was weakness, except on a yoga mat, where she was willing to be quite flexible. With a fierce intentness, she had ignored all her teachers who burbled on about it being possible to practice yoga off the mat. She confined yoga to yoga class. But maybe bending could also be seen as strength. Just as long as she wasn't the one doing it.

She wouldn't mind seeing other people bend, appearing graceful, agile, like dancers taking a bow. That's what the trees had been, part of a choreographed show, an outdoor show, a light show unlike any other she had seen. Better than lasers and fireworks and neon, better than bonfires and torches and luminaries. Better than film set lights and stadium bright nights.

The sky had been a stage for lightning to flash and ripple and tear across, and she had seen in the darkness the truth that light shone everywhere. And inside the cave, she felt warm and quiet, like a cub in its den. Everything that was needed would be provided. She had nothing to worry about. In the midst of the heavens opening up, she had a roof over her head. She was safe, secure. Nothing she would ever look for wouldn't be found.

And then in the morning, after sleeping in the cave, she had trudged back out to the road, and in the humming motion of wheels on blacktop she had lost whatever she had identified in the cave, left it back there along with the storm blasted tree limbs.

And not since this moment had she thought to wonder if it could ever be located again, not in the midst of a tornado-like deluge, not in the finding of random rock walls to shelter you, but right here and now, in a ridiculously comfortable living room, surrounded by people who for the moment at least, you could almost tolerate. What was the cave that could follow you here? Here amidst the shining floors and beauty you were starting to take for granted.

Pond took in the smoothness of the wood floors, the sheen of the glass windows, which were reflecting living room lights back at her, since darkness had fallen outside.

Cave walls were rough, not smooth. Cave walls didn't shine. She had happened upon them, and she didn't think such a happy accident came often. Especially not here, amidst the wealth of centuries, the weight of the past, family and money, history and everything she inherited and didn't want. This was what she had to flee.

"What are you doing here?" she demanded of Ferdinand, to change the subject of her inner monologue.

"Petting the dog," he said, demonstrating with overly elaborate gestures. Giselle closed her eyes, the picture of a contented being.

The dog looked a little like a happy Buddha statue Pond had seen somewhere, probably in California. She had seen more happy Buddha statues in the golden state than in any other. Other places Pond had traveled, and where people followed Buddha, they tended to go for the more severe forms, the ones where he wasn't dancing but looked as if he were willing Enlightenment to fall down upon him out of the tree.

"I'm not getting up until the answer comes upon me," his expression said, "even if it kills me." And it almost did.

Pond's brother had majored in Buddhism in college. Pond always thought it was just to annoy their mother, and during the times when Pond and her brother were talking without saying much of anything, he had told her more than she had ever wanted to know about the awakened one.

"But why are you petting your dog *here*, in my living room? You could be anywhere," she insisted.

"Here is where I am. There's nowhere else I can be at this moment."

"But you're in Baltimore, hanging out at my house."

"Waiting for my cousin." He was leaning on the couch, but looked like he was dancing away from her questions. "And her animal."

Pond gave up, crossed her arms and closed her eyes, leaning back into the cushions of the couch.

"I like traveling," Ferdinand said. "Haven't yet seen the place that would keep me there for good." He looked around the living room, his eyes taking in the odd characters gathered there.

Pond looked at Ferdinand. What he was saying wasn't different from how she lived, but *he* wasn't frantic.

"You're right," Duckie said in a rush. "Don't stay in one place. You stay in one place, it's likely to drive you crazy. Look at me," she said, pointing to her platinum hair and making a circling motion with one index finger.

"Not half as loony as you make out." Ferdinand chuckled.

"Don't be fooled," Duckie said. "I'm completely mad. My husband will tell you so for sure. And he's back home again, so he'll say so at least twenty times a day."

"Except now he can't," Pond pointed out. "Because you're here in my living room, and he's not."

"Exactly."

"You deserve a gentleman," Ferdinand said, making it clear by the severe expression on his face he both meant what he said and was taking himself well out of the running.

"You're right," Duckie agreed, her voice thoughtful.

"Goodnight," Pond interrupted in a rush, before she could regret her burst of good will. She almost ran out of the room.

"Our host is right. It is a good night," Ferdinand said.

# Thursday

The next morning, Pond had no idea if it had been a good night or not.

It was not calm, not quiet, a night both bright and dark. One of Baltimore's summer thunderstorms had rolled into town, opening up the skies with lightning flashes, so that sheets of water poured down, and all the power lines followed suit. The temperature dropped twenty degrees and the air became so saturated with water it was like breathing mid-ocean. She knew later in the morning hot steam would rise from the ground in visible waves.

The smell of earth and almost tropical vegetation wrapped around houses, blanketing the city with a rain forest atmosphere. The infrastructure was taxed almost to overload on the best of days, and when a storm came, you congratulated yourself if you *didn't* lose power.

It would not have been so much of a problem, electricity going out in the middle of the night— after all, everyone ought to have been sleeping in True's almost too comfortable beds. And they were in fact sleeping, all of them, in happy oblivion to the power outage, until an incessant thumping awoke the house.

And then there was sleepy consternation, in addition to the thumping, everyone stumbling around in the dark. They banged into True's odd-shaped furniture, which seemed to develop more shin-catching angles in the dark, and her limitless collection of oddities, which boasted eccentric corners to catch unwary toes. Mechanical arms grabbed at them as they attempted to slip by, moving toward the light.

There had to be light somewhere. All that dark made Pond aware she was groping to see. There had to be candles or lanterns, flashlights or portable floodlights, somewhere amidst that giant collection of human invention and oddities. But Pond didn't know where they were, and while she staggered along in heavy sleepiness and dark, the thumping continued.

It was not the same banging that had rattled through the house previously. This was a noise from outside of the house. Pond held onto walls to guide her steps, and made her way to the back door.

Outside, the wind lashed rain so hard it blew into her face, and the street lights, which were distant enough anyway, given the size of True's grounds, had also been darkened by the storm. So she couldn't see much of who she was talking to, rain streaked and windblown and groggy as she was. But she felt the person's presence and knew at once it had to be Luvreen, Ferdinand's cousin. Luvreen was as wide, tall, and formidable as Ferdinand was lithe and honed.

"Hey, girl," she boomed. "We have arrived. Any chance we could stay the night?"

Pond nodded, then realized she had to speak to be heard. Her nod wouldn't carry very far in the dark. And maybe her voice wouldn't either, in the wind-whipped air. "No problem," she shouted. "Help yourself." She stepped back into the kitchen to make room for Luvreen and her animal, expecting a small performing dog, or maybe a trained cat, if such a thing were possible.

But Luvreen pointed out toward the yard. "My animal's out here. So small she gets mistreated by the circus, but large enough she won't fit in the house."

Pond pointed toward the carriage house, found someone's shoes on the back porch and slipped them on. She was about to stumble down the back stairs when Nareen showed up, holding a hurricane lantern in one hand. Nareen gave the lantern to Pond. The lantern light flickered over enormous folds of skin, gray and brown, thick, deep lines, looking softer than tissue paper, but plusher than towels. And then the light flashed over an immense long body, and a beautiful, expressive trunk.

"Not an elephant." Pond believed she must be mistaken.

"Not a very big one," Luvreen said, on the defensive. "She's the runt, and she finally got fed up with being asked to do all the cute tricks. She wants more dignity. Just because she's tiny doesn't mean she doesn't need artistic freedom."

Pond shook her head. The artistic freedom of

elephants was something she had never before contemplated. But she showed Luvreen the carriage house, and the elephant looked quite content in that space, as happy amidst the hay bales as all the human beings were in their beds in the house. By now, of course, everyone was traipsing out to see what was going on. Except Duckie, who waved with good bleary cheer from the back porch. She pointed to her own bare feet, and Pond realized she was wearing Duckie's shoes.

"Wondered what that barn was for," Gruenbaum said, staring at the elephant without another word.

"Cuz!" Ferdinand threw his arms around Luvreen, and she was so tall in the lantern light he appeared to be hugging a gigantic animate rock formation. She appeared to tolerate his hug with good humor, not unlike a mountain allowed human beings to climb it, choosing with amusement to share its warmth and strata with tiny creatures who aspired to rappel off its heights. "You're as much a giant as ever, you runaway!" he exclaimed.

"Liberator," she said, her mouth almost prim.

"Hey," Pond shouted. "The elephant is the one who can stand on all four corners of the earth at once."

"Don't count on it," Luvreen said stiffly. "I didn't help her escape one bad situation only to land her in another."

"No," Pond blustered. "I mean, it won't inconvenience her at all. She just has to put one foot on each side of a map that's built into the floor. If she does that, she'll help find the secret of this house. Believe me, it's in everyone's interest. We have to figure out what's going on before the apocalypse gets here. My great-aunt was convinced this house had something to do with the last days. We've only got a few left before she said it's all over. Maybe we'll even stop the world from ending."

"Is the world ending, then?" Luvreen asked with obstinate calm, running her hands through her already wild hair, and managing only to make her outrageous wide black curls wilder. It looked as if her hair would spring right off her head one day, each coil had that much life to it. "Had to happen one time or another, I suppose."

"Fine," Pond said. "Have fun with that. Just let me borrow your elephant. We need her. And we will respect her freedom totally."

Luvreen pursed her lips in skepticism.

Pond sighed and decided to go back to sleep. Possibly in the morning, the elephant would have disappeared anyway, like dark in daylight, like a dream upon awakening. "Good night," she said, her voice fervent, hoping it was so. She scrambled upstairs, leaving them all to sort out whatever remained to be sorted out. They could sleep if they wanted, in the carriage house barn or anywhere else. They could find all the candles and all the lanterns and light them all, and hold the night at bay.

They could all leave, for that matter, she told herself with an impatient wave of her arm. And then she hoped they wouldn't. She needed the elephant. She hadn't seen an elephant since she'd attended a circus as a small girl. Her mother had taken her.

*Oh, Mother*, thought Pond, in exasperation, and

it was unclear even to her whether she was uttering a silent prayer or a curse.

***

The next morning, Pond looked at Nareen over a steaming cup of tea, which Nareen had managed to produce thanks to lighting a gas range by hand.

"Did that happen last night?" she asked, her voice tentative, no longer knowing whether she hoped it had or hadn't. She supposed it might be easier to deal with the day if it didn't include a runaway elephant. But part of her longed to stroke the animal's shoulder, run her fingers along those enormous folds of flesh and skin, lose herself next to that great height. And they had to have the elephant, after all. The mosaic earth was large, but not large enough those massive legs couldn't stand on all four corners.

Nareen nodded, and offered no further comment.

Pond began laughing, staring into the hot mug of tea, contemplating herself as the hapless owner of a house that now contained several houseguests—at this exact moment she had lost count, and also the ability to count. Not to mention a carriage house that contained an elephant.

She staggered over to the telephone, holding her sides to keep the laughter in. She picked up the receiver and began dialing.

"Bertram?" Nareen said, clearly expecting Pond to be calling the lawyer. After all, the power was still out. She would surely try what she could to call this off.

175

Instead, Pond said, "Mom?" Pond was laughing so hard, she had to repeat herself. "Mom," she said, getting a grip on herself. "Thank you for taking me to the circus when I was a kid." Pond became silent, and so did her laughter, but her sides shook with silent chortles. "That's it, Mom, no other reason. Just thank you for the circus." She hung up the phone with a bemused look.

"Take that, True," she said, wondering if True had known the circus would come to her house when she left it to her great-niece.

\*\*\*

And the circus did come to True's house, after a fashion. More than just the elephant, who turned out to be named Matilda. After breakfast, a self-important man wearing a bowler hat thudded on the front door.

Pond opened the door with a remarkable degree of self-composure, given the house still had no power, the elephant had eaten all the vegetables, and Gruenbaum had already made a run to the store at Nareen's request, to buy up all the cabbage, lettuce, and apples his van could carry. Even small elephants ate hundreds of pounds of food a day. With deliberation, Pond turned away from letting herself contemplate the heaping, steaming mounds of elephant droppings such food would produce. Forcing herself away from that thought, she focused on the man at the door.

"You have something that belongs to me," he said. He wore a comically small vest, but then, he was a comically small man, not that his air of importance was willing to concede size mattered.

Pond blinked. She was becoming expert in the strategic use of silence.

"An elephant." The bowler hat almost exploded off the top of the man's head.

Pond peered with elaborate care over her shoulder, beyond the foyer into the living room. "Don't see any elephants here. How'd you manage to misplace yours?"

"Misplaced itself, with the help of a rebel trainer," he grumbled. "I knew that trainer was trouble." He shook with outrage. "It's the animals that are the trained ones. *We* give them directions. Not the other way around."

"I do know what you mean." Pond figured agreement was easier than argument. "But you do realize I'm not one of your trained animals. You can't just show up on my porch and expect to give me instructions."

The man looked peevish and bossy, and his right hand twitched along his right leg, as if he wanted to grab a switch and flick it at her disagreeable shoulders. But he restrained himself, clenched his right hand, drew himself up to his full height, which wasn't very tall, and declared, "I demand you release my elephant or I'll have the cops after you."

Pond expected the Baltimore police wouldn't know what to do with the case of a missing—or a found—elephant, any more than she did.

"Good luck with the police," she said, her voice bright and encouraging, and managing not to laugh. He didn't know what he was getting into, making that call. "Is it really your elephant?" It seemed even more preposterous a man would claim to own an elephant than she would be saddled with a house. She felt more possessed by the house than possessing it, and she could tell Luvreen felt the same way about the elephant.

This man's ballooning self-importance was based upon something she wasn't ready to believe in: that he could point to another living being and say, "*Mine*." Pond didn't know what to say in response to the elephant, or the house, or other living beings, but surely it wasn't, "*Mine*."

Though even his expression betrayed the fact it wasn't truly *his* elephant, he merely grumbled his exact words inaudibly, and rushed off the porch, holding his hat as he ran. His trousers were tailored to fit his tiny legs, but looked no less incongruous. They were fashioned from dark serge fabric whose bright green pinstripes matched the band around the bowler.

\*\*\*

## Gruenbaum

Gruenbaum found Pond in the living room, closing the front door.

"I have news you might not want to hear," he said. "I thought the noise was coming from the geothermal heating system. Thought I had quieted things down. But maybe I don't know the system well enough to tell." He had adjusted the knobs yesterday, but now realized he didn't know if he had made it more or less likely that noise would resume, or whether the noise had come from the system in any case.

He was becoming frustrated, forced to admit to himself he understood the system so little he could no longer tell what noise he had caused and what had come from elsewhere. He was willing to work for two employers at once, making a little noise, stirring the pot, so to speak. But the indicators on the geothermal heating and cooling system were impossible for him to read.

Moreover, he wasn't at all willing to trust these currents of warmth in the earth, strong enough to power a heating and cooling system for a house big enough to lose yourself in. He was glad to play at being the ghost in the house, making odd noises, adding a little life to the place. But the vast life of the earth, which this heating and cooling system tapped into, made him aware of invisible energies he knew nothing about.

Today the dials looked almost like they were exhibiting an active intelligence, reading something beyond what he was able to interpret. He wasn't sure who or what was in charge of anything anymore. He wasn't sure what he knew and didn't know. How did you even know what you knew?

Moreover, his loyalties were starting to shift. He didn't object to banging on pipes to add a little noise to Pond's life. But all these other people had gathered, and here he stood, more and more subject to the same surprises as everyone else in this place. His position in the house, working with them, sharing meals with them, made him feel like he was part of their team, playing with them, not against them.

"I can't tell when the noise is coming back. Or if it is. Heating system powered by the earth. Who knows what the earth is doing. You think you can predict what the earth is doing next? *I* can't." He noticed his concern sounded genuine.

"*So* glad everything's more and more calm," Pond said dryly, in response to Gruenbaum's report. "If the world has gone crazy, then it must be my job to humor it along. And how would you like to contribute to the general craziness?"

Gruenbaum shrugged. "How about I take care of the chimney?" he asked, his expression hopeful.

"Be my guest," Pond said magnanimously. "Apparently you can't keep a small elephant from expressing her dignity, and you can't keep a chimney sweep from climbing chimneys."

***

## *Pond*

When Pond ran out to the carriage house and demanded to know how the circus man had tracked her so quickly, Luvreen admitted she had left information with the circus about where she had gone. Luvreen was helping the elephant drink from a giant bucket of water. Both elephant and Luvreen looked very happy.

Luvreen in daylight was no less intimidating than she had been in the middle of the night. Her hair spiraled even more freely this morning, and she would have looked fit to play Medusa if her face hadn't beamed with such bright joy and laughter, her arms wide enough to hold a small elephant and anything else that needed holding.

"What kind of an escape is that, announcing your destination?" Pond had never left word where she was going. Made it much easier to leave everything behind.

"A strategic one. I have a plan. I don't need to keep her away from the circus forever, just long enough to negotiate terms. She and I will go back under diplomatic immunity, and with the right to self-determination. No more jumping through other people's hoops. We will establish our own."

Pond sighed. "Next time, you can be the one who talks to that man in the bowler hat."

"Oh, I'll talk. And he'll listen."

"Then we can borrow your elephant later."

Luvreen glared at her.

Pond added, "Totally in keeping with her dignity, I promise."

"Heard that one before," Luvreen retorted.

*** 

## Duckie

Duckie had untangled all the beryls from all the topaz, and all the onyx from the jade, but by the time she reached aquamarines and yellow diamonds, she needed a break. She tromped out to the carriage house barn wearing a determined expression.

181

"It's like the jewels are speaking in their own language," she told Pond. *I'm really good at reading people*, Duckie told herself. She would just have to learn to read gemstones. "I'll be sure to tell you what they say."

"Do I even want to know?" Pond asked. "This house seems to encourage self-expression. You, the elephant, the earth. No shortage of communication going on around here."

Duckie placed a necklace around each of their necks, including one so long its strands fit even around and under that marvelous trunk, and so managed to charm Luvreen and Matilda that Luvreen voluntarily lifted the platinum haired woman onto Matilda's back. Matilda was gracious about carrying Duckie out into the gardens. Duckie would have squealed with delight, only she was too excited to make any noise at all.

Riding the swaying shoulders of an elephant was like nothing she had experienced before. Atop the elephant's back, Duckie the high society queen became the Infanta—royalty from another time and place, girlish, transported.

*Everything's worth it*, she told herself with delight, *everything's worth it after all*. She felt like she was again six years old, being placed by her mother on a white show pony in a riverfront park. All the world was before her. She was a princess, riding out to a parade, where she would be waved at by people with smiling faces, people who loved and honored her. The pony and the elephant merged in her mind, so her face dropped everything but innocence and clarity, sending forth a radiant glow.

That was how her husband saw her when he strode into the yard. He stopped, his mouth open, his eyes captivated by the sight of her on an elephant. He loosened the cravat around his throat—apparently doing his best to provide himself with more air—and then he tugged at the vest that encased his still powerful chest.

"*Damn,* you are beautiful," he muttered. "But you are my wife, and you are not being very ladylike. Look here," he called to her, his voice gaining strength, "you have to come home right now."

Duckie smiled with joy, the only thing she was very capable of exhibiting at the moment, and then focused more on her husband and what he was saying. Her smile became more tempered but didn't go away altogether. "I'm busy. I'm riding an elephant."

"I can see that," he said impatiently. "But I got you a Jaguar."

"A trained one?" Duckie asked. She was focused on circus animals for the time being.

"A shiny blue one. An *auto*mobile."

"That's nice, dear," Duckie said, her voice amiable and indifferent. "Thank you."

"You're not coming home," her husband concluded. "You look so…engrossed. I didn't know you already had a new ride."

"I'm not coming home right now, anyway," she said. "You're welcome to stay here with me. Maybe Matilda can carry both of us."

Her husband looked at Luvreen, who was beaming at Matilda, and at Pond, who was still wearing her old yoga pants and tunic, and had not yet showered that morning. Duckie's husband snorted. "Just because I was in California for a spot of fun didn't mean I gave my wife permission to go mad." He threw his arms up in the air and stalked back toward home. Then he stopped, long enough to shout back to Duckie, "Jack hammering? In the middle of the night. Is that really necessary?"

"Oh, no, not in the least, dear," she beamed. "It's not necessary. It's indispensable." She called out to Luvreen, "How anyone can ride anything else after being on an elephant is beyond me."

Luvreen grinned. "You're right. It's not possible. I walk everywhere, myself."

Duckie's husband shook his head. "Just remember, there's a sleek new Jaguar in my garage. I don't care what you say," he hollered stiffly to his wife. "There's no way you're walking everywhere. I won't have it."

She waved happily, and kept waving merrily when he reached the edge of True's property and walked onto theirs. She caught a glimpse of him running into a garden brigade that had descended upon their yard while he spoke with Duckie. She contemplated the thicket of rakes and pitchforks, buckets and trowels. She knew her husband's next move: He would have to go have a lie down on the couch and contemplate how to get her back.

*\*\*\*

## *Pond*

Nareen came out to the carriage house to tell Pond someone was on the phone.

Pond almost ran into the kitchen to pick up the line, hoping it was Bertram Something-Something. "Oh," she said, her voice falling into disappointed regions, "Mother." Pond listened grudgingly. "Thank you, Mom, I don't want to come to your place for dinner tonight, but you are welcome to come here." More silence on Pond's end. "I know I don't cook, but I can promise you it will be edible." Pond refrained from adding, *Unlike at your house.* "It might have lots of butter and salt. And it'll be delicious."

Pond was shocked the menace of tasty food was not enough to scare away her mom. Maybe her mom was becoming a renegade as she grew older. Maybe her mom would even eat a bite of dessert.

"Can we have something good for dessert?" Pond asked Nareen. She smiled a mischievous smile. "Something irresistible." She had never seen her mom eat sugar, but she would do her best to make it so tonight.

\*\*\*

## *Ferdinand*

Ferdinand and Giselle had visited the house's side garden, and from there discovered Gruenbaum atop the chimney. Ferdinand had rubbed Giselle's ears, lost in thought as he gazed up at the lightly

185

clambering sweep.

"It's a whole house full of performers," he told her, his face serious. "They just don't know it yet." He squinted at the chimney, four stories high when you considered the attic, and contemplated all the possibilities. He had been a tightrope walker as well as a dancer, when the occasion called for it, so he was comfortable thinking of the air as a usable element.

Rarely had he seen grounds that lent themselves to creating such a natural showplace. *Oh, what you could do with some good guy wire and pulleys.* He wished only that the old lady could have been here for the extravaganza. But no mind, he would repay her, show the way Giselle was able to perform, thanks to her help.

He and Giselle trudged back into the house. He had stumbled on an interesting aspect of True's collections the previous evening, and wanted to be sure he hadn't been imagining things. It seemed to him she had acquired an entire menagerie of monkeys and bears.

An entire room in the attic was devoted to the collections. Each piece appeared to be hand-carved, whittled with magnificent life-like, life-size, beautifully painted detail. The menagerie wasn't live, of course. Not yet. But any performance worth its name could see to that.

\*\*\*

## *Pond*

Pond was in the kitchen, talking to Bertram Something-Something. She wasn't laughing. She was listening. "Did True seem crazy to you?" she had asked, hoping he would confirm the conclusion.

True's madness seemed to her the type that was healthy, maybe even something to be cultivated. The world needed more craziness of the kind True demonstrated. Most of the world's madness, insofar as Pond had seen it, was much less delightful. More boring, for one thing, and more given to fear. True's madness was eccentric, all its own, and based upon laughter and something else. Maybe an outrageous joy.

Bertram seemed to feel compelled to defend his client. "I created a will for her, and she had to be in sound mind for that to happen, *dadgommit*."

"Spoonerisms," Pond teased.

"Far too sane." His voice sounded like he was delivering an official assessment like a bill or a pronouncement, a legal determination that left no room for doubt or discussion. But then he paused and backtracked. "Maybe she was scary sane. It could be she's so smart she is tricking all of us by *feigning* madness, making you ask such questions by setting up this whole codicil game. Which is more a matter of concern: the possibility she was quite rational, and in her fully rational state she set up a wacky and elaborate legal house of cards— while I *participated* in good faith—or that she was not at all reasonable, and convinced me otherwise? Was it more reassuring if someone was daft but looked quite right, or if they were quite right but looked a bit cracked?"

"Fine." Pond gave up. If True had been normal, then normality had a much larger definition and covered much more ground than she had ever before suspected. That kind of normal was fine by Pond. In fact, Pond herself was quite reasonable, had been her entire life, and was now confirming the new standard of moderation in taking in all these houseguests, including the elephant. Especially the elephant.

"There's another codicil," Bertram said, sounding reluctant. "I'm not going to laugh."

"Oh, good," Pond said, unsure whether she meant what she said.

"'All is not lost,'" Bertram read. "'All is found.'"

Shortest one yet, and the least helpful. At least she had managed not to lose herself in laughter. "You have no idea," she told the attorney, mentally going through all the things she had found. Especially the living beings. She just had no idea what any of it—what any of them—meant. Not being lost was one thing. Understanding was another entirely.

Bertram continued. "It also says, 'Open the inner sanctuary, while one stands on all four corners of the world, and then touch the sky.'"

"Of course. No problem. You can come help find the earth and the sky, all in this one house."

"I won't go near that madhouse. Won't go." He hung up the phone with a determined click.

Pond grabbed a quiet moment to consult the *I Ching*, her book that told her things she didn't understand, but knew she needed to know. "What is not lost?" she asked, six times. And it was good indeed she had grabbed that quiet moment, for another one did not come her way for a while.

A state of equilibrium had been achieved, the book told her. The old way had transitioned to the new. All was in place to move forward. At the same time, it was very important to maintain balance, not to take anything for granted. The lines symbolized a pot of water suspended over fire: and the right amount of energy needed to be applied, so the water boiled, but didn't evaporate entirely. In this way, one could direct natural and internal forces with appropriateness. And then the lines showed it was necessary to persevere, remaining unswerving in the face of obstacles—introspection was especially important in the face of obstruction.

*Glad I don't understand* that, Pond congratulated herself. If she understood what the book said, she would start to worry. *Balance*, she told herself, choosing one word out of the lot to hold onto. Balance.

\*\*\*

The man in the bowler hat came back much sooner than Pond expected, and he was still in his fierce and solitary state, unaccompanied by Baltimore's finest.

"Weren't the police interested in chasing elephants?" Pond asked, her voice cheerful as she opened the front door to him.

He scowled and shook his head. "Worse than

that."

Pond escorted him quickly out to the carriage house barn, making him walk all the way around the outside of the house.

"Murchison!" Luvreen exclaimed, to all appearances delighted to see him.

"He came back," Pond said. "But he didn't bring any cops."

"He can't," said Luvreen smugly.

"It's an undocumented elephant," Murchison told Pond. "No papers. Here completely illegally. How it got across the border *I* have no idea."

Luvreen cut her eyes at him. "You know very well. Your brother-in-law operates a highly successful smuggling operation, specializing mostly in colorful parrots from South America, but also in big game animals, many of them heading for private reserves in the American West. But some go toward circuses and every now and then a corrupt zoo or two."

Murchison paled.

"Also," Luvreen said, gathering herself up to her full height. "Your brother-in-law is not above forging papers for his parrots, elephants, and rhinos, and for his tigers and lions—but the papers often cost more than the bird or mammal did in the first place. So most clients, even super rich ones, take their animals without legal pedigree."

Murchison looked like a teakettle about to boil over.

"And circuses," Luvreen continued, her voice rising in triumphant conclusion, "are hardly in a financial position to hire animals who hold what look like official passports. Circus management has to cross their fingers and hope the authorities are too busy enjoying the show to care about such minor matters as zoological documentation."

Pond laughed, realizing Murchison had no legal standing to recapture the elephant he wanted to call his, just as she had no legal standing to rid herself of her house. The law was a funny business. Anyway, she didn't mind the police wouldn't be following in Murchison's tracks.

Matilda had no restraint. She loved everybody, and had already begun nuzzling even Murchison with her trunk, dripping water drops on his bowler hat. He was too annoyed to appreciate an elephant's attentions, though, and brushed her trunk away, along with the anointing droplets.

"Stop it," he said. "Behave yourself. Withhold your favors until you are commanded to distribute them. That's the problem," he complained to Luvreen. "You've let her do anything she wants."

"You want to stifle her. She won't have it. I won't have it. She's not coming back until we come to an agreement."

"We'll see about that," Murchison said, his mouth smug as he crossed his arms.

The man's certainty was making Pond nervous. She needed to get that elephant together with the earth map, and then all she had to do was find the inner sky and touch it.

***

Pond noticed that Murchison kept looking over

his shoulder toward the back driveway. His face was beginning to seem less composed, his sureness faltering, but then it looked like his continual scrutiny was rewarded.

Two clown-like individuals came into view, riding a four-wheeler motor scooter. One of the men would have barely fit on the scooter. Two were bulging out all over the place, making it look like a mound of humanity had acquired a slight metal frame and a motor, and was now propelling itself along, a ship of flesh. The ship was sailing in dignified slowness, its motor almost unable to keep up with its added weight.

"The circus police," Luvreen told Pond, who began to acquire a worried expression.

Pond didn't know if the circus police had any actual power, but she didn't want to tangle with such mobile marshmallows, either—or to have them interrupt the stability, the new order, her house had acquired.

"They're not welcome," Pond said. "The elephant has sanctuary here."

The two clown figures stumbled off the scooter and managed to right themselves. They looked dim and pleasant, cheerful and confused.

"There's the elephant," Murchison told them.

They nodded with enthusiasm. "Yes, there's the elephant."

"Get it," Murchison ordered.

They walked up to the elephant, who began blowing love droplets on them, a shower of water from her bucket. One of the clown figures giggled. There was no other word to describe it. He was huge, and his giggle was girlish and high pitched, the sound incongruous because it issued from such a large, puffy body. The other clown figure put up his arm to defend himself from the rain of elephant blessedness, and he slipped and went down.

"Fool!" Murchison said.

"The hay was wet," the fellow explained, from the ground. He looked much more comfortable lying down, as if gravity were a force he had to struggle against to remain upright.

Murchison went over to Matilda, arms outstretched. Matilda swerved away from him, her movement delicate, dancing backward and sideways with surprising grace. Luvreen grinned and nodded. "Good girl," she said.

"She's got you wrapped around her little finger," Murchison barked at Luvreen, following desperately after the elephant.

"Wouldn't have it any other way."

Meanwhile, Ferdinand and Giselle had also entered the back yard. "No problem," Ferdinand told Pond. "I got your chimney climber to help me lay guy wires. Add an almost invisible pulley system, and your aunt's army of monkeys and bears, and we're all set, ready to go. Ready for the show."

Ferdinand moved with such quickness and ease Pond hardly noticed he was there, much less that he was stepping in to save the elephant just in time. And Murchison never even saw what was coming.

Murchison persisted in going after Matilda, who led him on a backward dance through the carriage house, until she was up against a side door.

Murchison grinned with delight, seeming to believe he had maneuvered her into a corner. Pond ran up to the side door and swung it wide, a double panel door, tall and wide enough Matilda was able to exit with a sideways two-step.

Murchison growled. Matilda had already ambled forward almost all the way to the house when he exited the side door. He pulled up his trousers and prepared to grab her once and for all.

But as he ran toward the elephant, who had discovered True's lovely fish pond, and was gazing at her reflection, or maybe she was instead admiring the bright orange carp, Ferdinand issued an order to his monkeys, using pulleys to send them aloft, and those beautiful guy wires to guide them down again, so propelled by gravity, they began to descend from the sky.

Matilda remained cheerfully by the carp pond, while the menagerie began lavishing its attentions upon Murchison, inspiring him to step farther away from the pachyderm's quiet contemplative pool reflection.

Borne on an invisible guy wire, the mechanical monkeys—some of them carved, some of them cast, all of them painted to look brighter than the sun, with white faces expressing great fortitude, or black faces expressing great strength, or gray faces expressing great joy—the monkey troops began to descend from the sky. They came down in rows, although only in retrospect was that clear.

To Murchison, it must have felt like flying beasts were flinging themselves at him at random. Swooping down out of nowhere, materializing from thin air. First came one bearing a sword, and then another shooting a bow, and then another with a formidable club, and as he ducked to get out of the way of one, another came at him without pause. And then, just as it seemed he had weathered the storm of monkeys, the bears began to fall.

Matilda stayed at the carp pond, swinging her trunk in her own quiet dignity, not seeming bothered by anything at all. The mechanical animals weren't afflicting her, in any case. And Luvreen had run to her side, dodging the monkey cascade.

Ferdinand was grinning. Luvreen looked positively delighted.

"Oh, my God," Pond said, standing in the carriage house looking out at the madness. The two enormous clowns stood with her, jaws wide open, and in one fellow's mouth Pond thought she caught a glimpse of a gobstopper dyed to look like the world. She closed her eyes for a moment, and when she opened them, the monkeys were taking a momentary breather, while the bears entered the aerial battlefield.

The bears were obviously too much for Murchison. He had attempted to stand his ground while attacked by monkeys, perhaps partly frozen in place by shock. But when gigantic bears came winging their way toward him, he put his hand on his hat and ran, ran with considerable might toward the back gate, ran with visible energy toward freedom.

"Forget the elephant!" he shouted. "Just preserve me from the bears!"

The bears followed him, courtesy of Ferdinand,

who lightly lifted the wire and ran with it toward the gate, bowing aside at the appropriate moment. Just as Murchison turned around at the back of the property, where he could have gotten himself out of harm's way, a very cheerful specimen, tall and black and wearing a bright red smile, holding a salmon in one hand and a spear in another, propelled itself out of the sky onto Murchison's back.

"Oof!"

The spear had contacted his chest as he turned around, and he was thumped into immobility. Just at that moment, a great brown bear came flashing down from mid-air, and Murchison wailed, running, followed by the two clowns who'd abandoned their motor scooter and followed their boss, flailing and crying as they went. None of the three were attempting any longer to restrain the squalling noises trailing out behind them as they ran.

Murchison reached the gate and disappeared out of sight, followed by the two whose bodies wobbled as they went.

\*\*\*

Giselle broke away from Ferdinand and ran in a joyful gait to Luvreen, scampering around her and the elephant, letting loose as Pond had never seen her let loose. The dog was a whirling dervish, a black streak of joy, uncontained and uncontainable fur and love and enthusiasm. She looked like a dolphin cresting waves, except the land was now her element, and the sky. She looked like she would almost take flight, joining her distant cousins, the air bears and monkeys.

"She's beautiful," Pond exclaimed.

Ferdinand wiped the corner of one eye, watching her run. "She moves so effortlessly now," he said. "All because of the old lady's financing of surgery and rehab." He made his hands into the shape of a prayer. "Thank you," he said.

"What was that?" Pond laughed with relief, and cried a bit too. She didn't know whether to be alarmed or comforted that monkey and bear reserves could descend from the sky to hold the forces of conformity at bay. As long as the monkeys and bears were on her side, Pond decided, she welcomed them.

"Just a little circus," said Ferdinand, coming up and placing his hand on her shoulder. His hand was steady and warm, kind and reassuring.

"This place isn't a circus," Pond protested, then collapsed into helpless laughter, wiping a few streaks of water away from her eyes. "I mean, it wasn't."

Duckie was gasping with joy. She had watched the proceedings from the back porch. "Most often you have to go downtown to see the circus."

"Right," Ferdinand said. "Why limit yourself?"

The only possible response Duckie could offer was a smile.

"Let me summon my army of animals." Ferdinand, Gruenbaum, and Nareen walked around and collected all the troops, their movements gentle. They carried the animals into the living room, transforming it into a barracks and a mess hall and a hospital tent and a gigantic celebration, all in one. The animals had all survived, but in their aerial adventures some of them had acquired tiny chips in their paint.

"We have to take care of them," Ferdinand said. "All soldiers, and all performers, ought to be restored to their original condition as much as possible, treated with honor and love."

"I know carpentry," Gruenbaum offered, and True's basement yielded all the supplies they needed for repair, except paint, which Gruenbaum fetched from an artist's supply store in nearby Towson.

"They're not even really hurt," Duckie said, her voice filled with adoration. Pond saw Gruenbaum look suspiciously at Duckie, but then realize Duckie's adoration had become generalized, and was in no way directed at anyone in particular, especially not him. He breathed a sigh of relief.

"Haven't you heard the stories?" Ferdinand asked, filing an edge off a monkey claw. "Let's have this claw sharp, but not so piercing it endangers someone who has to handle it. Monkeys and bears are immortal, in all the old epics. They stand for undying love and devotion. As long as the monkeys and bears are with you, no opposing force can conquer you."

"As long as they're helping us," Pond said fervently. She didn't want to imagine facing down brightly painted hordes. She could take on most anything else, including her mother, but colorful animals might well undo her resolve.

"Monkeys and bears will never desert you,"

Ferdinand mused. "Much like a dog."

Pond winced. She thought of all the canines whose companionship she had declined over the course of her travels. She had always moved on in her lone condition, a single shadow passing across the land.

"There's another old story about that," Ferdinand said. "A man climbed a mountain, and his dog climbed with him. The incline was so steep he wondered if it was right to let his dog climb with him, but when he tried to get the animal to go back home, the animal only continued at his heels. So the two of them kept climbing, and they climbed past all the last inhabitants, past the final cabins which perched on the barely habitable rock ledges, and past the eagles' nests, and past the highest place birds would fly, and past the last place where winds would blow. And still they kept climbing. And at last, when it seemed impossible they could climb any farther, they arrived at the gates of Heaven.

"The gatekeeper said to the man, 'Welcome home. Well climbed. Well done. You may enter if you leave your dog behind.'

"The man shook his head. He was resolved upon it. The dog had climbed all that way with him. How could he possibly abandon the animal now, just outside the gates of Heaven?

"'Sorry,' the gatekeeper said with sympathy, and then his voice grew stern, admonishing. 'Animals aren't allowed into Heaven, you know. They don't have souls.'

"'Then I am not about to enter Heaven, either,' the man said, and he prepared to turn away, wondering how he and his dog would manage to climb back down all that distance, back through the places where winds blew, and birds flew, and eagles nested, and the last cabins perched, back down into the lands where people lived and cities buzzed and hummed with inhabitants, back down into civilization.

"'You're all right,' the gatekeeper shouted after the man, calling him back. 'You can enter. With your dog, after all.'

"And the dog turned out to be the man's own soul, his own highest truth and purpose. If he had left it outside the gates of Heaven, Heaven would have been nothing at all. So the man and his dog strode through the entryway, and all the streets were paved with gold, and all the buildings shone with precious gems built into the walls like stucco, and all the people smiled, and the man looked around and thought that it was very beautiful. In fact, it was very like where the man had lived, only with more gold and jewels, but after a short while, those faded into the background anyway, and became just the ground you stood upon, and the walls that lined the streets.

"And the dog scampered along with joy at his side, and the man took deep breaths of the air of Heaven, which after all was rather like the air of earth. But then the man noticed something important was missing. He gazed and gazed around, but none of his friends were there.

"'Where are my friends?' He had retraced his steps to ask the gatekeeper.

"'Oh, yes, I'm sorry to report they are in Hell.'

The gatekeeper was doing his job. His duties amounted to a kind of accounting. Nothing personal in it, nothing at all.

"'Then Heaven is misnamed,' the man said. 'I will go where my friends are.'

"And so in an instant the man and his dog found themselves in another place, and all the man's friends were there, and the man looked around and couldn't see what was so tormenting about this place. His friends' faces shone with light and welcome, and everything looked not unlike where the man had lived before, only now everything was lit by torches and flambeaus, and the food was rich and spiced, and the flowers were thick with scent. 'This can't be Hell,' the man said aloud, rubbing his dog's ears, and in fact, what the man experienced there was what he brought with him, just as had been the case far above and also in the middle lands.

"And the dog never left the man, and the man never left the dog." Ferdinand rubbed the monkey's claws and set them down. Pond reached out to feel what he had been working on. The claws were sharp but smooth under her fingers, perfect, honed with care.

*** 

Pond sat back on the couch, stunned by the story. She had thought she could take on anything except monkeys and bears, and now she realized she could take on anything except monkeys and bears and tales about dogs.

She was unable to keep herself from weeping in silence, tears wetting her face. She wanted her dog. She didn't have a dog, but she wanted it, with all her being. Where would she find her own dog?

Giselle nuzzled Pond's knee, and Pond forced herself to stifle a wail. She petted Giselle's ears, which the dog offered to her as if she were making available a soft, comforting blanket, a cure-all, a peace flag. And Pond rubbed the dog's ears until she felt no desire to weep, and just a quiet tiredness remained.

Armies of monkeys and bears were strewn around the parlor and the living room floor, propped up against one another, supporting each other while bits of paint dried. The touched-up paint was, if possible, even more beautiful than the original.

"You're an artist," Ferdinand had told Gruenbaum, who grinned, and continued applying his brush with ever more delicacy and vigor.

"I like working with these people in the house," Gruenbaum told Ferdinand. "Much better to work with people than against them."

Ferdinand straightened his back to stretch it out, and didn't say a word. But his eyes narrowed as he looked at Gruenbaum.

Duckie had promenaded back upstairs to collect more jewelry, bringing it back down with her to the living room. "Could be I imagined the idea of any pattern," she said out loud. "Could be it's all shimmer, all shine. Could be it just sparkles. So beauty is beauty, and doesn't have to say something besides. Maybe beauty itself is enough." She touched the back of her hair, looking radiant and for that single moment seeming unaware of how shimmering her eyes and face were.

"And I'm certainly not finding that dratted diamond," Duckie complained, just loud enough for Pond to hear.

Whatever it meant, it was okay—for now.

***

All afternoon, Pond stared out at the back gate and out the front window, expecting the reappearance of Murchison and at least a small coterie of circus police. But the street in front of the house stayed empty, and so did the back gate.

"When's he coming back?" she demanded of Luvreen.

Luvreen blinked her eyes mildly. "Whenever. I'm ready for him."

*But are we?* Pond's internal sense of disquiet asked. Meanwhile, she paced around the house looking for sky, but so far it was eluding her.

"I don't know where the inner sky is," Pond told Luvreen, when she couldn't put it off any longer, "but I can show you a great map of the earth. We need to get Matilda to stand on it." She had been telling herself she wasn't ready to take on an elephant, but it was really Luvreen she had to tangle with. And beyond that, whatever True had set up.

Luvreen rolled her eyes at Pond. "You need my elephant much more than my elephant needs you."

"Sure." Pond nodded, after taking a beat to consider the question. "Since Ferdinand asked, you're fine to stay here either way. But can't she also stand on the map? It won't affect her dignity."

"Show me this map," Luvreen said skeptically, and Pond marched her into the solarium and pointed silently to the unfurled earth. The map looked triumphant, as if its maker had envisioned someone turning the map into a banner and putting it on a flag pole at the head of a parade. All its edges appeared to be offering celebratory salutes: greetings and exultations to all who viewed it.

Luvreen snorted. The floor looked as innocuous as any other floor, and Pond shivered away a game-board memory and pushed away thoughts about what exactly might lie beneath where they now stood. "Looks fine," Luvreen said, stamping on the stones and jumping up and down to test their sturdiness.

*Don't mention the void, don't mention the void*, Pond told herself urgently. "Luckily Matilda's really small for an elephant, and that whole wall opens up into the gardens."

"Matilda doesn't make house calls," Luvreen said in a stuffy tone.

"Fine," Pond snapped. "Forget I asked." She would just have to find another way to carry out the directions about standing on all four corners of the earth.

"Teasing," Luvreen said in a soothing tone. "Humor."

Pond made a face at Luvreen. She knew humor, and it was in precious short supply at the moment. Then she imagined opening the solarium door, rolling back the whole wide wall, so that an elephant could step over the threshold and into the house, and she reconsidered. Maybe a small smile was justified.

"Look, this wall is on a track like a garage door. Can she make it through that entryway?"

Luvreen examined the wall of glass, which would peel away and open to the outside, and she took time to scan the solarium's dimensions, which were two stories high, but the whole time she also kept studying Pond's face. "If I ask her to," she said cautiously.

"Please. I wouldn't ask if it wasn't important."

"The world's got to end sometime. Not so sure my elephant has anything to do with it, one way or another."

"The world doesn't have to end *today*," Pond insisted.

When Matilda curtsied across the threshold of the solarium and first stepped onto the slate mosaic that formed the floor, preparing to stand on the earth itself, Pond held her breath. The elephant was so beautiful and elegant, and the look on her face was ancient and patient, as if she were declaring to Pond, *I will grant your request. I will play your silly game. But nothing you do to me can touch me. I am somewhere else. I am running with an elephant calf and the other mothers deep in the forest. I am not in this strange place.*

Luvreen was equally imperial, showing all the nobility of a queen in the way she carried her head atop her shoulders, the way she held herself high. She conveyed her skepticism silently, but guided Matilda farther into the room, sighing as she did so. *Sorry, girl,* her actions were saying. *I know you're greater than all this. I know we are asking you to perform again. I know you want to be free. But here we are, and here is this woman who asked us to help her. We wouldn't be doing this if we weren't so helpful. As long as we're here, we might as well be kind.*

The others stayed silently along the edge of the room nearest the rest of the house's interior. It wasn't like being in a house when the elephant walked in. It was like being in a movie, in a dream. People told stories about such things, and then when it happened to you, it just happened, and you went on breathing, and your heart went on beating, and later you would again be hungry and need to eat. But at the moment, everything vanished except for the wonder of what had to be an apparition and yet was real.

And Matilda's feet spanned the four corners of the earth, one giant foot placed on the N for North, and one on the S for South, and East and West were not left out. Staring at each massive foot, Pond couldn't imagine what a large elephant would look like. Matilda stood in place, Luvreen's hand on her neck, and the elephant placed her trunk on the ground and paused, and seeming to vibrate slightly in place.

Pond wondered what the elephant was doing. Matilda seemed to be hearing or sensing something that was beyond Pond's ability to register it—waves of sound or motion. Maybe Matilda knew all about the void. Maybe Matilda knew all the secrets of the house and just couldn't say what she knew.

Pond remembered hearing that elephants

recognized their own images in a mirror, that elephants remembered everything they had ever experienced, and that elephants brought good luck and the removal of obstacles.

*Please,* she implored silently. She could do with some good luck, and who needed obstacles, anyway? She waited in thrilled expectation, waited with her heart rate increasing in anticipation of some promised fulfillment. The floor would open up, and inner sky would be revealed. Hopefully, that sky had nothing to do with the void.

Nothing happened. Pond looked around the room, then strolled around, and then almost ran. Nothing to be seen here.

"Maybe it's happening somewhere else," she said impatiently, urging the rest to disperse throughout the house, to find what had happened now they had completed that part of the quest's instructions. One was standing on all four corners of the earth.

"Find the inner sky!" Pond ordered them, and then she ran to every room of the house, including Ferdinand's suite. The inner sky was nowhere to be found.

Pond raced back down to the solarium. The elephant was still standing dutifully on the cardinal compass points, shifting her weight a bit from foot to foot. The world was still unfurled around her. "I guess that's not it," Pond said, deflating.

"Maybe your aunt didn't know an elephant would show up," Nareen said.

Pond glared at her. The girl was probably right. Probably. She was beginning to think her great-aunt had some direct line to omniscience, the way she had set everything up. But maybe there were many possible ways the puzzle could be solved, rather than just one. Maybe the elephant was part of the answer, but not the whole thing. Pond frowned. Yesterday, someone had suggested people could work together, could stand together on the four corners of the earth. Pond had wanted to look to the elephant instead, rather than to people.

*Animals were easier to like,* she told herself, *easier to deal with. They didn't talk back.* Now, she paused.

"Okay," she said grudgingly. "It's obvious Matilda's not big enough." She couldn't yet bring herself to ask the others to help.

Luvreen uttered a sound halfway between a growl and a howl of protest, not even dignifying Pond's comment with a single word.

"Sorry," Pond said with haste, almost managing sincerity. "What if we all join the small elephant on the four corners of the earth?" And she took North, because it reminded her of the Yukon, where she had always wanted to go, hitching along the Trans-Alaska Highway. "You take West, Nareen, it's closest to you."

"I like the looks of this S," Ferdinand said, standing on the southern corner.

"East is the one that's left," Duckie said, taking her place there. And Pond sent her gaze far and wide, but could see not much that looked different.

"Go look," she told Gruenbaum, and then when he didn't move, she added, "Please," and he went.

He came back after what seemed a long time.

Staying in place on a cardinal compass point right next to an elephant leg was an unusual stance. The elephant leg made Pond aware of her own smallness, her own inconsequential status, so she almost threw up her hands and walked away from the whole thing. Surely nothing she could add to anything would make any difference at all. But when Gruenbaum returned, he said, "I think there's something on the third and a half story."

"Inner sky?" Pond asked.

"Maybe. Last time I checked, there wasn't a map in that ceiling. Now there is."

Pond hooted and whooped, then ran. The others, except Luvreen, followed in their own fashions, and they all saw Gruenbaum was right. A smaller, wooden version of the solarium floor's map was now visible in the ceiling of the third and a half floor. North, South, East, and West, the unfurled world lay spread out upon the wood, tempting Pond to solve the next part of the puzzle.

She stood on a chair and tapped the wood. Solid all around. Apparently a small panel had slid aside, revealing the new world map, about two hand spans wide, which was after all, much more modest in expanse than the one they had all been standing on.

"Matilda," Pond exclaimed, remembering she was still holding her position on the map, and ran back down to the solarium. "Thank you," she told Luvreen, while petting Matilda on the neck. "I think we uncovered the next part of it."

"Good," Luvreen said with satisfaction, leading Matilda back to the carriage house barn. "She needs to eat. Elephants only get to sleep about two hours a day, they have to eat so much to keep their beautiful little body going. At least now she can eat in peace, and without being so helpful."

And Pond investigated the new world map until she could investigate no more. By the time her annoyance grew so great that she could no longer continue, she had discovered nothing notable.

Rather than lasting triumph, frustration now came to settle around Pond's shoulders. Discovering the next map made her want to discover the next solution. Pond had to be able to solve the mystery of inner sky, even if it involved working again with an elephant. Even if it involved working again with *other people*.

The alternative was the quest was unsolvable, there was nothing she could do, there never had been anything she could do, she was a mere pawn in her great-aunt's house-sized chess game. *No,* Pond told herself, *each piece of the puzzle will click into place, and at last it will change everything.*

Pond scowled. She finally unclenched her grimace by transferring her fears to others, away from herself.

Despite herself, Pond was starting to feel a sense of responsibility for everyone in the house. Besides, if she couldn't solve her own problems, everyone else's became that much more engrossing.

Just before dinner, Pond found Duckie and asked her, "Aren't you worried your husband is going to come back again and demand you return home?"

Duckie had patted the back of her hair into something close to perfection, and now she blinked and grinned. "No, not at all. If he does return, I'll invite him to dinner, and that will be certain to do him in."

\*\*\*

Pond went back to the carriage house. "What if those men come while we're eating dinner?" she asked Luvreen testily.

"Easy. Teach the elephant to defend herself."

Pond shrugged. That sounded good. But how could an elephant protect itself? Especially an undocumented pachyderm. Weren't they at the mercy of any unscrupulous circus manager, any big game hunter stalking the streets of Baltimore?

Luvreen came close to Pond and whispered in her ear. "Matilda dances in the dark. Anyone who comes up to her while we're eating, she'll dance. She's actually very well-trained, and I've given her the cue. Woe betide anyone who attempts to take her now, because Matilda has moves she doesn't even know."

Pond winced, imagining someone crushed underfoot a giant elephant forepaw. She didn't want to see even Murchison in such a state. Not that she liked Murchison. It just sounded like it would create an inconvenient mess.

"She won't kill them," Luvreen said, watching Pond's face. "She'll only gather them up into a bouquet."

Pond didn't particularly want a Murchison bouquet, but figured it would be better than Murchison jam. Hosting an elephant apparently presented flower arranging questions Pond had

211

spent her entire life avoiding. She sighed and straightened her shoulders, and went to prepare herself to deal with the most peculiar event of the day, the arrival of her mother.

*\*\**

## *Mrs. Pond*

"I thought you were rattling around in this place by yourself," said Mrs. Pond to her daughter, taking in the figures who were swirling past her. Pond's mother had only just arrived and already looked completely undone, like a pearl who had slipped out of her setting and might roll away into a corner, absent the prongs of conventional approval and disapproval that usually held her in place. Nareen slipped by in a silent blur of hot steam and aromatic jasmine, holding a giant platter that contained a tureen, and Mrs. Pond wobbled a bit in her fragrant wake.

Duckie bobbed her head in welcome, and utterly charmed Mrs. Pond. "Your daughter is awesome," she said. Mrs. Pond nearly wept, an expression of surprise and dismay crossing her face.

"No one has ever said such a thing about my daughter." Mrs. Pond put her hand to her chest. "Still beating," she murmured. "It seems I have not entered the afterlife, only a very unusual dinner party."

Gruenbaum stalked into the dining room and nodded gruffly, and Mrs. Pond's eyes widened. He looked noble and grizzly, like something straight from the wilderness. To her eyes, unable to place him otherwise, he was a mysterious artist, his hair long, wavy, and an alluring gray, his clothes now streaked with beautiful paint colors. With that almost irresistible reserve, he had to be famous.

She turned to her daughter to demand an accounting of this company she was keeping. "I had this image," she said, gasping a bit as she reached for breath and steadiness, "you were all alone in this giant house. You were lonely." *You needed me*, she thought, grabbing at her hand-loomed but understated silk scarf for comfort, and only managing to disarray it, so she appeared even more askew, an uncharacteristic look for her.

"It's a full house, Mom," Pond said, frowning. "Almost. I've lost count. Maybe there's still an extra room or two."

At that moment, Ferdinand glided in, Giselle at his side, and Mrs. Pond almost yelped with astonishment. She had never seen so much beauty in one place. Everyone here looked like an exhibit for a living museum, a performer in an unbilled extravaganza, a spectacle to outdo all other shows.

And they were walking around as if nothing unusual were occurring, as if it were quite normal for these peculiar beings to gather together over a dinner table, to pass plates and forks and knives, to wipe their lips with *napkins*, of all things. Sure, you could call them serviettes, but it didn't change their basic function. These people looked like a gathering of strange angels, or renegade gods, or just the most interesting beings you could ever see in human form, and they were sitting around the table chatting, in Baltimore of all places.

And Mrs. Pond was pulling up a chair with them, and sitting there in amazed stillness, unable to comprehend what exactly was occurring in her life or her daughter's.

"I had no idea," she said. "I had no idea how things were with you. It's all a bit too much for me."

In came Luvreen, and Mrs. Pond was introduced to her as well. She was so tall indoors she seemed to fill the entire room, her laugh taking up all the extra space. In that laughter, she got lost, then found herself.

"The elephant's happy," Luvreen called. "She ate before we did, you slowpokes. Even more than humans, the elephant is always needing to eat."

*Oh my God,* Mrs. Pond thought, *an elephant.*

She didn't have much time to consider it. Her plate was now heaped high, and the bowls and platters and tureens kept coming, and never had she tasted such food. She couldn't resist the English peas, which had traveled all the way from True's garden, or the Eastern Shore peaches. She couldn't turn away the fingerling potatoes or the seaweed salad, or deny herself a bite or two of poppy-seed coated tuna, immersed for one sweet salty penetrating second in wasabi-soy dipping sauce. She devoured the oyster stew, all rich enticing creaminess.

And afterward, she couldn't help enjoying the cherry clafouti, irresistible in its simplicity, tartness softened but not eliminated, so she could tell herself she wasn't eating cream and sugar, but fruit of the trees, and how could one turn away from such abundant offerings, such pure delicacies, such a company of food and people.

For a time, Mrs. Pond lost herself in the flash of forks and spoons, in the ecstasies of eating, and so unaccustomed were such pleasures to her that she felt drugged, dazed, removed from all reality. She could have been floating above the table, suspended in her chair, and she would not have been any more or less surprised than she was already, using ordinary utensils to deliver nectar to her own mouth.

The flow of dishes and conversation went on around her, as if she were a rock in a moving stream, and the others were flashing by in the current, lit up by sunshine, glinting in the brightness of one another's conversation. *They* recognized *one another*, Mrs. Pond thought.

"How do you know one another?" she asked.

"We help each other out," Pond shrugged.

"Save a life here," Ferdinand said, grinning at Pond.

"And there," Luvreen offered, grinning in the general direction of the carriage house.

"We work together," Nareen said. "We had to help Pond last night."

"Today we had to defend ourselves against a circus attack."

"Oh, indeed?" Pond's mother quavered.

The faces around the table looked like mirror images of one another, allowing everyone to see their own smile reflected on the others' faces.

*How do I look to them?* Mrs. Pond wondered,

and realized she didn't know how she looked to herself. She had never thought about such a strange question. She was who she was. She did what she did. And now she paused and asked herself what that was, and had no idea.

She turned to her daughter. "What did you do out there on the road all those years?" She expected an angry reply. Every time she had asked such a thing before, she had gotten prickly Pond, thorny Pond, briar patch Pond.

Now, however, her daughter just shrugged. "I've been asking myself the same question."

Her mother's eyes widened. Maybe her daughter would settle down. Maybe being the owner of this house was prelude to joining the fold. Maybe her daughter would wear beige. Then Mrs. Pond looked around the dining room table and collapsed into helpless laughter. And maybe not.

Gruenbaum was tall, gray, and serious. Ferdinand and Giselle were a unit, joined in inseparable companionship, both quiet, piercing in their joy. Nareen was quicksilver, beautiful and mysterious, way too young to be so old in her demeanor. Duckie was a fountain of laughter bubbling over, cascading over everyone. Luvreen was enormity and glee, a rock face lit by direct sun. And Pond had to be dafter than ever, keeping such motley company, and yet she was also more settled than Mrs. Pond had ever seen her.

Sometime after Mrs. Pond was wondering if she had been actually intoxicated by the heavenly food, her head was so swimming with pleasure, she became aware of the talk surrounding her.

"Dunno about that geothermal system," Gruenbaum was saying. "It's hard to tell. What if something's gonna blow? You can tap into the earth, but what if the earth has its own ideas."

Things geothermal Mrs. Pond associated with Yellowstone, a place she had visited as a child. But this rugged man was talking as if long ago and far away were right here, as if Baltimore was about to blow. It could happen. She shrugged.

Living in Baltimore, you became accustomed to crumbling infrastructure and almost daily potential calamities. You crossed your fingers and told yourself it was part of the fun. Something like line dancing at the apocalypse. Something like a constantly shifting pressure valve. You bought your nonperishable foods, and kept your flashlights stocked with batteries, and stocked bottled water, and you smiled and raised your head up high.

In the store, you weren't the only one buying out the last loaves of bread, and clearing the shelves of all C and D cells before the hurricane hit, or the snow storm, or the chemical fire in the railroad tunnel burned for days upon days.

"We'll still be here come Monday," Mrs. Pond said.

"I won't," said Nareen. "My time's up then. I only stay one week in each place. At least I think I can stay here that long. If she lets me. I'll do my part to ensure it happens." Her expression looked determined.

Mrs. Pond looked at the child, for to her she was still only a child, despite her self-possession and her clear gaze.

Nareen caught Mrs. Pond's questioning glance, and smiled. "There'll be another house next week. There's always another house."

Mrs. Pond glanced at the nearly empty food platters. Nareen would be welcome, wherever she went, with talents like that. "You don't have a mother?" she asked, the question slipping out before she could retract it.

"Of course I do," Nareen said, slightly impatiently. "We all do. You have a mother," she told Mrs. Pond, a bit severely.

Mrs. Pond thought of her own aged Mater, and a flash of guilt ran through her. She didn't visit her nearly as often as she ought to. Last time she had gone to see her, her mom had been sharp as ever. That was maybe the problem. Her mom had spotted an albino squirrel, pure white, and had to point it out to her daughter three times before her daughter could see where it shimmered in the trees.

"You'll catch on," her mother had said, laughing, and Mrs. Pond couldn't tell if it was at her daughter or with her. "One of these days." *Fifty-six and still intimidated by my mother*, Mrs. Pond thought, swallowing, and wishing she hadn't brought up the topic.

"Never mind," Mrs. Pond told Nareen.

"A week is a good length of time. Long enough to get to know a place. Long enough to help a little. And not too long. Never get bored after a week, do you?" Nareen looked at Pond, but Pond looked away.

At the thought of her own mother, and at the thought of this girl's missing mother, Mrs. Pond longed to shriek into her pillow. Given her propensity for all things healthy and inconvenient, her pillow was filled with bits of natural rubber, little bits that cost as much as her husband had spent for an automobile, the first time he bought one. She told herself natural rubber was cheap; it contained multitudes. Lasting twenty years or more, think about how many wails it would catch and hold in its time. Pro-rated, that latex was a downright bargain.

Besides, that pillow helped keep Mrs. Pond sane and at home. Unlike her daughter, who just up and left. For one long moment, Mrs. Pond almost admired her for it. It took courage to lift your face up from the couch cushions and go. And then she nearly lost her breath again. What was she *thinking*? She objected on principle to everything her daughter did, everything her daughter had ever done, everything her daughter would ever do.

But she glanced down the long table, and everyone's faces gleamed. The table was set with a wild assortment of plates and cups and glasses, none of them matching. Porcelain consorted with pewter, and glass waltzed away with cut crystal. Bits of gold and silver and platinum shone next to polished marble urns and rough cut quartz vases, mirrored candlesticks sparkled in all directions, and an obsidian plate or two shone with all the dark light they absorbed and gave back. Red drinking goblets were climbed by intricate gold leaf vines, and Delft lay scattered the whole long span of the table—actual Delft—royal by its appearance, and from the seventeenth century, or maybe it was the eighteenth or the nineteenth.

By the looks of it, all the centuries sat down together at this table to take sup. And all the countries. Japanese cast iron tea pots sat next to Italian majolica sunburst platters. For his part, Gruenbaum was drinking out of an actual tin cup. Giselle had laid her head on the table next to Ferdinand, and the dog was so tall she had to lower herself a bit to set her head flat at arm's height. Ferdinand was rubbing Giselle's ears on one side of her head, and, seated only one large dog over from him, and showing a little surprise at her own actions, Duckie found herself rubbing the dog's ears on the other side of her head.

Mrs. Pond's earth shifted and tilted on its axis, and set itself back down again in new alignment. The scene was completely impossible, and yet had utterly charmed her. Maybe this wasn't so bad, after all.

***

## Pond

Pond wondered how the table cleared itself so quickly, but it was all explainable. So many hands made quick work of even such an allotment of dishes. Ferdinand juggled a few plates as he went. She frowned at him, not sure True wanted her dishes broken, or maybe it was that Pond didn't want *her* dishes broken.

And catching her frown, Ferdinand only grinned and added to the plates a water jug or two. Pond sighed and gave up. The plates and the jugs would take care of themselves. Or not. There were certainly enough to go around, even if a few ended up in pieces.

But it wasn't Ferdinand who broke one. It was Pond. She had placed an armful of oyster stew bowls on the counter, and was backing away with care when one tilted and fell, and shattered in an instant into more shards than Pond had known a single bowl could produce. Each shard glittered and glinted, its points and sides edged and keen, its fragments still following and carrying the curve of the bowl.

"It's even more beautiful that way than it was before," Pond noted.

"I can make more," Gruenbaum said, holding up another oyster stew bowl.

She put her hand up to stop him, and then saw he was joking. "One's enough. But look at it."

"Just don't step on it," Nareen said, sweeping up the pieces.

"Thanks," Pond said automatically. "I've never broken a dish before."

"Oh yes, you have," her mother said. "You were nineteen months old, and you refused to eat raw beets. You threw the bowl up above your head and it landed on the table's edge and broke in your lap, and the beets were so dark red it wasn't clear to me whether you were bleeding or not."

"No wonder I don't like beets." Pond made a face.

"You haven't had my roasted beet and fennel salad," Nareen said.

"Don't you ever want to stay anywhere longer

than a week?" Pond asked her, and then put her hand over her mouth. What had she said? Pond herself never wanted to stay anywhere longer than a week.

"Not yet," Nareen replied, and her expression made it clear she wanted to believe she spoke the truth.

***

In a happy post-eating blur, all the dishes were done and the plates put away, which was something like playing hide and seek. Since none of the items appeared to go anywhere in particular, you just had to find a place to tuck them away, and hope you would be able to find them again when you wanted.

And with these beautiful, precious pieces, every place was suitable, and none. You could match up articles by color, or shape, or size, by country, or century, and all of the pairings made sense, and none of them did. These dishes could never be arranged the same way twice—not on the scullery shelves, and not on the table. It would drive a neat person crazy, but for anyone who loved profusions of light and color, it was like playing with finger paints, only more solid.

After all the lights in the kitchen had been turned off, Pond noticed the electricity had come on sometime during the day when she hadn't been looking. She felt like she had been watching water, waiting for it to boil, and only after she had turned away and forgotten she had meant to make tea, the pot had come to a rolling bubbling readiness. It was that way with the electricity. In the middle of the night, it seemed both impossible and unreasonable for power not to be there. Flip a switch and the current was meant to flow. Light on demand. And in all the darkness of mid-night, being awaked from deep sleep, light's absence seemed unbearable.

Now that she noticed it, looking around the living room, the light seemed a benediction. All through dinner, their table had been illuminated from above by a gorgeous chandelier that had to be hand-blown glass from Venice. Even in this house, the chandelier was extravagant, but the shine it dispensed was almost palpable. And now the living room was full of soft glowing lamps, each one bright and warm, and each one casting a circle of light so everyone seated in this space was golden and anointed. The light appeared to be liquid, fluid, a stream flowing through their shared space.

"Everything's beautiful." Pond hadn't meant to speak the words aloud. At least she hadn't said every*one* was beautiful, which she had also been thinking.

Luvreen spoke Pond's silent observation. "You know everyone's beautiful because of love," she said, laughing at Pond's expression of protest.

"I've never been less in love in my entire life," Pond said. "There's no one here to whom I feel the slightest bit of romantic attraction. They are fantastic, sure, or at least tolerable, but not in *that* way." She made sure to keep herself from looking at Ferdinand.

"There are lots of ways to love," Luvreen continued, rolling her eyes at Pond. "I love Matilda, for instance. And I know a walrus handler who loves his giant sea beast. Love makes everything beautiful. Even management. That's what has made it so difficult to leave the circus."

"Surely not," Pond said. None of the bosses she had ever worked for had been beautiful. She glanced out of the corner of her eye at Luvreen and all the rest of them gathered here. This *lot, yes,* she was willing to admit it. *Even my mother. Oh, my God, even my mother. But not management.* "Mom," said Pond idly, and then kicked herself for saying it, "are you coming to dinner tomorrow?"

Mrs. Pond shook her head. "Couldn't possibly."

"But that's the circus," Pond heard her mother telling Luvreen before she went. "The world out here is a lot different from the circus."

Luvreen laughed. "You might be surprised," she said.

# Friday

## *Bertram*

Bertram Something-Something stared at his phone. It was too early to call—not even quite nine o'clock in the morning—and yet his finger was itching to jab those numbers. He put one hand over his eyes. *What had he been thinking*, he again asked himself, *allowing Gertrude to set up such a ploy, such a series of ploys?*

He was almost certain she was *not* playing with her grand-niece after all. Pond seemed far too unruffled when he called her up to deliver these absurd codicils. She simply couldn't be the butt of the joke. Instead, he was now almost sure the one Gertrude was playing with was *him*. And he had made a point of not only not playing with life, but not allowing life to play with him.

He had made it almost to fifty without being overly inconvenienced by fun. Fun was what frivolous people engaged in. Serious people had to carry on with the business of the world. The world would stop running, all the planets would fly out of their orbits, if determination and resolve were allowed to crumble.

The clock clicked over to nine that morning, and he opened the file containing today's codicil. He sighed, again taking a deep breath to compensate, and setting off another round of stifled giggles.

*I don't giggle*, he told himself severely, and managed only to laugh out loud. He was still laughing out loud when Pond answered the phone. It was like the winds had begun blowing, and once that happened, good luck to you halting them. He remembered seeing a production of *King Lear*, with the old king bellowing at the storm at the top of his lungs, and you can't outshout a storm, you can't out blow the wind, was Shakespeare's message, at least that was what Bertram had gathered, so he let another gust of laughter rush forth.

The laughter now threatened to burst one of the brass buttons on his dark blue blazer, which set off his broad shoulders and narrow waist to fine advantage, he told himself, since there was no one else in his life to pay him such a compliment.

His eminently discreet secretary chose that exact moment to show Bertram's client into his office, before closing the door with a silent click behind herself. Bertram's secretary effaced herself so effectively that she almost didn't exist, except his practice ran like a quiet, efficient machine due to her invisible grace. The timing couldn't have been more appropriate.

Her arrival provided a sudden, startling impetus to control himself. He nearly choked himself swallowing a last laugh, and waved his right ring finger and pinky in acknowledgement of his guest while she took a seat, her every motion cool, smooth, conveying all the unruffled dignity of a queen. She was so physically small to project such definite power. Her eyes remained steady as she listened to the lawyer's side of the conversation.

"Oh, Mr. Something-Something. I mean, Bertram," Pond said, on the other end of the line. "I recognized you even before you identified yourself. I'd know that laugh anywhere."

Pond was met by a long pause while Bertram considered his options. He could hang up on Pond and deal with his client, the architect of all the ploys, the one who showed herself to be more outrageously alive the more she pretended to be dead. He could continue the conversation and let his client know he would be with her soon. This client showed up at unpredictable moments, the only one who had ever managed to set her own terms and times with the attorney. She simply demanded it as her due.

"One moment," he mouthed to his client, and she nodded, settling herself a little more firmly in her chair. Her feet barely reached the floor, but she carried herself as if she owned the floor along with the office's elegant dark wood paneling, precious carpets, and possibly even its air. For all Bertram knew or could research, she might well—despite whatever his deed and right of possession seemed to say. All legal expertise and protocols failed to contain her.

Bertram did his best to suppress his hypersensitive response to his client's presence. She was way too petite to be so intimidating, way too far away from him to fill his entire awareness with a fragrance both earthly and unearthly at the same time—some sort of tantalizing, maddening flower essence or tree resin. She was way too silent to be making his ears ring, but they were already echoing with a memory of all the words she had inflicted upon him, and anticipation of all the ones still to be inflicted.

Pushing away his fascination and his frustration for the moment, and hoping it was a good idea, Bertram put Pond on speaker phone, so her voice sounded in the room, audible now to his client, too.

"I assume there's a message," Pond prompted him. "We've had so much fun talking every day lately that I wouldn't mind so much if you called just for no reason. But somehow you seem the type to make phone calls only if they are required."

"I'm not laughing," Bertram told Pond, and his client, allowing a note of severity to enter his voice. He wanted to establish the seriousness of this business, while he had an attentive audience. He was drawing an important line. He, at any rate, was not to be toyed with.

"Not at the moment." Pond's voice carried a mocking grin.

"The codicil says," Bertram cleared his throat, "'What you think is far from inconsequential, your thoughts determine what happens to you. Now open the inner sanctum, stand on the four corners of the earth, touch the sky, and prepare to fly.'"

"Oh, dear," Pond retorted with an almost cheerful bitterness. "Perhaps it's a good idea not to think at all. Or maybe what I have to do is think the quest will be easily solved. Today is the day I will figure out all the mysteries of the house, and the universe, and myself, while I'm at it.

"Your latest message makes even less sense than ever. Although the more time I spend in this house, the more I think nothing makes sense. So it's perfectly appropriate those things you read me don't make sense. If they made sense, something would be wrong. They wouldn't go with the house. But then if I think things don't make sense, would that *make* them not make sense? That's what the codicil says. My head is buzzing a bit. Is yours?"

Bertram, for his part, was beginning to get a headache at the idea things didn't have to make sense. With a mournful motion, he plucked at one of his brass buttons, recalling how bright he had felt, putting his blazer on earlier that morning. "Of course everything has to make sense," he said, staring at the codicil, and shooting a sidelong glance at his client, a plea she would help make it so. "It's in plain English. I wrote it. Nothing I write doesn't make sense."

"The *words* make sense," Pond told him, "but their meaning goes beyond what they actually say."

"Of course. That's what words do." He considered denotation, connotation, implication, and application. And that was without even taking into account intonation and inflection. Things could mean lots of things, couldn't they?

A sudden image appeared, with a pathway laid out before him, but it wasn't a single pathway. In every direction, ways branched off, winding and spiraling everywhere. He had been looking for an orderly garden walk, and instead what he was seeing was an image of fractals. There was order within chaos, and then more chaos within order, and if he looked closely enough, order within that. Maybe the planets in their orbits were wobbling drunkenly, and he had only *imagined* they were part of a regular pattern. Maybe he who had forced himself to walk through life in one straight line, not looking to either side, had been the deluded one. He again stared at his client, sending her a silent beseeching appeal for help, and this time she responded.

She waved a small hand at him, as if she were directing an invisible orchestra and he was the cello. He took the line off of speaker phone and placed a hand over the receiver. Since this was the only client ever allowed to interrupt him, he could only manage to work the mute button at odd, random, moments, but on the other end of the line, Pond heard nothing but muffled, distorted sound.

"What the hell," said the client with a sharp grin and an arched eyebrow, "what is that girl's problem? And yours? Goddamn, and tell her not to curse. Cursing's not ladylike. That house is the easiest thing in the world, and she can't get it. I suppose you can't get it, either. Remember to disguise my voice."

Bertram sighed. He stared at this woman, who had to be human, but who right now looked like a laughing angry bird who might take flight at any moment, or peck his eyes out. And she had a mouth on her worse than a bloody sailor. In setting up the house per her instructions, he had had to go to great lengths to mask her saltiness.

He did his best to avoid her eyes, which were piercing, their precise color unidentifiable. What came across was a wild, pure, uncontainable glee and fierceness. This woman had power, and she knew it, but Bertram had never been able to determine the source of her power. It wasn't just money. It went way beyond that. If it hadn't, she wouldn't have been able to walk away from the house and the money, not to mention her life.

Without some sort of extraordinary inner will— or maybe just crazed determination—she wouldn't have been able to hand everything over through such an elaborate and questionable legal scheme, all concocted with the assistance of a lawyer who would as soon laugh as lose his integrity. Now he was laughing, now he was almost certain Gertrude was laughing at *him*, did that indeed confirm he had abandoned integrity forever? He almost groaned at the idea. What was an attorney without integrity? An empty signature stamp.

He pulled himself together and relayed True's message to Pond, moving back onto speaker phone. "Cursing is not required. When you curse, what you say returns back to you." He wondered again if his translation had lost the original's spirit along with its salt.

"Great," Pond said, her voice melting into sarcasm, and added, "you realize that doesn't help at all. I hadn't been cursing before, but maybe a blue streak is quite in order now."

"I'm doing my best," Bertram said, waving his

hands palm up at True in a rolling motion so she would say something more. He toggled the phone off speaker and put his hand over the mouthpiece again. "Come on," he told True. "Help her out."

"Codswallop," pronounced True in a decided tone. "She's the one who's got to figure it out. No one else can do it for her. Next she'll want someone to wipe her bottom." Her eyes told the lawyer the message also applied to him, but he did his best to ignore it. That was one of the drawbacks of having a client who seemed to know things about him she couldn't possibly know. She would let drop the most inconvenient and unwanted observations, which he would then have to exert tremendous effort to forget.

"Dear one," said the lawyer, calling upon his best, most refined translating abilities, "work with yourself. No self-opposition, no self-division."

"I've been working with myself," Pond protested. "This whole shenanigan has made me work with other people. *That's* what I've never done before." She let out a huff of deep self-commiseration.

The lawyer sighed for thirty long seconds and asked himself why and how he had gotten caught in the middle of an impossible conversation, between a living client and a legally dead one. He listened to True's reply and then relayed it to Pond, vowing all the while he had to learn that mute button.

"Might as well give up now," True snorted. "Might as well bury your head in your armpit. Stinks to high heaven, but at least it reminds you you're not dead yet."

"You're fine," the lawyer told Pond, wishing he weren't serving as a relay station between nonsense and sense. Was nonsense contagious, and now he would in turn pass it along to others, in an invisible and ineluctable momentum he could neither help nor stop? "Others are fine. It's all about not minding one way or another. Either way, don't work against yourself, and then you're working for yourself."

As he spoke, his eyes took on a blank glaze, staring at the elegant wood-paneled wall. He didn't understand what he was saying, so how could Pond? But it was his best effort to capture what True might mean, since her instructions were strict: neither her words nor her tone could be captured in these communications. They would serve as a direct reveal.

Pond said nothing, so he again found himself bewildered by both of his clients. In fact, now he considered it, the living one was only a little easier to understand than the legally dead one.

"How are things over at the house?" he asked Pond, taking refuge in more concrete matters, and meaning to be sympathetic, and thinking his client might not mind an update, either. "I don't expect you have been able to find anything, based upon the directions I've been delivering."

"I'm not sure what I've found, or that anything I've found has anything to do with True's directions. But I also don't want to rule out the possibility. I don't know," she said, her voice clear and ringing. "Things here may not be completely terrible. There's a lot of life here. A dog. A man. An elephant."

233

Bertram studied his fingernails and decided to ignore that last part of what she had said, it made so little sense. "What have you found?" he asked, holding his breath while he waited for her reply.

For some odd reason, he found himself hoping Pond would be able to answer his questions, tell him which of those oddly branching paths he should take. He knew Gertrude never answered questions, only asked them. And right now, strangely enough, he was the one who wanted to know: had he been correct or mistaken in looking only straight ahead? Had he eaten enough peaches? *One thing was for certain,* he told himself sternly. *I have delivered more than enough codicils.* He attempted to smooth out his forehead, but the worry lines only took new shapes.

"It's hard to describe," Pond said. "I don't mean to be evasive. Not really. It's just hard to say. Why don't you come see for yourself?" Her voice sounded sincere, in a mocking way. "Do you look the same way you sound over the phone?"

"How do I sound?" Bertram asked, straightening his jacket.

"Well," Pond said, and it sounded like she was equivocating. "If you come to this house, one thing is sure. You will either snap, or you will learn to relax."

*I will not go,* Bertram told himself after hanging up the phone. *Too much to do.* He could possibly dispense with keeping the planets in their orbits, but the moon and the sun also depended upon his maintaining his regular course. *I will* not *go.*

But Gertrude went, vanishing as suddenly from

234

his office as she had arrived in it. *Where did a legally dead person spend her time?* he asked himself, and then resolved not to add to his list of unanswerable questions.

\*\*\*

## *Pond*

Pond stared at the phone. The first conversation they had had, he had supplemented the codicil with statements he called forth from memory, helping clarify—or muddle—things based on what Gertrude had told him. But this time he had seemed distracted. Their dialogue was interrupted again and again by his need to consult something, probably notes, and he was also talking to himself, by the sound of it. He was in two places at once, or his attention was divided in some other way. Pond shrugged and dismissed her observation. Attorneys were one of the things she assured herself she would never understand, and she was to be congratulated for that.

She felt pulled in two directions right now. The codicil had talked again about opening the inner sanctum. Maybe that had something to do with the instructions about thoughts determining what happened to you.

*In which case,* Pond made a wry face, *I am doomed, doomed, before I even began.* Her brief and intermittent attempts to meditate at the ashram had taught her that her mind was a fierce tangle of sensations and desires and memories and impressions and dreams and wants. No sooner would she sit down and watch the breath than a volcano would erupt inside her. All the things she had ever wanted or not wanted came forth, all the things she had to do or not do. If her future in the house depended upon a quiet mind, then the whole quest was over before it had begun.

*But I'm not* that *bad,* another part of Pond's awareness interrupted. *I've been playing nicely with the guests.*

*Now you have to play nicely with yourself,* another inner voice declared. Pond couldn't tell whether it was one she ought to listen to or not. But there it was, saying something very much like what the lawyer had told her. She had to avoid self-division.

*You mean like multiple directions and potentials inside me?* Pond scoffed at herself. *Good luck with that.*

Pond stomped out toward the carriage house. While she had been on the phone with Bertram, Giselle had scampered out of the kitchen after Ferdinand, heading in the direction of the carriage house barn.

Many of those in the house seemed drawn to the elephant. When she reached the carriage house, she found Gruenbaum had slept outside with the elephant without telling anyone.

"I couldn't stop worrying about that little lady," he said. "She's such a cute little flirt. Besides, the house was quiet last night."

Pond frowned. If he had slept outside the house, how had he known the house was quiet? Then her mind skipped into another groove, thinking about flirts. The elephant wasn't a flirt, just a charmer. One house guest *did* qualify as a flirt. Duckie sprang into Pond's inner awareness, her silver hair arranged to a meringue perfection.

Luvreen was also in the carriage house, feeding Matilda. "Come on," she said, "more food for the modest mouse."

*Food*, Pond thought, visions of a lemon meringue dancing in her head. "Let me find Nareen."

"The cook is indispensable," Luvreen said. "It's always that way."

Pond brushed away the thought any person could be described as indispensable to her. "*I'm* Pond," she told herself silently, forming her hands into determined fists of independence.

*** 

And so rather than tracking down Nareen, Pond stalked off to the inner sanctum, only to flee it before she could bring herself to sit down in attempted stillness for even a single moment. She ran instead to the upper third and a half story, where she stared at the newest map of the world. The small map was just as beautiful in its construction and detailing as the larger one, the wooden image just as compelling as the stone corollary in the solarium. Each piece was a work of art, executed with brilliance and precision.

It made Pond almost happy, seeing that people were capable of imagining and creating such a thing, each part of the world nestled into the whole, at once intricate and simple. She pulled over a chair and clambered onto it. The ceiling was low enough here that reaching out her arms at full length she could touch it, and she did so now, stretching her hands across the world's span. With fingers extended, this earth was two of her hands across. To look at, the map had layers and textures, but to touch, it was all one smooth surface. *She's got the whole world in her hands*, Pond said to herself, making a face in protest. *Not that it was doing any good.*

Pond stared at the world. She was sure the next piece of the puzzle was here. Touching the sky had to have something to do with this map. And it had to be the sky lay just on the other side of this ceiling, of this roof, but for now nothing Pond did opened the gateway between the room and the outer world. The earth was separating her from where she thought she had to go.

*I'll get it*, Pond vowed to herself, and then noticed if thoughts determined what happened, that was one she wanted to entertain, for once.

She sighed, and directed her attention back to the map, and didn't register how much time was passing, so absorbed in the world and the sky she didn't know what was going on elsewhere on the property she was beginning to consider hers.

\*\*\*

Pond disappeared all morning. Ferdinand and Giselle tracked her down in True's third and a half story, one of the places in the house where time itself seemed not to enter. The light here was clear and lovely, the air warm and fresh. At the moment, the air was filled with a slight tinge of cedar, and maybe sandalwood. Beyond just the inner sanctum, Gertrude had to have installed some sort of ventilation system throughout the house.

"Beautiful," Ferdinand said, his voice gentle, and Pond's awareness was called back into the rest of the house.

"I can't control what I think," Pond said defensively. "So I might as well open the sky." Not that either one of her statements was showing any results. For the moment, the two parts of the day's codicil seemed to contradict one another, adding to Pond's sense of frustration. Without knowing it, she was becoming more aware of her own state, so she now found herself saying, "But I also don't know how to do it, how to work with myself in that way."

She took refuge in externals. They would have to put the elephant back into action when they discovered the sky they had to touch, anyway. That was more like it: focus on the elephant. That was more familiar. Keeping her attention there felt more like the Pond who had gone at the world with elbows out and limbs akimbo, rushing madly here and there and everywhere. She made a face at herself. "What's going on?"

"Not much. Everything's under control. That is, if you don't mind a little action taking place while you work here."

"How do I know?" Pond asked, bristling. "Do I even want to know?"

"Probably not."

\*\*\*

## *Ferdinand*

"The morning started smoothly," Ferdinand reported. "Everyone ambling around taking care of business. The paint dried on all the monkeys and bears overnight, so first I tucked them away in their storage places. Then Giselle and I danced through the downstairs. We practiced all our steps for the next time we go back on tour. We were moving quicker and lighter than sunlight glinting on waves, baby."

Pond shot him a suspicious look, before she realized he wasn't calling her by any kind of an affectionate name, just being exuberant.

"Gruenbaum clambered up onto the chimney," Ferdinand continued. "He wanted to check the rigging he had strung the day before. I saw him testing the pulleys, and they were still in place. You can barely see them, even if you know they are there. He used the wire I found in the attic alongside Gertrude's menagerie of monkeys and bears, and it's holding strong, probably durable enough to carry much more weight than it did yesterday.

"Nareen sat down and read her book for a while, after she did the morning dishes. But when I saw her a little later, she was closing its pages and shaking her head. She said she couldn't tell if what it was describing had already happened, or was going to happen. When it came to that book, she said time was bendable and fluid, and sometimes when she read, time became bendable and fluid for her. She said she had memories she wasn't sure had happened yet, and she didn't always know if she had dreamed or read them, or seen them in another state that was still coming into view. She's an interesting one. You've collected a whole house full of interesting ones."

"Speaking of which," Pond snorted, tilting her head in his direction.

"Duckie got herself into a fuss," Ferdinand said, ignoring Pond's comment, "and said the jewelry didn't have to tell her anything at all, didn't have to have a code for her to undo. The jewelry could sparkle and shine, could glint and glimmer, and that would be enough. It could continue being an offense against good taste, and that could be tolerated.

"She said it was becoming clear to her the jewels had the same pattern the dishes did, and everything else in this place. It meant what you wanted it to say. It was like the pieces of a language had been laid out in all different forms. Some were precious metals and stones. Some were valuable plates and stemware, china and crystal. Some were contraptions she didn't care to encounter. But it all added up to a grammar, containing its own magic. 'Maybe it's about us,' she told me, 'what we say through them, how we arrange them, how we use them.' And then she went home."

"Really? She went home? That's the first surprising thing you've said to me all day."

Ferdinand's face lit up with laughter.

\*\*\*

## *Luvreen*

Meanwhile, that morning Luvreen had been hanging out with Matilda, watching the modest mouse enjoy a dirt bath. The carriage house floor hadn't been quite dirty enough to satisfy a pachyderm's grooming needs. So Luvreen had carried in a few shovelfuls of soil from the garden, and now Matilda was calling out delicate approval and rubbing dirt over herself gleefully. And then Matilda's calls turned more to snorts and rumbles, and Luvreen became aware she and the elephant had company.

The engagement had begun mildly enough. The two circus clowns, or circus police, had returned in disguise. They pretended to be a delivery service, showing up with a bushel or two of paper whites. Their mission was complicated by their unmistakable girth, which bulged out over the fake uniforms. The uniforms were borrowed from a clown costume trailer, so they added a note of unintentional humor to the act.

"Here's a package," said one of the delivery clowns to Matilda, forgetting to address Luvreen, the human, who would have to sign for the box.

"Didn't order anything," Luvreen said, drawing the man's gaze to her. "What's in the box?"

"Paper whites."

"Flower bulbs," Luvreen said slowly. "Matilda might be able to eat those. Usually they bloom in the middle of the winter on people's windowsills inside their houses. You're a bit off with your timing."

"He didn't tell me it was flower bulbs," said the first clown. "He told me it was an elephant catcher. Bait." Then he realized what he had said and put his hand over his mouth.

"No problem," Luvreen said, grinning. "Whatever's in the box, I think you'll find it doesn't quite work the way you'd like." And she called to Matilda with a clicking sound she'd perfected, one that would be quite hard for anyone else to duplicate.

Matilda came to Luvreen and the two of them began moving, in a pattern both mesmerizing and potentially deadly to slow-moving delivery men. The elephant's feet shuffled and slid and tapped along, in enormous graceful waves.

One man stared at the hooves, another man at the trunk, which Matilda was wielding in sinuous billows, making it seem like an entire ocean of elephant was moving inexorably toward them. The first delivery man dropped the box and began to run backward, tripping over his own feet as he scrambled. The second one's eyes grew large, and he froze in place, until the tip of Matilda's trunk brushed up against his neck, and he yelped and melted into a slick of fear, a fluid dark streak. He scarpered away after his friend, but not before his foot caught on the box they had dutifully delivered. And he tripped as he ran, and tore the box slightly, bringing it within Matilda's orbit.

She stepped upon the cardboard, her movement light and graceful, almost gentle, and the container crushed, allowing round white flower bulbs to scatter forth, a small flood of them. Matilda paused long enough to sniff at the bulbs, and decided not to eat them for the moment.

She scooped up several and tossed them at the fleeing clowns, who must have remembered the monkeys and bears of yesterday, and thought they were being attacked by flying hordes of animals, and not just a lone elephant. Either that, or the roof was flinging itself at them in its fury at their insolent trespass.

At that point, as the men scrambled away in a flurry of paper white bulbs, Murchison drove through the back gate with a circus truck. He backed it in so the loading gate was toward the elephant, and he had already opened the door for ease of stowing a small large animal.

From Luvreen's vantage point it was clear: all he had to do was put the truck in place, set the emergency brake, lower the ramp, and scoot the elephant up into its interior. And the elephant would be imprisoned.

But the timing wasn't quite right, so he was still maneuvering the truck backward when his assistants were running toward him. Luvreen caught a glimpse of his face in the rearview mirror. He must have seen his assistants flailing in the mirror and been inspired to stop too soon, and without setting the brake or putting the truck in gear.

He ran around to pull out the ramp. The ramp mechanism must have been well greased, as it unrolled with ease, making no sound. But no sooner had he unrolled the ramp than it was occupied—and not by the desired elephant, but by his incompetent assistants.

"Fools!" he shouted, as they ran to hide in the interior of the truck. They must have wanted to believe they were making themselves safe. Instead, they made themselves a perfect target through the open truck door, with nowhere to run and hide.

More showers of paper whites poured down upon them. As soon as the bulbs began raining down upon Murchison, he fled into the interior of the truck as well, hugging the walls at the end of the truck nearest the cab, with nowhere else to go.

Luvreen grinned, rolled up the ramp, rolled down the door, and was looking about for a means of securing the latch, when the men inside began thumping and calling for help. Luvreen sighed, just as Gruenbaum arrived on the scene. "They wanted to put Matilda in there," Luvreen explained. "But they ended up in their own trap."

"Good," Gruenbaum grunted. "Serves 'em right." Then he paused to listen to the thumping. "You don't actually want those three to hang around, do you?"

Luvreen shook her head. From the way she was twitching her trunk, showing mild agitation, Matilda didn't like the noise they were making, and truth be told, neither did she.

"I'll drive the truck." Gruenbaum went to take the wheel, but before he could get into the cab, the truck began rolling. The rocking protests of the three occupants had set things in motion, again a bit too soon.

"Hey," he yelped, but the truck was moving, and

he couldn't get into the cab in time to stop it.

The driveway here was on a slight incline down to the back gate, and at first Luvreen figured, watching and running behind the truck as it rolled down the hill, that it was on a trajectory to be able to negotiate the gate, slotting itself straight through the only open space available to it. Of course, beyond that was another neighbor's garage, and that could get messy.

But instead, the truck hit a slight bump, and turned to the left, and picked up just enough speed to launch itself squarely into the wall that divided True's property from Duckie's. It was a beautiful old stone wall, and the truck had such momentum its front wheels made it over the wall, crushing it in the process, and then lodged itself in full straddle fashion, middle of the truck body pinned securely on the wall, so the vehicle could move neither forward nor backward.

Luvreen stopped mid-stride and shook her righteous fist. "Wish they'd kept going."

By now, the thumping racket had called Duckie out of the house, and she said, "They're not going to move anywhere in particular, are they?" She looked at the wall with a critical eye. "I can set my stone masons to work on that in no time. I've got a small army of them. Don't really want to take them away from their basement duties, but sometimes a great cause requires shifting resources around. Having them fix the wall won't inconvenience my husband nearly to the same degree. I'll have to come up with some other tender attention to lavish upon him."

Luvreen batted her eyelashes. "Elephants are

much easier to understand than men. Or women. What are we going to do with them?" Luvreen asked, of no one in particular.

"Let them go," Nareen said, appearing out of nowhere and taking in the situation. "You don't want them here, do you? The thumping alone is aggravating enough."

Luvreen sighed and shook her head. She didn't want them coming back, either, unless it was to talk terms. She went to the back of the truck and opened it.

Murchison poked his head out into the sunlight, kneeling down a bit to do so, and his expression was even more sour than usual. "Runaway truck," he said. "Runaway elephant and trainer. What *isn't* running away?"

"Not you," said Luvreen, with as much patience as she could muster. "You three had better run away quickly until you can return and talk nicely. Talking nicely does *not* include stealing elephants. It also doesn't include fake flower deliveries."

"Those were real paper whites," Murchison said with justifiable pride. "I don't like to let on, but I am *something* of a gardener. I've got my own circus trailer, and all winter long, paper whites bloom on every available surface. That was a serious sacrifice I made this morning. Now I have to collect an entire new set of bulbs, and the new ones won't be able to come from every stop we made all the rest of the year, as *these* did. But without replacement bulbs, my trailer will be completely barren all winter long." He groaned.

"I know just what you mean," Duckie chirped.

"A winter without flowers cannot be tolerated."

Luvreen glared at Duckie, and Duckie blinked and seemed to realize she was being wanton with her sympathy, spreading it all around to those who didn't deserve it, at least from the perspective of the elephant's rightful champion.

"And now I have to *walk* back to the circus," Murchison said. "I thought we would be returning in triumph, bearing an elephant. And now we don't have the elephant or the truck. The circus needs that truck. Have to have it to move on to the next show. Either that, or they'll have to leave something behind. Like *me*, probably. I'm not going to stand for it. I'll be back," he said, his voice heavy and threatening.

"You'll see me again when I come to collect the elephant and the truck," he promised Luvreen. "Come on," he growled at his delivery clowns. "We've got work to do." Then he looked at all the bulbs strewn around. It appeared to Luvreen very much like he wiped a single angry tear away from the corner of one eye.

\*\*\*

## Pond

"So now the back driveway's blocked with half a truck," Ferdinand reported. "Duckie's already got men working on the wall. They ought to be able to set things right, let us be able to drive in and out that way again."

Gruenbaum liked to go on runs to the various

stores, picking up food for humans and animals, paint supplies, whatever else the household needed. He had told Pond it was most convenient to pull right up to the back door, through the back drive. Soon enough he would be able to resume his supply trips.

"While you all were mucking up the wall, *I* was trying to solve the whole earth problem," Pond said, with growing testiness.

She, who didn't want to consider anyone else indispensable to her, didn't mind thinking she was indispensable to everyone else. And all this drama had gone on without her. At least the others had taken care of the elephant. Now if only she could figure out this blasted earth and sky business. Not to mention her own thoughts.

"I don't know what to think about anything," she said aloud. No, that wasn't really true. "I know what I think. I just don't know if what I think is helpful. We have to touch the sky," she said, grimacing to show she wasn't much of a cheerleader. "Besides, those men will be back. We need to protect that elephant."

"We'll be ready for them," Ferdinand promised. "They're in for a show."

"Tell me it doesn't involve a snake charmer."

Ferdinand threw back his head and laughed. "Giselle's afraid of snakes."

\*\*\*

After lunch, Pond investigated the stone wall. The men working on the masonry had cleared away

249

the wall to either side of the truck, and laid the stones in neat piles, so it now looked like the wall had gotten tired of being laid out in a straight line, and had gone leaping and bounding away into assorted dotted lines.

The current formations reminded Pond of the *I Ching*. She would have to pay it a visit, see if it made any more or less sense after her lack of success in confronting the world that morning.

Duckie was supervising the workers. "I can't decide which of them is handsomer," she confided to Pond in a quiet voice.

"Mmmm," Pond said, indifferent.

"Maybe they're all equally good looking. They look so different, of course, but that's part of the picture they make." She stood on one side of the workers, and Pond caught that Duckie was pretending not to be staring, and the men were pretending not to notice that Duckie couldn't tear her eyes away from their rippling shoulders. "Beautiful, isn't it?" Duckie asked Pond.

"The stones they are laying are gorgeous," Pond said, her voice pointed.

Duckie sighed and didn't bother correcting her host. "Why don't we have them rebuild the entire wall?" she suggested brightly. "If we only rebuild part of it, the new part will stick out and be very awkward. It's like painting a house. If you refresh one wing, you might as well do all the rest. I've learned many things over my years of home maintenance, including how to draw out projects as long as possible. Especially the more picturesque ones." She sighed with joy.

"Fine," Pond said, not paying much attention.

"I can't imagine a better morning. I get to admire bodies in motion. It's poetry! It's art! Now I just have to come up with another way to favor my husband. If the foundation is no longer being reinforced because the stone masons have to work out here, under my watchful eye, what else can I do to brighten his day?"

"I'm sure you'll manage somehow," Pond said. "Preserve us all from such thoughtfulness."

Duckie gave her a hurt, innocent-little-girl look and then turned back to admire the workers.

\*\*\*

## Gruenbaum

Gruenbaum went back to his room, looking for his wallet, wanting to be ready to go on a supply run when it was possible. Murchison was far from being his favorite, intruding upon that well-mannered elephant. *Trouble with people*, grunted Gruenbaum to himself, *was they had no* manners. They might well benefit from the little lady's example. Never had he seen such an appealing, communicative nose.

And then he grabbed his wallet and froze in place, a chill running down his spine.

While he had been rescuing elephants, someone had paid his room a visit. A note now lay under his wallet. He took a deep breath and studied what he was being told, but the words didn't sink in.

Whoever had delivered this note had been into

this room while he wasn't here. Whoever had delivered this note *might still be in the room*. He whipped his head around in all directions. No sight or sound of anything. Nonetheless, he crouched and looked under the bed. He checked the closets. The messenger was gone. But not the message.

He sat down on the edge of the bed and told his heart to stop booming in his ears. His heart obeyed, and its sound quieted, but compensated by thudding along ever faster. He gave up and decided to ignore his inconvenient heart for the moment. The problem was, the note couldn't have been written by anyone in the house. He had ascertained that much by observing everyone over the course of the week.

The note read:

**STERLING, DON'T BE SO QUICK TO CONSIGN ME TO DEATH. WHAT MAKES YOU THINK I'M NOT MORE ALIVE THAN EVER BEFORE?**

So who had written the note to him, and who had delivered it, and what was he supposed to do now?

\*\*\*

Life did not become any easier for Gruenbaum when he gathered himself together enough to make it back down to the kitchen, ready to ask Nareen for a grocery list. He told himself he was proceeding in a way that wouldn't attract notice. But that damn girl was too suspicious.

At the same time she handed him a list, she said, "Thanks for getting all the food for the house every day. Not to mention all the paint supplies. And the elephant's vegetables. How very nice of you to do so." She shot Pond a momentous look to make sure Pond was listening, "Especially when you're not taking any money from the house to pay for it."

Gruenbaum swallowed and congratulated himself on being so weathered, so grim, so *old* he was sure no one could tell exactly what he was thinking or feeling. "No problem," he said, keeping his tone light, patting his pocket. "Put it on the plastic."

Pond stared at Gruenbaum. "You don't look any more like the credit card type than I do. You're saving the receipts? I suppose I can reimburse you from the house money roll, although that's more work. I gave Nareen a money roll for a reason—so I don't have to handle it myself."

Gruenbaum had adopted an aggrieved air that could not hide a tinge of embarrassment. Of course he hadn't thought to save receipts, being so unaccustomed to the way this magic plastic worked. He had waved the card at all the stores, pleased and delighted to be able to buy anything, anything at all, and to not have to think about bills, for the first time in his life. And by his doing so, Pond was also not thinking about bills.

"Thought I was doing you a favor," he told Pond, glaring at Nareen. He knew that girl was going to be annoying, from the first time he saw her. And now she was more than fulfilling his expectations.

He waited for Pond to say something more, and she didn't, and so he trudged out the back, waiting for the workers to clear the way, so he could hightail it out of there. Of course, he would have to return, not in triumph, but bearing boxes and bags and crates of supplies, and the whole time he would be wondering how much that girl knew, and how much Pond suspected.

How could he get in trouble for doing something nice? How was it fair his generosity would be suspected, when the part of his actions that deserved scrutiny had so far evaded attention?

*Must mean I'm a miserable failure. They have no idea I'm the ghost in the house. They think I'm an ass backward benefactor.*

He sighed, and decided to buy Matilda a kohlrabi out of his own pocket. He had always liked kohlrabi, and he thought the elephant might, too. At least *she* wasn't looking at him like he had two heads.

* * *

Gruenbaum got back with his load of elephant vegetables, not to mention a few additional artistic supplies for Ferdinand, and a long list of obscure spices, condiments, and ingredients for Nareen, which he had never heard of and had to ask again and again for help in finding. He loaded everything into the kitchen, saw no sign of Pond or Nareen, and shrugged his shoulders. He went through all the bags and boxes, cartons and crates, taking the perishable items, as far as he could identify them, and placing them in the refrigerator.

The upstairs refrigerator was almost full already,

so he ended up carrying several armfuls down to the basement cooling unit. He placed the goods on the shelves, straightened his back to relieve it from the loads he had been carrying, and decided a little daytime noise would not be amiss.

He looked around the basement. All still, all silent. He walked over to the far corner, the one hidden in shadows, and where all the pipes of the house converged, branching off from this central entry point. He reached out for the lever, the one he had only to turn in order to set a noise, and he gripped the handle, noting how familiar its heft was becoming in his hand, and turned it. And unlike the last time he had produced the noise, there was no delay this time: the noise rocketed forth, broadcast throughout the house by all the pipes, traveling forth in rolling, sounding, booming waves.

He grinned with satisfaction. He wasn't doing anything wrong, he told himself. A little friendly noise never hurt anyone.

But he heard a definite step behind him, and turned around hastily, and saw Pond staring at him, her face blank. That was the worst of it, he couldn't see if she were angry or sad or disappointed. He couldn't see anything at all in her. She wasn't letting anything show. Her face had gradually become more open, to Gruenbaum and to all of them, and now a shutter had closed over it, shut tight, so her eyes and her skin appeared to belong to someone else, not to the Pond he knew, or was beginning to know, but to a stranger.

Pond's expression made him feel again like he didn't belong, here or anywhere—a feeling he was long accustomed to, and had begun to shed. And now it was back again, the sense of drifting, of not being quite connected to anyone or anywhere else.

*That is fine*, he told himself. *Not a problem.* He was tough. He could deal with it. The pay his other employer offered was too good, the opportunity too great, to pass up. It didn't matter if Pond had found out.

Then he caught a glimpse of Nareen farther away in the basement, and he knew she had set him up. *Fair enough*, one part of him said. He might well have done the same, if things were reversed. She was smart, that was for sure. If she had just accused him, he could have accused her right back. She had instead shown Pond what was going on, so Pond saw it for herself. Now there was no denying it. He shrugged. He would still get paid, and the pay was still good.

Pond told Nareen to get the others. And while Nareen vanished silently up the stairs, Pond continued staring at Gruenbaum, until he withdrew within himself to avoid her gaze.

Then he noticed she might as well have been looking at a blank wall, as if he were as unimportant to her as rock. When she did switch her glance from the fieldstone walls to him, nothing changed. No flicker of recognition went his way. No relief. It was sheer unremitting emptiness.

\*\*\*

## *Pond*

It took time for the others to gather while Pond waited. Luvreen hadn't wanted to leave the elephant. Duckie hadn't wanted to leave the stone masons. Ferdinand couldn't get Giselle down the basement stairs. She balked, and he didn't want to force her, so he left her up in the kitchen, even though he didn't like to do so. She lay on the floor with her head on her paws, staring down into the cellar dimness after him.

When she had gathered them all, and they had all clambered down the basement steps in Nareen's wake, Pond walked over to the lever, which she had shut off after catching Gruenbaum in the act.

"Look what I found," she told the others. She placed her hand on the lever, and pulled it dramatically. The banging commenced. She placed the lever back in line, hidden along the pipe, so you wouldn't even know to look for it. "He was in the act."

Ferdinand nodded, with an air that looked like appreciation. "I thought some of the people in this house might have more up their sleeves than they've shown. So you're the ghost," he told Gruenbaum. "I've had to play at many things in the various circuses and non-circuses where I've performed. I don't judge, at least not usually. People often have a reason for what they do."

"There's a ghost?" Duckie asked, her face bright, grinning at Gruenbaum.

"He's the noisemaker," Pond barked, suddenly very tired, tired in her bones, tired in a way she

257

hadn't been since she had been sleeping in this house, she now realized. "He's the one been waking us up at night, banging around."

"Oh," Duckie said, making her mouth and eyes very round. She looked again at Gruenbaum. "Why did you do that?"

Pond hadn't thought to ask, and wanted to brush Duckie away impatiently.

"It was a job," Gruenbaum said. "I needed the work."

"*I* was paying you," Pond burst out sharply. "I *told* you to take all the money you wanted from the money roll."

"Someone else was paying me first," Gruenbaum explained. "That's what gave me the idea to come to this house. I wouldn't have thought to leave Arkansas otherwise."

"But your mother," Pond said blankly.

"That's another reason why I was glad to come. But without the job…"

"Who are you working for?" Ferdinand asked.

Gruenbaum twisted his lips. "I don't know. I got a letter in the mail, outlining the work, telling me where to go, giving me a credit card with access to unlimited funds. That's why I didn't pay for groceries out of the money you carried," he told Nareen, but he was looking at Pond the whole time, and she could tell he wanted to explain himself to her.

She closed her eyes. She didn't know what to think, that's why her face was blank. She felt equal impulses to erupt in laughter and tears and rage. "What fun you must have been having, amusing yourself by scaring us."

"You weren't really scared," he said, his whole face and body looking lame, like he had lost the ability to set them in motion.

It was the truth, but for an instant Pond felt a rush of foolishness, of shame. Someone she had thought was on her side had been working against her, or at least for someone else.

"So what," she said, her face cold and dismissive. "Doesn't mean I want you running around my house banging on pipes. It's an odd way to amuse someone else, if you're not doing it to amuse yourself."

She had *known* the house wasn't haunted, and every unaccounted for noise, or smell, or sight could be accounted for with ease. She just hadn't expected such a dreary explanation. "Well, you can't stay in the house," she announced in a decided tone.

"I didn't expect *that*. You can't just toss me out. Why would you do that? I have to be here."

"Because your boss is telling you to," Pond said. "Too bad. You'll have to go find someone else to work for."

"I can't. I have to stay. There's the elephant to help take care of, and the whole earth up in the third and a half story. There's an added mystery too."

But Pond wasn't hearing every word he said. "Not that you're going to be any good if you stay here. You've been betraying us. Not just waking us all up. We might as well have been your enemies, for how you've been treating us."

"That's not it," he said. "I've been helping you

every way possible. I'm speaking the truth. I can see why you wouldn't believe me, since I'm the one who's been making noise. I was making noise, but that wasn't important. That was just a job. The whole time my true work was to help you and your house."

"While also taking care of your *real* employer."

"Come on," Gruenbaum pleaded. "I didn't cause any harm. I wouldn't have accepted the job if it caused any harm."

"You're a gentleman," Duckie said, and she sounded like she meant it. "I believe you. He's way too graceful and gray for me to disbelieve him," she told Pond. "He can bang around all he wants, and I won't mind. I don't see why you do."

"He helped a lot with the monkeys and the bears," Ferdinand said. "I have a commitment to give credit where credit is due. He was a major player."

"Behind the scenes," Gruenbaum said.

"He helped a lot with the household supplies," Nareen said, surprising Pond.

She hadn't expected Gruenbaum would find support from Nareen of all people.

"Are you telling me not to kick him out?" Pond snapped at everyone, in disbelief.

No one replied.

"Okay, so he's gone," Pond pronounced his sentence. She gestured with her thumb over her shoulder. "Out of here."

"You don't understand," Gruenbaum defended himself. "Something is really going on in this house. I was hired to make it *seem* like something was going on, but now something is actually happening."

"The elephant catchers," Pond said, with all the ample sarcasm she could muster.

"No, worse than that. I mean, I don't know how bad the elephant catchers will get. But there's an actual ghost in the house. Someone delivered another message to me, the same kind of message that brought me here in the first place. This one was delivered this morning. To my bedroom. That means the ghost is in the house. For real."

"There aren't any ghosts," Pond sniffed with utter disdain. "We've just proved that. So a messenger delivered a note." She looked around at all the faces of those gathered in the basement.

None looked back at her suspiciously, but who was to know? Gruenbaum hadn't seemed worthy of extra scrutiny, and he had been a double agent all along. "Maybe one of these people." A slight shiver went down her spine as she said it. She didn't want them *all* to be working against her, for some invisible outside employer.

"No. It couldn't have been anyone here, because we were all helping take care of the elephant. *Except you*," he said, looking at Pond. "But I know you couldn't have been the delivery person."

"That's true," Ferdinand said. "We all were outside. Did you hear anything while you were upstairs?"

Pond thought back, then shook her head. No sight, no sound, no sign of anyone or anything. Maybe she *had* learned how to focus on what she was doing, despite herself. Or maybe something had happened, and she had missed what was most crucial.

"But I still don't see why you're convinced it's a ghost," she told Gruenbaum impatiently. He sounded like he meant what he said, and the suggestion of an actual ghost merely added to her discontent. "So someone else came into the house while everyone was outside *elephanting* around."

Gruenbaum shook his head, and his eyes showed real fear. "The note calls me by the name only my mother used. No one else knows that name."

"So your mother wrote the note!" Duckie exclaimed with glee.

Gruenbaum's fear intensified visibly.

"His mother's in the ground," Pond reminded Duckie. She managed to muster a bitter grin. "That's strange. What name?"

He coughed. "Sterling."

"The name you aren't living up to. What a shame. Well, Sterling, or Gruenbaum, or whoever you are, this is goodbye."

"For now," Gruenbaum said. "You're really going to send me into exile? I can't leave this house. I have to figure out what's going on, how my mother is writing me notes. Has my *mother* been my employer all along? She's a very determined woman, a very strong one. But how would she have gotten a credit card from beyond the grave? I've never had a credit card before, so I don't know. Do they give these out to dead people now?"

Pond stared, her eyes cold. She wanted to laugh, and she didn't know why. Was it hilarity or hysteria?

"Good luck to you," Gruenbaum muttered. "Finding that note in my room may well mean it's safer outside this house than in. I'll just go visit the little lady," he said, his voice gruff.

Pond pretended like she hadn't heard him. She pushed away his words.

\*\*\*

After everyone disbanded in Gruenbaum's wake, Pond stalked up to the solarium and stared at the map of the earth. They could open the wall of glass, walk Matilda in here, get her to again stand on the four corners, joined by four humans—Nareen, Duckie, Luvreen, and Ferdinand.

Then Pond could go upstairs and figure out how to open the sky, after which flying might be a simple matter.

Pond hoped her face didn't look the way she felt.

Ferdinand followed her into the solarium, his demeanor expressing a clear desire to be helpful.

Pond scowled at him. When she had first opened the door to him, she hadn't noticed how many questions she could have asked him. Why had he been living there?

"I suppose you have some horrible and obscure motive about coming to this house," Pond concluded, her voice drenched with bitterness. "What are you doing here?"

Ferdinand grinned, his face warm and open and bright. "I did live here. But you're right, that's not the only reason I came back. A year ago, I visited this house."

Pond felt a shiver go down her spine. She didn't like to think of the other reason that might have brought him back. All these things she hadn't known she didn't know about her guests. "At least you knew True," she said hopefully.

"I don't know if anyone really *knew* True. But I met her, and she helped me. I mentioned it to you before." He patted Giselle's head, and blinked away sudden tears. "Giselle could barely walk at that point. She was only a year old, but her hips were going out. I didn't have any money. I would have had to put her to sleep. Gertrude paid for Giselle to have surgery, and then for twelve weeks of rehab."

Now Pond wanted to give way to tears of relief. The dog had received an extended lease on life, not to mention entire months of therapy, thanks to her crazy old aunt. "And you lived here during the meantime."

Ferdinand nodded.

"So you may know this place better than anyone," Pond decided. "And True. You have to help open the sky." *After that, we can figure out flying.*

"I came back to pay my debt. If True's not here, I'll still help any way possible."

Pond looked at Giselle. She was glad the dog could walk. In fact, the dog could amble and stroll, sit and stand with ease, which made Pond happy to be able to move her own legs. She had never thought much about walking before, how good it was to stride through the house or run up and down the stairs. Being able to do so would make it that much easier to solve the sky.

"Help me open the sky," she told Ferdinand. "Otherwise I might take an axe to it." And she didn't really want to destroy something so beautiful, just convince it to open.

"I'm your partner for sky opening," he said, bowing his head, "Giselle and I."

\*\*\*

Pond and Ferdinand rounded up everyone else, including Nareen and Duckie. They had to pull Nareen away from the kitchen and Duckie away from the jewels, and Luvreen away from the elephant. When they went out to the barn to find Luvreen, they noticed Gruenbaum in the far side of the barn. He made a motion as if to indicate he would soon be on his way out of the carriage house, but didn't say a word.

"We have to figure out the sky," Pond announced. "And then we know Matilda will help us again by stepping on all four corners of the earth."

"See about that," Luvreen muttered, but she smirked and winked as she spoke, so Pond told herself Luvreen was only teasing.

"Check all the ceilings," Pond told everyone. "It might not be the map of the world we have to figure out. Check other possible skyways, too. Don't be shy. Bang on ceilings with broomsticks or whatever it takes."

And so everyone grabbed some sort of implement—a yardstick, a mop, a broom, a rake—and went roaming throughout the house. The ceilings offered interesting designs and patterns, some of them pressed tin, with gorgeous patterns, some of them exposed wooden beams, some painted with trompe l'oeil murals, but none of them appeared to be anything other than a ceiling. And yet the directions promised it was possible to touch the sky.

Not everyone was equally enthusiastic about banging overhead with long-handled implements.

"The sky's the sky," Pond moped, after some time, "and the ceiling's the ceiling." She had gone from room to room on the second floor, and not found anything. Everything was steady and quiet, unobjectionable and functional as an overhead surface. Some of them were even immensely beautiful. But none appeared to be anything other than what they were.

She sighed and checked in with everyone else. No one else had discovered anything of note, either, on the ceilings they had been examining.

Nareen and Duckie had worked methodically through the ground floor. Duckie reported to Pond she had developed a crick in her neck after one room, and Nareen took over doing most of the work.

"I didn't mind," Nareen said. "I like helping." She looked shy, and as if she felt her position in the house to be less secure than before Gruenbaum had been caught serving as chief noisemaker.

She'd seen Pond staring dubiously at all of them now—even Nareen, the good cook, the one who had noticed the noisemaker and waited until the right moment to reveal his malfeasance. And yet Pond was still rumbling with general dissatisfaction, and even Nareen was not immune from it.

"I don't like to start over mid-week," Nareen told Pond. "Without knowing where my mother is, it's quite difficult to gain entry to another house."

"You'll be fine," Duckie murmured, her voice so vague Pond wasn't sure if she had heard what Nareen had said.

"Stay with it," Pond said.

"The ceilings are only ceilings," Nareen said. "But maybe I can come across a story that will turn them into sky, roll them back and show the constellations wheeling above all the ceilings. Those constellations light up the night, but they're present even during the day. Orion's belt, the hunter's dog who is always accompanying him, Cassiopeia seated on a throne, and Pegasus leaping the heavens."

Pond shrugged. She was more into eating than astronomy.

"Fine," Nareen said. "Ceilings it is," and she resumed tapping on them.

Pond found Luvreen on floor three, wandering through the rooms, almost too large to be contained, even by such an ample house. "I feel like an Amazon," she told Pond. "Give me a barn or a circus tent any time. I bang on these ceilings and small showers of dust trickle down, so every time I have to pull back and restrain myself. Makes me want to yodel or yelp or something. Don't want to get plaster dust on beds and other furniture. Don't want to be confined in this house, either."

"Thanks for your help," Pond said, wowed by

Luvreen's size and energy.

"I'm going to find that sky if it's the last thing I do. Sky's the limit," she told Pond. "These ceilings are just temporary. Just barriers." She frowned, her eyes thoughtful.

Pond found Ferdinand and Giselle had gone to the top story and were lying on their backs staring at the wooden patterns. The ceiling here looked like an unfolded fan, opening out from the earth.

"What would it look like if the fan folded in on itself? Something that opens out could close up again," he told Pond, "which would in turn open the ceiling. So far I can't identify the mechanism, but I am almost certain it involves hidden wheels and pulleys, an elegant orchestration of forces. We just have to see how it can be triggered." He got up and began tapping systematically all the surface areas he could reach. Nothing. No area sounded different than any other.

"I can't identify any hollow spots along the walls," he said, "and they are mostly glass anyway."

He was staring at the floor when Luvreen came up to find him, followed after not too long by Nareen and Duckie.

"We're looking for open sky," Pond told him. She found herself wanting to argue with him as she followed his gaze to the carpet, which was gorgeous hand-dyed, hand-loomed wool.

"Standing place," Ferdinand said. "Sometimes you need to find a standing place, and then it's easier to reach the sky." His face showed a flash of satisfaction.

Pond scowled at him. "My aunt was into the end

of the world," she reminded him. "Something like that, anyway. The lawyer told me she thought everything was changing, and this house had something to do with it. All the old ways fall away, and then the new ones can arise."

"Sure." Ferdinand grinned. "And Baltimore's the perfect place for the apocalypse."

Pond nodded. She could recall manhole covers being rocketed into the sky on downtown streets, erupting from the force of some underground pressure: gas, or water, who knew. All the infrastructure here was crumbling, so the local natural gas utility took for granted they lost a full thirty percent of the gas they transmitted through pipes to heat houses and provide cooking fuel.

All that natural gas in the air, leaking up through storm drains and along sidewalks, leaking through streets and crosswalks, leaking into people's houses, no wonder everyone in Baltimore was quirky. They were all drunk on natural gas—literally intoxicated.

"I have a very serious question, though," she told Ferdinand. "If the end of the world came to Baltimore, how would anyone know?"

Baltimore was not behind the rest of the world, as everyone was so quick to assume; Baltimore was at the forefront, at the vanguard, at the leading edge of the new. The world had already ended, and only Baltimore had survived. Or Baltimore was in constant training for the end, and as a result, all its inhabitants had been prepared, as a way of daily life, to receive revelations.

Anyone who listened could hear angels singing, on all the street corners of the city, twenty-four hours a day. They just didn't sound the way we expect angels to sound like. They were there in the rumble of exhaust and blat of horns and bone-shaking bass beat that rumbles through drivers and cars and travels miles, and in the helicopters hovering over another crime scene, and sirens that fill sky day and night, present here in the same way church bells occupy the atmosphere in some other cities.

Ferdinand threw back his head and laughed. "You have a point," he said.

"You got used to even the apocalypse," Pond said. "Even the end times could become part of your daily routine, what you saw on your way to work, what you bumped into at the grocery store, what you stepped over or around on the sidewalk, what you looked past, everywhere you looked.

"So the lawyer," Pond continued, turning her laugh into a frown. "He almost implied this house might have been rigged. Something here might really be giving way, what's been might be letting go. What's to come might be arriving. All these clues, this whole quest. It's leading up to *something*."

"Be careful what you wish for," Ferdinand said. "You might find the end of the world as we know it."

"That'll be fine." Pond clenched her teeth, and determined to make it so. The world as she knew it was what she had been avoiding for so many years. She didn't mind the world as she was discovering it in this house. She looked at Ferdinand, really looked at him. He had nice eyes.

At that moment, Ferdinand's gaze went again to the floor.

"Sky," Pond chided him.

"I *know*," he told her, kneeling and tapping. "Listen." He tapped a few more times. "Something's odd here. One part of the floor sounds empty, or not solid, while another part thuds as if the wood goes all the way down to the center of the earth."

"Pull back the rug," Nareen said, but Pond had already begun doing so.

She looked up at Nareen, noting her peculiar expression, doubt and anxiety comingling. "It's okay," Pond offered brusquely. "You can help."

"I can still stay here until my mom comes back. I don't know why," she added. "It's odd. I don't like him very much, and I was very angry at him, but I miss Gruenbaum. Maybe I was too quick to point a finger at him."

Pond nodded, not paying much attention to Nareen's words. She was focused on rolling back the rug. The floor had a clear demarcation, one that corresponded to the pattern in the ceiling. In the center of the floor, as in the center of the ceiling, a small earth, two hands' span across, unfurled itself.

"As above, so below," Ferdinand said.

"Sounds like you've attended too many yoga classes for your own good," said Pond, groaning. But secretly she agreed. The correspondences between inner and outer that the *I Ching* was pointing out to her seemed mapped into this house.

The whole world was in this house, in the solarium. The earth and the sky were right here.

"*That*'s what Gertrude's clues mean," Pond exclaimed. "She built everything into her house."

At that moment, the clanging began again, the same clanging that reverberated through all the pipes, through all the nights and days they had been in the house, the same clanging they had just assigned to Gruenbaum as the cause. But he was now out in the carriage house barn.

Luvreen rushed to the window. "I locked the doors. The doors are all locked." She ran down a half-story and looked out a back window, running up to report. "Besides, he's out there with the elephant. He was visible when I looked out the window. He was petting Matilda, and looking like he was in mourning. Matilda was showering him with a few select drops of water. She likes to anoint people. Makes them laugh. Makes her laugh. But Gruenbaum looked like he was missing human company. He looked up at the house, and saw me in the window. I waved, and he waved right back, too eagerly. He misses us."

"Maybe he has a key, and that's where the noise came from," Pond grumbled, not believing her own suggestion.

"Ferdinand, go check him. Search him. See if he has a key." She turned to Nareen and Duckie. "Please go check and make sure all the doors and windows were locked."

Luvreen put her hand on her own impressive hip, watching Pond.

"Let's go down to the basement," Pond suggested to Luvreen, not very enthusiastically. "Let's all meet back in the living room."

\*\*\*

By the time they reconvened in the living room, the mystery had only increased. While Pond and Luvreen were in the basement, standing right in front of the noisemaking pipe, the banging had commenced again. But this time the handle on the pipe was aligned to allow heat to flow and the system to work in silence. The noise was not coming from here. Pond felt its question echoing in her bones. "*We* are not making that racket," she told Luvreen, her expression severe.

Luvreen nodded. "That is one thing you are right about."

Pond sniffed in disdain and reassured herself there weren't any other things she wasn't right about, but her unease only intensified when Ferdinand reported Gruenbaum was free of all keys, and had seemed both mystified and afraid, upon learning the noise was continuing in his absence. "His face got all white," Ferdinand said. "He put his head in his hands and said, 'Oh, Mother.' Of course it's not really his mother," Ferdinand said, and his voice remained confident as he said it.

"Of course it's not," Pond agreed impatiently.

Nareen and Duckie had checked the doors, and all were locked. "How many keys do you have for this house?" Nareen asked Pond. Pond had every key in her patch pockets, and she checked. They hadn't left her possession. An unfamiliar thrill of fear shot through Pond.

"*Something* made that noise." She believed in explanations, in beginnings and ends, in causes and

273

effects. They had only to discover what it was, and they could stop it. "Maybe it wasn't Gruenbaum," she said, her words slowing as she thought aloud. She wasn't willing to invite him back in the house, not yet.

But she was willing to entertain the possibility some other person was in the house. That was the logical account for how a message had made its way into Gruenbaum's room that morning, and how the noise had returned, even in his almost certain absence. "Maybe he came back into the house and back out again without being noticed. Maybe he came through the chimney."

"He's not *so* skinny," Duckie said. "I do like his build. He's so rangy, tall, and strong."

Pond sent her a look of reprimand. "We have to search the house. Let's go together."

And so all five of them, working together and accompanied by Giselle, began in the basement, inspecting every room. They opened all the closets, cabinets, and cupboards, and found nothing. Not until they entered the secret room, the hidden inner sanctum, did Pond again have the feeling someone or something else had just been in the room.

The scent had changed, once again. Now it was jasmine, or something like it—high and fragrant and so delicious she wanted to eat it and wear it at the same time.

"Something has been here," Pond said, announcing what was the truth, even if it didn't make sense to her.

"Whatever it is, we'll find it," Ferdinand said, his voice easy and kind. "There's no reason it has to be scary."

"Really?" Pond was annoyed the explanation was eluding her. And yes, she was frightened something invisible was making itself visible in this house.

For years she had traveled in all sorts of impossible conditions, and had never let herself feel fear. And now a cold shiver flashed down her spine, and she knew there were many things she didn't know or understand. She could search her whole life, and not be able to explore everything.

But now she only had the remnant of seven days, and she had to discover the secret that would unlock this house's mystery. Maybe that one secret would explain everything else. Maybe you could find a key that would lead you to all doors.

*There was nothing to be afraid of after all,* she told herself, straightening her shoulders and swallowing past a knot in her throat in order to resume brash fearlessness, her more habitual stance.

"We'll find it," she promised herself and everyone else in the room. "We'll figure it out."

But for now, no sign, no token, no explanation was in the offing. From room to room they went, looking for truth, and seeing only the steady walls of the house, the beautiful, sturdy floors and ceilings. They observed all the inventions True had acquired that remained inexplicable in their purpose and function and attested if nothing else to human ingenuity and imagination, the need to take disparate elements and make something new and unexpected out of them.

And if what emerged seemed superfluous, it was

part of the game. They might come up with something everyone needed. Or they might not.

\*\*\*

Not until the group had made its way to the top of the house again did Pond think to ask a question that ought to have occurred to her earlier.

"What did the note tell Gruenbaum?" she asked, hitting herself on the forehead with the back of her own hand. "We'll have to ask him." And so they headed back to the carriage house barn, and found Gruenbaum sitting on a bale of hay.

He looked up as if he had been expecting them. "I was just hoping something might bring me back into contact with my friends. If you are my friends." He changed his tone, seeing the look on Pond's face, which wasn't angry but also wasn't welcoming. "Don't worry. Everything's fine. You don't have to be my friend," he said.

"What did the note say?" Pond asked, her voice betraying exhaustion. "The one you found in your room?"

"Crapola. Please don't ask that. It's my secret. You can't just expose it to the light of the world. As long as I'm the only one who knows about the secret, I can pretend everything makes sense, that I'm not insane. If I tell you, you'll know. I've gone off the deep end. Not my idea."

But still, he took a deep breath, dug out his wallet and unfolded a piece of paper, drew the note forth, and handed it to Pond. He clenched his eyes tightly, as if she was going to shriek at him, to accuse him of madness or something worse.

Despite herself, Pond felt a flash of sympathy.

"I don't want you to think of me as someone who gets visited by ghosts," he said. "I didn't ask for it. First time it's happened. I'm not a freak. Don't put me in a sideshow."

Pond stared at the note, which was written in block letters and yet somehow seemed familiar. But she didn't want to read what the words said, didn't want to let her mind register their meaning. It couldn't be that they said what they did.

**STERLING, DO NOT CONSIGN ME TO DEATH SO QUICKLY.**

"That can't be," she said. "That makes it sound like your mom wrote this note."

"I know." Gruenbaum groaned. "That's why it's so terrible. It's not possible, but there you go."

"Well, if it's not possible, then there's some other explanation for it," resolved Pond, determined to clear everything up. "If your mom is dead, then someone else wrote it. I didn't know your name was Sterling, but someone does. Who else knows?"

"That's the thing," Gruenbaum said. "No one. It was the name my mom gave me, and the one she called me, but only she ever called me that name. Even my birth certificate says something else."

Pond felt something electric at the back of her head and brushed at her head to rid herself of the sensation. "Your mom is dead," she said, her voice severe, precise. "So someone else wrote this note. We just have to find whoever it is, and everything will be clear."

Pond was willing to admit the house was strange, that it contained many unexpected devices, not to mention all these unexpected people, but she was not willing to admit the house could be haunted. Houses just *weren't*, in this day and age.

Maybe one hundred years ago, when people lived in shrouds of suspicion and unknowingness, or two hundred years ago, when they thought the simple act of looking at someone's tattoos could transfer those designs to the viewer's unborn children. But that was then, and this was now, when the light of clear reason and GPS shone everywhere.

There was an explanation. Pond was certain she would find it, as certain as she had ever been about anything. It was only a matter of time. She sighed.

For now, they had been given another quest to pursue. They had to open the sky, they had to find Gruenbaum's mother or whoever it was who was posing as such, and they had to figure out this house before it figured them out.

For a moment, Pond felt unsure. She seemed to be part of a play, but she didn't know whether she was writing her own scene or not. If she was acting as a marionette, who was pulling the strings?

"Back upstairs," she said. "We've got to get that sky figured out."

"Did you find it?" Gruenbaum asked, his face eager, lit up, as if he was being welcomed back into sunshine.

"Maybe," Pond said. "We found something in the floor, and then we got distracted by more noise."

Gruenbaum paled at hearing of the new noise. "Let me back inside," he pleaded, but Pond shook her head. She wasn't quite ready for that. After the noise had commenced again in his absence, she was almost convinced he hadn't been behind it, but she wanted to let herself settle in, arrive at a new understanding of Gruenbaum. Maybe he hadn't betrayed her. Maybe he was as confused as anyone else.

She almost laughed, looking at his face, which was now a picture of longing and bewilderment. He so much wanted to help, and didn't know how.

"Just wait here," Pond told him. "For now." She had to refrain from kicking herself. She was becoming kind without meaning to. *Stop it*, she told herself. *He of all people deserves to sweat a little.*

But now his face was again beaded with perspiration and chagrin, and his discomfort wasn't making her feel any better. She steeled herself and turned to go back inside.

"The sky is calling," she told the others, with mock heroism.

They pulled themselves away from Matilda and her human escort, Duckie patting Gruenbaum's shoulder in sympathy, and Nareen smiling at him. Pond saw Gruenbaum rubbing his own eyes, as if he didn't believe what he'd seen. Ferdinand nodded his head in silence. Luvreen winked at Gruenbaum, a giant wink that occupied her entire face.

Pond didn't look back as she went into the house, but she could feel Gruenbaum's stare upon her, could feel him willing her to call him back inside, back into the ranks of human beings.

She ignored the call, and kept going, not that it helped much. She just needed more time. That was all she needed, with regard to both Gruenbaum and the house. And it was what she didn't have.

\*\*\*

Back in the house's upper third and a half story, Pond stared at the floor, the unfurled earth mirroring the ceiling. "They look like they both can roll away, open out, do something," she spluttered. "It's only a question of finding the mechanism." The correspondence between the floor and the ceiling was too clear for it to be meaningless. "But how does it work?" Pond asked. "How do we open it up?"

*That was always the question*, she realized, looking back over every bit of her travels, and even before that, over every bit of her life. *It wasn't that life lacked meaning, necessarily, it was that we didn't know how to find what it meant. We didn't know how to interpret it.*

Maybe there was beauty and significance there all along, even in what seemed arbitrary, in the people we bumped into, in the jobs we worked, in the places we lived, whether they were efficiencies or culverts or mansions. Maybe the opening was there all along, and we didn't recognize it, didn't know how to access it. Pond rubbed at her eyes.

Or maybe this house was a trick, a tease, an invitation that couldn't be responded to. The house was making her want to feel everything did have a solution, questions got answered, if you sought you would find.

"Why isn't it happening?" Pond asked. All the clues fit together, creating a trajectory that led somewhere. She willed it to make sense. She would continue knocking, and the door would open.

She knelt on the floor, and knocked on every bit of the wooden earth, her hand moving with a steady pace in its exploration. Nothing. But she felt better.

The wood held such depth of beauty, its every grain telling a story of earth in which the trees had grown, sun and rain had nourished the tree, years upon years of growth, until the tree spired to the sky. And then the tree had fallen, or had been cut, and had become transformed into something new, into this design, into this beauty.

*Anything so gorgeous couldn't be all bad*, Pond told herself. Not a lot of her life had been devoted to the conscious pursuit of beauty, and yet looking back, she now saw beauty everywhere she had traveled.

Much of it wasn't this kind of beauty, the crafted, artistic, lovingly assembled kind. Much of it was just ever-present, sunlight flashing across a winding river, a road following a river's contours, white birch trees standing between river and road. *It is all so beautiful,* Pond thought. She hadn't noticed, and it had been so beautiful, even when she wasn't looking for it, even when she was looking past it or through it.

She had been rushing along, and all the time a feast of beauty had been laid out before her. Even if nothing much made sense, it was somehow comforting to know loveliness was present everywhere she thought to look, even in the harshest moments.

All of it was beautiful, she saw now, in a flash. Even the ugliness she remembered from the most downtrodden districts she'd visited in the past was beautiful. Even that added to the whole picture. Her mind reeled and she felt a bit dizzy.

Even in the midst of a waking nightmare, beauty could be found.

"It's *all* beautiful," Pond said. "Even the things we don't know. Even the things we don't like." She sat back on her heels and threw up her hands, giving up for the moment. "I don't know how to open the earth, or maybe move aside the earth, open the door.

"Look at it. Both the ceiling and the floor look like they want to fold back. They want to roll back and reveal what's been there all along." Pond knelt down to the floor's design, staring at it so intently her eyes began to blur. She thought she had seen tiny letters along the forty-ninth parallel, the line between Canada and the United States. And then she couldn't see the characters anymore.

"Get a magnifying glass," she begged the room in general, and Nareen ran down the steps.

"It was in the office, in the antique dentist's cabinet." She returned panting, holding out a magnifying glass that was a work of art in its own right.

Pond held out the glass with eagerness and trepidation, wondering what it might or might not reveal. "Look," she said. "It's true. The forty-ninth parallel is not a solid line. It's formed by letters. The letters say, 'What do you think it is?'" And

Pond wanted to shout with protest and also with something like reluctant admiration. True was nothing if not consistent. She was every bit as maddening as ever in the questions she asked and the puzzles she set.

"What do I think it is?" Pond mused manically. "I think it's a barrier. It's something that's blocking me, obstructing me. It's keeping me from the sky." She looked at the ceiling's earth and shook her fist. "Get out of the way already." And the dual earths almost seemed to wink at her in their stubborn persistence, their beauty now an affront.

"That's not helping," Ferdinand said.

"Do tell." Pond's sarcasm was withering. She sighed. What had the lawyer said earlier? *What you think has something to do with what happens.* "If I think it's in the way, it's in the way. But if I think it's not, it's not just going to vanish." She stared at the ceiling, hoping despite herself it would do exactly that.

"Try it this way," Ferdinand said. "Think it's not going to be a problem."

"Fine. The earth is not a problem. The sky's open. We can touch it."

And she threw up her hands and sat back on her heels, and the doors in floor and ceiling opened. She whooped in surprise.

"That's impossible," she shouted, near tears. But right above her, the ceiling gave way, revealing sky.

The earth furled itself closed, and the rest of the ceiling followed, as if it were a stadium roof opening to the air, a fan closing itself. Pond wasn't tall enough to reach, but now the roof was open, and someone who *was* tall enough could touch the sky. Maybe. Pond looked at Luvreen.

"Can you reach the sky?" she asked. Luvreen was the one person in the room who could conceivably reach up and have her hand stretch past the bounds of the house.

But that might not be what the instructions meant. For at Pond's feet, as the ceiling rolled back, the floor also fanned apart, a clear circle folding back out of the way, and revealing an inner door that now could be accessed.

"That's ridiculous," Pond protested. "Maps don't have ears. Why did they move aside just then? It was like they heard me and responded." But despite her protest, she looked at the inner door and at the others, and her eyes were bright. "Who wants to do the honors?" she asked.

"Go for it," Ferdinand urged her, and she leaned over and grabbed the half-circle handle and tugged, and the inner door swung up slightly and the entire surface of the door eased itself into a hidden pocket, so what was revealed was a basket nestled into the floor, a perfectly formed basket that contained two seats and was attached to strong tensile ropes and to shiny fabric that appeared to feature all the colors of the rainbow.

Red, orange, yellow, green, blue, violet, and a shimmering white-gold so brilliant it almost couldn't be looked at. The eyes skipped past its gleaming radiance and then returned, enticed and dazzled at the same time.

"It's a hot air balloon," protested Pond. She wanted to collapse into hooting laughter, wanted to shout at Gertrude in anger and in praise, and wanted to roll on the floor in wonder and relief tempered only by mistrust.

"Looks like one to me," Ferdinand said, his voice tart. "There're two seats. That means two of us can take a ride. But which two?" His legs looked like they were itching to leap into the basket. "Who are you taking with you?" he asked, his voice gruff with some emotion Pond couldn't identify, and then shook his head.

He brushed his hand over his face, and when Pond saw him next, he was back to his usual calm expression. "Let's help figure out what there is to figure out," he said, so Pond thought she must have imagined his unexplained outburst of feeling.

"What makes you think I'm going anywhere?" she asked, her eyes narrowed, not noticing her question made no sense at all, in fact contradicted everything she had been wanting since she inherited the house. From the moment she had learned of her legal ownership of the place, she had longed to be rid of it, longed to cast off the dust of her feet upon it, longed to be on the road again.

And now a new kind of road unrolled before her, one that would open pathways in the sky, and she didn't know what to do with it. "I'm not going anywhere," she said, crossing her arms in resolution.

"Stand on the four corners of the earth and touch the sky, and prepare to fly," Nareen said. "Looks to me like we've figured it out. Matilda and four of us stand on the mosaic downstairs and then somehow that activates the hot air balloon. And you can fly away." She sounded forlorn. "I'm not sure why, but it doesn't make me feel triumphant. I want to be the storyteller, weaving together all the strands we have discovered, so the story is whole, as solid and bright as the hot air balloon material. I think we have all the pieces now, and know how to fit them together. So why do I feel like I'm losing something, rather than gaining something?"

Pond shrugged.

"I don't want you to go," Nareen continued. "Even if I can be the one to go with you. I still don't want you to go. I like it here." She gestured around them.

"It's a good room," Pond admitted, her tone grudging.

"It's not the *room* I'm talking about." Nareen sighed and straightened her shoulders. "So, who will go with you?"

"Why does everyone keep asking me that? There's a hole in the house. Do you think I can just go off and leave a hole in the house? It lets in sky."

Duckie looked at the two seats. "Well," she said, her expression coy, clasping her hands, "Gruenbaum and I could always go together." She winked and sent a smile in the direction of the carriage house barn. "Doesn't Mexico sound delicious? I could take Gruenbaum off your hands."

Pond snorted. "No chance. I'm not sure anyone's going anywhere. I have a feeling this hot air balloon is a distraction. It's a red herring, something that seems to be the answer but really leads us away from the real solution. The hot air balloon doesn't explain the knocking sound. The noise has been going all through the house, even after Gruenbaum has been banished to the barn. The hot air balloon doesn't explain the note Gruenbaum received, the one that called him Sterling, his mother's name for him. It's pretty, but the hot air balloon's not doing it for me," Pond said decisively. "There's something else going on."

"You have to decide who to take with you," Luvreen said.

"I'm not going anywhere," Pond screeched. "Not until I figure out this house."

\*\*\*

Despite herself, and despite meaning what she said with every ounce of her being, while she helped set the table for dinner, Pond knew everyone was watching her. Waiting.

"Okay," she said, attempting to brush off their gazes and speculation. "Go get Gruenbaum." No need for him to starve. He could sit at their table and eat and then go back out to the carriage house barn. Locking him out hadn't stopped anything. The house's quest had its own momentum, and it didn't seem to depend as much upon Gruenbaum as they'd thought.

Luvreen nodded and went rushing out. She entered the kitchen again, announcing, "Castaway's back. Redeemed! Brought again into the fold." She turned around to welcome Gruenbaum in. "What are you waiting for?" she asked.

Gruenbaum offered a shy part-smile. "Am I forgiven?"

Pond shrugged. "You get to eat dinner."

"Not everyone's appetite will be as good as usual," Luvreen said. "We're all wondering who Pond will take with her," she told Gruenbaum. "There's a flipping hot air balloon tucked away into the floor on the third and a half story, and there are only two seats in it. It's weird in here right now. Consider yourself warned."

Gruenbaum frowned. "Won't be me who goes anywhere," he told Luvreen, looking at her and Pond, and all the rest of them. "I'm staying here to find out what's going on. Maybe I can solve everything, clear my name, show all I did was provide my friends with a little extra noise. Noise isn't bad. Besides, if my mother is following me, she can track me down anywhere. Leaving this place won't help. Might as well stay and confront it, whatever it is."

"Yeah, I'm not going anywhere, either," Luvreen said. "There's Matilda to look out for. Maybe I should eat dinner with her, things are that much more peaceful out in the barn than they are inside. Matilda is content, which is more than I can say for everyone here."

\*\*\*

Pond had discovered bringing Gruenbaum back didn't divert attention away from the question of the two-seater.

Which two rear ends would occupy those perches was the question on everyone's mind. Walking between the kitchen and the dining room, she and Ferdinand bumped into each other in the narrower pantry. "I'm not asking you to go with me," she said, "because I'm not going anywhere. But if I did ask you to go with me, would you go?"

She didn't look at him while she spoke, but after she had posed the question, she glanced at him.

His face was frozen. "No. I can't." His gaze rested on Giselle. He shook his head. "Giselle wouldn't fit in the basket."

"That's good." Her voice was fierce with something she didn't recognize. "I'm not asking you."

"Good," he said helplessly, and it seemed even he had no idea what he meant.

***

Dinner would have been awkward enough without Pond's parents showing up.

Pond's dad looked almost entirely bemused by the crew of people gathered around the table, the mismatched flatware and plates, the flagons and goblets and glasses and china, the crystal and tin that adorned every place setting in a completely unique formation.

"You have gathered some unlikely dinner guests," he told his daughter. "You could put out a call to central casting, ask them for the ones who don't fit anywhere, and gather this bunch around a single table, and here is where you'd be." He smirked.

"You don't have to stay here," Pond said, but despite herself, she couldn't manage to summon

289

anger.

"Not going anywhere. I like movies, I'm willing to admit. It just doesn't often happen I feel like I'm on a set." He turned to his wife. "Take two," he told her in a stage whisper, his beautifully smooth jowls taut with his enthusiasm.

"Two what?" she whispered back. "Dinner rolls? Servings of potatoes? I'm already on my third helping."

Pond suppressed a grin. Nareen had taken paper thin slices of potatoes and baked them in layers with onions and duck fat. Pond's mother, the one who thought of food as fuel, was putting away the dinner like she hadn't eaten in ages, like she *enjoyed* food. And Pond knew her mother had eaten this well, just last night, because her mother had also been right here at *this* dinner table.

Everyone fixed their stares on the whispering guests. Pond's mother looked demure, while Pond's father looked expansive, not just in body but also in spirit—as if *he* were the host who had thought to gather everyone around this table. Meanwhile, Pond caught the rest of the more long-time dinner guests shooting suspicious gazes at the latest arrivals, as if they could be considered intruders.

"Two what?" Luvreen whispered to Pond. "They can't know about the hot air balloon, with its two seats, but what are they talking about?"

"You do look like a movie star, darling," Pond's father told her mother.

"You're just noticing my natural brightness," she said, patting her lips with her napkin. "Often a person doesn't see what's right in front of him."

Duckie sighed. "I just remembered. I forgot to attend to my husband. He spent an entire day languishing, all by himself, no stone masons to take care of him. The basement would have been silent at my place, no clangor at all." She laughed. "Maybe all the noise migrated over to this place, and *that* explains why the pipes kept ringing even after Gruenbaum went out to the elephant guest house. Mexico," she continued, addressing Gruenbaum. "They have good snorkeling there." She gave him a coquettish look he seemed to look past.

"I'm not going snorkeling," Gruenbaum told Duckie. "I'm staying right here. That's the truth. Even if I have to spend my time in Matilda's company. I'll do what I can to help. Maybe I can also ask my mother what's going on."

"Always a good idea," said Pond's mother.

"Ma," Gruenbaum began, as if his mother were sitting right there at the dinner table, "you're not really bothering me." He turned to Pond. "My mother wouldn't do anything to bother me. It has to be she wants to help me. She has a good message for us. We were wrong. She's not trying to torment us. Where *is* she anyway? It's almost certain she didn't go snorkeling, so I won't either."

\*\*\*

"Dinner was remarkable," Pond's father announced before he left for the evening.

She'd been so focused on other things she hadn't

291

thought to mind the presence of her parents at the table.

"Glad you could join us," she said absently, and in a not unfriendly tone, so he reached out and kissed his daughter's cheek.

His aftershave smelled startlingly familiar, even though she hadn't been close enough to catch his signature fragrance for years. She put her hand on her cheek, surprised. Her dad hadn't kissed her in a long time. The last time had to have been on her thirteenth birthday.

"You didn't say anything," he said. "But then again, you didn't say anything in protest, insult, or outrage, either." His eyes looked bright, as if he were congratulating himself on his good and surprising fortune.

"Goodnight, dear," her mother said.

"Goodnight," Pond told them, and she didn't even regret the exchange of pleasantries.

# Saturday

## *Murchison*

Murchison grumbled all the way to Pond's house, and he walked the entire way so as not to lose another circus vehicle. *Next thing you know, I'll lose my own head.*

This time he took note of the city as he walked, all the torn-up streets, all the steel plates piled on top of gaping chasms so cars would be able to drive over giant pits that had opened up. There were sinkholes created by leaking water pipes and erosion, some created by men and a few women with backhoes, digging in ostensible attempts to stop the holes. Instead, they added to them, and in the process created vast crevasses through almost every city neighborhood. Some streets were now composed of steel plates bolted atop steel plates, and in such cases drivers sailed by, traveling always over an abyss. They looked comfortable with the situation, as if they perceived nothing remarkable in such an arrangement.

Murchison had wandered through enormous

numbers of cities, but he had seen few that were coming apart at the seams in such a visible way. *Hope we make it out of here alive*, he told himself, watching as a worker vented natural gas from the ground.

"Is that safe?" he asked the worker.

"Safer than the alternative," said the man with the white hard hat.

"Will it explode?" Murchison's gaze followed a hissing line of holes that had been drilled in the street off into the distance as far as his line of vision could follow.

The man shrugged, his face remaining calm and cheerful. "Or it might just burn like an Olympic torch. Lots of them. Little flames shooting out of every one of those holes. Why have only one Olympic torch when you can have a hundred?"

Despite himself, Murchison choked out a laugh. "The Olympics at the end of the world."

By the time he made it to the carriage house barn, Murchison had run through every possible angle, every argument. He was almost sure he could convince anyone. Except Luvreen didn't seem very convincible.

What he wasn't prepared for was the smile Luvreen turned upon him as soon as he entered the elephant's current living area. *Never trust a smile,* he told himself. Performers could put on and take off a smile as easily as others put on and took off clothes. But Luvreen's seemed sincere. *Good reason to trust it even less.*

"Good morning," she said with elaborate sarcasm. "Don't know as I can say it's good to see you, but here we are anyway."

"Can we talk?" he asked her.

"What else are we doing?"

"No, I mean…" He opened his hands and showed his empty palms. "What would it take to get you back to the circus?"

She glared at him, and he put up a hand in self-defense.

"Maybe we can talk," she acquiesced. "It's all well and good, hanging out at Pond's place, but Pond is also going to ask my elephant to perform again." She looked at Matilda and sighed. "Maybe an elephant's lot in this world is to perform. Maybe everyone has to play in some sort of show or other. Maybe your main choice is what kind of performance you get to put in."

\*\*\*

*It was going well*, Murchison told himself later. *Everything was perfect.* He was certain he would have gotten the elephant back, along with the circus truck and the trainer, if he hadn't been interrupted.

A silver haired woman came waltzing in first, sidling up to Matilda with an apple for her. Murchison noticed everything the silver haired woman did seemed to involve a bit of seduction, even if she was interacting with an elephant.

A tall, sooty man, lean and quiet, had already been hanging out in the back of the carriage house barn, and when the silver haired woman entered, he slunk down even lower on a bale of hay, but no one seemed to pay him much mind. Despite or maybe because of that omission, he let out a mournful sigh that was audible from where Murchison stood.

Matilda was so expressive and loving by nature that it didn't take much to prevail upon her. She trumpeted with joy and took the apple from the silver haired woman's hand, while the woman stroked her deep gray crosshatched folds of flesh, every one of them at once strong and delicate.

"Look at you," the woman said.

"Who's she?" Murchison asked Luvreen, not appreciating the interruption.

"Duckie," the silver haired woman introduced herself. "Look," she said, ignoring Murchison. "This elephant is a beautiful lady, out of her element. She's used to being appreciated by the crowds. Or maybe she's found her element. She looks pretty happy. Like me! I'm used to country clubs and private dining rooms, but somehow I've never been happier." Duckie looked like she would topple over in surprise at what she had just said, if her wispy weight hadn't been supported by the elephant.

Meanwhile, Duckie made a point of ignoring Murchison, as if he weren't there, as if she had the ability to dismiss someone with a flick of her eyes, to erase someone's existence with a glance or a lack of a glance.

Murchison returned the favor, registering and then dismissing the flirtatious woman. Thank God she was employing her wiles on an elephant, and not a man.

He straightened his shoulders and told himself to focus on the concessions. Usually the only concessions he considered were cotton candy and caramel corn, not to mention a few hot dogs. But he was intending to broach making a concession in elephant negotiations. He was even planning to admit it out loud.

And then another man entered the carriage house barn, whistling, and everything Murchison had been endeavoring for went out the window. This man reminded Murchison of someone he had seen in a movie. Robert Redford, playing some rich guy in the twenties, before the market crashed. Some fake millionaire who wore white suits and drove a gold Cadillac, who walked with a cane especially because he didn't need it.

"Hello, Old Sport," the obviously rich man said.

Murchison growled aloud in displeasure.

"You sound like one of those circus animals," Duckie told Murchison, and it was clear she was turning her attention to him in order to ignore the new man's arrival. Had to be her husband, Murchison concluded. Only a husband could be treated with that particular form of disdain.

"It's a job hazard." Murchison growled at Duckie and at the new arrival. "Spend time with animals, you become like them."

"You mean, displaying much better manners than humans?" Luvreen said, arching one eyebrow. "My main concern is animals might take on humans' negative characteristics. That's much more of a risk than the reverse."

But even so, Murchison told himself, doing a play-by-play later, he could have salvaged everything then, if Duckie's husband hadn't bumbled onward.

"You're coming home now," he said to Duckie insistently. "That place is enormous without you."

"Oh, really?" Duckie asked, with elaborate sarcasm. "Oh, I see. I'm looking back over all the time we've been together. You've never spent time alone in the house without me, have you? Poor thing. It's always been me rattling around in that vast emptiness by myself. I hadn't noticed what it's like to be alone in that place. Do tell."

"It's miserable," he said, his expression plaintive, putting his hand to his throat, and seeming to manage only to obstruct his breath. He gasped slightly, adding a note of authenticity to his appeal. "You have to come back."

"No such thing. I'm having far more fun here. Besides, that old homestead feels cramped with the two of us."

"You make no sense at all," he said, broadcasting exasperation. "There are all these...people here." He glared at the elephant. "And you're all crammed into this one house. I do understand it's as large as ours, and perhaps even lovelier, but still. There can't be any room to think here."

"Maybe *that's* why it's so nice," Duckie said stubbornly. "Too much room to think at home."

"You're telling me you're not coming back?" her husband said, as if such a response were inconceivable. "But you're my wife."

"True enough. Not that you have been acting like you knew it before."

Murchison raised an eyebrow.

"There's plenty of room for you here," she told her husband. "You can get to know the elephant."

Murchison groaned, a deep bone-rattling aching sound. "No," he said. "The elephant has to come back to the circus."

"The elephant's very nice," Duckie said primly to her husband. "*And* she has a name. Meet Matilda." She turned to Luvreen. "Matilda wouldn't go snorkeling with me in Mexico, but then again, Matilda also wouldn't go to California and gallivant around with a nymphet who wasn't even of legal age. Maybe I ought to stick to elephants from now on. Less romantic, and they do have big noses, but I could overlook a minor flaw like that."

Luvreen snorted.

"What I can't ignore is that I don't want to go home," she continued. "My home hasn't been a home for years, and I'm not going back. Not without some significant changes. If you get tired of staying here," she told Luvreen, "you and the beautiful lady can come stay in our garage."

"No, you can't," blustered Duckie's husband. "My cars are in the garage."

"For now, they might be," Duckie said sweetly. "Haven't you noticed how everything can change?"

Duckie's husband looked like he had just felt the ground liquefy beneath his feet. That happened in earthquakes, Murchison had heard. It had happened in Christchurch last year. He just hadn't seen it happen to anyone standing right in front of him.

"No, everything can't change. I won't allow it," the husband insisted again, but even as he spoke, his voice sounded hollow. He looked at his watch. "My watch stopped," he said, and put his hand to his head. "I don't know what to do."

"I'm not going anywhere," Luvreen announced, in response to Duckie's invitation, and Murchison felt his hopes fade like dry ice evaporating into the upper recesses of a big top. It all seemed so solid, and then it was gone.

Duckie's husband looked at his watch, shook it, and looked at it again. His expression of dissatisfaction did not leave him. "My heart is still marching along," he said. "So it's not like everything has stopped moving. Just my wife and my watch." He sighed and threw up his hands at no one in particular, then trudged out of the carriage house. "What has gotten into this world?"

\*\*\*

## *Pond*

Pond had spent the entire morning scowling at everyone again, so anyone who could manage it scattered as far out of her way as possible.

Somewhere deep in her inner recesses, Pond found it charming that Ferdinand and Giselle pretended not to notice she was back in her prickly, elbows-out stage, and just proceeded to busy themselves with the monkeys and bears.

"Reviewing performance protocols," he told Pond. "In case Murchison returns. If the house requires another aerial defense, it'll be ready to go."

Pond had been glowering in the kitchen, when she yelped with surprise. A strange man was walking through the pantry toward her, and didn't pause, even when she squawked in protest.

"Who are *you*?" she asked.

"Same old, same old," grunted the man cheerfully, tipping his hat to her. He kept walking toward the basement stairs.

"*Excuse* me," Pond said, "but this is my house. What are you doing in it?" The place might be full of strange people, but they were all strange people she had invited in—more or less. Still, that didn't mean she was ready for someone else to waltz in unannounced.

"Oh, sorry," the man said. "Didn't notice you were new. I'm the pool guy. I come to clean the pool every Saturday."

"This house doesn't even have a pool!" she burst.

"What are you talking about? It's a beautiful pool, especially after I clean it." He kept walking down the basement stairs, and Pond followed him.

"That's funny," he said, pausing at one of the blank fieldstone walls. "I left the door open last time I was here." He squinted at Pond. It looked like he was gauging what she knew, perhaps if she had been the one to close the door to the pool. But if she had closed the door she would have noticed there was a pool behind the door.

Pond shook her head and held out her empty hands.

"Okay," he said, "let's get 'er open." He pressed alongside one of the fieldstones, one that looked indistinguishable from all the others, and a doorway revealed itself in the wall. The pool guy threw the door open.

Pond gasped. Far from looking like a murky basement pool, the room was flooded with light. Gertrude had figured out a way to create shafts that brought actual full daylight into the room.

With the light dancing on the water, it was almost too bright for Pond's eyes to focus. She laughed despite herself. This pool had to be under the solarium, which meant the void she had been threatened with was only a pool. Even if she had fallen during the game board puzzle, she would have enjoyed a soft landing. A wet landing, but a safe one.

She shook her fist at True. And then she laughed some more.

She left the pool guy to his cleaning and returned upstairs to her glowering. Some things had their own momentum.

\*\*\*

## *Nareen*

Nareen read. She loved the *Eighth Book of Secrets*, but was finding it less compelling than usual. Life had overtaken her, and for once she found she couldn't focus on reading. Almost always she managed to remain at a distance from the places she visited, the houses she occupied. It was sometimes easier to consider everyone family that way—not let them get to you in particular. Consider them your family in general. Temporary, your kin for a single week, and then you'd be moving on.

And now she didn't know if she could pick up and go as lightly as before. Her mom had warned her against such a thing, letting herself get too involved.

*Keep a distance,* her mom cautioned her. *Keep moving. Air doesn't settle. It's always going.*

Nareen sighed again, and turned a page, and realized she had absorbed nothing from the one she had just read.

*What kind of storyteller are you?* she asked herself. She realized with a shock she was getting involved in the story. In the past, she had let events unfold, far removed from her. It made it easier to pull all the threads together into a single whole. And now she was in the events, and unclear about how they all fit together, and didn't much like either sensation.

But it was too late. She couldn't extricate herself.

\*\*\*

## Pond

That entire morning, Pond devoted a good deal of attention to not thinking about the two-seater hot air balloon. She instead recalled other two-seaters, such as a tandem bicycle she had ridden with a random woman on a boardwalk somewhere. Maybe Delaware. Maybe one of the Jersey shore towns. The woman wanted to wheel along the boardwalk and couldn't operate a bicycle by herself, so she had talked Pond into being the lead bike rider. Pond had found the whole experience unwieldy. She was used to being solo.

*No wonder I don't like two-seaters*, Pond told herself. *You have to stop and think before you move. You can't just up and go.*

And then there was a two-seater outhouse she had seen somewhere in Idaho or Washington State, one of those isolated mountainous regions where people built houses amidst trees so they wouldn't have to see their neighbors, even if they had them. Some of those places lacked indoor plumbing, and people still walked outside, even amidst the snow and ice, when they felt the call. One woman Pond had stayed with kept a toilet seat by the fire, so it at least would be warm when she had to trudge out along the snowy path to sit on the outdoor throne.

Pond had asked the people why they had a two-seater. "We went all out," the woman explained. "Dug a big enough pit that if two people had to go at once, they could. You know how some people want two bathrooms." The woman's laughter rang out. "We have ours."

"Do you ever use it with anyone else?" Pond asked, imagining the woman and the woman's husband perched next to one another, shoulders bumping amiably. The berth was narrow, and Pond thought you would not be able to help coming into physical contact with anyone else who wanted to sit next to you.

But no one would admit to having used the tandem outhouse in tandem, and Pond knew very well why. It was cleaner and easier to travel alone. Just because two seats existed didn't mean they both had to be occupied at the same time.

304

Pond grouched and grumbled her way around the house, ending up at last in the quiet room, the inner sanctum. She was beginning to love this space, but even its calm atmosphere wasn't helping today. Somehow the light and the peace weren't finding their way into her heart. Instead, she had a feeling that in the past she would have satisfied herself by running wildly in the direction of the nearest horizon.

It was an itchy feeling, an itch that couldn't be scratched because it had no physical location. It was a burning that could only be soothed by being in motion. It was discomfort and a drive that propelled Pond along, making her move on, always moving onward. And now she was trapped, confined, locked in this house.

*But there's that hot air balloon*, part of her said. She could run up to the open roof, she could activate the balloon with Matilda's help. She could soar away.

But then she would never know the house's secret. The house's secret had to involve more than just an escape mechanism. An escape mechanism was what Pond had spent her whole life cultivating, and she was now beginning to recognize it as only a temporary answer.

If you lived that way, you would always have another place to run from. *Where have I been running to?* Pond asked, and had no answer. She didn't know what she was looking for, but she couldn't run from this house until she had figured it out. It had something to tell her.

"What are you telling me?" she asked out loud,

as if the walls and the roof, the floor and the air, could speak. "What are you *saying*? I'm not going anywhere until I figure out what's going on in this house. Do you hear me? I'm not going anywhere, not in that hot air balloon, not anywhere."

Everything remained quiet, almost too quiet. No banging on the pipes today. Only her heartbeat remained almost audible, its urgency reminding her time was passing, and she didn't know what to do.

When she left the inner sanctum room, Pond locked it, something she hadn't done before. She followed some unbidden prompting, and closed the door, removed the key from the lamp stand, and pocketed it.

Calling the lawyer provided no answers. Of course it was Saturday. *Why he would be at work made no sense at all*, Pond told herself, but she couldn't help ringing him anyway. She left a message with his answering service and stalked over to the couch, throwing herself down. She couldn't bring herself to read any of the books lining the office shelves, not even the ones that promised salvation in every paragraph.

When the doorbell rang, Pond almost leaped up. Something was happening, thank God. Maybe Murchison was back. She almost hoped so. She would rather something move forward than stay becalmed in this waiting and wondering.

She opened the front door to reveal a stranger, but a familiar one. "You're Bertram Something-Something," she said, almost leaving the question out of her voice. He had to be. He looked the way she had imagined him, except he was wearing a blue gray tweed hat, one so appropriate to him she wondered how she could have omitted it from the picture she had been forming of the man. His shirttails were not rumpled—in fact he looked so starched she could almost smell the unyielding cleanliness, even from a distance—but she would see what she and the house could do about that.

He tipped his hat to her. "I shouldn't be surprised you know who I am. Your great-aunt always managed to surprise me too."

"I thought you'd come visit." Pond had indeed expected him to come, but had then gotten so absorbed in her maundering about she'd forgotten. "Is there a codicil today? I don't know whether to hope there is or pray there isn't."

Maybe further instructions would ease her dissatisfaction, lift her up into the sky on a floating balloon. She couldn't go there until she had figured everything out, but who knew? Maybe the directions could bring peace, just as they had brought unease.

Bertram shook his head. A note of embarrassment entered his voice. "Your great-aunt believed in taking a Shabbat," he said. "Today is that day."

"She wasn't Jewish," Pond complained. She had never considered it one way or another, True's Jewishness or lack of Jewishness, but now True was taking a Shabbat, it seemed highly annoying that she *hadn't* been Jewish. "Do goyim get to take a Shabbat?"

Bertram cocked his head to one side, looking like a very learned parrot. "I don't know the answer to that question in general," he admitted. "But for True, the answer is clear. She took one anyway, whether it was allowed or not. She said she needed a break from nonsense. One day a week at least."

"So, she considered the directions nonsense." She felt a hot wave flood through her, and identified it a moment later as a flash of embarrassment, a flood of shame. All week long she had been dutiful and sometimes frantic in following—or not following—directions the issuer had considered meaningless.

"Oh, no," Bertram said. It looked like he was rushing to reassure her. "She considered lawyers nonsense, I'm afraid." He coughed in a gently rattled way.

"Oh, good." Pond laughed aloud with relief. "They are, of course." She put her hand over her mouth. "I mean, maybe not you."

Bertram shrugged. "After all the hoops I've been jumping through this week in accordance with True's instructions, I have to be willing to concede the possibility. She's been making nonsense out of me."

Pond stared at him. A lawyer did indeed make an ally she never would have anticipated, but she felt a sudden rush of sympathy for him. "That's two of us, then," she said, opening the door and inviting him in.

He had been standing on the porch, which was a bit awkward, although clearly he was doing his best to look poised and in command of the situation.

"Lawyers don't make house calls," he said. "At least, I don't. But I wasn't able to stay away. When your message came through, forwarded from my answering service, I found myself in my car without thinking about it, and here I am. I still can't quite understand the sequence of events. What have you been finding? Those instructions don't make any sense."

"Oh, yes, they do," Pond said, her expression ominous. "How would you like to take a ride in a hot air balloon?"

Bertram shook his head.

"Don't worry," she assured him. "I haven't gone crazy. Neither have you, as far as I can tell." She took him around the house.

Nareen was reading on the downstairs window seat.

"Who is that?" he asked.

"She's staying the week." Pond wondered how it was possible to explain Nareen. "That's what she does."

Bertram shook his head.

He put his hand to his eyes and rubbed them when he saw Ferdinand and Giselle. Ferdinand was working with the carved monkeys and bears.

"What is this place?" he asked Pond. "It looks like a theater. Or maybe a dream."

"Sure, call it whatever you like." She didn't feel like talking with Ferdinand.

"Duckie," Pond said, introducing him to the silver haired woman, and Bertram smiled at Duckie until the moment when she began flirting with him.

"I have a cuff link right here," he told Pond. "I can poke her with its pin."

"No need to get violent." She suppressed a

laugh.

Duckie batted her eyes at him lovingly. "You *are* a dear. A bit stiff, but you could be encouraged to loosen up."

Out in the carriage house barn, it looked like he almost staggered when meeting Matilda and Luvreen.

He was then introduced to Gruenbaum, who emerged from the shadows to shake his hand.

"I can't believe it," Bertram said. "But I'm starting to sound repetitive." He took a deep breath and straightened his shoulders. He shook hands all around.

Pond watched the process. He couldn't shake Matilda's hand, but he put out a hand in her direction without thinking, and looked startled to have her trunk move forward and twine around his fingers.

"*Whaaa*," he exclaimed, and stepped backward.

"Despite all of the directions," he told Pond, "until now I didn't think anything out of the ordinary was occurring. But this place is unbelievable."

"Not really. At least, you haven't seen anything yet." Pond guided him to the upper third and a half story and pointed to the hot air balloon. "Care to take a ride?"

He sat down with a thump. It looked as if he'd let go of all the air he'd been carrying in his lungs in one outpouring puff. And then he remained in stunned, breathless stillness for a few moments. "I thought I was conferring with a client," Bertram said. "But now I'm wordless. Wordless is something I have never been before."

An indefinite time passed, during which Pond stared at the hot air balloon, her face lapsing into gloom. Then Bertram spoke.

"I can't believe it," he said. "But I feel so adrift it's like I'm already flying through the air, wheeling along in total silence. You can feel it." His voice became dreamy. "What it would be like to be carried by updrafts and downdrafts of the wind, the silence singing, the quiet so complete. Traffic sounds muffled and died away, and then there are the high currents of air, the clear atmosphere empty except for a few birds, a world so calm. Hushed silence carries its own power, its own force buoying you aloft, so you feel you could stride across the sky in three steps, one foot on earth, one foot on heaven, and the next step, who knows where, but it would take you on beyond the universe somewhere."

"It's okay. You're right here." Pond frowned, lost in thought. "Maybe that's True's plan. Set up a house so odd and beautiful it inspires imaginary flights."

Bertram patted his arms and his legs. "Maybe you're not as crazy as your great-aunt." He laughed, his voice weak but honest. "Never before have I laughed with a client. Not over the phone. Not in person." He raised one eyebrow. "Must be the first sign of losing my acumen. Next, I'll begin talking to myself, and forgetting crucial elements of my daily to-do list. I might even find myself longing for a friend."

He squeezed his eyes shut. "*Friend*. That word

hasn't crossed my mind for ages, when I decided friends took too much time. You know how it is. Anything other than work is a time vampire, no matter how it presents itself. You have to watch out in particular for friends."

He opened his eyes long enough to assess Pond. "You look neither friendly nor unfriendly."

"Good," she said. "I think."

"It is good. Maybe that's why I find myself liking you. I've never had a niece, but you look like a good one. Of course Gertrude would have left her house and estate to such a niece. And so you and I are both mired in the same dilemma. What are you doing with the hot air balloon?"

She shrugged, and said nothing.

"I can tell you what I know from my experience," he continued. "You might have to get rid of it before you sell the place. You know how some people fill in swimming pools before selling." He nodded at the hot air balloon, his gaze suggesting for the moment, as long as he was talking real estate, that he knew everything there was to know.

"Oh, nonsense," Pond declared abruptly. She had no intention of closing up that swimming pool, and had forgotten she once meant to sell the house as quickly as she could. Now she wanted to wrestle the house to the ground, hold it down and pin it until it conceded defeat. "I'm not going anywhere. Come on. You haven't seen the most interesting thing."

But when she unveiled the mystery room, Bertram didn't seem surprised.

"Sure," he shrugged. "I read novels in my youth,

novels which featured hidden compartments in automobiles and trains and houses, so it feels as if I'm seeing something come to life I had already known about." He nodded, as if he were a wise sage, once more adopting what had to be his ordinary superior expression.

Pond was disappointed at the lack of reaction he showed. He had been so predictable in showing astonishment at everything else in the house she had thought he would be dazed by this place, her favorite. She sat down on the Spartan couch and stared around the room.

And then she drew a ragged breath when she saw it. *It couldn't be*, she told herself, willing her lungs to resume taking in air. *It's not what you think. Everything is always explainable. You just don't know what the explanation is yet.* She rose with her muscles tensed, her spine stiff, and the hair on the back of her neck standing up in alarm. She walked gingerly over to the nearest plain straight backed chair.

It was a note, an innocuous looking piece of paper on the chair's seat, as if pieces of paper could materialize out of thin air in a locked room. This bit of paper looked like the one Gruenbaum had shown her. And the printing was the same, too—all capital block letters, and tugging at her with a feeling of recognition.

She pushed aside the exterior conditions of the note to read what it said, but that didn't help.

**POND, DEAR, STERLING IS MISTAKEN, BUT NOT IN THE WAY YOU THINK HE IS.**

Pond held the note out to Bertram.

He took it from her in silence and read it. "You don't look so good. I've seen that shade of green and white appear only on corpses—and those already prepared for burial, and treated to the most expensive cosmetic routines undertakers have at their command."

Pond grimaced. "So, I'm innovative."

"It can't be all that bad." He tapped clumsily at the paper. "Besides, this message seems to be from someone who likes you."

Pond took a shuddering breath. "The last thing I want is a ghost murmuring endearments at me. Ghosts don't exist."

"Of course not. I would never suggest they do. I'm far too rational, not to mention dull, to consider such a possibility. Besides, dullness is a virtue that ought to be cultivated, and ghosts violate that principle in a most unseemly manner. Dullness is in such short supply these days. Look at this house, for instance. Everyone and everything has gone to the far opposite side of dull. Even my guide, and you seemed so sympathetic earlier. Now you appear to be most unusual. But…ghosts don't exist."

"Good to hear it. So, who wrote this note?" She called forth some inner strength she didn't know she had so that she was now able to find a weary amusement in the situation. Before he could answer, she said, "I have to tell the others. This means someone has been in this room while it was locked. And I have the only key."

\*\*\*

## *Bertram*

After Pond had gotten everyone into the living room, including Gruenbaum, she explained about the note.

Bertram still didn't understand anyone's concern, so Gruenbaum explained his mother's name for him, which made the lawyer's eyebrows rise.

"And only your mother knew that name," Bertram muttered, crossing his arms and leaning back in a quietly elegant chair. "A recollection is tugging at me. But it doesn't match the name Sterling.

"We have to figure this out," Pond shrilled, impatient at how calm everyone appeared. "Someone—or something—was in that locked room. This note didn't just appear from nowhere."

Gruenbaum nodded, narrowing his eyes. "I know how you feel. Same thing happened to me the other day, and no one in particular listened to me then, either. Has there been any more noise in the house?"

Bertram again adopted an expression that made him appear like an angel of surprise, so everyone clarified to him the way the house had been broadcasting noises.

"I thought I was the one making the noise," Gruenbaum explained, his eyes rueful. "And then even after I left, the racket continued."

"Why on earth would you make noise?" Bertram asked, his voice careful. Meanwhile, he kept tapping his front teeth with his thumbnail.

"It was a job," Gruenbaum said gruffly, not explaining much, but seeming to give Bertram reason enough to nod.

"My logical wheels are starting to turn." Bertram scratched his chin. "It has to be the same one who made the noise left the notes."

"My mother," Gruenbaum said, his voice mournful, as if his mother were dying all over again. "I thought she had been resting in the ground all these years, enjoying a bit of quiet, and I just visited her to show my respects and confirm she was gone, and then here she is again, resurrected, and rattling around the place, disturbing the peace— and not only mine, but everyone else's."

"Most men of a certain age no longer have their mothers with them," Bertram prompted, and then kept staring until he propelled an answer.

"She's dearly departed. I took her flowers this week. To her *grave*."

Duckie had moved to the edge of her seat all of a sudden, as if she believed he had presented flowers to another woman, and saw a problem with his paying attentions to anyone else. "I suppose that's permissible. A dead mother doesn't seem to pose much competition." But then she frowned. "Maybe she's not dead after all," she said, her voice sounding like a complaint. And then she seemed to catch the impropriety of her comment. "Not that I mean she ought to be. But maybe I do. At least, if she's dead she ought to have the consideration to stay that way."

"She's dead all right," Gruenbaum confirmed. "Only question is whether she's also still alive."

Ferdinand shook his head. "I don't disbelieve in ghosts. I just don't believe we are dealing with a ghost. I'm not sure spirits write notes, for one thing. Don't they use other methods instead? Rapping, knocking, banging on pipes…"

"I'm sure *I* don't know," Pond said, refusing to look at him, and then giving up and looking at him anyway. At least his eyes were already focused somewhere else, and she didn't have to fight not to fall into them.

Nareen had been quiet, seeming to follow the conversation, looking unsure about what she could add. "Maybe it connects with the secret we're supposed to discover," she offered tentatively.

"You're right! The hot air balloon is a decoy. The real question is what sort of puzzle this house is giving us, beyond the obvious." She rubbed her eyes. "What did you say about Gertrude?" she turned to Bertram. "She believed in the end times."

"Let me see." Bertram pulled his shoulders back. "I have to remember. I'm translating a bit. She said the old ways fall away, and the new ones arise. Maybe that was the hot air balloon. And maybe not. She said by the time you find the secret, it will be too late, but if you don't find the secret, then it will be even worse." He put his hand over his mouth. "Sorry. I didn't intend to say such a thing."

Luvreen groaned. "Me and my elephant have to get out of here. That is, if I decide to believe the apocalypse is happening right here in this house. When I was a kid, I went to a Sunday school taught by a pastor's wife. She had a mania for all things end of the world. As a young girl, I expected the

317

world to end any day, but it never did, so I just kept going."

She grinned. "Calamity is just another name for life. That's my philosophy, and I love life, every bit of it. Even the messy, crazy parts. It's all a hoot and a holler, all a part of the show. If the world is ending, might as well enjoy it here. Stay here, and I still have a chance to make things right with the circus before returning. I'm pretty sure the circus will continue on past the end of the world, anyway. And I bet this house will too. It's just as wild as any circus I have seen or been in. In fact, being here, I'm starting to be convinced there's no difference between the big tents, show trucks, performing trailers, clown suits and the whole rest of the world."

They were all quiet for a moment, until Luvreen spoke again.

"Or maybe the end of the world has already come and gone. What makes you think the end of the world is a problem?" Luvreen asked Bertram cheerfully.

He snorted, and everyone laughed. The moment of darkness passed.

"If the world's ending, I want it to end right here," Pond said fiercely, not looking at anyone. But she could feel Ferdinand's gaze on her now, and she didn't mind. She didn't mind at all.

\*\*\*

## *Pond*

"I want us to find who or what is writing these notes," Pond declared, bringing everyone's chatter to a halt. The lawyer kept telling them that according to Gertrude, the time was at hand. Something big was going to happen. Something up to and including the end of everything. And yet the atmosphere prevailing here was closer to a party.

"You can celebrate later," she chided everyone. They had to find out what was going on. "First find the note-writer."

She looked at Bertram, expecting him to depart, but he rose with the others, moving more slowly than they. They began to scatter in one direction or another. "Thanks for coming by," she told him. "It's never boring here."

"I can see that. I normally seek out the humdrum, the predictable. Tedious is not a bad quality. I lived in England for a time, and still follow English radio and television, thanks to podcasts and online subscription services. I don't even mind admitting I am a bit of a Herbert, someone so dull most people consider it objectionable. So what am I doing standing in this living room? Why am I not fleeing, the first chance I get? Perhaps I'm not completely useless. I can help."

Pond shook her head, keeping her expression serious. "No, I'm afraid you can't."

Bertram's face fell. "But you're letting all those others help." He suddenly looked about five years old, the only kid standing alone on a playground.

Pond smirked. "Rumple your shirt a little.

Untuck your shirt tails. And then you can stay."

Bertram blushed, a hot, bright red blush that swept across his entire face. He looked askance at Pond for a moment.

She glared back at him, to make it clear she was not flirting with him. He was safe, and so was she.

He took a deep breath and looked like he was willing the heat to leave his face. It took a while, but finally, a semblance of cool returned to him. He drew a deep breath. "I won't tuck my shirt back in," he promised, making an extravagant mock bow, "if it happens to become disarrayed while searching."

Pond kept a straight face. "If that's the best you can do," she said, pausing to taunt him a little more. "Be my guest."

She stared after him as he wandered off into the rest of the house. This place seemed to form a mirror for everyone who entered it, showing them what they were looking for, or what they *weren't* looking for.

Pond shook her head. Part of her wanted to run off into the house with the others, banging on walls and searching under beds, but she needed to pull her thoughts together first. Stray pieces of information floating through her head felt to her like they were related, even though they didn't fit into a logical pattern, at least not one she could identify yet.

She sat back down in a wing chair, a gold one, and absentmindedly stroked the swirled pattern built into the fabric. Some sort of burnout velvet design, beautiful, and easy to lose oneself in.

\*\*\*

*I'm not running*, Pond noticed sometime later with a start. *I should be running, from this house altogether, or on the hot air balloon, or through the house, searching with everyone else. And I'm not. I'm sitting still. I'm contemplating what I know and what I don't.* She felt smug for a moment, as if she were growing up, and had recognized her own advancing maturity.

And then she felt silly. She knew nothing, nothing at all. Perhaps less than nothing.

She stared at the note again. If Gruenbaum wasn't mistaken—or not in the way she thought he was—did it mean his mom was alive? Maybe someone else had been buried under that name, and he had taken flowers to someone else's grave. But why Gruenbaum's mother would be rattling around this place made no sense. *Because Gruenbaum's here*, she told herself. *Get rid of Gruenbaum and maybe his mother's ghost will go. Or his mother, if his mother wasn't yet a ghost.*

It somehow seemed more polite of her to be a ghost, if she was tormenting everyone. A living being could bother to show more consideration: could march right up and knock on the door and shake hands and sit down for dinner. There was plenty of room at the table. Pond had been demonstrating that all week.

Pond shook her head and the *I Ching* caught her eye. She hadn't consulted the book of changes in quite a while, partly because she had been so busy, partly because she wasn't sure what to ask it anymore. But now the note gave her another idea.

"Is Gruenbaum's mother alive?" she asked the

coins six times, falling with ease into the meditative rhythm of focusing on the question and on the coins' patterns.

With gentle movements, Pond recorded the designs and looked them up, then her eyes focused off in the distance, looking past the walls of the house, looking into invisible realms where her eyes could not see. The patterns were beginning to speak to her beyond the words they indicated.

This time the answer seemed to her to focus not at all on Gruenbaum or his mother. They seemed to focus on Pond. The designs spoke of a ruler who accomplished good by putting others' interests first, who prospered by helping others prosper, who let go of negative personal qualities in order to foster positive qualities, and as a result, created a realm not too far from heaven on earth. This time of abundance and blessing was such that even things that often would turn out in an unfortunate way became transformed into an advantage for all.

Pond sighed and laughed at the same time. Surely *she* was not that ruler. She was no ruler at all. She couldn't even command herself.

But the book of changes went on. It described a leader acting in natural innocence, so fresh that even unplanned events worked in accord with the good so that all flourished and prospered.

Pond giggled, her laughter helpless. The book was pointing toward a ruler so wise he or she could be complete, whole, spontaneous, and from that impulse could in turn choose the right course of events.

*But I'm no leader.* She looked around the house,

its quiet beauty embracing her. *I'm just the temporary person in charge of this place,* she thought, shrugging away a deeper glimpse that had been pulling at her. *Maybe it didn't matter what you called yourself, maybe it mattered what you did.*

*So I'm not a leader, nor a ruler,* she decided. *Doesn't matter. I'll just do the best I can, whatever happens, whatever visitors or elephants or ghosts show up, I'll do what seems called for. Even if my mom comes back for dinner tonight.* She grinned.

"Who is leaving these notes?" she asked the *I Ching* next. It might not vouchsafe to answer the question she asked, but it would say something interesting, she was certain.

This time the response started off in a straightforward direction, talking about providing nourishment to oneself and others, both in terms of the words that left one's mouth, and the food and drink that one took in.

Pond felt a flash of nervousness shoot through her.

The next part of the answer pointed to a female principle, a maternal principle.

*It's not my mother, and not Gruenbaum's, certainly. It has to be an abstract idea. Not me,* she assured herself. She wasn't anyone's mother anymore than she was anyone's leader.

Ah, and the next lines went on to advise that she should indeed follow rather than lead, and in so doing she would find all the guidance necessary, as well as friends and helpers to act in accordance with the situation at hand.

*Got the friends and helpers covered,* she told

herself, thinking about the crew knocking around the house searching for whatever intruder had been interrupting them with inconvenient notes and with pipe banging.

She frowned. The house's silence was now beginning to grate on her. What was the note-writer doing, waiting so long in between pipe-reverberations? This silence was becoming ridiculous. Any moment, Pond expected a humming, a thumping, a vibration that would echo throughout all the walls, and set her own bones singing.

*Good God*, thought Pond, *I haven't gotten* used *to it, have I?* It seemed people could get accustomed to anything.

The final line of the *I Ching*'s answer was that the earth was broad, and steady, and firm, and carried all who walked upon it.

*Umm*, responded Pond. So the note-bringer was walking upon the earth, which must rule out it being a dead person. Surely dead people, in the event they were inspired to go wandering about, would float above the ground with delicacy, leaving the earth itself for those who had to stick with more pedestrian forms of ambulation.

Or maybe the book of changes was indicating that whatever was going on had more to do with earth than with heaven, with what we all had to deal with right here and right now, not somewhere else, not someone else, not later.

*This is it, this time,* Pond told herself. *Got to figure it out.*

\*\*\*

Pond searched the basement first, pausing to dip her hand in the pool's water—perfect temperature, but no time to swim now. She didn't expect to find anything, and indeed came across only an odd contraption she hadn't noticed before, something that appeared to be a seal for a business, an embossing stamp, a letterpress.

She found a blank page from one of the cookbooks stashed on the cellar shelves, eased it into the machine, and lowered the crank handle. She gently worked the paper back out again, and yes, a raised ridge now spelled out a beautiful pattern.

*Pond Elixir, Inc.*, read the design, its words forming a circle. Pond had no idea which of her ancestors had fashioned an elixir, had needed to sign letters or papers with such a device. She shrugged and kept moving.

But the basement, with its gigantic fieldstone foundation, seemed utterly quiet. Pond was disappointed, in a vague way. She had halfway hoped the pipes would start ringing, as they had before when she had discovered Gruenbaum mid-act, busy sabotaging the house's peace and quiet.

*Much worse this is,* Pond thought. Now the sense of disquiet was internalized. She herself was providing the soundtrack, jumping at every moment of non-noise.

When she found Duckie looking slightly furtive in the parlor, Pond stopped to put together a question that had been floating just out of conscious range. She had figured out what Nareen was doing in this house, and Gruenbaum, and Ferdinand. And Luvreen seemed clear enough, with her whole entire elephant.

"What are you doing here?" she demanded of Duckie.

Duckie cleared her throat beautifully.

*Only Duckie could clear her throat beautifully*, Pond thought, watching the platinum haired woman turn her charm on Pond. Often she didn't bother, reserving such brightness for the men she bumped into.

"Why, helping you search," she said. "We'll find whoever did it," she said, her smile shining.

"I get that you don't like being in your own house," said Pond, her voice as kind as possible, given her words. "And your husband," she shook her head and declined to say anything more. It wasn't necessary to be cruel. "But why are you here? You're looking for something," she said out of nowhere, at once certain it was true. "You are helping but you're also doing something else."

"Oh, well," Duckie laughed lightly. "You have me there. I do like jewels."

Pond squinted at her. "I said you could wear anything," she said.

"There's one I haven't found," said Duckie. "I've been looking and looking, and it doesn't seem to be here. It's an old European diamond. True used to wear it."

She took a deep breath. "Not that I'm very shy. It's a two-carat diamond at least. If you found that, I'd sure be glad to borrow it. I was half thinking of borrowing it in another, longer-term, and more indefinite, sense," she admitted. "But something's changed. Now I don't care if it's a loan rather than a theft. That would do. Do you know what happened to your aunt's two-carat pendant?"

Pond shook her head. "No idea," she said, and made sure Duckie knew she meant it. "I'm not a two-carat diamond woman. If I did have such a thing, I'd give it away, or lose it, or lend it out to a friend."

"I know you would," Duckie chirped. "I mean, just look at what you're wearing. Unreasonably comfortable clothes. I mean, such a dear you are." Her voice became hopeful. "If you find it, let me know."

***

Pond went on a rampage through the house, feeling like she had to knock all the books off the shelves, even the ones she had managed to look through. Who knew what was *behind* all the books? Maybe secret messages were painted on the walls. Maybe it wasn't that she had been invited to find something in the books, maybe the secret lay beyond the books.

She also felt like she had to turn on all the inventions that could be turned on, whether they were operated by electricity or hand-crank, pulley or some lever or other invisible mechanism Pond couldn't understand. Just set them all in motion, and she might find something. She might see something that was still eluding her.

She stacked books on the floor in her bedroom,

something she hadn't done before. But the plaster beyond the built-in bookcases was quiet and unobjectionable, unlettered, not speaking except in silence and blankness.

Pond punched her pillow, just to let out frustration. She felt relieved and daffy, all at once. In the old days, punching a pillow would have been more satisfying. Now she just looked at her fist print she had left in the down and wanted to laugh at herself. She sighed instead.

One contraption she didn't understand at first glance but liked. It was a wooden box, carved out of a solid piece of wood, and the box nestled into one's hands, so you wanted to hold its shape, investigate it. The box had a handle on two sides, opposite each other. Pond was right-handed, so she turned that handle first, and was rewarded by being startled when a jester jack-in-the-box jumped out at her.

*The box didn't have any musical prelude*, she told herself. That's why she was surprised. All the jack-in-the-boxes she had seen before, when she was a kid, made noise, letting you know something might jump out at you. You kept turning through the dancing notes, knowing a surprise was coming, knowing the happy music masked fear.

This one was quiet until the harlequin figure sprang out. That made it eerie.

She next, more awkwardly, operated the lever on the left-hand side, gripping it with her less dexterous hand. That cranking, too, was silent, and also led to the figure emerging without warning. She knew to expect it this time, and yet still leapt back from the box, almost dropping it in the process.

She studied the figure's face. Maybe it was a fool, a court clown, one of those licensed to mock king and queen, the only one for whom it was safe to speak truth, even to those who had power of life and death over all their subjects, because when the fool spoke, the truth was clothed in laughter, the barb hidden behind a joke.

She loved this little clown figure, and yet also felt a bit terrified by it. She couldn't tell whether the anatomy depicted in the figure represented a male or female. Its face was painted so both its age and its gender were indefinite.

Something about the figure kept speaking to her. That was it: its eyes had followed her as she had leaned away in surprise, and now followed her again as she leaned closer to study its grin. The contraption was silent, and yet inescapable.

Pond again became aware of the house's silence, and realized the box reminded her of her own current situation. The house itself felt to her like it was waiting to jump out at her. The silence prevailing at the moment didn't take away the fact everything was building to a release. The balloon might float away on its accord; or someone gathered in the house might take it upon themselves to get in the wooden basket and go. Ferdinand and Giselle, for instance—what was keeping them here? Or something else she didn't even know to anticipate might happen, something worse.

After drawing a blank with bookshelves and with contraptions, Pond left the stacks of books piled in her bedroom. She decided to check the inner sanctum again, for no particular reason, other than it had become her favorite place in the house. She had locked the door after discovering the note there, so she now had to dig the key out and go through the steps of opening everything up.

Ferdinand and Giselle approached behind her as she opened the door, so all three of them found themselves in the room together.

*It's not awkward,* Pond told herself. *We are searching for an intruder. Focus on that.*

"I have to tell you something," Ferdinand said. Pond took a deep breath, which was audible, and then almost choked on her own air in attempt to keep herself looking calm and smooth and not ridiculous. She turned her face to him, hoping her expression looked relaxed and alert, ready to respond to whatever he said.

"I think we need to investigate this room further," he said.

She nodded intently, remaining composed.

"I agree," she said. She didn't know what they could investigate, the room was so bare.

"Have you tapped all these walls?" Ferdinand asked.

Pond nodded, and then shook her head. She wasn't sure. This place was so quiet she did let herself relax when she came here, and so maybe she had and maybe she hadn't. She shrugged and the two of them began working their way around the room.

This room was so unadorned they were able to complete the inspection more quickly than in some of the others. Giselle lay down in front of the wall hanging, the three beautiful white cranes. She put her head on her paws and stared at the birds.

"They're beautiful, aren't they?" Pond told the dog. And then she frowned. Dogs didn't understand representation. Giselle wouldn't know she was looking at bird paintings. Giselle was staring in that direction for another reason.

Pond took a deep breath and went over to the dog, kneeling at her side. She put out a hand slowly, her movement reluctant, and pulled the hanging away from the wall. She didn't want to believe it, but yes, she thought a faint seam was just visible in the plaster. It had been hidden by the cranes. The birds flying away off into the distance had distracted Pond; her gaze had followed the birds' motion, up and away, rather than down and behind.

Pond stood and removed the hanging from the wall. Yes, it was a door. A door-shaped outline, anyway, built into the plaster. She sighed. "I didn't want to find an opening there," she said. "I liked this room the way it was. Surprises aren't all they are cut out to be. I wouldn't mind a few less at the moment."

Ferdinand had noticed Pond's discovery and moved closer to her. It felt like he was providing back-up.

Pond reached out a hand, exploring the outline, starting at the lower right-hand corner and working her way upward. When she got to the area where one would expect a door handle to be, at about hip height, she felt a difference in the plaster on the right of the outline, outside the seam. She pressed, and a small rectangular area became visible, one that swiveled out from the rest of the plaster, and one that must have served as a lever, for the seam now opened wider, revealing itself as indeed a door. Pond put her hand into the now visible seam and urged it further apart.

When the new door was open, Pond and Ferdinand stared at what they had discovered. A bare space, a clean space, one even more silent and still than what Pond had been calling the inner sanctum, but which was now revealed as an outer room.

The deeper chamber felt even more quiet and mysterious. It was completely bare, but not barren. Waves of peace reached out to enfold Pond, drawing her in. She went into the room tentatively, motioning Ferdinand to follow her if he wanted. There was room for them both, and for Giselle. The area was small, but not cramped.

"Someone's been here," said Pond, stating the obvious. The room felt like someone had just left it, even though no visible signs of anyone's presence were evident.

"So the note-writer has been here," Ferdinand said. "And now the note-writer is gone. Made an escape just before we arrived."

A small glint had caught Pond's eye. She reached down and picked up a piece of metal. "Tell me it's not what I think it is," she implored, holding a bullet out to Ferdinand.

She had seen bullet casings, especially out West, where people seemed to enjoy going up into the mountains and shooting at gravel pits, beer cans,

"No Trespassing" signs, fences, rocks. Shell casings littered some of these places, but Pond had usually seen them after they had been fired. This one had yet to be fired, and it was different from all the rest, made of a metal unique in Pond's exposure to bullets. "It's silver," she said.

Ferdinand laughed. "So the note-writer probably isn't a werewolf," he offered, his eyes filled with glee.

"Oh, good," said Pond, her face dour. She hadn't considered the possibility before he mentioned and eliminated it in one breath. "Werewolves don't exist, any more than ghosts do. Besides, ghosts wouldn't need to carry guns. They are scary enough in their own right."

The bullet meant the note-writer needed a human weapon, couldn't call upon supernatural lightning strikes and thunder bolts, or whatever weapons a ghost might want to wield. They were still dealing with reality, Pond was entirely convinced of it. Thinking about that aspect of the bullet made her feel more cheerful. Reality she could handle.

But another part of her felt bereft. She had grown so fond of the inner sanctum that finding this door was like finding a door in her own head, one she hadn't known had lurked there all along. Her privacy had been violated, her interior space, her place of retreat, had all along been harboring an intruder, an invader, someone invisible who liked writing notes to disturb her peace and Gruenbaum's, not to mention everyone else's, someone who carried a silver bullet.

Pond stared at the bullet. Presumably one who

carried a single bullet also had access to more. It didn't mean the note-writer was disarmed, even if Pond now had this ammunition. *Maybe so,* Pond told herself, wanting to hope. Maybe the note-writer was quiet because there was no more damage to do. The entire household had mobilized, and this was nothing less than war. The note-taker had been vanquished. Pond weighed the silver charge in her hand and doubted it was so.

"Thanks anyway," she told Ferdinand.

"It's better to know," he told her. He must have been reading her face. "Whatever we're dealing with, we can't hide."

"I don't want to hide. I just want my sanctuary back. Now it feels open, instead of closed, unsafe, rather than a retreat. Who knows what will come whirling out of that door, even if I close it and cover it back up with the three beautiful cranes? And where's the note-writer now, while we are here talking?"

Pond contemplated a note-writer armed with a gun; the notes had already felt like they had launched small bits of shrapnel at her. She wanted the munitions to stay metaphors, though, rather than actual material armaments.

"You might kill someone with that thing," she said out loud.

"That is usually the idea," said Ferdinand, laughing at her, so that she felt better.

The world couldn't end as long as you were still able to laugh, she told herself. Or if it ended and you could still laugh, then things weren't so bad anyway, on beyond the world's end.

\*\*\*

Later, at dinner, Pond willed herself to focus on laughter. All day she and the others had searched, and had found nothing. Adding nothing to a silver bullet and a note was an activity Pond did not find very satisfying, so she felt she was suffering from a giant case of cosmic indigestion by the time dinner rolled around.

Plus, her mother and her father had come to join the ever-more well-occupied table, which wasn't adding to Pond's appetite for food. And her brother, for the first time, had accompanied them. Pond had a history of not being able to talk with her brother even when they were speaking. They directed words past one another, and somehow managed not to connect at all.

After such conversations, Pond might realize weeks later what her brother had been meaning to say, and by then she had forgotten what she herself had been aiming to articulate, and had no idea if any of her own intentions had reached her sibling.

But this time, tonight, her brother looked straight at her, and she didn't look away, and he spoke, and she was somehow able to hear right away. She tapped at one of her ears, suspicious. She didn't believe in ear doctors, any more than she believed in any other kind of physician, and had certainly not had any check-up in longer than she could recall. And yet somehow the frequency on which her brother was speaking was now coming in loud and clear.

"Congratulations, sis," he told her, nodding

ironically around the dining room, a shock of black hair falling over one eye in a manner Pond had always considered affected, but which now struck her as charming, so that she rubbed at her own eyes.

Her brother declined to look at the other guests, as if he were too scrupulous to have contact with other human beings.

Pond suppressed a smile, noting he was focusing on studying the things in the room. So far all the live human beings and the one dog were too much for him to take in. But he adjusted his far too hip designer Belgian glasses and let his eyes grow mock wide at the elegant wood and museum quality paintings and eccentric table settings. "Only one as crazy as our great-aunt could do proper justice to this place."

Pond nodded, her face serious, pretending she didn't get what he was saying. "But then she would have left it to you," she said.

He shook his head with vehemence, patting his sweater vest in self-satisfaction. "I wouldn't have anything to do with her estate," he said. "I know too much about its origins."

Pond's face went blank. She had never thought about where the house or its money had come from. In her mind it had been Great-Aunt Gertrude's. Where it had come from before that had never occurred to her.

"Unmentionable," her brother said, with a sharp glint in his smile. "The elixir was probably poison, first of all, not that such things were regulated in those days. So it was legal, strictly speaking. But it also fostered a serious addiction. If you got used to being on Pond's Elixir, that was how you stayed. It became a lifelong need. Who knows what was in it? That remained a secret. But it could and did make some go insane. You can see it in the family still," he winked at her, nodding at their dad.

Their father maintained his composure. Pond couldn't tell if it was because he had understood the insult and was impervious to it, or had simply remained oblivious. Either way, she kept a straight face. "Not at all," she said. "It skips generations. You have it next."

Had Pond's Elixir really made people go mad? Not that she knew if that was a bad thing. Or maybe it was that she was becoming more and more convinced there were all kinds and degrees of insanity. Maybe mad was the reasonable way to be. Maybe Pond's Elixir freed people to express the truth, and everyone concluded they were mad, when in truth they were most sane of all, and simply not meeting everyone's expectations.

Pond's brother smirked. "It goes with the money," he said. "Follow the money, and you'll find the madness." He looked at her with a significant expression. "But even worse than the elixir," he paused, "or at least, even more embarrassing, is what the next generations did to multiply the family jewels. They fabricated an unmentionable ointment to apply to everyone's unmentionables." He made a ghastly face and waggled his eyebrows in a facsimile of a grotesque mask.

Pond felt queasy and wanted to burst out laughing. "Why, to what exactly are you referring?"

she said, her face delicate, exaggerating her own natural modesty. Surely they hadn't applied it to everyone's unmentionables. Everyone would have had to apply it to their *own* unmentionables.

"It's unmentionable," said her brother, "but some would say the ointment was exactly formulated for goolies. And some would say danglies benefit even more."

Pond felt her face grow red, despite her best attempts to not react. She looked around the dining room. She had known she didn't want the family jewels that came with this place, but she hadn't known her family's jewels were based upon anointing others' family jewels with some unmentionable cream. She put her head into her hands, cupping her face with her palms, and dissolved into hysterical laughter.

"It's okay," Duckie told Pond, for once playing the part of a wise sage. It seemed she had, with uncharacteristic keenness, picked up on the gist of Pond's conversation with her brother, perhaps because it focused on two of her favorite subjects. "There's nothing that's all *that* unmentionable. Besides, family jewels are rather nice."

She arched one eyebrow at Pond's brother, in both a reprimand and an invitation. Pond felt her stomach do a slow tumble, watching Duckie flirt with her brother, whom Pond now admitted to herself was cute after all.

Talk about unmentionable.

\*\*\*

## *Duckie*

Duckie listened to the amusing exchange between the family members, enjoying the conversation about jewels.

"Mom," Pond said sometime later, seeming to remember her earlier conversation with Duckie, "do you know anything about Gertrude's two-carat diamond pendant? We can't find it."

Duckie almost stopped breathing while waiting for the reply.

Pond's mother paused, fork raised mid-air. "I think she was buried with it," she said off-handedly. "Do you know anything about it?" she asked her husband.

He shook his head. "I let women handle the jewels around here," he said. It looked like he had no idea how his words related to the previous part of their conversation.

"Disappointing," Pond's brother said. "If all the previous generations of our fine family had taken such an approach, we wouldn't be where we are. Pond wouldn't have this fabulous dining room. You," he told his father, "would have to find gainful employment. Such a prospect is, of course," he paused for effect, "unmentionable."

"Sorry," Pond told Duckie. "Apparently you're out of luck with the two-carat diamond."

Duckie swallowed nervously. She patted her cleavage delicately. "Just a moment," she said. "It's taking me a bit to catch up with where the conversation just went. Are you sure she was *buried* with her two-carat diamond?" she asked Pond's

339

mother, her voice verging on tremulous.

Pond's mother nodded. "Especially if you haven't been able to find it," she said. "That was a nice diamond."

Duckie coughed to cover a groan. She patted her cleavage, where not long ago she had nestled a two-carat diamond.

*I put it there just for safekeeping*, she thought to herself. It had showed up in her bedroom not long after she had admitted her interest to Pond. When she first saw the jewel, her response was glee.

But her second reaction was dismay. The jewel had appeared on her pillow, right where she had been sleeping all week.

Her face became pale and flushed at the same time, recalling that moment. She was aware she was not always the quickest person in drawing connections between events. But she was almost certain she hadn't been laying herself down to sleep at night and pressing her face the entire while into an enormous pendant. Especially since it was the gem she had been looking everywhere for. It couldn't have been there all along.

"The diamond must have been buried with True," she said. "If the diamond was laying around anywhere in plain sight, I would have seen it." That much was true. It hadn't been in plain sight. "And if I hadn't seen it, I would have felt it. And if I hadn't felt it, I would have heard it."

"Heard it?" Bertram asked.

"Diamonds make a slight singing sound," Duckie explained.

"Do they? I've never noticed," Pond said.

"My ears are very finely tuned. Diamonds are a higher pitch than the ones normally registered by human beings. But I have acquired a special sense for valuables, and my ears can be relied upon to tell me when a new diamond is around. And if I hadn't heard it, I would have smelled it," she added, defying anyone to challenge her ability to smell out precious stones. "You know there are wild pigs in France who hunt truffles. I'm like that, but with money. And if I hadn't smelled it, I would have tasted it," she concluded. "A special tingling on the tip of my tongue always alerts me, in the event my other senses haven't already kicked in."

For instance, Duckie now recalled, to confirm what she was telling herself, as soon as she had seen this diamond, all her senses had activated at once, so that her eyes became sharp and determined, her ears rang, her mouth, nose, and skin tingled with the sensations they were receiving.

*This is it!* Duckie had exclaimed in silent awe, reaching out to take the diamond. Yes, it was definitely True's. An old European diamond, the one Duckie had been seeking all week. There was no mistaking it. She grabbed it and tucked it close to her heart, keeping it safe, before anyone else could see what she had found. Then she had started thinking, an activity that never moved as quickly with her as it did for some. Logic was linear, she told herself, and she went straight to the core. It was okay if it took her a little longer to arrive. She didn't follow all the steps, she cared about the heart of what mattered. Love and valuables—how could you tell the two apart, anyway?

She now came to an unavoidable conclusion. *If the diamond hadn't been there all week, it had appeared this afternoon, right after talking with Pond about it, which meant someone had placed the diamond in my room.*

She stopped coughing and raised her voice, turning to Pond. "Did *you* put the diamond in my room?" she asked. Then she turned white. She hadn't meant to admit that she had found it. Did that mean she would have to hand it over? Having just gotten her perfectly manicured paws on it, she didn't want to relinquish possession, at least not so soon.

But if Pond had not served as a diamond delivery person, then someone else had, and Duckie also didn't like that idea. Unless, of course, it was one of the men. She wouldn't mind if any of them had visited her room. Although why they had waited until she was not in the room she didn't know, and couldn't bring herself to contemplate.

Pond shook her head. "Of course not." Her face became stiff. "Do you mean you found the diamond, after we talked about it?" She looked fierce.

Duckie paused. It was a decisive moment. She had to determine forever which of two paths she would take. She could be honest and lose what she had been intent upon finding this whole entire time. Or she could lie, and keep what she had smuggled away.

But in that moment she felt naked. If she kept the diamond, she would then be losing something that mattered even more. Something that had become as close to her as her own clothes.

She looked around the table. Gruenbaum was staring into his tin cup, avoiding her gaze as only he did, managing to be so charming even while looking away from her. Ferdinand had finished his course and was patting Giselle's head. Luvreen had her arms crossed, and was looking amused. Something told Duckie no matter what she decided, that girl would find it at least a little funny, worth at least a little laugh.

Duckie felt as if her life were passing before her eyes in a burst of light. She could say nothing, finish her dinner, and excuse herself, taking herself and her new diamond back to her husband. Or she could confess, admit what was going on, and stay here. And lose the diamond.

*Dammit,* she told herself. *I know it's the wrong thing, but I can't help it. I have to do the wrong thing if it's what my heart says I must do.* She took a deep breath. Here she went, forever launching herself onto the path of wrong. Take this step, and there was no turning back. Ever.

"I found the diamond this afternoon," she told Pond, placing her dinner napkin discreetly over her cleavage so she could extract the gem from her bosom. She flashed it in the gleaming radiance of the chandelier. "It was in my bedroom. On my pillow."

Duckie sighed. Not everyone could be strong and upright and choose the path of good. She had given in to her weaker instincts, and now there was no taking back what she had done.

\*\*\*

## *Pond*

"So True wasn't buried with her diamond," Pond said, a few heartbeats later, feeling her cosmic indigestion was now complete.

As if this morning's note to her hadn't been enough, it had been followed by the silver bullet. And as if that hadn't been enough, there had been the complete and total silence of the house, building up to a deafening crescendo. Something had to happen, Pond knew. And indeed, it had.

Now the diamond True had been buried in had arrived at her dinner table, along with her parents and brother. Pond laughed and groaned at the same time.

"You're forgetting another possibility," Gruenbaum told Pond. "She *was* buried with the diamond." He drew a deep breath. "Maybe my mother isn't the only one haunting this place. Maybe your aunt is, too." He paused. "Or maybe all ghosts know each other, and they're cooperating somehow. Teamwork." He made an attempt at an uncomfortable grin. He looked around the table, gesturing at everyone who was gathered there, as if that explained his comment.

"I don't think so," Pond shook her head. "Haunting doesn't happen by committee." At least, she wasn't willing to admit the possibility they were dealing with two ghosts. The simplest explanation was always the best.

"We're dealing with one note-writer," she said,

"who carries a gun, and used to carry a two-carat diamond." But who or what that note-writer was remained to be seen.

"What was your mother's name?" she asked Gruenbaum.

He paused. "She's my mother. I hardly have her name in my mind. She's just *Mother*. Stella," he said finally.

"We'll find the note-writer," Pond said, "the silver bullet carrier, and the diamond bringer." She didn't know why in the world the messenger, whoever or whatever it was, would care to divest itself of such a diamond.

"We will not stop looking until we find it. Whatever it is." Her voice was steady and determined. If they hadn't found it today, then tonight they would continue searching.

Pond's brother had been following the conversation as best he could. "You mean the house has a mystery?" he said, with mock eagerness and sympathy.

Pond scrupulously ignored him.

"I've always been better than you at solving mysteries," he told his sister emphatically.

"Maybe that's why you didn't inherit the house," she smiled with mock sweetness, and he subsided into silence.

But she did allow her family to hover over the note she had discovered in the inner sanctum, and they all shook their heads. Their expressions told Pond as loudly as if they were speaking that they thought someone besides Pond had written the note as a joke, and Pond was exaggerating its significance—and *that* explanation was the kindest possible one they could summon.

Pond could identify their train of thought as clearly as she could see the dinner plate in front of her. If Pond had written the note herself, it was even worse: she was becoming a crazy old bat far before her time. But if she were right, and the note did have something mysterious about it, that would be truly inconceivable.

Pond patted Duckie's hand.

Duckie stared at the diamond, clearly wishing she could whisk it back into her possession. "What's done is done," Duckie said glumly. "Not everyone can stand firm in the face of temptation. Some of us give in at the blink of an eye." She blinked her eyelashes with a thoughtful expression and turned them in the direction of Pond's dad. "Now, you," she said, loud enough for Pond to hear, but apparently out of earshot of her father, "are as finely tuned as a piece of wood, but it's not one that's been fashioned into a responsive guitar or violin. More like a two-by-four."

Pond could tell her father wasn't noticing Duckie's overtures, and gave a sigh of relief. At least there were still some things to be grateful for. She ate, and then barked orders to everyone to clean up and search.

"You're welcome to stay here," she told her family, "but if you're going to be here, we'd appreciate your help in looking."

"For someone or something that writes notes, carries a gun, and used to have a thing for fine diamonds." Her brother shook his head. "You sure you and your friends aren't playing an elaborate murder mystery game?" He looked at them, his eyes sharp. "That would explain your otherwise outlandish garb and demeanors."

"It's no game," Pond told him sharply, and her voice indicated she meant it.

Her parents and brother decided to leave. They didn't appear to be certain whether they were leaving her because they didn't believe her, or because they did.

"You don't have to stay here," Pond's mother told her daughter on the way out.

"Of course I do," Pond barked. "Whatever it is would never let me go."

Even if Pond left, the mystery would follow her everywhere she went, and she had a feeling her statement wasn't just metaphorical. The gun-toting note-writer would do the same.

Pond's mother patted her daughter's cheek. "What does one say to a family member who is convinced the impossible is true?" she said, her voice vague, as if she were speaking of something that had nothing to do with Pond, or with herself.

For her part, Pond was thinking a mirror thought. "You have no idea what's going on," she said. The look on her face was almost sympathetic. "You can choose to pretend the truth doesn't exist. I no longer have that option."

They had never been closer to one another, even as they stood right next to each other and each felt she was looking at the other through the wrong end of a telescope, so what was nearest appeared farthest.

# Sunday

## *Pond*

The banquet table overflowed with food and actual flagons, baroque dinnerware, mismatched flatware, and rare linens. There were flowers flown in from what seemed like every gardening corner of the world: the Netherlands and Chile, Venezuela and Mexico, not to mention Colombia, Israel, and Italy. Numberless vases bloomed with flowers that flashed their sepals, petals, stamens, and pistils in every color, every size, and every form.

Crystal, silver plates and flatware, brass and gold cups and glasses gleamed in the light of towering candles and glinting chandeliers. Even the floors and walls glinted with brightness and festivity, but nothing shone as brightly as the faces gathered around the table. An apparently endless chain of human beings had assembled themselves to form an improbable peace garland.

The impossible had occurred. Murchison was seated next to Luvreen. Duckie's husband was serving as his wife's gallant dinner escort. Bertram

348

was patting his lips with an Irish linen napkin, and not quite managing to hide his astonishment at the assembly or at his own presence. Ferdinand was perched next to Pond, and it looked like he was actually sitting on one hand to restrain himself from reaching out to someone, probably Giselle. On Pond's other side was her mother, and then her father and brother. Then there were Gruenbaum and Nareen. The circle was complete.

There shouldn't have been room for everyone at the table, not physically or in any other way, but they had managed to add leaves to it, expanding it into the living room, so that all were included. Not one had to sit at a distant satellite table. All were in the same orbit, joining in the same round of gracious laughter.

Pond raised a glass, proposing a toast, and found herself momentarily wordless. Then she drew a deep breath and declared, "Thank you, and welcome!"

The dinner almost hadn't happened. There were so many moments in which it all could have gone wrong, and yet here they were, having passed through the impossible. Peace on earth had come to Baltimore, at least in this room, at least for this time.

So why did she feel such a pressing sense of uneasiness? Something tugged at her, asking for her attention. She pushed the feeling away for a moment, long enough to add, "To friends and family, all of you. Enjoy."

And then while the hubbub of happy conversation rose around her, she ran through

349

mental thickets, attempting to identify what was wrong.

It wasn't anything to do with the elephant. Murchison had shown up after lunch and had knocked on the front door. "Can you put in a good word for me?" he'd asked Pond, who answered the door. "I always seem to get off on the wrong foot with Luvreen. I think we can make a deal she and I are both happy with. Only thing is, if I propose it, it might make her crazy. Please tell her, if she comes back to the circus, the elephant can do the tricks the elephant wants to do." He swallowed tightly. The expression on his face announced he was hoping offering such a deal didn't mean he had lost all reason.

Pond had put her hands on her hips and stared at Murchison. "The elephant has to stay here through this evening," she said, counting the days.

This was Day Seven. Today, all would be decided. Everything would become clear. At least, she hoped with all her might it was so, for today was the day the codicil had said would be her last chance to figure out the house's mystery. Today, she would get the house or the house would get her.

"Fine, fine," Murchison agreed hastily.

He trailed behind Pond, staying out of Luvreen's sight, and heard Pond deliver his message.

Luvreen laughed, a slow, rich-as-molasses laugh, and asked Matilda, "What do *you* think, girl?"

Matilda was always agreeable. Pond had never seen Matilda not being agreeable, and considered it possible Luvreen was more sensitive on the elephant's behalf than the elephant was on her own behalf. Maybe the one who didn't want Matilda to perform in particular ways was the trainer, and not the star.

But at the moment, Matilda was extra pleasant, trumpeting and showering Luvreen with little water droplets of affection, offering to dance right there in the carriage house barn. Her eyes were bright and clear, her skin groomed to perfection.

*Maybe elephants understand more than we know*, Pond thought, watching her response.

"Sounds like it's a yes," she told Murchison, over her shoulder, and he stepped forward gingerly, hand held out in an almost universal symbol of peace.

Matilda tapped him on the palm with her trunk, and he drew his hand back in alarm. It had looked like a reprimand, but now that he registered her former disapproval, Matilda drew him in for a hug, wrapping her trunk around his shoulder.

It looked like he was fighting to keep himself from smiling, and then gave in. "Maybe it was worth it, after all," he said, "sacrificing every single paper white bulb in my entire collection. Maybe I can acquire more as we travel, and create a garden in honor of the elephant's homecoming. I can rename my trailer Fields of Matilda. You'd make a good queen," he told Matilda, and Luvreen nodded.

"I am beginning to consider an unlikely scenario," she told him, her voice grave, but her eyes dancing with laughter. "You could possibly even be human."

And so they began to speak, their voices tentative and awkward, but reaching toward understanding, as Pond left them in the carriage house barn.

\*\*\*

Duckie's husband, whose name turned out to be Stanley, was a harder case.

He had come sidling around the corner of the front porch when Pond had stepped outside to pick up the newspaper.

"Don't mind me," he told Pond, who sighed. Pond *did* mind his presence on her porch, and felt he qualified as a truly annoying trespasser. She had gained a good deal of experience this past week, evaluating those who showed up unasked.

She looked down her nose at him, without knowing she was borrowing one of Duckie's moves, so that Duckie's husband stopped and looked at Pond with a quizzical expression.

"Where do I know that from?" he asked out loud. "It makes me miss my wife all the more. Look here," he told Pond, his voice carrying even more emotion than he was articulating, "you have my wife, and I've about had it with that."

"I don't *have* your wife," Pond told him. "She is a mature adult. She can go where she likes." Pond had to fight away a grin. She knew Duckie would want to be called anything but mature. *Girlish, yes. Mature, oh...please don't mention it, darling.*

"But right now she's staying here," Duckie's husband complained. "Our beautiful house is right next door, and she's staying here of all places." He didn't say it, but his tone showed he considered

Pond's house amounted to nothing less than a temporary insane asylum, a collection of mad refugees, bedlam in Baltimore.

"That's true," Pond said, keeping it noncommittal, responding to what he'd said, rather than what he implied. "You're welcome to join her." Not that she particularly wanted him to do so.

The more she saw of Duckie's husband, the more Pond understood why Duckie had remained in the house. It was no longer just because she had to find the two-carat diamond, though it could have been because she wanted to keep wearing it.

After Pond's parents and brother had left last night, Pond had given the jewel right back to Duckie and told her to place it around her neck if she wanted.

Duckie had looked confused, as if she had been expecting to receive blame rather than a reward, and then she had glowed, joyful and radiant.

"That's what *she* said," her husband complained. He might as well have been proclaiming, loudly and repeatedly, "Woe is me." His tone was querulous, as if he had been eating bees.

"So what's stopping you?" Pond demanded. She unrolled the newspaper. The only news in Baltimore these days seemed to consist of various vague and contradictory but obviously apocalyptic omens.

Meanwhile, people were becoming more and more alarmed by both arbitrary fire bombings and random acts of kindness, so newspaper columnists didn't know whether to be more concerned with Molotov cocktails thrown onto lawns in the northwest quadrant, or by acts of seemingly unwarranted generosity.

Crime was to be expected, but *kindness*?

People smiled and sometimes laughed, for no reason at all. Strangers now and then sang to one another in grocery stores. Small children ran for the sheer pleasure of being alive. Young couples danced along the inner harbor walkways, and so far had managed to evade arrest by short-tempered officers, who demonstrated a misconception that both skateboards in particular and happiness in general constituted illegal insubordination.

Everything was falling apart, and no one knew what the future would hold. It was perhaps the most reasonable thing for everyone to give up hope. And still people persisted in the perfectly unreasonable act of not only hoping but believing. All was not lost, such dreamers proposed; all was just beginning to come into view. If everything was crumbling, it only let in more light.

So far, Pond's house had managed to stay out of the papers, and she wasn't sure why. The events therein were remarkable enough that they proved True right. Her house formed an epicenter of some sort or other; the time was at hand for a new way of seeing, a new way of being, and those who had gathered together in this house were at the forefront, at the vanguard, of the nascent reality.

Or else they had all gone insane, and Duckie's husband was there to remind Pond that convention favored the latter explanation.

"Wives don't just pick up and go," he snapped, bringing Pond away from her thoughts. "It doesn't happen."

"Really?" Pond said, with false politeness.

"Mine never has. It would disrupt everything." His voice had been confident, his eyes far from it.

"You know it's not all that bad. You can enjoy the luxury of having dinner with yourself sometimes."

Duckie's husband looked startled.

"Get to know your own thoughts," Pond told him, suppressing a grin. As for herself, she hadn't learned her own mind until she found herself coming smack up against the colorful crew gathered in this house. "Get to know yourself. You might not be as terrible as you appear," she told him.

He spluttered with rage, and then with laughter. "You might not be as terrible as you appear, either," he told her.

\*\*\*

## Duckie

Duckie found out later that when he entered the house, her husband did not go straight to find his wife.

He had asked Pond how he could help, and busied himself looking for the note-writer, so when Duckie first caught a glimpse of him, it was from the back. He was kneeling next to Ferdinand and Giselle, tapping on wainscoting in the third-floor hall, and so unexpected was his presence that his wife did not at once identify him as her husband.

*Who is that handsome fellow?* she thought, catching a glimpse of the back of his always perfectly coiffed head. *I haven't seen him around here before.* And then with a warm flash of recognition, she identified him, and ran up behind him, putting her hands over his eyes.

"Stanley!" she exclaimed, entirely giving away the surprise. His hand felt warm on hers, and not unwelcome. Familiar, like an old friend she'd forgotten she had been missing. "What are you doing here?" she asked.

"Little of this, little of that," he said. His voice told her he was telling the truth but also flirting with her, prolonging the time when he would let her know she had won. She had left, and he'd had to follow. The terms had changed now. He was showing he knew that. But he waited a few moments before letting on that he knew.

He turned around to look at her, and caught a glimpse of her new diamond necklace. "It's beautiful!" he exclaimed. And then he looked suspiciously at Ferdinand. "Who gave it to you?"

"It's not mine," Duckie said airily. "I'm just borrowing it from a friend." She still couldn't get over having done the wrong thing, having betrayed her lifelong loyalty to diamonds, entirely renounced her glittering allegiance, and then having been rewarded rather than punished. She thought what you left behind got left behind. Who knew that it could come back again, and in a better way, with less guilt and trouble this time?

Her husband nodded. "There's something different about you. I can't put my finger on it, but I look forward to finding out what it is."

\*\*\*

## *Bertram*

And then there was Bertram.

Bertram had sighed heavily upon awakening that morning, aware Gertrude's, and therefore his, Shabbat was over.

Today there was another codicil to be opened, read, and delivered. *I could call that niece on the phone*, he told himself, wanting to take refuge in being stern. He could stay the heck away from that mad place. He could hold onto his reason and his sanity, his peace and quiet and his own dear company.

But ever since he had visited Pond's place yesterday, his own sleek estate had lost some of its natural luster. It seemed more and more like a barren little bachelor's castle, and also like it was boasting, protesting too much its own self-sufficiency and well-being.

The leather consisted of the most expensive grades one could acquire, of course, but it now felt too smooth, as if he would slide off his own furniture, and too cold, as if he were attempting to sit on the sleek exterior of a leather coat, rather than a couch, as if he were always on the outside of his own life, and never on the inside.

His hand itched as he reached toward the codicil. *All right*, he grumbled. *I'll just head on over for a minute. Won't go inside. Stand on the porch and deliver it. Then get out of there while I still can.*

But in the end, he got to Pond's door and rang

the bell.

When she answered, she put her hands on her hips and said, "I was wondering when you'd get here. *Finally*," and she grabbed his hand and drew him inside, so he stood panting for a moment in the entry foyer, wondering how his fortunes had changed in such a drastic way that he, who was always in control, always planned everything, had been pulled inescapably into a situation he had no intention of allowing himself to enter.

Bertram shook his head, and came up with no words at all.

"You have a codicil," Pond pressed onward, "read it to me."

He returned to himself long enough to nod, reaching inside his breast coat pocket and tangling with his bright white silk handkerchief to withdraw the legal document. He took a deep breath as he opened it.

For her part, it looked like Pond had stopped breathing, dispensing with air temporarily.

He read through the document once, raising his eyebrows as he went. He had written them, certainly, but he had also honored True's directions that he not read them until sharing them with Pond. This one was perfect, if he did say so himself. Not any more understandable than the others, but a perfectly fitting final codicil.

He wiped a grin off his face and announced, "'You're looking in all the wrong places, of course. What you see visibly is only the most obvious part of the puzzle. Learn what defines life and death and then all is clear.'"

Without meaning to, Bertram had replaced one word in the codicil with another. The codicil actually read, "Learn what *divides* life and death and then all is clear." But his brain had skipped over such an obvious mistake. What divided life and death was self-evident. What defined life and death, that was worth discovering, and so without meaning to, Bertram muddied the waters a bit more.

"That's what we're *doing*," Pond said with frustration. "Of course it's all about life and death." She hit herself on the forehead with the back of one hand.

Bertram mused. When everything was obvious, why was it so hard to figure out what was going on?

"The gun-carrying note-writer is still eluding me. I have no idea if Gruenbaum's mother is dead or alive. Maybe that's what the codicil means. I have to determine what defines death and life, in relation to Stella, and then everyone else's death and life will also make sense.

"But the other codicil instructions have been more about life than death," Pond said. "All the puzzles have been about life, really. Even the ones that seemed to be about the void. It's not that Gertrude was so fixated upon death. How do you define life and death?" Pond asked, as if Bertram was attempting to stop her from doing so.

He paused, a blank look on his face. "I deal with clients. It's usually clear whether they are alive or dead, and I don't have to make much of a determination."

"Baltimore makes life and death particularly visible," Pond said wryly. "Time doesn't work the same way here as it does in other places. Gertrude's house could only exist in Baltimore. The mystery she set could only unfold in this place, where time races ahead in eddies and flurries and then becalms itself in doldrums—and you can see both impulses coalesce all at once, right in the space of one block, right in one living human face."

"Baltimore is my favorite place in the entire world," Bertram said. "It's the demimonde, where time stands still, where nothing ever happens. Baltimore is secure and obscure. It knows and accepts it will never be the center of the world, or of anywhere really, and so it has freedom to be itself. It's ever-charming. I have no idea what you mean," he protested. "Baltimore's terrific."

"Didn't say it wasn't," Pond said, her voice acid. "I said it has something to do with life and death. Everything's coming to a crescendo now."

"That sounds dangerously loud and stimulating, like it might involve hundreds of shimmering cymbals." He raised one eyebrow and tugged at one earlobe cautiously. "Are you certain? I hope you're not. Or maybe if you are right, earplugs will be needed."

"You've been saying it yourself, all week long," Pond insisted. "The codicil just did, too. The mystery we have to solve is about death. And life. And what the difference is between them. You can't avoid that question." She stared at Bertram in such a way that he could not escape her gaze.

He blushed. Then he caught sight of himself, reflected in wavy outline in one of Gertrude's display cases—this one bursting with pressed flowers of all kinds—and for a moment he also let himself see a momentary glimpse of Pond's meaning.

He was standing in a client's foyer on a Sunday, because he couldn't stay away. The house or something in it had drawn him more surely than catnip drew a feline.

Right then he ought to have made a break for it. But he didn't.

He sat down on the couch when Pond invited him to do so. He sighed and settled in. This couch didn't make him feel he was sliding off it. This couch made him want to stay a while.

Even then, he could have run for it. But he didn't.

"Tell me anything you can about Gertrude," Pond said, staring at him with unavoidable eyes, so that Bertram felt he were being cross-examined by a very intent young bird.

He found that gaze much more intimidating than the lawyers and judges and other clients he was used to working with. Something about Pond's stare unnerved him. Maybe because it was so like her great-aunt's, and becoming more so all the time.

"Do you think this house is rubbing off on you, too?" he wanted to ask Pond, but he didn't. He frowned and thought back to what he knew of Gertrude. Was there anything he hadn't mentioned about the great-aunt that might help her niece? He grinned. He couldn't mention how alive she was, of course.

"She suggested the house was like one of those Russian dolls," he said. "But you know that, probably."

Pond nodded. "Russian dolls nestle into one another, so inside every doll is another. Just the way the inner sanctuary had contained another chamber. We're looking all over," she said. "For all the good it's doing. We haven't discovered anything that illuminates much of anything that encloses much of anything else. Maybe that explains life and death," Pond said. "One encloses the other. But which is which?"

***

## Gruenbaum

Gruenbaum came rushing in, waving a yellowed newspaper clipping. Pond and Bertram had been sitting on the couch.

"Look," he spluttered, nearly unable to speak. "She *is* dead."

He didn't know how he felt. For a while he had been holding out hope that perhaps his mother hadn't passed on, that he had delivered flowers to some other person's grave, or maybe just to an empty headstone. He knew some people paid for their headstone, even had their names engraved on it, while they were still alive. Maybe someone shared his mother's name.

But no, this clipping proved it. Yellow with age, a small obituary notice, but a clear one. Ma was gone. The note-writer wasn't his ma. It could have been someone impersonating her, but why anyone would do that, he wasn't quite clear.

Pond read the brief notice of departure. Stella Moritz.

Gruenbaum had already memorized it. Dearly missed by her husband and sons, and by her employer.

"Who employed your mom in Baltimore?" Pond asked him.

He shook his head. He had missed that part of the notice, focusing only on the bare life and death of it all.

"She was only here to visit a friend," Pond said.

Bertram read the clipping. "The memory wheels are turning," he said. "I've seen that name, Stella Moritz. I've seen that name in Gertrude's files. I do believe Gertrude might have employed her."

Gruenbaum stared at the lawyer. "Does that mean you're my boss?" he asked, half hoping and half dreading the answer. If the lawyer had been sending him directions, at least he could now look his employer in the eye and resign, make clear where his loyalties lay once and for all—with Pond, with his friends here. Not with the nameless person who had contacted him.

But did that make Bertram the note-writer who had been visiting his room? Gruenbaum's spine shivered and his vertebrae contracted into a defensive posture.

"Not a chance of it," Bertram said.

"We're supposed to find out what defines life and death," Pond told Gruenbaum, her face giddy. "So the obituary helps us do that."

Gruenbaum stared at the death notice in Bertram's hand. The paper proved his mom had left this world, departed her body just as he had always grown up believing was the case. So why did he feel disappointed? It wasn't like he wanted her to have stayed away this whole time, living life in Baltimore without him. And it wasn't like he wanted her to be a ghost, wandering without end and without rest.

But it felt like something had concluded—a chapter had closed, and he again wasn't sure what came next.

"So where'd the clipping come from?" Pond asked. "I hadn't thought to ask before. I have been focusing on the definition of life and death, which this notice seems to exemplify. Stella is dead, and we are alive, and so is the note-writer."

"Oh, that." Gruenbaum shifted uncomfortably from one foot to another. "It was on my pillow," he said. "Sweet dreams." He laughed, unable to contain a slight note of hysteria.

"The note-writer is still here, and it's not your mom."

"Unless it is," Gruenbaum said, almost hopefully. "Maybe she's still visiting me."

Pond shook her head, dismissing the possibility. "After they've died, people don't write notes or use bullets or hand out newspaper clippings."

"How do *you* know?" Gruenbaum asked. "Have you ever been a ghost?"

Pond laughed scornfully. "Of course not. Well, I did wander those seven years, drifting all across the land. Not in a strict sense, anyway," she amended her previous comment. And then, apparently to be sure Gruenbaum understood, she stated adamantly,

"Ghosts don't exist in the way you mean."

"Good." Gruenbaum said. If his mom was a ghost, he was disappointed she hadn't had more to say to him along the lines of a motherly greeting. This ghost had been much more distant than his mother should have been.

*Not that I want ghostly arms to embrace me*, he insisted silently and fiercely. Not at all.

And after the obituary was delivered, the ghost persisted in remaining completely unobtrusive.

\*\*\*

### Nareen

They had almost lost their cook earlier that day, which would have been a disaster, not only for the dinner, but for Nareen.

Nareen's mother had called, and told Nareen to prepare to visit another house. Colleen didn't mention it, but Nareen knew such a call meant Colleen was in the midst of an emotional conflagration. Colleen was dancing around the fire's edges, fascinated, admiring, drawn by the danger, and wanted her daughter to serve as her mother's safety, her back-up, to make sure she didn't get burned up entirely by the flames. Colleen wanted her daughter with her.

"Mom," Nareen said, staying patient. "I'm not done here. I haven't finished out the week. You can't just interrupt me at your convenience."

On the other end of the phone, her mom was silent for a moment. "Children grow up, don't they, when you're looking the other way?"

"Mom, I don't know if I want to keep living the way you live."

"It's good enough for me," said her mom defensively. "It was good enough for my father before me. On down through the generations the pattern marched, and now my own daughter is threatening to break it."

"I'm not you, Mom," Nareen said, choosing every word with care. "You can do what you need to do, but then I have to do the same. I love you."

Colleen sighed. "We're at a crossroads. The way I go through life, we're always at a crossroads, but this particular intersection divides one way of living from another. If you choose the other fork in the road, you might be lost forever to your mother. Some choices there are no going back to. I'm happy with my life," Colleen told her daughter.

"And I'm happy with mine."

Nareen knew her mother meant she was happy with the way she had been living her life, and couldn't quite stop her daughter from doing the same, even though she wanted to. "It's okay, Mom." She knew her mother was feeling helpless, seeing in her mind's eye a vision of her girl running out the door into the wide, wide world, and without a backward glance at her mother, who was now the one left behind, the one watching while the other went on.

"It had to come," Colleen said. "The day had to come when you made up your own mind. I can do everything to keep it from arriving, and still that day will come, so I might as well not fight it. When will

I see you again?" she asked Nareen, with a new note of respect in her voice.

"I don't know," Nareen said, pressing the phone against her ear. It was all she could do not to run into her mother's arms at the moment—find out where her mother was and drop everything and everyone here in that instant, and scamper off to whatever new adventure her mother had chosen for the thrill of it. But her mother would tire of it in a day or less, and then Nareen would be left holding the pieces for one week, cleaning up after her mother had enjoyed the exploit and moved on.

They had different attention spans, Nareen realized, with a rueful smile. Her mom couldn't be blamed for that, but it needn't determine her daughter's life forever, either.

"You can call me," Nareen offered, feeling like she and her mother had traded places. She was now the stable one, the caretaking one, serving as an anchor for the loose-footed youth. "Call me anytime. I'll always answer if you call."

"Yeah. That'll work until that one time I can't make the call. You're a darling," she said, hanging up the phone, and Nareen knew it might be a long while before she heard from her mother again, and that her mother was right. One day, no call would come at all.

Nareen sighed heavily and slipped her phone back in her pocket. She straightened her shoulders and went to see Pond.

"Look," she told Pond. "I know I told you I didn't want to stay longer than a week. What would you say if I changed my mind?"

"Plenty of room for that," Pond said, staring at Nareen's face, and clearly seeing the tears that weren't falling.

Nareen presented a wobbly grin, and that night surpassed herself with the best dinner she'd ever made.

*** 

## *Pond*

"You came back," Pond told her brother, when he showed up in the late afternoon. She hadn't expected him to return, but didn't mind. "Are you sure you can stand to eat here again? Food provided by such an embarrassing fortune."

He grinned. "I can force another meal down."

*Past all your objections,* she wanted to say, but didn't.

"Thought having dinner here would make you feel itchy," she said. "Although I hear there's an ointment for that."

She invited him to search for the gun-carrying note-writing obituary-leaving ghost that wasn't a ghost because ghosts didn't exist. "Find it," she said, "and you'll find the answer to everything."

"I'm pretty sure the answer to everything is nothing. At least, that's what I learned in college."

Pond had always thought he had chosen his Buddhist studies major to annoy their mother—but maybe there was more to it, she conceded.

"Whatever," Pond said. "Find it."

Her brother winked. "I can almost guarantee I

can help you find nothing," he promised.

***

Pond's parents said hardly a word when they arrived, right before everyone sat down at the table.

Her father had insisted they go back to the house, while Pond's mother insisted they couldn't. Now they stood arm in arm, the better to elbow one another under the guise of amity.

They continued battling each other in silence, shooting death's-eye grins at one another, in the belief they were masking their enmity and presenting a perfect and very agreeable social face to the world.

Pond stared at them and her expression said, *These are the people I have to thank for bringing me into this existence?* It looked like she wanted to close the door in their faces, but couldn't bring herself to do it.

Instead, she said, "You can only come into this house if you leave all your weapons outside. Drop them at the door."

"No weapons," her dad said, showing her his bare hands.

"That's not what I meant," Pond corrected him.

"Ah." He nodded punctiliously. "You want your mother to leave her mouth at the door."

Pond's mother snorted with scorn. "Only if you take off your ass-hat and leave *it* at the door."

He flared his nostrils and looked like he was considering saying something he might have regretted forever.

369

Then he held a hand out to his wife, reaching across his body to do so, and said, "Deal."

Pond's mother took his hand. Her expression asked, *What have I let myself in for? Unprotected in a madhouse, unarmed in an apocalypse—social if not actual. And who knew, the final end of the world might well come between the second and third courses.*

But not too much later, she was smiling at the banter and enjoying another kind of wine.

***

Pond couldn't eat, not even a single bite, despite the delectable food and the happy hubbub rising up from the table. She pushed herself back from the table, eased away from the feast in silence, slipped out toward the kitchen, and then kept going, moving through the other side of the bathroom, through the formal parlor, and back all the way around to the formal entry foyer.

An impulse was calling her outside. None of her guests noticed as she opened the front door and slid out onto the porch. Taking the long way around ensured they assumed she had vanished into the parlor or kitchen.

She walked around the front of the porch and turned the corner to the far side of the house, the dark side, where Duckie's husband had emerged from earlier that day.

It wasn't that Pond had expected to see someone there. It was simply inevitability.

Pond had arrived on the porch the same way

waves arrived on the ocean shore, the same way migrating birds returned home, and leaves fell from trees in autumn, and flowers bloomed again in spring. There was no fear, no sense of anguish.

"What defines life and death?" Pond asked the shadowy woman.

"This little dandy does," said the shadow in a tart voice. The shadow pulled out a gun and showed it to Pond. It was a beautiful gun, tiny and deadly, the counterpart and origin of the bullet Pond had discovered, and she did not want to learn what it was capable of.

"No need to get violent," Pond said cautiously, holding her arms out in front of her, and all but closing her eyes.

"Come on, Nelly," the woman said. "Pull yourself together. A little violence is just the thing on the right occasion."

"I didn't expect to see you again," Pond said, feeling slightly dizzy.

"Rumors of my death have been greatly exaggerated." The woman laughed, and her laugh cascaded forth in brays and nickers, caws and cackles, and confirmed what Pond had known without knowing.

"But..."

"Oh, you ridiculous child," True said. "You're not going to let yourself be ruled by ignoramus stop signs? Why should I die on anyone else's schedule? Going to die on my own sweet time," she declared.

"No one asked you to die," Pond spluttered with anger. Just like no one had asked True to come back to life, either.

371

"Oh, they would have if I gave them half a chance, which I certainly was not about to do. Look here," she continued, jabbing the air with the gun. "You have to stay in this house, because I have places to go."

Pond spluttered with anger. "All week I've *been* staying here, following your instructions. All according to your schedule," she added bitterly.

Despite the gun True held, she wanted to reach over and grab the old woman, shake some reason into her, or some delusion out of her.

"Tut-tut," True chided, and Pond couldn't tell if her great-aunt was angry or amused. "I had to know if you could be trusted. None of the rest of the family could be. You proved yourself tolerable when you didn't go flying off in that balloon. I will allow you to remain in the house. You have to stay here, attend to things while I duke it out with perpetuity. Perpetuity and I eat each other for breakfast, and you know what *that* means."

"You're crazy."

True again snorted with laughter, but the gesture she made with her head indicated both agreement and disagreement. "I'm not any crazier than you," she said, her voice sharper than ever.

Pond swallowed hard, looking at the gun flying erratically through the air in True's hand.

"And I'm perfectly sane," Pond said dryly, although both points were debatable.

True whinnied with laughter. "You're not a complete loss," she told her, with a note of actual fondness in her voice.

"*Why* did you do this to me?"

"That's what I'm telling you, if you'd shut up and listen. I have to go to Oregon. Best state in the union to choose your own ending at the right time. Time for me to finish everything. Don't you want the end to be just as good as the rest of the adventure?"

Pond sighed. She didn't want to admit to herself that True had lost it, whatever *it* was, but that was the kindest conclusion she could draw. All week she had been fighting to figure out the house's secret, and now she wasn't sure she wanted to know anymore.

"So you go to Oregon," Pond said with elaborate sarcasm. "And as a matter of convenience you choose your own ending. Time to die, bye-bye. Fine. I refuse, by the way, to mourn you twice. Meanwhile, I stay here and keep the world from ending, per your instructions. Good of you to give me such a job. So thoughtful. Besides, what you're saying means the world hasn't already ended."

"I didn't say that." True snorted. "We're way beyond the end in this city. But as long as some good people remain here, it's all bound to continue somehow. There's nothing more you can ask."

There was a *lot* more Pond could ask, like who had died and appointed True God. Especially when not even True had died.

"You're not dead yet," Pond pointedly announced to her great-aunt. She reached an arm out toward True, wanting to touch her, to prove her observation. But True was holding a gun—not aiming it at Pond, not exactly, but also not aiming it away from her, either.

"You can touch me. I'm flesh and blood. Your own flesh and blood. Gives you that sweet warm feeling, doesn't it. *Family*," she hooted softly.

Pond reached out her fingers and tentatively placed two of them on True's forearm, the forearm that was not in turn attached to the gun. True was tiny, the bone of her forearm birdlike, delicate, so frail it felt it could snap at the slightest pressure, but warm and very much alive. "I don't understand," she said blankly.

"You don't need to understand. There's nothing you can do to change it."

"But *you're not dead now*. I can run in there and show everyone how alive you are."

"Oh, no you can't," True said, raising the gun with a flourish.

"Don't shoot me." In a flash, at gunpoint, Pond realized that with her entire being, she loved life, all of it, even the bits she had considered horrible. All of it was beautiful, or miserable, in exactly the ways it had to be.

Besides, she hadn't kissed Ferdinand yet. She couldn't die without kissing him at least once. Although, if she ever started, she wasn't sure she would be able to stop.

"I have no intention of shooting you," True said. "Don't be so ridiculously self-centered. Besides, I'm quite fond of this porch. Wouldn't want to see it covered in blood."

Pond almost laughed, she found the suggestion so startling. How had she been self-centered?

"The gun's not for the likes of you," True said sharply. "You're too pedestrian yet. This gun's for a real queen." She pointed its delicate barrel at herself, just to be sure Pond saw what she meant.

"What?" Pond said blankly, understanding suddenly how Duckie must have felt quite often, attempting to track conversations, as if she were floating and bobbing along, carried by a rushing stream without knowing where she was going.

"It would be far too tedious to use the gun on you," True explained with a sigh. "Plus, I'd have to look at the mess. I've got no problem going full blast on myself, however." She cackled with glee.

Pond stared at her great-aunt.

This much she was beginning to understand. If she went running in to grab all her friends and family to show them True was alive, by the time they got out to the porch, True would be dead. What defined life and death here was the truth. What Pond couldn't say was the truth. Because someone's life was protected by it.

"You're asking me to lie," she told her great-aunt. And so, was life a lie? And death the truth? At least in this moment, death would be the consequence of telling the truth.

Pond felt more and more dizzy, as if everything she had ever believed were whirling around and trading places with everything she hadn't believed.

"You don't have to lie. And you don't have to tell the truth. Like you have the foggiest idea which is which, anyway, bird breath." She lowered the gun and sat back into the recesses of the bench. "You can't say you don't like the house," she said, shifting suddenly to a tone Pond would have expected someone to use if she were visiting a friendly neighbor for tea, and being offered any selection she wanted from a plate of cookies.

"You're right," Pond admitted. "I can't say that." She let herself recognize she loved the house. And for a moment, despite the abyss she felt she were walking over, she loved True, too, the one who had given her the house, the one who had assembled or created such a place.

Pond leaned one shoulder into the side of the house. The house felt like more than shelter; it felt like a friend. How True could leave it behind, she didn't understand. Maybe True didn't really want to go. "There's plenty of room," she told True, the same way she had ended up telling all the other guests all week long—always despite herself. "You can stay here."

"You do specialize in nonsense, child," True said sharply, but with a strong dose of humor in her voice as well.

"Why not?" Pond asked, unable to keep petulance out of her question. The house was good enough for everyone else who was gathered around the banquet table. By what right did True remove herself from such company?

"It wouldn't do." True smiled gleefully in the shadows. "I'm not dead enough yet for you to set a place for me."

Pond goggled at her great-aunt. Was True saying the rest of them *were* dead, because they were accepting Pond's invitation? Or simply that True was now too alive to be confined in any single place? Pond shook away both possibilities. Focus on what made sense. "I *knew* there wasn't a ghost," she said, her voice rising in triumph.

"Of course there was a ghost, child. It just wasn't dead."

"Not yet."

"Now you're getting the idea. Part of it."

"But if you shoot yourself, then you can't go to Oregon," Pond said with exasperation.

"Almost the same difference," Gertrude said impatiently, and in a tone that made it clear Pond's objection was nothing short of meaningless to her. "It's still *my* ending."

And the two of them remained silent for a while. A burst of laughter spilled out onto the porch, reverberating through the glass of the parlor window.

Pond felt a sudden sharp longing to be back among the laughing people, the ones who hadn't left everything behind. She once *thought* she had left everything behind, but this week had proved it wasn't so at all. She had her whole life ahead of her to live.

True's age was impossible to read in the dark. It had been impossible to read in the light, when Pond had last seen her, so that was not very surprising. True was inscrutable, always young and always old at the same time, possessed of herself in a mind-boggling way that went far beyond this world. If True had decided her life here was over, who was Pond to stop her? Besides, True's gun would make sure of it. True's life here was over, and she would go forth one way or another, by walking off her former porch, or by being carried off it.

*Why argue*, Pond decided. True had made up her

mind. Pond now made up hers.

"I won't tell anyone," she said aloud. And then she felt in that instant she must run inside and shout, "Aunt True's outside!" and grab the whole lot of them and drag them forth to see reality, this living, breathing woman right before her.

But if she did that, the woman had made it more than clear her gun would fulfill its intended purpose. True was dead, whether Pond liked it or not, whether she said anything or not, whether she did anything or not. But True was also more alive than many people Pond had met.

True laughed, and it was all Pond could do not to join her. Then she gave in, and their voices mingled and rose in currents of buoyant humor.

And then Pond felt the next instant like weeping, floods of tears rising up within her. "I don't understand at *all*," Pond wailed, through her laughter. "I thought figuring out the house's secret would explain everything. And instead it's much worse. Talking to you, I know less than I ever did."

"Good. Maybe now you can listen. Why wouldn't you want the end to be just as important and good as the whole rest of it? Have you *seen* what they do to old people? My friend Josie's still hooked up to all those tubes, looking exactly like a stuffed vulture in a hospital gown. She would have despised that gown. Of course, Josie's been gone for all these long days, but not her electrified bird body in its hideous green gown.

"And if you think that's bad, consider Myrtle. She was so rich her family decided they loved her too much to burden her with food. She starved away into the vapors. Of course, she always was scrawny. Didn't take long once they gave instructions to the nurses. The nurses might have nightmares about it, but the beloved family is off enjoying their new private island in the Maldives."

True shook her head with vehemence, and the gun wobbled through the air in concert with her movements. "It's Oregon for me. You have to stay here and keep things open."

"*What* things?"

"It can't have escaped you, charming little rat face, that in this house there are doorways within doorways. The house is like a Russian nesting doll. Open one door and you'll find another. Open that, and another one reveals itself. It never ends."

Pond closed her eyes. When she opened them, True was still there.

Having spent a week in the house, and having not stopped being surprised, Pond was willing to consider the possibility that the house could continue surprising her. So far, so reasonable. But there was no way a house in Baltimore had anything to do with worlds ending or continuing, which made Pond want to reject all the rest of it, too.

"What does that have to do with me?" she asked, crossing her arms.

"You have to stay in the house." True's eyes looked darker, more penetrating, than before. "You have to stay in the house, attend to it, or the doors start closing."

"I can hire a caretaker," Pond said. She loved the house, but she might love freedom even more. Who was True to demand what Pond do?

True shook her head. "It's got to be one who understands, and will stay with it."

"I can tell her," Pond said. Or him.

True shook her head.

"I can write it down."

"Why do you think I'm talking to you in person?" True sighed. "A torch has to be handed from one person to another."

"You're not handing me a torch," Pond protested.

"That's what you think," True said, reaching around with her non-gun hand to tap Pond once sharply on the breastbone, so Pond felt a burning sensation right in the middle of her body.

"What are you doing?" Pond waved her hands in consternation. Talking to dead relatives was enough to ask. Heartburn before dinner was taking it a step too far.

"You get used to it," True said.

"I don't *want* to get used to it," Pond complained.

"Then don't. Keep opening doors and you'll begin to figure everything out." True paused, and then said, "He's gorgeous, you know."

Pond blushed, grateful that the shadows hid her face. She pretended for an instant that she didn't know what True was talking about. Then she swallowed and said, in a very shy voice, "I think so, too."

"He thinks the same of you."

Then there was a steady silence, in which Pond became aware of the crickets, which were always there as background noise in Baltimore summers, a wall of sound so thick and ever-present you stopped noticing it, until sometimes you became aware it was there as reliably as gravity, as humidity, as air. You could lean into that sound, let it enfold you. And then you could break through it again later, when you knew what you wanted to say.

"Did you talk to him?" Pond asked, when she could gather her words about her to speak.

"No need," True said. "He can't keep his eyes off you. If I'm not mistaken, his hands want very much to follow suit."

Pond laughed. She wasn't playing any games; she hadn't noticed. She had been too busy trying to keep herself from falling into Ferdinand's depths. "It feels like diving into an ocean," she said. "Like I'll lose myself."

"Heaven and hell," True growled. "Of course you will."

"That doesn't help," Pond said fiercely. She looked at True through the shadows.

True's face seemed ignited by an inner light. Of course it was a trick of the eye, an effect of the shifting dark and the glimmering light streaming through the wavy window onto the porch outside. The inside of the house seemed more and more vivid, as Pond gazed into the brightness. Where she was standing felt more and more dreamlike.

She looked back through the window, into the light, and admitted she loved every one of them gathered there, all the crazy ones, all the mad ones, all the happy and the sad ones. All of them, the ones who frustrated her and delighted her, she loved them all.

"Time for me to move on to the next new world," True announced. "I may set things up in Oregon and then be back."

"Wait," Pond said, her mind whirling again into a flurry of questions. "Gruenbaum."

"I employed his mother." True nodded. "The lawyer's not completely useless, at least when it comes to that kind of ending."

"And you were Gruenbaum's boss."

True nodded noncommittally.

"Can I at least travel?" Pond asked.

"If you must, but not for too long. You don't want the doors to slam shut while you're off burning yourself on the beaches of Barcelona."

"Right," Pond said.

Pond walked around the corner of the porch, back toward the front door. She wanted to be the one to leave, rather than having True leave her. She reached out her hand toward the front door. Then she paused.

Before she touched the handle, she drew her arm back, walked back around the corner to where True had been seated. She was gone. No sign of any woman in the shadows.

The shadows remained, dancing and shimmering in the wavy light pouring through the windows. How had True disappeared so silently and completely? Pond stepped to the edge of the porch. It wasn't possible for her to have vanished. There was nowhere for her to have gone. If she had walked away, she would still be walking, and Pond would be able to see her, follow her path.

But there was no trace of her at all.

Pond put her hand on the bench where True had been sitting. Warm. A living being had been here, moments before. And now was gone. Pond stood still, and didn't know what to say or feel.

She waited until her lungs, of their own accord, had taken several deep breaths. And then there was nothing more to say or do here, so Pond walked back to the front door.

The handle felt smooth and polished in her grip. Through the glass on either side of the door she could see the laughing faces around the table, the figures of her friends and family in motion and rest, eating and drinking, telling stories. She could feel the camaraderie all the way out here, in the dark. She sighed, and then she grinned.

Looking in at the happy glow, Pond felt she was simultaneously standing inside the house and outside. She was at once bathed in the light of the banquet table, and comfortable out here, watching what was going on in the interior.

For the first time in her life, Pond knew she was actually free to stay or go, at least for a while, at least for now. She could choose. She gripped the handle, turned it, opened the door, and walked straight to the table.

"What have you been doing?" Ferdinand asked, gazing up at her.

"Looking forward to this," Pond said, and she let herself focus on his eyes.

She shouldn't have been surprised that a simple exchange of glances felt like a door opening, but she was astonished anyway.

True was looking in all the wrong places for new

worlds, Pond told herself, pulling a chair up to the dinner table. Everything you could ever discover was right here.

# Acknowledgements

Pond consults the Wilhelm/Baynes edition of the *I Ching*, published by Princeton University Press.

Joyful thanks to beloved friends and family, meditation community and teacher, and readers, especially Antje, a brilliant first reader. Good humor and love to everyone, and to Tim in particular, amazing husband, reader, and friend.

# About the Author

Juniper Ellis is an award-winning professor and a speaker-in-demand from Paris to Chicago, reaching people from all walks of life. Audiences say her words are "*challenging and inspiring, life-changing, smart and relatable, radiant, uplifting and funny, eloquent*". Her nonfiction book **Tattooing the World** (Columbia University Press, 2008) was listed as "required reading" in the *New York Post* and won the 2008 City Paper award for best book by a Baltimore author.

**Website:**
http://www.juniperellis.com/

20768779R00236

Made in the USA
Middletown, DE
07 June 2015